Unravel
THE
Dusk

THE BLOOD OF STARS DUOLOGY

Spin the Dawn

Unravel the Dusk

UNRAVEL
THE
DUSK

THE BLOOD OF STARS

Book II

ELIZABETH LIM

Alfred A. Knopf
New York

Text copyright © 2020 by Elizabeth Lim
Jacket art copyright © 2020 by Tran Nguyen
Map copyright © 2019 by Virginia Allyn

All rights reserved. Published in the United States by Alfred A. Knopf, an imprint of Random House Children's Books, a division of Penguin Random House LLC, New York.

Knopf, Borzoi Books, and the colophon are registered trademarks of Penguin Random House LLC.

Visit us on the Web! GetUnderlined.com

Educators and librarians, for a variety of teaching tools, visit us at RHTeachersLibrarians.com

Library of Congress Cataloging-in-Publication Data is available upon request.
ISBN 978-0-525-64702-7 (trade) — ISBN 978-0-525-64703-4 (lib. bdg.) —
ISBN 978-0-525-64704-1 (ebook)

The text of this book is set in 11.35-point Sabon MT Pro.

Printed in the United States of America
July 2020
10 9 8 7 6 5 4 3 2 1

First Edition

To Mom, for giving me courage,
to Dad, for feeding my imagination,
and to Victoria, for always laughing with me along the way

I had a mother once.

She taught me to spin the finest yarn and thread, made from silkworms raised in our courtyard of mulberry trees. Patiently, she would soak thousands of cocoons, and together we'd wind the gossamer threads onto wooden spools. When she saw how nimbly my little fingers worked the wheel, spinning silk like strands of moonlight, she urged my father to take me on as his seamstress.

"Learn well from Baba," she told me when he agreed. "He is the best tailor in Gangsun, and if you study hard, one day you will be too."

"Yes, Mama," I'd said obediently.

Perhaps if she'd told me then that girls couldn't become tailors, my story would have turned out differently. But alas.

While Mama raised my brothers—brave Finlei, thoughtful Sendo, and wild Keton—Baba taught me to cut and stitch and embroider. He trained my eyes to see beyond simple lines and shapes, to manipulate shadows and balance beauty with structure. He made me handle every kind of cloth, from coarse cottons to fine silks, to gain mastery over fabrics and feel how they draped over the skin. He made me redo all my stitches if I skipped one, and from my mistakes I learned how a single seam could be the difference between a garment that fit and one that did not. How a careless rip could be mended but not undone.

Without Baba's training, I could never have become the

emperor's tailor. But it was Mama's faith in me that gave me the heart to even try.

In the evenings, after our shop closed, she'd rub balm onto my sore fingers. "Baba's working you hard," she would say.

"I don't mind, Mama. I like sewing."

She lifted my chin so our eyes were level. Whatever she saw made her sigh. "You really are your father's daughter. All right, but remember: tailoring is a craft, but it's also an art. Sit by the window, feel the light, and watch the clouds and the birds." She paused, looking over my shoulder at the patterns I'd been cutting all day. "And don't forget to have fun, Maia. You should make something for yourself, too."

"But I don't want anything."

Mama tilted her head thoughtfully. As she changed the burnt-out joss sticks by our family altar, she picked up one of the three statues of Amana lining the shrine. They were plainly carved, faces and dresses washed out by the sun. "Why don't you make three dresses for our mother goddess?"

My eyes widened. "Mama, I couldn't. They would have to be—"

"—the most beautiful dresses in the world," she finished for me. She tousled my hair and kissed my forehead. "I'll help you. We'll dream them together."

I hugged Mama, burying my face in her chest and holding her so tight a laugh tinkled out of her throat, like the soft strokes of a dulcimer.

What I would give to hear that laugh again. To see Mama one more time—to touch her face and comb my fingers through her thick braid of black hair as it loosened into waves rippling against her back. I remember I could never weave silk as soft as her hair, no matter how I tried, and I remember I used to think the freckles on her cheeks and arms were stars. Keton and I would sit on her lap, me trying to count them, Keton trying to sweep them off.

The stories she'd tell us! It was Mama who dreamed of leaving Gangsun and living by the sea. She recounted to us the tales she'd grown up with—of fearless sailors, water dragons, and golden fish that granted wishes—tales Sendo drank in with his soul.

She believed in fairies and ghosts, in demons and gods. She taught me to sew amulets for passing travelers, to cut paper clothes to burn for our ancestors, to write charms to ward off evil spirits. Most of all, she believed in fate.

"Keton says it isn't my fate to become a tailor like Baba," I sobbed to her one afternoon, weeping from the sting of my brother's words. "He says girls can only become seamstresses, and if I work too hard I won't have any friends, and no boy will ever want me—"

"Don't listen to your brother," Mama said. "He doesn't understand what a gift you have, Maia. Not yet." She dried my tears with the edge of her sleeve. "What matters is, do *you* want to be a tailor?"

"Yes," I said in a small voice. "More than anything. But I don't want to be alone."

"You won't be," she promised. "It isn't your fate. Tailors are closer to fate than most. Do you know why?"

I thought hard. "Baba says the threads he stitches into his work give it life."

"It's more than that," replied Mama. "Tailoring is a craft that even the gods respect. There's something magical about it. Even the simplest thread has great power."

"Power?"

"Have I told you about the thread of fate?"

I shook my head.

"Everyone has a thread tied to someone—a person who's meant to be by your side and make you happy. Mine is tied to Baba."

I glanced at my wrists and ankles. "I don't see anything."

"You can't *see* it." Mama chuckled gently. "Only the gods can. The thread may be long, stretching over mountains and rivers, and it may be years before you find its end. But you'll know when you meet the right one."

"What if someone cuts it?" I worried.

"Nothing can break it, for destiny is the strongest promise. You'll be bound to each other no matter what happens."

"The way I'm bound to you and Baba, and Finlei? And Sendo?" I was mad at Keton, so I didn't care if my youngest brother and I were tied together.

"It's similar, but different." Mama touched my nose and rubbed it affectionately. "One day you'll see."

That night I took a spool of red thread and cut a string to tie around my ankle. I didn't want my brothers to see it and make fun of me, so I tucked the loose end under the cuff of my pant leg. But as I walked with my secret tickling my ankle, I wondered if I'd feel something when I met the person I was fated to be with. Would the string give a little tug? Would it stretch and bind to its other half?

I wore that string around my ankle for months. Little by little it frayed, but my faith in fate did not.

Until fate took Mama from me.

It came for her slowly, over many months, like it came for the cypress tree outside our shophouse. Every day, leaves trickled from its spindly arms—only a few at first, but more and more as autumn loomed. Then, one day, I woke up to find all the branches bare. And our cypress tree was no more, at least until spring.

Mama had no spring.

Her autumn began with a stray cough here and there, always covered up with a smile. She forgot to add cabbage to the pork dumplings Finlei loved so much, and she forgot the names of the heroes in the stories she'd tell Sendo and me before we went to sleep. She even let Keton win at cards and gave him too much money to spend on his errands in the marketplace.

I hadn't given much thought to these slips. Mama would have told us if she wasn't feeling well.

Then one winter morning, just as I'd finished adorning our statues of Amana with our three dresses—of the sun, the moon, and the stars—Mama fainted in the kitchen.

I shook her. I was still small, and her head was heavy when I lifted it to rest on my lap.

"Baba!" I screamed. "Baba! She won't wake up!"

That morning, everything changed. Instead of praying to my ancestors to wish them well in their afterlife, I prayed that they spare Mama. I prayed to Amana, to the three statues I'd painted and clothed, to let her live. To let Mama see my brothers and me grow up, and not to let her leave Baba, who loved her so much, alone.

Every time I closed my eyes and pictured the future, I saw my family whole. I saw Mama next to Baba, laughing, and teasing us all with the fragrant smells of her cooking. I saw my brothers surrounding me—Finlei reminding me to sit straight, Sendo slipping me an extra tangerine, and Keton pulling on my braids.

How wrong I was.

Mama died a week before my eighth birthday. I spent my birthday sewing white mourning clothes for my family, which we wore for the next one hundred days. That year, the winter felt especially cold.

I cut the red thread off my ankle. Seeing how broken Baba was without Mama, I didn't want to be tied to anyone and suffer the same pain.

As the years passed, my faith in the gods faded, and I stopped believing in magic. I shuttered my dreams and poured myself into keeping our family together, into being strong for Baba, for my brothers, for myself.

Every time a little happiness dared to seep into the cracks of my heart and tried to make it full again, fate intervened to remind me I couldn't escape my destiny. Fate took my heart and crushed it little by little: when Finlei died, then Sendo, and when Keton returned with broken legs and ghosts in his eyes.

The Maia of yesterday picked up those pieces and painstakingly sewed them back together. But I was no longer that Maia.

Beginning today, things would be different. Beginning today, when fate caught me, I'd meet it head-on and make it my own.

Beginning today, I would have no heart.

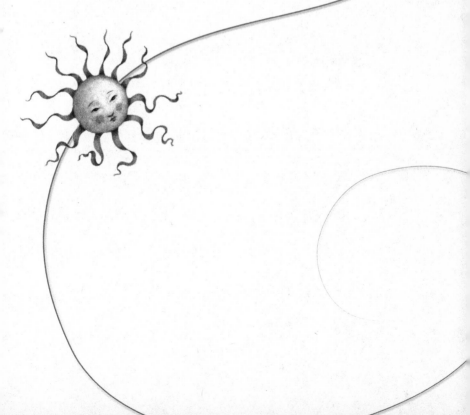

PART ONE

THE LAUGHTER
OF THE SUN

CHAPTER ONE

Thousands of red lanterns illuminated the Autumn Palace, suspended on strings so fine the lights looked like kites floating from roof to roof. I could have watched them all night, dancing on the wind and painting the twilight with a burnished glow—but my mind was elsewhere. For beneath the sea of bobbing lights, the Square of Splendid Harmony was staged for an imperial wedding.

Seeing all this red, in celebration of Emperor Khanujin's marriage to Lady Sarnai, should have gladdened me. I'd worked so hard and sacrificed so much for the peace their union would finally bring to A'landi.

But I wasn't the same Maia as before.

The Autumn Palace's vermillion gates rumbled, and I pushed through the throng of servants to catch a glimpse of the wedding procession. At its helm would be Lady Sarnai's father, the shansen. I wanted to see the man who had bled my country from within, whose war had taken two of my brothers, and whose name alone made grown men shudder.

The shansen, his gold-plated armor shining like dragon scales from under his rich emerald robes, rode on a majestic white stallion. Gray touched the tips of his beard and eyebrows. He did not look as fearsome as I had pictured—until I saw his eyes; they gleamed like black pearls, fierce as his daughter's, but crueler.

Behind him rode his favored warrior, Lord Xina, followed by the shansen's three sons, all with their father's dark, unsettling eyes, and a legion of soldiers wearing patches on their sleeves embroidered with the shansen's emblem—a tiger.

"The shansen will mount the steps to the Hall of Harmony," announced Chief Minister Yun loudly, "where his daughter, Sarnai Opai'a Makang, will be presented as our emperor's bride.

"Tomorrow," Chief Minister Yun continued, "the Procession of Gifts will be presented to the emperor's court. On the third day, Lady Sarnai will formally ascend to her place as empress beside Emperor Khanujin, Son of Heaven. A final banquet will be held to celebrate their marriage in the eyes of the gods."

The wedding music swelled and merged with the clatter of the shansen and his men marching up the stairs. Firecrackers clapped, loud as thunder, and each stroke of the wedding drums boomed so deep the earth beneath my soles thrummed. Eight men strode across the hall bearing a golden carriage draped with embroidered silk and armored with glazed tiles painted with turquoise-and-gold dragons.

When the shansen took his place before the hall, Emperor Khanujin stepped out of his palanquin. The music ceased, and we all bowed to the ground.

"Ruler of a hundred lands," we chanted, "Khagan of Kings, Son of Heaven, Favored of Amana, our Glorious Sovereign of A'landi. May you live ten thousand years."

"Welcome, Lord Makangis," Emperor Khanujin greeted him. "It is an honor to receive you at the Autumn Palace."

Fireworks exploded from behind the palace, shooting high beyond the stars.

"Ah!" everyone gasped, marveling at the sight.

Briefly, I marveled too. I'd never seen fireworks before. Sendo tried to describe them to me once, though he'd never seen them either.

"They're like lotuses blooming in the sky, made of fire and light," he'd said.

"How do they get up so high?"

"Someone shoots them." He'd shrugged when I frowned at him, skeptical. *"Don't make that face at me, Maia. I don't know everything. Maybe it's magic."*

"You say that about everything you don't know how to explain."

"What's wrong with that?"

I had laughed. *"I don't believe in magic."*

But as the fireworks burst into the sky now, lurid splatters of yellow and red against the black night, I knew magic looked nothing like this. Magic was the blood of stars falling from the sky, the song of my enchanted scissors—eager to make a miracle out of thread and hope. Not colored dust flung into the sky.

While those around me cheered, eight more young men carried another golden palanquin toward the emperor. Lanterns hung from its every side, illuminating an elaborately painted phoenix.

A phoenix to match the emperor's dragon. To breathe new life into the country, helping it rise from the ashes of war.

The attendants lowered the palanquin, but Lady Sarnai didn't step out. She was wailing so loudly that even from the back of the square, I could hear her. In some villages, it was the tradition for a bride to wail before her wedding, a sign of respect for her parents to show that she was distressed to leave them.

But how unlike the shansen's daughter.

A soldier parted the carriage's curtains, and Lady Sarnai tottered forward to join the emperor and her father. An embroidered veil of ruby silk covered her face, and the train of her gown dragged behind her, crimson in the fragile moonlight. It did not even shimmer, as any of the dresses I'd made for her would have: woven with the laughter of the sun, embroidered with the tears of the moon, and painted with the blood of stars. Strange, that Khanujin would not have insisted she wear one of Amana's dresses to show off to the shansen.

I frowned as she continued to wail, a shrill sound that pierced the tense silence.

She bowed before her father, then before the emperor, falling to her knees.

Slowly, ceremoniously, Emperor Khanujin began to lift her veil. The drumming began again, growing louder, faster, until it was so deafening my ears buzzed and the world began to spin.

Then—as the drums reached their thunderous climax—someone let out a scream.

My eyes snapped open. The shansen had shoved Khanujin aside and seized his daughter by the neck. Now he held her, shrieking and kicking, above the Hall of Harmony's eighty-eight steps—and he ripped off her veil.

The bride was not Lady Sarnai.

CHAPTER TWO

The false princess's legs thrashed wildly beneath her skirts, the long satin train of her wedding robes rippling beneath her.

"Where is my daughter?" the shansen roared.

Already, everyone around me was placing bets on the poor girl's fate. Would the shansen slit her throat—or would the emperor beat him to it? No, they'd let her live until she talked. Then they'd kill her.

"I—I—I—I d-don't know," she blubbered, her wailing intensifying before she repeated, "I don't know."

She let out a scream as the shansen dropped her onto the stone steps.

"Find my daughter!" he barked at the emperor. "Find Sarnai, or there will be no wedding—only war."

The warning hushed everyone in the square.

Where was Lady Sarnai? Didn't she care that thousands would die if this marriage did not proceed?

"The war would never end," Keton had told me. My youngest brother so rarely spoke of his time fighting for Khanujin, I could not forget his words: *"Not unless the emperor and the shansen came to a truce. At dawn of the New Year, they met to make peace. The shansen agreed to withdraw his men from the South and reaffirm his loyalty to the emperor. In return,*

Emperor Khanujin would take the shansen's daughter to be his empress and tie their bloodlines together.

"But the shansen's daughter refused. She had fought alongside her father's army. I'd seen her myself—fierce as any warrior. She must have killed at least fifty men that day." Keton had paused. "It was said she threatened to kill herself rather than marry the emperor."

When Keton had shared this story, I doubted its truth. What girl wouldn't want to marry a man as magnificent as Emperor Khanujin?

But now that I had met Lady Sarnai—and the emperor—I knew better.

Gods, I hoped she hadn't done anything rash.

I stood on my toes to get a better look at what was happening, but a shooting pain stabbed the back of my eyes and they began to burn. Urgently, I rubbed them. Tears came, trying to wash out the heat. But my pupils only burned more fiercely, and I saw a blood-red sheen reflect onto the track of tears smeared on my palm.

No, no, no—not now. I covered my face, hiding the mark of Bandur's curse, the terrible price I had paid to make Lady Sarnai's dresses and secure peace for A'landi.

My heart began to pound in my chest, my stomach fluttering wildly. A rush of heat boiled through my body, and I crumpled to the ground.

Then, suddenly the burning in my eyes vanished.

My vision cleared. I no longer saw the people around me clamoring in commotion. I heard them chattering and fidgeting, but they were far, far away. My eyes and ears were somewhere else, outside of my body.

I was there, on the steps of the Hall of Harmony. The air reeked of sulfur and saltpeter from the fireworks; the sky was scarred with stripes of white smoke.

I saw the girl, her rose-painted lips and tear-streaked cheeks, and I recognized her—she was one of Lady Sarnai's maids. Imperial guards pulled her up the steps as the emperor approached.

He struggled to contain his ire—his fingers twitching at his sides, inches from his dagger, whose golden hilt was artfully hidden under layers of silk robes and a thick sash with dangling jade amulets.

He knelt beside her, taking her hands into his and untying the cords that bound her wrists. Once, he'd crouched beside me the same way, when I'd been a prisoner. How marvelous I'd thought him then, unaware that I was under a powerful spell the emperor's Lord Enchanter had cast over him.

Without Edan's magic, sweat glistened down the nape of Khanujin's neck, and his back strained under the heavy weight of his imperial robes.

I wondered if the shansen noticed.

The emperor tilted the maid's chin up to him, his fingers pressed so hard against her jaw they would leave bruises. Cold fury raked his black eyes.

"Speak," he commanded.

"Her Highness . . . didn't say. She . . . she asked us to drink some tea with her to celebrate her betrothal to you, and we couldn't refuse." The maid buried her face into the hem of Khanujin's robes.

"So, she poisoned you."

Fear punctuated her sharp, gulping breaths. "When I woke,

I was dressed in her clothes, and she said that if I did not pretend to be her, she would kill me."

Khanujin let go of her. He raised an arm, likely to order that she be taken away and executed somewhere quietly, when—

"Lord Xina is gone!" one of the shansen's men cried.

Like whiplash, my sight broke. Whatever had stolen me from my body hurled me back again, until I was among the emperor's servants as before, ears ringing with the uproar over Lord Xina's disappearance.

"Find them!" Khanujin shouted. "Ten thousand jens to whoever finds the shansen's daughter and brings her to me. And death by nine degrees to anyone caught aiding her escape."

Death by nine degrees. That meant not only the execution of the guilty party, but also their parents, children, grandparents, aunts, uncles—the entire bloodline.

Numbly, I watched the crowd scatter, eunuchs and craftsmen and soldiers and servants all searching for Lady Sarnai. I needed to move too, before someone noticed me—or in case someone had seen my eyes glowing red.

But I couldn't move, not while the drums boomed so violently the clouds themselves seemed to shake. They rattled me, each thud resonating deeply into my bones and reminding me of what I was becoming.

"Did you know they used to play drums to scare off demons?" I could still hear Bandur taunting me. *"Soon the drums will only remind you of the heart you once had. Every beat you miss, every chill that touches you, is a sign of the darkness folding over you. One day, it will take you away from all that you know and cherish: your memories, your face, your name. Not even your enchanter will love you when you wake as a demon."*

16

"*No,*" I whispered, pressing my hand over my heart, feeling its unsteady rhythm.

Still there.

I wasn't a demon. Yet.

Once the emperor married Lady Sarnai and peace for A'landi was secured—once Baba, Keton, and all A'landans were safe—I would spend every waking moment trying to break my curse. Until then—

Someone seized my elbow, pulling me out of my thoughts—and out of the square.

"Ammi!"

"Get moving, *Master* Tamarin," she said brusquely. She tossed a braid over her shoulder. "You'll get yourself sent to the dungeon standing around like that, especially now that everyone knows your leg isn't really broken."

Then she turned abruptly and disappeared into a throng of serving girls.

I was stunned. My hands fell to my sides, my feet forgetting where they'd meant to go.

Why had Ammi spoken to me so curtly, as if I'd offended her?

Master Tamarin.

A lump rose in my throat. The way she'd said my name, I suddenly understood why she was angry with me.

She'd known me as the tailor Keton Tamarin, not as Maia. The morning I'd returned to the palace, the emperor had divulged to all my true identity. How betrayed she must have felt to learn of my lie from him, not from me, after all her kindness to me during the competition to become the imperial tailor.

"Ammi!" I called, running after her. "Please, let me explain."

"Explain?" Her round eyes narrowed at me, trying to be

cold but not entirely succeeding. "I don't have time for you. There's ten thousand jens at stake. Might not be much to you anymore, but it's a fortune to the rest of us."

"I can help you."

"I don't need your—"

"I can find her."

My friend's words died on her lips, and she drew in a sharp breath. "What do you know?"

To be honest, I didn't know anything. The old Maia, being a terrible liar, would have confessed that right away. But in this small, seemingly insignificant way, I had already changed.

"I'll show you."

I started off before Ammi could refuse, and when I heard her reluctant footsteps following me out of the square, I headed for Lady Sarnai's residence. I should have been glad that she'd come, and I should have tried apologizing to her again, but I didn't want her asking more questions about Lady Sarnai's whereabouts. Besides, something else weighed me down. A leaden heaviness in my chest that took me a moment to recognize.

I *envied* Lady Sarnai. Envied her the chance to be together with the man she loved.

The chance I couldn't have with Edan.

Come with me, I could still hear him plead.

How I'd wanted to, more than anything. The warmth of his hand on my cheek, the press of his lips on mine—they were enough to melt me.

But even if I could relive that moment, I would still have told that painful lie to make him leave. It was better to endure whatever suffering that would befall me alone—Edan would be free from the bonds that had held him captive for so long.

"Where are we going?" Ammi said, sounding irritated. "Everyone else is looking outside the gates."

"This way," I said, cutting into the garden. My voice came out strangled, but I hoped Ammi wouldn't notice. "I know a shortcut to her apartments."

"Why would she still be there?"

I didn't reply. Just started running.

I pushed Lady Sarnai's doors open. Incense burned, a thick haze pervading the room. I grabbed a lantern, waving it around for any signs of a struggle.

A shadow fluttered from within the bedchamber.

Ammi shivered. "Maybe we should g—"

I put my finger to my lips and beckoned to her with my other hand.

Quietly, we followed the movement into Lady Sarnai's resting chambers. The bed's silk curtains were swaying, but the air was still; there was no wind tonight.

Setting down the lantern, I flung open the curtains.

Lady Sarnai's attendants lay on her bed, gagged, their wrists and ankles tied together with the bedsheets. Unconscious, but beginning to stir.

I spun away from the bed. A pile of clothes had been strewn across the floor, a torn yellow sleeve peeking out from under a table. I crouched and picked up the scrap, examining it.

Lady Sarnai despised yellow, and neither she nor her maids would ever have worn material so coarse.

It was from an imperial guard's uniform. The rip looked recent, the edges of the sleeve wrinkled as though someone had clutched the fabric tightly.

I scanned the rest of the bedchamber. A sword, too thick

and unwieldy to be Lady Sarnai's, leaned against one of the large trunks by her changing screen.

In a burning flash I could not control, I saw Lady Sarnai and Lord Xina just outside the palace. They were dressed as imperial guards, blending in with the search parties sent to look for them. My eyes flickered back to normal.

"She's not in the palace," I murmured. "She's disguised as a guard."

"How do you know that?"

Instead of replying, I grabbed the sword off the trunk. "Don't look," I ordered Ammi.

She paled, but she obediently backed out of the room. Holding the sword high, I smashed open the lock and lifted the lid. From the stench that rushed out, I knew what I'd find inside.

An imperial guard, his eyes cloudy with death.

Dried blood, nearly black, clotted above his lips. His nose had been broken, his throat, neatly sliced—by someone with a steady hand who knew where to deliver the quickest, quietest death. His uniform, stolen.

Outside the bedchamber, Ammi screamed. I guessed she'd found the other dead guards.

. . .

"Well done," Emperor Khanujin said when we reported what we'd found.

Bowing low at my side, Ammi beamed. The whole walk over to the emperor's royal apartments, her emotions had wavered between horror at finding the dead bodies and eagerness to be in the emperor's presence.

Now the horror was forgotten, but I couldn't fault her. Even a glimpse of the emperor's receiving chamber was more than a maid of her station might ever hope to see.

I wished I shared her excitement, but I felt only the sharp sting of regret.

"She'll be dressed as a guard," I said quietly. "Lord Xina, too. They left with the search parties so they wouldn't draw attention. They can't have gotten too far."

From behind a tall wooden screen that obscured our view of him, the emperor spoke again.

"The two of you discovered this? No one else?"

"Yes, Your Majesty."

"If what you say is true, then you will be rewarded. You are dismissed."

I started to lift myself, but the emperor's headdress tinkled. "Master Tamarin." Dread washed over me before he even uttered his next words. "A moment."

Ammi flicked me a curious glance, and I mustered a smile to assure her everything would be all right. But, in truth, I had a bad feeling about this.

He waited until the doors shut with a snap and we were alone. "You were not in the palace this afternoon."

"His Majesty had graciously given me the day off from my duties as imperial tailor."

The emperor's tone became harsh. Deadly. "Where were you?"

No more games. He knew I was aware of the enchantment Edan had cast over him, and why he hid himself behind that wooden screen.

"I went to the shrine to pray," I lied, "for good fortune, in anticipation of His Majesty's wedding."

The emperor's shadow leaned back, and he sniffed, sounding unconvinced. "I'm sure you are aware the Lord Enchanter is missing."

So, he hadn't found Edan.

"I was not," I lied again.

Irritation pricked Khanujin's voice. "I find that difficult to believe, Master Tamarin, given I am told he was last seen with you."

My pulse quickened. "Your Majesty, I have not seen the Lord Enchanter since I presented the dresses to Lady Sarnai."

"You dare to tell me more lies?" Angrily, Emperor Khanujin rose and stepped into the light. I bent into a bow, not daring to look up.

The cold tip of a dagger lifted my chin, hooking me like a fish from the water.

The glow of the emperor's glorious former self had faded, but it wasn't all gone yet. His height was still imposing, his shoulders still square and proud, his voice still smooth enough to charm a tiger into its cage.

But his face had begun to change. Cosmetics disguised the sallowness of his skin. His mouth pursed with cruelty, his teeth were larger and more crooked, and his eyes, which I'd once thought radiated the warmth of midsummer, were cold as a snake's.

The emperor flinched, noticing me stare. "I'll not ask you again. Where has the Lord Enchanter gone?"

His dagger bit into my skin, and I glanced at my reflection on its smooth blade. I hardly recognized the girl I saw, or the calm voice that uttered, "I would not dare lie to His Majesty. Truly, I do not know."

Emperor Khanujin stared at me, his gaze narrow and calculating.

I waited, my pulse pounding, until he finally set down his blade.

"He did something when you put on that dress," he hissed. "There was a flash of light—that was magic, I know it. You two planned it together."

"If I planned to leave with the Lord Enchanter, why am I still here?"

"My guards found this in your chambers."

The emperor held up a single black feather. A hawk's.

Edan's.

My pulse roared in my ears, but curiously, I held my calm. It was unlike me: yesterday, I would have stared at the ground, stammering a barely coherent response—begging for the emperor not to hurt Edan. Today, I simply clasped my hands and bowed my head. "The Lord Enchanter is known for taking the form of a hawk to facilitate his service to Your Majesty. If he visited my chambers, it was no doubt to ensure that I was working on my tasks for Lady Sarnai."

"You've developed a courtier's tongue while you were away, Tamarin," said Emperor Khanujin. The praise rang hollow in my ears, as it was meant to. "You traveled with him for months. Why did he leave?"

That, I knew the answer to. Edan had left because I'd begged him to. Because I'd lied to him and told him I'd be fine without him. Because I had broken his oath to the emperor, and if he didn't leave . . . gods knew what Khanujin would do to him.

But I couldn't tell the emperor that.

I could lie, but no lie would keep Edan safe from Khanujin's wrath forever. Unless . . .

I licked my lips, tasting the sweetness of a new possibility. I glanced at Emperor Khanujin's throat, barely protected by the richly embroidered collar of his jacket.

Think how easy it would be, a dark voice bubbled within me. *My* voice.

If you want to protect Edan, this is what you must do. You have the strength. Khanujin is weak and alone.

Heat prickled my eyes, and my fingers twitched with temptation.

Yes. Do it. The voice resonated deeply, overthrowing my senses and my reason. *Kill him.*

No! I dug my nails into my palms. *Go away.*

The voice in my head chuckled. *Little Maia. You know it's only a matter of time. I grow stronger every minute. Soon my thoughts will be your thoughts. Our thoughts will be one. You won't even notice it.*

That was what I was afraid of. I gritted my teeth. *LEAVE ME.*

When the laughter floated away and finally faded, I uncurled my fingers and rubbed the bloody half-moons imprinted on my palms.

"Tamarin!" the emperor growled. "If you lie to me, I'll have your father and brother brought here to be hanged."

A flare of anger shot up to my chest, squeezing it so tight I could hardly breathe. I wanted to tell him I would kill him before that happened, that I'd give in to the darkness in me and shatter his bones one by one before I let him touch my family.

But I did not. The anger was gone as quickly as it came. I touched my head to the ground in a deep bow.

"Forgive me, Your Majesty, but I do not know. I pray the

Lord Enchanter and Lady Sarnai will both be found." I paused, waiting for the sharp sting of regret rising in my chest to dull. I wished I had never searched Lady Sarnai's room, had never helped the emperor gather clues to find her.

I bowed again, and finally, Khanujin flicked his hand in dismissal.

"Thank you, Your Majesty." My voice was ice once more, gravid with lies. "May you live ten thousand years."

CHAPTER THREE

A calamity of bells startled me awake. It was an hour or two before dawn, the sky still dark but bright enough for me to make out the gray fumes curling up from the exhausted lanterns.

Over and over, the bells pealed, the sound resonating through my windows. When I finally rose to close them, I caught a flash of movement outside—and heard the snap of a whip biting into flesh.

Lady Sarnai. Lord Xina. They had been found, and the guards were thrashing them.

Bamboo leaves clung to Sarnai's back, and water dripped from her long black hair. From the looks of it, they'd made it to the Leyang River before the guards captured her and her lover.

"You won't be slaughtering any more of my men," one of the guards was telling her. "Not on my watch. Take her back to her residence, and bring this one to the dungeon."

I leaned against the wall. A cold knot twisted in my stomach. If not for me, maybe they would have gotten away.

Lady Sarnai's happiness was a small price to pay for peace, I reminded myself. No more families would suffer the loss that Baba, Keton, and I had felt, when Finlei and Sendo were killed in the war.

So, why did my relief taste bitter?

An hour later, I had my answer. Minister Lorsa barged into my chamber to announce that the wedding would resume this afternoon with the Procession of Gifts. I was to fit Lady Sarnai into "the stars dress." Immediately.

. . .

A troop of soldiers patrolled the front of Lady Sarnai's apartments, and a line of archers stood at the windows behind the rustling willow trees.

No incense burned on her table this morning, and all the lanterns hanging from the ceilings had been taken down. Anything she might have used as a weapon was confiscated.

Wind seeped in through the broken windows, which had been hastily patched with cotton sheets and parchment. The chill raised goose bumps on my skin.

I bowed. "Your Highness, I've arrived to dress you for the wedding cele—" I caught my tongue; Lady Sarnai would not view tonight's festivities as a celebration. "—For the banquet tonight."

She didn't rise from her chair. Her rich black hair had been oiled and plaited; in the gleaming sunlight, it shone. But her full lips were cracked with dryness, and her eyes stared glassily ahead. She looked like she might shatter.

But Lady Sarnai was not glass. Stone, perhaps. And stones did not break.

"I could wring your neck with those dresses," she spoke, her voice low, a growl from a tiger's throat. "If not for you . . ."

She gritted her teeth. Hatred unsteadied her breath, and I knew if it weren't for the guards outside and her lover in prison, she'd make good on her threat.

I lowered my gaze to the ground and chose my next words with care. "I am relieved Your Highness has been returned safely to the Autumn Palace. Ten thousand years of joy and happiness to the Lady Sarnai and His Majesty—"

"Enough!" she barked. "You think by helping Khanujin you will win his favor?"

"No, Your Highness, I do not."

She leaned back in her chair, her long fingers clasping the wooden arms. "When I am empress, you will be the first to pay."

Her words were a deadly promise, but I wasn't afraid of her anymore.

"As you wish, Your Highness."

Lady Sarnai frowned. "You've changed," she observed. "Something about you is different." A cruel smile formed on her lips. "It's the enchanter, isn't it?"

Now my eyes flew up, meeting hers with my own cool stare. That pleased her, and I regretted it.

"There are rumors that he is missing. I assure you such news will greatly interest my father, particularly when I confirm it tonight."

"The Lord Enchanter is not missing," I lied.

"Oh? I would not have gotten as far as the Leyang River if Edan were still here." A little laugh rasped from her throat. "Don't worry, tailor. Khanujin will hunt him to the ends of the earth to get him back. Or is that not what you want?"

She was trying to hurt me. I'd done her a terrible wrong, and she had nothing left but words to hurl at me.

"I want you to marry the emperor," I replied. "The wedding is our only hope for peace."

Contempt spilled across her face. "It is too late for peace."

Keton had told me before that the Five Winters' War ended only because of a stalemate. The shansen feared Edan, and Edan was wary of the dark forces behind the shansen's enormous power.

But if Edan was truly gone, how would the emperor prevail against the shansen?

This wedding had to happen.

"Time grows short, Your Highness," I said quietly. "I must fit you into your dress."

Lady Sarnai's two maids—her two *new* maids, Jun and Zaini—brought forward a large walnut trunk. Bitter wistfulness washed over me as I opened it and lifted out the dresses of the sun, the moon, and the stars. Their radiance flooded Lady Sarnai's dark chambers, beams of gold and silver light darting across the ceiling.

"How beautiful," the maids breathed. "They're—"

"I suppose he wants me in that one." Sarnai pointed curtly at the dress of the blood of stars. Stripes of sunlight danced over its black silk, igniting bursts of otherworldly color, like shooting stars across the night sky.

Before I could reply, the maids snatched the dress from me and accompanied Lady Sarnai to her changing area.

While I waited, I turned to the large rosewood mirror on my left. Sunken eyes peered back at me, tired from worry and lack of sleep, and wisps of black hair escaped my hat. I touched the freckles peppering my cheeks, and my pale, bloodless lips.

I was a shadow of my old self.

Lady Sarnai had stepped out from behind the changing screen, the dress of the stars' skirts blooming behind her. The bodice cinched her small waist, the neckline accentuating the sharp contours of her shoulders and chest. Our measurements were nearly the same, and everything fit her perfectly, as I knew it would.

But the fabric, which had come alive only moments ago from my touch, now hung flat and dull—the color of charred wood, of an endless night.

"You call *this* a wedding gown?" she asked, scowling.

I didn't know what to say. The dress had *changed* when I wore it. The skirts had danced with azures and indigos and purples richer than any dyes found on the Spice Road, casting my skin with a silvery sheen that had made even the emperor gaze at me with wonder.

But on Lady Sarnai, it was lackluster. Lifeless.

I angled closer to her with my measuring string, and I tried to get her to step into the light. "Let me see if—"

"Perhaps Your Highness should try on another dress," the younger maid, Jun, interrupted. "The dress of the sun."

Lady Sarnai's eyes narrowed. "Fetch it."

She meant me, not the maids. I rolled my measuring string over my arm and lifted the dress of the sun from the chair to bring it forth.

She blinked, her eyes watering at its brightness.

"Your Highness, are you all right?"

"I don't want that one," she began. "I—" Sarnai stopped. Her jaw slackened, and her shoulders jerked back and forth. Her arms flailed, and she began gasping as if she could not breathe.

"Your Highness?" Jun and Zaini fanned her, tapped her wrist as if that would help. "Your Highness, are you feeling ill?"

Sarnai coughed and wheezed. Her lips moved, but only

a strangled sound came out. "Demons," she mouthed. Her bloodshot eyes widened with panic. She shrieked, "Demons! They're burning me."

She trembled violently as she clawed at her bodice, trying to tear it off. The maids grabbed her arms to steady her, but she writhed and twisted away. Blindly, she stumbled back against the wall, tripping over her long skirt. "Tamarin, get it off," she rasped. "Get it o—"

Then her body thudded to the ground.

The maids screamed, and I dropped the dress of the sun, hurrying to Lady Sarnai. I lifted her head onto my lap, holding her neck still as the rest of her body shook.

It was the dress. I had to get it off before it killed her.

I rolled her onto her stomach and fumbled at my belt for my scissors. There wasn't time to undo dozens of buttons, so I cut into the back of the dress. Or, at least, I tried to. The fabric was so strong it resisted my scissor blades. I cut again and again, until the threads loosened and the maids and I could pry the dress off.

"Thank the gods," I breathed when Lady Sarnai finally stopped trembling. But my relief was short-lived. Her arms had gone limp at her sides, and when I turned her over, her eyes wouldn't open.

I let go of my scissors. I'd been gripping them so hard the bows had made indents into my fingers. What was happening to the shansen's daughter?

The older maid, Zaini, pressed her ear to Lady Sarnai's chest.

"She isn't breathing!" she cried, her pitch rising with distress. "She isn't breathing!"

"Hush," I said. "Bring me water."

Zaini obeyed, and I poured it over Sarnai's face, but still she didn't stir.

Soundlessly, the two lifted Lady Sarnai onto her bed.

Her eyes were swollen, lips twisted in pain. Bruises had flowered up her chest and neck, and her skin had turned a wretched shade of blue and gray. But worst—and strangest—of all, clusters of inky violet marks traveled up her body, shimmering horrifically like burning stars.

"Is she . . . alive?" I asked. I couldn't say *dead*. I wouldn't.

Zaini hedged by chewing on her lip. "Barely."

My stomach clenched. Sarnai's pulse beat, but only if I touched her mouth did I feel the faintest of breaths. It was as if she were deep asleep, unable to wake.

Edan's warning came back to me. *"The dresses are not meant for mere mortals."*

He would have known what to do. But he wasn't here, and I had no magic of my own . . . except for the scissors. What could my scissors do for Lady Sarnai?

What was I to do?

The Procession of Gifts would begin in less than an hour. There would be no wedding without Lady Sarnai. Only war.

"Tend to Lady Sarnai," I said. "Until she is well, I will take her place at the imperial wedding."

Jun and Zaini shot looks at me, their fear replaced by alarm and shock.

I tilted my chin to confirm my intent. "Speak of this to no one."

No other words needed to be said; they understood my meaning. Both their lives and mine depended on their silence, and on Lady Sarnai's recovering.

My gaze lingered on the dress of the stars, a puddle of black silk on the floor. Its seams were ripped, the bodice torn, and the layers of the skirts in disarray. No time to repair it now.

I reached for the dress of the sun and headed to the changing screen.

By the Nine Heavens, I prayed this would work. If it didn't, A'landi would be back at war before the night was over.

CHAPTER FOUR

What I dreaded most was meeting the shansen face to face. He did not seem like a man easily fooled.

"People will see what they want to see," I murmured to myself. It seemed so long ago that Keton had given me that advice. Only then, I'd been disguising myself as him, not as the shansen's daughter. Though, I supposed—ironically, the penalty for being caught was the same for both.

Death did not frighten me as much as it once had.

Jun and Zaini painted my face to erase the freckles on my nose and cheeks, and made my lips as full and red as Lady Sarnai's. They plaited my hair so tight it hurt to think, and a dozen emerald and ruby pins dangled from my crown, tinkling every time I moved my head.

I didn't need a veil to hide behind. My dress was so blinding no one could look at me for longer than an instant. The laughter of the sun must have fed off my excitement and nervousness, for the dress had never flared so vibrantly before. Light radiated from its every fiber, piercing even the dark clouds outside.

My arrival inside the Hall of Harmony roused murmurs of awe from the court. Many had to shield their eyes from my splendor, and even Emperor Khanujin could not look directly at me. As we walked together down the hall, the heat from my sun-woven dress drew beads of sweat that trickled down his forehead, ruining the cosmetics that covered his faded glory.

This displeased him, but I ignored his scowls and smiled at the court. Better I than he capture everyone's attention. Better that he was too irritated to notice that I was the imperial tailor and not Lady Sarnai, the Jewel of the North.

Once we reached the front of the hall, he took a seat in a comfortable satin-cushioned chair, and I stood at his side, the brilliance of my dress waning as my legs throbbed from balancing on heeled shoes.

One after another, the nobles and ministers in Khanujin's court presented their gifts. Then came the ambassadors from every corner of the world—Kiata, Samaran, Frevera, the Tambu Islands, and Balar. Trunks full of the finest lace, and jade-carved dragons with scales so delicately chiseled they looked like they'd been stolen from tiny fish, hand-painted ceramics gilded with bulls' heads by the finest Samaran artisans, and wood carvings from lands I had never even heard of.

Finally, the shansen arrived. As Lady Sarnai's father, he had the honor of presenting his gifts last.

For such a large man, he moved quietly. Scars roughened his cheeks, his gray beard curving from his chin like the tip of a ceremonial dagger. Up close, the angles of his face were sharp and unforgiving. Carved by war.

"I present to you, Emperor Khanujin, a scepter crafted by the blind monks in the Singing Mountains. It is meant to bring prosperity to he who rules A'landi."

He turned to me next, his piercing gaze falling on my heavily powdered face. My dress flared brighter as my pulse quickened.

The shansen harrumphed, and though he did not shield his

eyes, he looked away. "And to you, my daughter—the finest archer in A'landi—I give the ash bow you sought to wield when you were a girl." I caught the tiniest ripple of pride in his next words. "Of all my children, you were the only one who could draw it."

The bow was so tall that the bottom of the curved limb rested just above my foot. Its lightness surprised me, but I kept my lips twisted in a scowl even as I inclined my chin to acknowledge the gift. I knew Lady Sarnai held little regard for her father.

"With the shansen's offering, the Procession of Gifts is concluded," Chief Minister Yun proclaimed.

I could hardly suppress my relief. All the guests fell to their knees and bowed to the emperor, wishing him "ten thousand years," a phrase I was beginning to wish I'd never have to hear or mumble again. Then finally, stiffly, I followed the emperor out of the hall.

He heedlessly took a pace that required me to hustle to keep up. I kept my head down, staring at the long stretch of gold tiles leading outdoors, ignoring the faces of our bowing guests. But as I followed, a hawk's cry tore my attention away from the floor. My eyes flew to the windows and up to the sky.

A hawk soared above the palace, but its feathers were gray not black, and its eyes did not glow the familiar yellow that haunted my dreams.

Of course it isn't Edan, you fool, I rebuked myself. *He hasn't the magic to turn anymore.*

When we exited the hall, the hawk still flew above us, its tapered wings skimming the clouds. It followed us until the emperor stopped at the nearest pavilion.

I desperately hoped he would dismiss me so I could rest before the banquet tonight. My feet ached from standing.

No such luck.

He clapped for one of the attendants to bring me the shansen's gift.

"You must be keen to test out your bow," he said. "See that hawk in the sky? I'll have the cooks roast it for the banquet tonight."

"It would be inauspicious for me to hunt," I said tightly, "given it is our wedding day."

"*Now* you care about decorum? There's been plenty of death in the palace, thanks to you. Surely the gods will overlook the death of one measly bird."

He thrust the bow at me, and my pulse shot up, my dress flaring in response. I clenched my fists, calming myself. "No, thank you."

"Why so dour, Sarnai?" the emperor taunted. "I've your lover in the dungeon. Aren't you curious about him? Whether he's still alive?"

He circled me so I couldn't pass him. "A hundred lashes last night," he continued, "and a hundred this morning. That's more than most men can survive, yet Xina is still alive. *Barely*. A quiet one, he's always been." Khanujin leaned closer to whisper in my ear, "They tell him if he'll scream, they'll stop. But he won't. Wouldn't you like to see him, Sarnai? His blood stains the walls of his cell. They had to send in two girls to mop up the mess when he fainted. When they were done, my guards woke him again for another hundred lashes. I wonder if you'd recognize him. He's more of a *thing* now than a warrior. That is what Northern pride will do for you."

I raised my chin, my tongue heavy with a retort that I bit back.

Pathetic, Maia, the voice inside me taunted. *Why hold back? Have a taste of your power. The emperor is weak. Show him his place.*

Tensing, I pushed aside the voice. Tempting as it would be to punish Khanujin—for what he'd done to Lord Xina, to Edan, and to me—I was not Maia right now. I was Lady Sarnai.

But the shansen's daughter would have shown him his place. She would have crushed his toes with her heel and vowed to kill him in his sleep. She would have strangled him with the gold chains hanging from his neck. She would have sworn revenge.

Too late, I realized it had been a mistake to bite back my anger.

Khanujin grabbed my wrist and pulled me close, the power of my dress making his cheeks redden and his temples perspire.

"You are not Sarnai."

My mask of calm faltered. "I—"

I gave a sharp gasp as he tore off my headdress, my neck jerking up as the pearls and jeweled tassels clinked against the pavilion's marbled floor. He stared at me. Recognition dawned, and his lips thinned with displeasure. "Tamarin."

"Your Majesty, I can explain—"

"Consider your words carefully, tailor," he warned, "lest they be your last. Where is she?"

"In her residence. The dress, Your Majesty . . . she could not wear it. It . . . it harmed her."

A beat of silence. He deliberated my answer. Then—

"And how is she now?"

I wavered on how to answer. How was she? Truthfully, the

dress's magic had marked her beyond recognition. I couldn't imagine the pain she suffered. Only someone as stubborn and hard-hearted as she would cling to life so tenaciously. Still, I wasn't sure she would survive the week.

But if I told the emperor Lady Sarnai was on the brink of death, I would endanger the wedding. For the sake of A'landi's peace, I needed time to figure out what to do.

"She is . . . recovering," I replied. "Her maids are caring for her."

I expected him to lash out at me for deceiving him, but the corners of his mouth lifted. "You did well taking her place. Not even her father knows it is you."

He leaned forward, his dry lips brushing against my cheek in what everyone else perceived as a kiss. Except he whispered harshly, "Perhaps it is better this way, though I urge you not to be so taken with birds in the sky."

I swallowed. So that was what had given me away. I hadn't known Khanujin to be such an observant man. Then again, I knew little of my emperor.

"Edan will not be a hawk when my men find him," he intoned. "He will be a man, like Xina. And he will be punished accordingly."

He rested his hand on my shoulder, squeezed the bone so hard I flinched. "I can be merciful, Maia Tamarin. I can be more merciful to him than I will be to Lord Xina. But that all depends on you."

"I don't know where he's gone," I repeated. *Even if I did, I wouldn't tell you.*

The emperor's smirk vanished, and he gave my shoulder another cruel press before finally letting go. "Then pray the banquet tonight goes well."

. . .

A hundred dishes were spread out before Khanujin and me, enough to satiate a thousand. An artist could have blissfully died after capturing such a glorious buffet of food with his brush, every color and texture represented, every plate a thoughtfully curated piece of art for both the eyes as well as the tongue.

The old Maia would have hated being seated at the center of this culinary theater. She would have bitten her lower lip and stared at the ground, fidgeting with the ends of her sleeves to ignore the rumbles in her belly. Yet she would have lusted after the spicy mung bean jelly lightly tossed with peanuts, the wood ear mushrooms marinated in vinegar and garlic, the fried fish fritters with ginger and plum sauce.

Not tonight. Tonight, in my radiant gown of the sun, I sat rigid in my chair, coolly ignoring every stare and glance that darted my way. Every morsel of food that went into my mouth was forced.

"You aren't eating, daughter," the shansen remarked.

I picked up a chunk of roasted carp. Swallowed. A fish bone poked the roof of my mouth, and I swallowed it too, almost hoping I'd choke and be sent back to my chambers.

Khanujin chuckled. "She is angry with me for putting her lover in the dungeon."

"She is fortunate Lord Xina is only in prison," replied the shansen darkly. "If it had been me, his head would be mounted on a pole in the center of the banquet hall. And I would have forced Sarnai to drink his blood."

"That would be inauspicious, Lord Makangis." Khanujin lowered his hand to my shoulder, and squeezed it tightly. "We shall wait until after the wedding for his execution."

I could feel the shansen studying me, as if waiting for the

color to drain from my face. But it was his next words that made me pale.

"I notice your most formidable guest is missing. Where is the enchanter?"

"Away in service to me."

I nearly choked at the lie, but the shansen frowned. "He pays me no respect with his absence."

"You pay *me* no respect by bringing a legion of your soldiers to camp outside my palace."

The shansen smiled. "Insurance that the wedding will go as planned."

"My enchanter is preparing his own insurance."

All lies. I stared blankly ahead as the servants brought out a new dish, one of the final courses. It was a whole pheasant, braised with imported red wine and resting on a bed of glowing embers that sent sparks flying up to the ceiling. The guests clapped at the chef's finesse and skill.

The smoke wafted to my nose, tickling my anxiety. Edan no longer protected A'landi. That duty was now left to me—to make sure this wedding happened.

If not, the shansen would strike. And A'landi would burn.

I barely heard Chief Minister Yun announce, "Let us toast Lady Sarnai."

"Yes," Emperor Khanujin said. "To her health and beauty."

The court raised their cups to me, unaware of the gleam in the emperor's eye. *I* knew he was reveling in the secret knowledge that the shansen's daughter was writhing in her apartments, brutally injured.

I raised my cup and drank. The alcohol sent a wash of heat over my cheeks and made my lips tingle, but it was not strong enough to wash away the cold seeping into my blood.

As I set down my cup, a familiar face swirled in the cloudy liquid. A low, thick laugh rumbled from its depths, making my hands tremble.

Bandur.

Suddenly, the shansen and emperor's guests vanished. In their places appeared ghosts with long white hair and sharp, gleaming teeth. Shadows leaked from their lips.

Sentur'na, they called, a word—a *name*—I did not know. Their arms reached out to touch me, and I jerked away.

Go back to Lapzur! I wanted to scream. *Stop following me!*

Sentur'na, we are waiting for you. It is beginning. You cannot escape.

All ghosts, except one: in the shansen's place sat a demon.

It wasn't Bandur, who took on the form of a wolf. But a tiger I'd never seen before. A tiger whose scorching red eyes seared into me.

You cannot escape.

Fear bristled the back of my neck. "Who are you?"

The demon merely smiled, raising its cup to me while the ghosts clamored:

GIVE IN, SENTUR'NA. YOU CANNOT ESCAPE. GIVE IN—

The fire in the center of the table burned higher and higher as the ghosts chanted. Wine splashed out of their cups, staining my vision red.

Enough! My dress flared, and I flung my wine into the fire.

The ghosts vanished. The tiger demon in the shansen's place vanished. The fire roared, and my bronze cup rattled and rolled off the table until a servant caught it.

I blinked.

No more ghosts. Only ministers, their wiry beards wet with

wine, gawked at me. Even the servants had frozen in place to stare.

The shansen stared too, a deep frown furrowing his thick brows.

"Are you all right, Sarnai?" the emperor asked icily.

Wine dripped from my fingers, and a servant hastily dabbed a napkin at my hands. Another servant refilled my wine.

"Yes . . . ," I started to say, but then I looked into my cup.

Bandur was gone, but the red eyes weren't. They flickered like two pomegranate seeds floating in the cloudy white wine.

My eyes.

Terror seized me. I bolted up, throwing my napkin onto the table to cover my eyes with my hands.

Spinning away from the attendants who tried to force me back into my chair, I fled the banquet.

CHAPTER FIVE

I didn't remember collapsing in the middle of the Autumn Palace, but I woke in chambers that were not my own.

A cushion supported my head, and my eyes were so dry it hurt to blink. When my vision focused, the sight of Emperor Khanujin standing before me made me leap out of bed.

He greeted me in a menacing tone. "You've slept the day away, Tamarin. Unfortunate, given it may have been your last."

My heart skipped with panic. Had he seen my eyes turn red? Had the shansen?

No. I'd be in the dungeon if he had. Not in one of Lady Sarnai's rooms.

"That outburst of yours last night will not happen again."

My voice came out hoarse. Raw. "Yes, Your Majesty."

"What happened?"

"I don't know," I whispered. It was the truth.

"They're saying you've gone mad over Lord Xina's imprisonment," he said. Still fuming, he regarded me. "You will resume your masquerade tonight. You will eat and celebrate in silence. Should the shansen grow suspicious, you will do everything in your power to reassure him. Lives hang in the balance, Tamarin."

He spoke as if he cared about A'landi's well-being. As if this wedding truly mattered to him. That surprised me, but I hated him too much to believe his words.

"Why not kill him?" I asked, scarcely recognizing my words as I spoke them. "Why not poison the shansen? Or have an assassin murder him in the middle of the night?"

Khanujin scoffed. "I don't expect you, a peasant, to understand the intricacies of court."

"I'm not a peasant—"

"You are what I say you are," he interrupted. "I am the emperor, and I am trying to prevent a war, not start a new one. If you want your country to survive, I suggest you put on the damned dress and finish this wedding." He pivoted for the door. "Fail me tonight, and I will have your father and brother hanged while you watch."

I bit back a stinging retort. *How dare you threaten my family!* I wanted to scream at him. But instead I knelt, glowering mutinously at the floor as I did. For all his palaces and his armies and his threats, the emperor was just a man. I was beginning to believe the shansen, however, might be more.

I waited for the rustle of the emperor's clothing to become silence, for the guards' footsteps to fade into the sound of the distant wedding music, before I moved again.

It took me some time to stand. My knees wobbled, and my skull pounded with echoes of the voices I had heard last night.

Sentur'na, the ghosts had called me.

Simply remembering the name brought a shiver racing down my spine. I didn't know what that meant. Nor did I know how long I had left before my transformation. Once it happened, I'd never see my face in the mirror again. I'd never hear my name being called again.

Never see my family again. Or Edan.

From the back of Lady Sarnai's chambers, a whimper broke the chilled silence.

I called out, "Lady Sarnai?"

I went to her. Her eyes were shut tight, dark metallic veins blistering across her neck and chest. There was a stack of folded towels on the table next to her, and I dipped one into the bowl of water and pressed it on her forehead.

Guilt swept over me. It was because of my dress that she'd become disfigured like this. Kneeling by her side, I prayed to whichever gods might listen.

"Please allow Lady Sarnai to recover," I whispered. "For the sake of A'landi."

Jun and Zaini were there already, preparing the moon-embroidered gown for me to wear tonight. From their cowed silence, I knew Emperor Khanujin had threatened them the same way he'd threatened me. Their lives depended on my success with the shansen.

"My father sought to unleash their powers on Emperor Khanujin," Lady Sarnai had said, *"but . . . one does not bargain with demons without paying a steep price."*

What had that price been? I wondered. Did it have something to do with the tiger demon I'd seen in the shansen's place last night when the ghosts came to me?

"I can dress myself," I said, dismissing Jun and Zaini.

When they left, I lifted the dress of the moon. It was the most serene of the three gowns I had made, its silvery brocade casting a soft sheen over my skin like moonlight shimmering on a quiet pond. Whereas the dress of the sun's skirt flared like a bell, this one was sleek. The skirt cascaded from my hips in a slim line, like a flute, and the hem brushed against my heels, soft and light as the feathers of a swan.

I took out my magical scissors and cut a deep slit into the

skirt. Invisible threads stitched themselves in place as I fashioned a pocket within the inner folds of the skirt.

Then, before I could change my mind, I reached for the dagger I kept hidden against my spine and raised it to my lips.

"Jinn," I whispered. The secret word that unlocked the power in the dagger. One of Edan's first names.

I unsheathed the weapon, fingers trembling, and caught my reflection in the gleaming iron blade. But it was the other side of the dagger that I watched.

How harmless it looked. Like gray, unpolished stone—at least to the unknowing eye.

But I knew it wasn't stone. It was meteorite. The dust of the stars.

I'd seen firsthand what it could do to demons and ghosts. A mere graze of the blade had burned Bandur's flesh into plumes of smoke.

Holding my breath, I splayed my fingers above the meteorite, hovering there until I gathered enough courage to touch it.

Now, I told myself, lowering my fingers to brush the blade. A silent gasp jumped from my lips as the blade stung my skin. Just a sting. The touch had not burned.

My flesh was still mine. Still human. For now.

As I set the dagger down, slowly the weapon's glow died away. Then I sheathed the blade and tucked it into the pocket I'd created.

I'd been wearing the dagger because I valued it and didn't trust leaving it in my room for the emperor's men to find. But now, if the shansen was not all he seemed, I had a feeling I would actually need it.

I prayed I was wrong.

CHAPTER SIX

Three enormous incense burners blazed in front of the Grand Temple. On this last day of the imperial wedding, the emperor and Lady Sarnai were to make an offering—to ask the gods to bless their union. Monks chanted in ancient A'landan.

"Bow three times to the South," the priest instructed us, "for the Immortals of the Water and Wind to bless this royal marriage and welcome Her Highness, the Lady Sarnai, as Empress of A'landi, Daughter of Heaven."

The emperor and I knelt side by side, thick silk cushions under our knees. Once we had finished bowing, a gong signaled for us to change direction. I numbed my mind as the priest gave the new blessing. All I needed to do was get through today. A'landi would be whole again, and I would have done everything I could for my country.

When the ceremony was complete, the emperor and I proceeded to the final wedding banquet. Afterward, there would be a ritual to make sure the marriage was consummated.

I wasn't planning to stay in the palace long enough for that.

The emperor strode three steps ahead of me, and I followed, my head held high, bearing an enormous phoenix crown with strands of pearls obscuring my face. Whereas the dress of the sun was so brilliant no one could even look at me, the dress of the moon shone gently, its silvery light more radiant than the thousands of lanterns illuminating the palace. Even under the afternoon sun, it was a beacon of splendor, and again, everyone looked at me instead of at the emperor. This time, he was not irked. It was part of his plan.

Wine perfumed the air, sharpened by the pungent aromas of three hundred different dishes: fried fish and braised pork, eight-spiced bean curd, and crispy shrimp fried with pineapples brought over from the Tambu Islands. The best acrobats, dancers, and musicians had come from throughout A'landi, and the afternoon was spent reveling in their talents. I might have enjoyed their performances were I anywhere but here.

When at last the banquet began, the shansen sat in the same seat as before, across from the emperor and me. He laughed and drank with his men, throwing subtle insults at the emperor, but I could feel him watching me. The empty chair on his right would have been Lord Xina's; I wondered whether everyone truly believed my outburst last night was an act of grief.

Something told me the shansen did not.

"Lady Sarnai," said one of his warriors, slightly drunk, "your dress outshines the moon. We thought it impossible there could be a gown more beautiful than the one you wore yesterday, but the Jewel of the North has set an example for these Southern court ladies." He chuckled. "My wife should like to commission your tailor for a dress of her own."

I opened my mouth to speak, but Khanujin interrupted, "We shall ask the imperial tailor on your wife's behalf, Lord Lawar, as a token of peace between the North and South."

"I've heard the imperial tailor is a woman," the lord continued. "She must be gifted, to be able to sew the dresses of Amana."

The shansen grunted. "Bring her forth. I should like to meet this girl."

I held my breath, trying hard not to glance at Khanujin.

"I've a better idea," said the emperor smoothly. "Lady Sarnai, why don't you demonstrate the tremendous power of your dress?"

It took all my control not to glower at him. Surely he had to be joking.

"The goddess's power is not mine to invoke," I said in the flattest tone I could muster.

"My daughter speaks at last," rumbled the shansen. His eyes narrowed. He *knew* there was something different about me. "It's not like you to be shy, Sarnai. Come, show us what the dress can do."

I wouldn't rise. I forced a morsel of roasted squab into my mouth, chewing defiantly.

"She's still angry with me," Khanujin said, laughing. A chorus of awkward chuckles joined him. "Stand, Sarnai. Show us Amana's strength."

The emperor's calm surprised me. Had I underestimated him? Edan's enchantment had brought upon him the appearance of majesty, but I was starting to wonder if the charm of his tongue was his own entirely.

He left me no choice, so I made a show of leisurely setting down my napkin and rising from my seat, deliberately taking my time.

The dress of the moon had the most fabric of all the three gowns, with long sleeves and a sheer jacket over the bodice tied with a wide embroidered sash. Tiny pearls studded every inch of the gown, representing the tears of the moon. It had been painstaking work, sewing them onto the fabric, and it had paid off. The pearls rippled, almost like the reflection of the moon over water—a breathtaking effect.

I unrolled the sleeves, letting them hang loose and brush against the ground. Slowly, I turned, ignoring the loud cheers and cries as silvery lights cascaded over the fabric.

Only the shansen was unimpressed. "A few sparkles and shiny silks are hardly representative of Amana's power. Are you sure the tailor did not fleece you, daughter?"

"This gown is embroidered with the tears of the moon," I said, an edge to my voice now. I'd gone through so much to make these dresses. How could anyone doubt them?

I gripped the sides of my skirts, bunching as much fabric as I could into my fists and squeezing. How could I show him?

I sought the moon through one of the latticed windows, the curtains sheer, dancing slightly in the autumn wind. The moon was as starved as it had been the night before, a fragile crescent—according to legend, that meant the goddess of the moon could not see her lover, the god of the sun. When the moon was full, she could see him, so she was happier.

Remembering the story made me think of Edan. I'd likely never see him again, never feel his arms around me, or inhale the warmth of his skin touching mine, never hear his voice caress my name.

We were like the sun and the moon, sharing the same stars and the same sky.

Somehow, that made him feel less far away. And made my heart feel slightly less alone. Less cold. For a moment, the darkness inside me weakened, and my dress came alive—

"Look!" one of the ministers cried. "The dress . . . it's . . ."

Glowing wasn't the right word. I could understand why he stumbled to find the right one. Light burst from my dress, permeating the entire hall as if stars were shooting forth from the ceiling. A powerful gust of wind rushed across the room, followed by a sudden *flash*.

The flames on the candles went out with a snap, and the bronze goblets and porcelain plates sang from the sting of an invisible kiss. Some of the guests ducked under the banquet table, while others marveled at my dress.

When it was over, the servants hastened to relight the candles, and the chamber broke into applause. Even the shansen's lips curled with interest. The emperor basked in everyone's praise—as if *he* had been the one to make Amana's dresses.

Maia Tamarin, the imperial tailor, was forgotten. Lady Sarnai, the Jewel of the North, was forgotten.

But I, whoever I was at this moment, did not forget.

I returned to my seat, my mind reeling. The dress had glowed beautifully, and its fabrics had shone with the mysterious light of the moon—enough to impress the shansen.

But this couldn't be *all* Amana's dresses could do. I'd seen their power destroy Lady Sarnai, disfigure her beyond recognition. What other secrets did they hold?

Would they turn against me when I became a demon? Or join me in my fall?

Hiding my troubled thoughts, I sat quietly at the emperor's side.

"Very impressive," allowed the shansen. "But unlike you Southerners, I know my lore: the power of Amana's dresses can only be wielded by the tailor who creates them." His eyes, glittering like two polished stones, darkened at me. "So either you are not my daughter, or this is not Amana's dress."

My throat tightened. "I am your daughter. And this is Amana's dress."

"It is not the latter that I doubt," the shansen replied with a grunt. He pointed at the ash bow he had given me. It hung in the middle of the banquet hall, displayed prominently among the other wedding gifts.

One of his attendants brought the weapon, and the shansen thrust it into my hands. "Only the Jewel of the North has the strength to wield this weapon."

The attendant presented me with a box of scarlet-painted arrows, and as I picked one up and nocked it, he guided me away from the banquet table toward a clear place to demonstrate my ability with the bow.

It was a miracle my hands did not tremble. I'd never drawn a bow or fired an arrow before. There was no way I could pass the shansen's test.

"Where shall I aim?" I asked evenly.

The shansen stroked his beard. "The tiger on my banner across the hall. That should be easy enough for you, Sarnai."

I squinted at the emerald banner, embroidered with a regal white tiger arising from a mountain bed.

"Is this necessary?" Khanujin interrupted. "This is a banquet, Lord Makangis, not a test."

"If Sarnai is who she says she is, this would not be a test, but child's play. Her favorite sport."

I swallowed and lifted the bow. Within a panicked second of pulling, I knew that I could not draw its taut bowstring.

Help me, I implored, appealing to the magic shimmering in my dress. *If I cannot do this, A'landi will be lost.*

Something held back the power of my dress. Something was choking its magic. Choking me.

A wicked frost bubbled up my throat. It tasted metallic and bitter, like iron left in the snow. Like moonlight that had gone stale.

Amana cannot help you, the cold whispered, sounding distressingly like my own voice. *But I can.*

Shadows folded into my thoughts, weaving darkness into my mind. *No!*

Before I could turn it away, supernatural strength filled me, and I snapped the bowstring back against my cheek. My hands moved without my control, directing the bow. I tried to resist, but I was torn. If I failed this test, the shansen would know I wasn't his daughter.

This is your chance, my voice enticed. *Kill the shansen. Save A'landi.*

If he dies, there will be no war.

Sweat beaded my temples, my focus blurring as I fought to ignore the voice blaring inside me. I couldn't breathe, couldn't even hear my heart. The green banner ahead seemed to sway. No, the entire world was swaying, the walls boiling in shadows only I could see.

Do it, Maia. Kill him. KILL HIM.

The darkness swallowed me whole—just for an instant. But an instant was just long enough to change everything. I swerved the bow to the left and pointed my arrow at the shansen's chest. And released.

The scarlet arrow shrieked across the hall, my shot straight and true. I froze in terror. There was no chance I'd missed. No man could move fast enough to escape the death I had just delivered.

And yet, the arrow diverged from its path ever so slightly, so at the last moment it pierced the white tiger embroidered on his cloak—instead of the shansen's heart.

Once again, the court burst into applause. Beside me, Emperor Khanujin wore a thinly veiled smirk, and the shansen crossed his arms.

"Only the Jewel of the North has the strength to wield the bow," the emperor repeated. "She is your daughter."

The shansen merely grunted, snapping the arrow out of his cloak—but I caught the dark look he passed me. It vanished before I could read it, and he flung the broken arrow onto the ground.

"Let the festivities continue!" declared Emperor Khanujin.

Everyone returned to the food and wine, and the shansen escorted me back to my seat. My pulse was thundering in my ears and my eyes began to burn again, flares of crimson speckling the pearls dangling in front of my face.

Panic rose in me. *Run,* I warned myself. *Get out of here before anyone sees.*

But I couldn't. I'd run off last night. If I left again, Khanujin would kill Baba and Keton.

Besides, no one was paying attention to me.

No one except the shansen.

Praying he wouldn't notice, I counted my steps the way I used to count my stitches, to calm the storm rising within me. *Ten paces until I reach my seat. Nine. Eight. Seven.*

Six. One of the servants brought a tray of candles to replace the ones that my dress had extinguished. The glow from the flames made my pupils burn, and tears tracked down my face.

Five. I couldn't bear it any longer. I made the mistake of looking up, away from the lights.

The shansen seized my arm. "There is something amiss with your eyes, daughter."

I tried to twist out of his grip, but he was too strong. "Let me go."

As I struggled, I spied a flash of black stone within his robes. An amulet, like the one Bandur wore, only with a tiger's head engraved on the face. Before I could make out anything more, the amulet fell back into the folds of the shansen's cloak, and he knocked my crown off my head.

A hush fell over the hall.

"You are not my daughter," he snarled.

With more strength than an ordinary man should have, he hurled me against the wall and overturned the banquet table. Plates shattered, and guests screamed.

"I declare this marriage invalid," he growled. "The truce is over."

Daggers and poisoned needles flashed in his men's hands. A blink later, knives were buried in the throats of the guards nearest Emperor Khanujin.

I lay stunned on the floor. I didn't hear the screams and shouts, the thuds of the dead guards falling to the ground. I didn't see their blood seeping through the silken red tablecloths, smearing the gold-embroidered symbols of the emperor and Lady Sarnai's names.

My attention was completely riveted by the shansen. His pupils constricted, the tiger fur on his cloak melting over him. And his fingernails grew long and sharp—into claws.

The amulet I'd spied in his coat dangled from his chest, the brutal beast carved on its surface darkening, like ink spreading into a painting coming to life.

White smoke curled from the amulet, and the shansen inhaled it through his nostrils. When I looked at him next, he was not a man at all.

But a demon—a tiger with bone-white fur and glistening black eyes—that lunged for Emperor Khanujin.

CHAPTER SEVEN

He moved in flashes, faster than my eye could follow, lethal and precise. Everywhere he danced struck a tempest of blood and death.

Chopsticks clattered against porcelain bowls, and teacups shattered on the ground. Furniture cracked, or was it the sound of bones breaking? I could not tell. My vision went in and out of focus, the flashing red of swiveling lanterns hurting my eyes.

I should have run, yet I could not. I could not do anything but stare at the shansen's cinder-black eyes, knowing, with a shiver, that someday mine would be just as empty. Just as soulless.

A platter of steamed fish flew over me, and I ducked, taking cover under one of the banquet tables.

Three servants already hid there, teeth chattering and necks shiny with sweat. They held each other, covering one another's ears to block the clamor of the screaming guests and praying for survival.

As the air grew pungent with salt and iron, nausea gripped my throat, thickening until I wished I could vomit. I tried to focus on the flying food instead of the falling bodies. There were too many to count.

A minister dropped beside me, his bright blue robes ripped at the torso. The servants jumped away in horror, but I pulled the minister under the table for protection.

A dark blossom of blood seeped through the silk of his robes, turning even the gold-knotted buttons crimson and staining the jade plaques on his belt, which many of the ministers wore—believing the jade protected them from illness and ill luck.

I started to press my hand against his wound to stop the bleeding, but he grabbed my hands. His lips were already graying, final words dying on his breath. It was then I noticed my skin was colder than his, colder than death.

His mouth parted, and he spluttered sounds. "H-help me," he pleaded. He gripped my sleeve, pulling it over his face as if its magic might resurrect him.

I pressed a hand to his chest and gently uncurled his fingers from my sleeve. But he had already passed into the next world.

Remorse clotted my throat as I closed his eyes. I started to murmur a prayer for him, but the table shook, the servants shouting that it was about to collapse.

I crawled out quickly and backed against the wall. The emperor's guards were still attacking the shansen, and one staggered my way, bloody claw marks etched deep into his chest. When I leaned onto my side to get out of his way, something hard hit my thigh.

My dagger!

I pulled it out of my pocket, my hands curling over the walnut hilt.

"Jinn," I whispered to the weapon, quickly unsheathing it. The blade's meteorite edge began to glow a faint gray.

I held the dagger close. I'd only used its power once—against Bandur on the Isles of Lapzur. Gods, I hoped it would work tonight.

Springing to my feet, I shouted, "Lord Makangis! You've missed me!"

He turned to pounce on me, taking the entire width of the banquet hall in three fleet leaps. He would have crushed my bones with his heft, but his hind legs stumbled at the last moment and he landed farther from me than he should have.

Surprise flitted across his beastly features, and as he snarled in confusion, I raised my dagger to show my strength. The power of the meteorite made him balk.

He's not a demon, I realized, stunned. His eyes were black, not red like Bandur's—or mine. His wounds bled not smoke but bright human blood. What was he?

Whatever he was, I swung at him. Even on four legs, he stood taller than I, so I had to jump to attack his neck. The meteorite grazed his skin, and he let out a terrible roar.

His claws swiped at me, and blood trickled down my arm.

I felt no pain, only anger, and I drove my weapon into the shansen's ribs. He writhed and twisted, his face contorting until it was more man than tiger.

Finally, the shansen stood in front of me. But before the emperor's soldiers could capture him, he pulled up the hood of his fur-lined cloak and shouted, "Gyiu'rak!"

A terrible gale erupted, and from a storm of wind and ash, the shadow of an enormous tiger emerged behind the warlord, folding over him.

The shansen's demon.

It gazed at me for a moment that seemed to stretch for eternity. Its eyes were red as the cinnabar used to tint A'landi's prized scarlet lacquer, so depthless they had no reflection, no soul.

Then I blinked, and the shansen was gone.

An eerie silence fell over the banquet hall. A few red lanterns still swung from the rafters, round shadows flickering as ash settled.

Heart pounding, I lowered my dagger and scanned the room. Dozens of servants and ministers and guests were dead, many more wounded. The emperor himself cowered behind a broken screen, the corpses of his bodyguards strewn about him.

He pushed the bodies aside and stood, his robes bloody and streaked with soot, unharmed.

I needed to go—I needed to leave this graveyard before anyone realized what I had done.

Ducking into a shadow, I sheathed my dagger and slipped out of the hall into the night.

. . .

I was not fool enough to believe that the emperor would reward me for protecting him against the shansen. Now that he had seen I could wield magic, he would never let me leave his side.

I tore off the dress of the moon, and my body gave a violent shudder. All of me ached, and an agonizing heat buzzed through my fingertips as I hurriedly gathered my things.

The tattered threads of my enchanted carpet poked out from under my bed. It seemed a lifetime ago that I'd woven it with just two bundles of blue and red yarn, only half believing it would ever fly. Now I understood the costs of magic better. Like me, my rug didn't have much time left.

I seized it, along with my letters from Baba and my sketchbook. I didn't know where I would go, but I didn't have much time.

The only pause I allowed myself was to drink a cup of water

to soothe my parched throat. A sudden coldness gripped my heart when the candles on my table flickered, most of them snuffed by an eerie wind.

But what wind? All my windows were shuttered.

Then I saw the wolf lurking at my door. His name boiled out of my throat:

"Bandur."

The demon entered and leaned against my wall, paws scraping the floor. "The power is irresistible, isn't it?"

My hand slid behind my back for my dagger, gripped the hilt. "Get out of here."

"You feel it leaving you now. It's becoming hard to breathe, little by little it suffocates you; you feel the fire within you dying." His voice was matter-of-fact. "Stoke the flames, Maia. Let it burn."

I threw my bundle over my shoulder and headed for the door.

Bandur leapt to block me. "Now that you have tasted it, it will consume you faster than before. You don't have long, Maia Tamarin. The Forgotten Isles call for you." His paw curled over my wrist, claws sinking into my flesh. "Surely, you've heard the voices."

I had.

Sentur'na, they begged me. *Sentur'na, come back to us. We need you.*

His claws sank deeper into my wrist. Trying not to wince from the pain, I wrenched my arm away and pulled out my dagger.

"Jinn!" I cried.

The blade shot out of its sheath, its meteorite surface glittering. Holding it high, I whirled for Bandur and stabbed at his heart—

But he dissipated into smoke, and my dagger met only air.

His laugh resonated across the walls of my chamber. "So much fight. You'll make a fine guardian."

"Show yourself," I demanded. My voice shook, the dagger in my hand trembling.

Bandur reappeared in the mirror. "Hurry, Maia. Any longer, and I will send my ghosts to destroy all that you love." He mused, "I will start with this palace."

"Go ahead," I snapped. "I care nothing for the emperor."

"But what about your friends here? All these innocent lives. You already have blood on your hands, dear Maia, especially after tonight."

I glanced down at the wound on my arm. A plume of smoke curled out from Bandur's reflection, brushing my skin. To my horror, its touch had healed me.

"What is the shansen?" I whispered.

"He struck a deal with Gyiu'rak," Bandur replied, "the demon of the northern forests."

"Gyiu'rak," I repeated. So that was the name of the shansen's demon.

"Her power lives in him now until the bargain is complete."

"To conquer A'landi." I sucked in my breath. "What then?"

"Then she will claim her reward. Her blood price."

I shuddered. "What is that?"

"Why should it matter to you?" Bandur asked, stroking my hair now. I jerked away, and he laughed. "Soon you will be bound to the Isles of Lapzur, and I will finally be free."

"I will never go to Lapzur," I said through my teeth.

"You know that is not true. Every night, its waters beckon you, and its ghosts call to you."

I curled my fists. *Sentur'na*.

His shadow loomed over the dress of the moon, smothering its silvery light.

"Stop lying to yourself," he said in a pitying tone. "Amana cannot save you. Soon the dresses too will be consumed by the power inside you. What a guardian you will be then, armed with the sun and the moon and the stars."

Then, as swiftly and silently as he had arrived, he was gone.

I started out the door, refusing to be shaken by Bandur's visit. What if he was right? Maybe I had no choice but to obey the calling. But I wouldn't go without a fight.

Gritting my teeth, I probed the newly healed skin on my arm. So the stories about the shansen were true. He *had* made a bargain with a demon to conquer A'landi.

Without Edan, Emperor Khanujin would have no chance against him.

You could stay, a voice inside me nagged. *You could help. You have the power of a demon stirring inside you.*

It was true . . . if I stayed, maybe I could help. Maybe I could—

"No!" I balked. I buried the voice deep into my thoughts, knowing that behind its cloying words was the demon Maia, trying to needle her way into my mind. The more I used the dark powers stirring inside me, the faster I would turn into a monster.

Then A'landi is without hope. All that you sacrificed will be for nothing.

I clenched my fists. Edan had called me the hope of A'landi. He'd left believing I could save it.

I should have told him the truth.

I looked in the mirror. My face was pale, no color flushed my cheeks, and the warm, earthy brown that had once lit my eyes was flat and dull. "I will be of no help to A'landi if I am a demon," I told my reflection.

My duty to the emperor was done. I could stay here no longer.

Instead, I would find a way to defeat Bandur and free myself of his curse. Even if it meant returning to the Isles of Lapzur.

First things first. I couldn't expect to escape the palace unnoticed carrying the dress of the moon. I opened my trunk, searching for the two walnuts and the glass vial I'd used to store the sun, the moon, and the stars on my journey with Edan.

I found them wrapped in layers of silk and satin scraps and scooped them up with my palm. At my touch the walnuts and the vial trembled as if possessed, rattling onto the floor until— they snapped together.

In their place was a round walnut pendant made of glass, with a smooth crack in the center: my two walnuts and the vial forged together. It dangled from a thin chain, melded of gold and silver.

The pendant was smaller than my palm, about the same size as the amulet Emperor Khanujin wore—and Bandur, too.

Bandur's had a crack in the center.

A shiver tingled across my skin as I slipped the chain over my head and grasped the pendant. It began to glow, and I held my breath as the dress of the moon spun and spun, its silvery ribbons whirling as the dress spiraled smaller and smaller, then disappeared into the pendant's crack.

When the dress had fully returned inside, the pendant weighed lighter against my chest. But the absence of the other two dresses was a hollow ache. The sun and the moon and the stars yearned to be together.

The other two dresses are in Lady Sarnai's apartments, I thought, swallowing hard. I didn't have time to retrieve them. I needed to leave now. Too many had witnessed the power of my dress and my dagger against the shansen. If the emperor found me, he'd force me to stay at his side to defend the palace. I'd never be able to break my curse.

But deep down, I knew Bandur was right. Amana's dresses were my lifeblood now.

I couldn't leave without them. Without all of them.

CHAPTER EIGHT

"We heard the warning bells," Jun said when she let me inside Lady Sarnai's chambers. Her voice trembled. "Is . . . is the emperor in danger? Has the shansen attacked?"

"Yes," I replied solemnly, "but he's retreated for now."

"Why did he attack?" she asked. "Did he find out that you weren't—"

She couldn't finish the words, and I couldn't bring myself to confirm her fears.

"It's over now." I hesitated, hating myself for the lie I was about to tell. "The emperor's commanded me to take the dresses for safekeeping."

"Thank the gods," Zaini said fervently. "They're cursed."

She and Jun pointed me to Lady Sarnai's trunks. "Take them. Please."

I scooped the dress of the sun and the dress of the stars— still damaged from my cutting it off Lady Sarnai's body—into my arms and funneled their essence into my pendant.

Then, I heard a hoarse cry from behind the bedchamber's closed doors.

At first, it sounded more like an animal than a person. Low and reedy, like the whimper of an injured fox. But when I heard it again, I recognized the voice.

Lady Sarnai. The air around her was thick with incense

meant to drive away the evil spirits Jun and Zaini were convinced had attacked her.

The sight of her made me shudder. Jun and Zaini had bandaged most of her skin and treated it with salve, but they hadn't wrapped her nose, mouth, and ears, which were a motley mess of violet and blue burns and ore-colored splotches—the pigments not unlike the blood of stars.

"Demon's breath," I whispered. "She looks worse than before."

Ghosts haunted Jun and Zaini's eyes. The maids looked like they hadn't eaten or slept in the past two days. Knowing Khanujin, I bet they hadn't even left Lady Sarnai's apartments, on pain of death. The way their voices trembled confirmed my suspicions.

"We've . . . we've tried everything, Master Tamarin."

"No matter what we feed her, she will not wake. And her skin . . . where the dress touched her—it keeps changing, sometimes blue, sometimes gray. We've never seen anything like it."

The two maids huddled together fearfully. "She can't be long for this world."

The calmness of my voice surprised me. "His Majesty hasn't sent for a doctor?"

Jun and Zaini shook their heads.

No surprise. The emperor probably feared that the royal physicians might divulge the secret that Lady Sarnai was near death. Not that it mattered anymore, after what had happened at the banquet.

I swallowed. I couldn't leave Lady Sarnai like this.

Darkness crawled in me. *Let her be. She's never been kind to you. Let her die.*

I turned to the door, but then Lady Sarnai coughed. The

sound was so pitiful, so unlike the fierce princess who had once terrified me.

Think of how she slit the throats of those guards. She wouldn't have a second thought about leaving you behind.

I had no doubt this was true.

Then leave her.

It would be so easy to listen to the dark reason in my head, to let the demon strip me of my humanity one thought at a time. But the old Maia was still there, for now. *You're stronger than this*, she urged. *Resist.*

Leave her, the demon insisted. *She wouldn't hesitate to abandon you.*

Yes, but I wasn't Lady Sarnai.

I was Maia Tamarin.

I let my satchel slide from my shoulder onto the ground. It landed with a soft thump, and I knelt beside Lady Sarnai, ignoring the relentless whispers buzzing within me.

How could I save her?

Even if they'd been permitted to visit, doctors couldn't do anything for Lady Sarnai. The only person who could help her wasn't here.

"Where are the Lord Enchanter's chambers?" I asked.

Jun blinked at me, her wide-set eyes blank with confusion.

"In the Summer Palace, they were by the Great Temple," I said impatiently, grabbing a spare sheet draped on one of Lady Sarnai's chairs. "Where are they here?"

"But the Lord—"

"Yes, I know he's away. This is urgent."

They blurted their answer, and I was gone.

. . .

A palace-wide search for me had begun. At every turn, I heard the guards shouting my name, "Master Tamarin, reveal yourself! Master Tamarin!"

Under a somber veil of clouds, I quickly fashioned a disguise out of Lady Sarnai's bedsheet. I pulled it over my head and hurried to the north end of the Autumn Palace.

The entire courtyard was empty. Shadows haunted the path to Edan's residence, which boasted no celebratory lanterns or flowers or any sign of the earlier festivities. I slipped through the doors to his apartments and slid them shut.

His rooms had been ransacked. Books and scrolls lay sprawled across the floor, having been thrown without care from their shelves. His desk was a mess of inkpots and brushes, his bed an upheaval of feathers and sheets. Dust rose in clouds as I sidestepped a smashed bamboo birdcage and shuffled deeper into his chambers.

I wasn't sure where to look for something that might heal Lady Sarnai, but Edan's workspace seemed like the best place to start.

Maps littered his desk. Some pages were yellowed with age and smelled of spices I couldn't name. There were journals in his careful handwriting, with illustrations of countries I'd never heard of. I thumbed through the top one, pausing over a drawing of a familiar Niwa spider. These must have been the notes Edan consulted before we'd left for the Halakmarat Desert. His writing was in a language I couldn't read.

Nelrat, I supposed.

"Do you not write anything in A'landan, Edan?" I murmured, moving on to his cabinets. From the deep dents in the wood, it appeared the emperor's men had tried to smash the locks open, but without success. They'd given up, maybe too frightened by what magic still lurked in the Lord Enchanter's chambers.

Not long ago, I hadn't been too different. Well, I'd never been frightened of Edan, but I remembered the air of mystery surrounding him during our early meetings. It had taken months before I saw the earnest boy beneath the enchanter's cloak of arrogance and magic.

I touched the lacquered cabinet doors, tracing my fingers from the strange words inscribed on the surface down to the bronze lock in the middle. There was no keyhole, but the lock was shaped like a hawk, its two spread wings latching either side of the doors.

My curious fingers folded the wings together, not expecting anything to happen. But the metal warmed under my touch, the bronze melting into a black lacquer like the rest of the wood. The doors cracked open, as if they recognized me.

Inside, I found drawers containing glass vials, filled to the brim with liquids of every color imaginable. There were plants and flowers and herbs I did not recognize, most dried and still in their whole form; some were crushed or ground and stored in hemp pouches. I found seeds that bloomed into flowers when I touched them, feathers and scales and molted snakeskins. At the bottom of the cabinet, I found a tray of objects. Talisman boxes inlaid with iridescent shell, a teak comb with missing teeth, an hourglass, a tin cup, an empty inkpot. The bottomless leather pouch that allowed Edan to carry so many books with him during our trip. I quickly exchanged my satchel for it, then picked up a familiar-looking mirror.

A reflection of the truth, he'd called it. When I was pretending to be my brother, its glass had revealed my reflection as my true self. Maia, not Keton.

I swept the dust from its glass and looked at myself. Without powder caking my cheeks and rouge painting my lips, I could see the familiar constellation of freckles on my face, the tired eyes that looked older than I remembered, the chapped lips.

"Still Maia," I murmured, relieved. For now.

Tucked beside his bed was the little flute he had brought on our journey. I raised it to my lips, but I could not coax a sound out. How forlorn it was, without its master. Longing for Edan flooded over me, and for those carefree days when I could sit by a campfire listening to him play.

You're not here to relive memories of Edan, I chided myself sternly.

Setting down the flute, I rifled through the books on the ground. Most were in languages I could not read.

A loose page peeking out of one of his journals caught my eye. Edan had brought it with him on our journey. Sand from the desert still spilled from its pages.

With trembling fingers, I picked up the loose page.

Maia. My name jumped out at me in Edan's elegant script— finally, something written in A'landan.

Knees suddenly weak, I sank into the chair by his desk.

Xitara—my brightest one. Forgive me for leaving you.
It is not what I would choose, but I would pay any
price for your freedom—for your happiness. You say
you will not be happy without me, but I know that is
not true. Live your life, xitara.

His writing ended there, unfinished. It was the farewell letter he had intended to give me when he left for Lapzur.

I held it to my heart, the page crinkled from the strained press of my fingertips. I missed Edan so, so much.

"Where are you?" I murmured, reaching for my pendant. The walnut shell was warm, the light of my dresses pulsing within.

I turned back to the pile of books when a chill came over me, a sudden breeze tickling the back of my neck.

"Maia?" a voice called, faint yet near. A voice I dreamed of these nights, so tender and dear was it to me.

Again, "Maia?"

I trembled. The sound came from the mirror of truth. Was this my demon sight again?

I picked up the mirror and looked within: Edan sat by a tall stack of books, his black hair falling over his eyes. Trees rustled behind him, and the sky above was blue and clear. It was day, whereas here, it was night.

"Edan?" I called urgently.

He looked up and jumped to his feet. "Maia? Maia, can you hear me?"

"Yes." I reached out to touch him, but my fingers only slid along the cold glass of the mirror.

"Are you safe?" Edan asked. Dark circles bruised the skin under his eyes. He hadn't been sleeping well. Yet somehow, without the weight of his oath upon him, he seemed more carefree than before. What torture it was to see him so clearly yet not be able to touch him.

I nodded.

"I was hoping you'd find the mirror."

His smile was infectious even from a thousand miles away. I couldn't help smiling back, until I remembered why I was here.

"I need your help," I started. "Lady Sarnai was badly hurt by the dress of the stars—it attacked her, and now she will not wake. Is there something here that can help her?"

His brow wrinkled in thought. "Check the third drawer. In the cabinet with the hawk. The lock will open to your touch—"

"It's open already," I said, managing to sound both sheepish and brusque.

"A small glass bottle labeled AN EXTRACT USED FOR THE GRAVEST OF INJURIES. I used it to save the emperor during the Five Winters' War. A few drops will ease her pain, but I can't promise it'll wake her."

I stared at the array of bottles. "I can't read any of them."

"Use the mirror."

I held it over the bottles until I found the one Edan had described. "Does this mirror always translate ancient texts?"

"Only for you."

I raised an eyebrow.

"I had a feeling you wouldn't be able to stay away from my chambers for long," Edan said with a roguish grin, then his voice softened. "When Khanujin forbade me to see you, I spent the time preparing to leave you. Everything I have is yours now, Maia. My possessions will speak to you, the way your scissors do."

A flood of warmth crept up in my chest, and I savored it, wishing the cold would never come back. "Thank you."

Edan started to speak, but I interrupted. He was going to ask about the wedding, or how I was, and I wanted to avoid those questions. "Did you make it to Agoria? Khanujin is looking for you."

Edan shook his head. "The master I sought never left. He's at the Temple of Nandun."

So Edan wasn't in Agoria at all—but still in A'landi, high in the mountains somewhere, tucked away in a shrine to the beggar god.

I let out a sigh of relief and leaned toward the mirror. "Has he been able to help you?"

Edan's dark brows knotted, and the color drained from his face.

"Maia," he whispered hoarsely. "Maia, you said you were free of Bandur."

"What?" I drew back. How did he know I wasn't? My eyes weren't burning, and he couldn't have heard about what had happened to Lady Sarnai.

"You are wearing a demon's amulet."

I looked down and saw my pendant had slid out of its place inside my tunic.

"No, it's just the walnuts you gave me." I held it out, showing him. "This isn't—"

His jaw tensed, his voice thick with dread, with fear. "Don't go to Lapzur."

"I have to," I said. "I have to fight him before . . ." *Before I lose too much of myself.*

"You can't win if you go alone," said Edan. "Wait for me. I'll go with you."

The strain in his voice touched me, but I wasn't going to change my mind. "I'm getting worse every day, Edan. Soon I won't be able to resist."

A grimace tore apart Edan's careful composure. "Come here, then," he urged. "My teacher, Master Tsring, can help you. He's mortal now, but he knows more about magic than anyone, save the gods themselves. He's dealt with Bandur before."

"I don't have much time," I said in a small voice. "I don't even know where you—"

"The Tura Mountains. They're not far from Lapzur. Call for me when you see them, and I will find you."

"With the mirror?"

"Yes," replied Edan, "but be careful. The demon inside you will grow stronger every day, and whenever you use magic, you open yourself to its influence. Do not use its power. It will corrupt you, and you will turn faster."

To that, I said nothing.

"Maia!" Edan had raised his voice, and I flinched. His eyes were so blue, not the blazing yellow they'd once turned when he was angry. "Swear it on my life, Maia, that you will not use the demon's power. Swear you will not go to Lapzur without me."

Sudden rage rose in me. It flared white and hot and so dazzlingly intense I could not control it.

How dare he! He does not control you, Sentur'na.

The whispers grew louder, deafening. Edan's furniture vanished. Trees sprang from the carpets, their branches withered and gnarled. The Forgotten Isles of Lapzur. I shut my eyes, pushing out the hallucination. "No!"

The mirror slipped from my grasp, and I lunged for it, but whatever connection Edan and I had had was broken.

"Edan?" I whispered, clutching the mirror. Only my reflection stared back at me. "Edan, I'm sorry."

But Edan was gone.

I crumpled onto the ground in despair. My pendant whirled around my neck. I grasped it and forced it to still.

Edan was wrong. It *wasn't* a demon's amulet. The dresses inside belonged to the mother goddess, Amana. There was nothing sinister about them.

Still, a pinprick of doubt stabbed me. *Then why is there a crack in the center, like in Bandur's amulet?*

That, I couldn't answer.

I tucked the pendant back inside my tunic. The dresses inside thrummed softly, a steady pulse against my heart's. Unlike my scissors' song, it did not stop when I let go.

I inhaled a deep, shaky breath. At least Edan was safe. That would have to do for now.

CHAPTER NINE

I didn't hear the window open.

It was morning, and I was still in Edan's chambers reading through the books at my feet when, from behind, someone shook me.

"They're coming for you!"

Ammi pried the book from my hands. "Master Tamarin," she pressed, "are you listening? You have to get out of here!"

"What?" I rasped. My tongue was so dry it clicked against the roof of my mouth. "Who?"

"The emperor!" Ammi pulled me to my feet. "Jun and Zaini won't be able to hold their tongues for long. You must hurry!"

I grabbed my things, including the medicine I'd found in Edan's cabinets. "What of Lady Sarnai?"

"She's alive, but barely. They took her to the dungeon this morning. That's what will happen to you if you don't—"

The dungeon! "I have to help her."

"Are you listening?" Ammi grabbed my arm. "Half of the palace guards are looking for you, and the other half are watching Lady Sarnai. You can't—"

I twisted out of her grip and grabbed Edan's pouch, slipping the vial, his flute, and his mirror inside. "You don't have to come if you don't want to."

Ammi wrinkled her nose. "I'm not letting you go alone. I doubt you even know where the dungeon is."

I didn't.

My expression must have been easy to read, for she let out a sigh. "I'm going to regret this, aren't I?"

I slipped the pouch's straps over my head. "Why are you helping me? I thought you were upset with me."

"I *am*," she replied, "but that doesn't mean I want you killed. You're too good a tailor for that, Master Tamarin."

I might have smiled if the morning hadn't taken such a dire turn. Still, the iciness creeping into my heart thawed just enough for me to smile at my friend. "Call me Maia."

A tight smile graced Ammi's lips in return. "Hurry up, Maia. The last thing I want is to be caught with you." She started climbing out the window. "This way. We'll cut through the gardens. By the gods, I hope the guards are having lunch."

. . .

They weren't. And unfortunately, Ammi was right about the dungeon teeming with security. I would have no chance of getting inside to see Lady Sarnai. Not without help.

Bamboo fences surrounded the prison, a box-shaped structure constructed of large, mismatched stones. No windows, and no doors but for the entrance. It seemed more like a crypt than a dungeon.

Then again, most prisoners weren't meant to live long inside.

After ducking behind a bush, I mentally marked the guard with the keys dangling from his hip, and reached for my pendant. My thumb edged along the side of the walnut that carried the dress of the sun.

Here goes.

"Wrap your sash around your eyes," I whispered to Ammi. "Shut them as tight as you can. Don't open them—no matter what you hear. Not until the light is gone. Then run back to the kitchens."

Before she could ask any questions, I darted out of my hiding place and counted to three— "Now!"

I reached for my pendant and released the power of the dress of the sun, aiming it at the guards. The light blinded them. One by one, they staggered, dropping their weapons and trying to shield their eyes before crumpling against the fence.

There was no time to waste. I knocked past them and crouched beside the guard with the keys, snipping off his belt with my scissors.

Only when I was well inside the dungeon did I shut the laughter of the sun back into my pendant, but I kept a hand on it in case I encountered more guards.

I scrambled down the stairs, scanning the prison for Lady Sarnai. Most of the cells were empty. A few held servants caught for stealing, or soldiers who drank too much. I didn't spare them a glance. According to Ammi, the more important prisoners would be on the lower level.

When I reached the floor below, Lady Sarnai's labored breathing gave her away. I hurried toward the sound, the iron keys slippery with sweat in my palm, and opened the door.

Shock flew through me, and I gasped.

Overnight, Lady Sarnai's condition had worsened. Her ivory skin was now a pale, unnatural gray-blue. Even more worrisome were the black and violet splotches flaring under her robes; they blazed over her chest, coming dangerously close to her heart.

Jun and Zaini had been right—she wouldn't be long for this world, not if the blood of stars continued to consume her.

Someone groaned in the cell across from hers. Lord Xina. The space for him was too small, and he was curled against a corner, a rivulet of blood dripping from his temple to the ground. "Get away from her," he croaked. Chains rattled as Lord Xina feebly struggled to rise. "Get!"

I had to hurry before the guards heard him. Collecting myself, I stepped closer to Lady Sarnai and reached into my pouch for Edan's extract.

Using my teeth, I uncorked the bottle, then poured half its contents down her throat, covering her mouth with my hand so it wouldn't dribble out. A grunt escaped her lips when I touched her, and I winced; I couldn't imagine the pain she must be in.

At last she swallowed, and gradually, her breathing evened. I waited expectantly, praying that the blood of stars would cease to spread across her body. That she might at least stir and wake.

But Edan's medicine hadn't worked.

I panicked. *What now?*

Desperately I tried to pull her to her feet, but I couldn't budge her. Either I gave up now and made my escape or I risked the guards catching me.

Think, Maia. Think.

Out of habit, I started to reach for my scissors before my fingers twitched with revelation. My pendant still throbbed against my chest, and when I touched it, a soft tingle of comforting warmth rushed through my fingertips.

A silvery thread, so thin at first I was sure I had imagined it, spun out of the pendant through my fingers and shimmered over Lady Sarnai's face. Like tears.

Could the tears of the moon help her?

In legend, the goddess of the moon had been a healer, the counterpart to her fiery husband, the sun. It was worth a try.

I unwound the dress of the moon from my pendant. Even in the dungeon's thin air, it rose like a kite on a breeze before settling gently over Lady Sarnai's body.

I knelt beside her, watching the argent satin ripple over her arms and legs. Slowly, ever so slowly, a soft white glow spread over her body, soothing the blood of stars' vicious flares until the marks, dark and glittering, receded from her heart. Then Sarnai's eyelids fluttered, and her ashen blue complexion began to change color and bloom with the faint promise of life.

As the moonlight woke her, I eyed the shackles chaining her to the wall and hesitantly took out my scissors. Would they work on metal?

Their silver blades shone brightly against the chains, and as I held them to the iron links, they began to hum. They were telling me to try.

Slipping my fingers into the bows, I parted the blades and cut at the shackles. Each snip took far more strength than cutting through fabric—so much that I needed to use both hands to clamp the scissor blades down on the links.

With a brittle clatter, a wrist shackle fell to the ground.

"Thank the Nine Heavens," I whispered. Working more quickly now, I moved to Lady Sarnai's other wrist, then to her ankles—until she was free.

Footsteps thumped above. The guards were also waking.

I shook Sarnai until she moved, breathing hard. She jolted

up in a delirious panic, tossing aside the dress of the moon and lashing at the vial still at my side. She thought I'd come to poison her.

"Shhh." I tried to calm her. "I'm here to—"

Sarnai snatched my scissors and pressed their blades against my neck. The metal sang violently into my ears.

She meant to slit my throat with them, but her wrist wobbled, her face twisting with bewilderment as she saw what had happened to her. Faded were the fiery blue splotches on her skin, the marks of the dress of the stars. But in their place were silver-white scars, like brushstrokes across her face and body. The tears of the moon.

As the blades quivered in her grasp, I pried them gently from her.

"Why?" she whispered.

It took me a moment to realize she was asking why I had risked my life to help her. I had asked myself that too. I didn't like her. No doubt she felt the same about me.

I returned the scissors to my belt. My tongue felt leaden, and my mouth became dry. I didn't know what to tell her.

Before he left, Edan had called me the hope of A'landi. But he'd been wrong. I couldn't be the hope of A'landi, not when I was turning into a demon. But Lady Sarnai, daughter of the shansen and bride of the emperor, could unite the North and South. She was a princess and a warrior in her own right.

"Because you are the hope of A'landi," I replied softly.

She licked her lips, still cracked and parched. "Khanujin will punish you for this."

"I'm not afraid."

Lady Sarnai raised an eyebrow as if she didn't believe me. But she said no more.

"We have to go now," I urged her. "The guards are wakening."

"How many?"

Ever practical was the shansen's daughter.

"At least three in the dungeon. Four at the entrance. More outside."

Sarnai barely flinched at the numbers. Her strength was returning.

Without a word of thanks, she rose and slipped out of the cell. Moments later, I heard a guard exclaim, "You—"

Bones cracked, and swords clanged against the iron doors and stone walls. Bodies fell.

I winced, regretting I hadn't asked her to leave the men alive.

Once the threat of the guards had been eliminated, Lady Sarnai returned. I was one step ahead of her; I'd already opened the door to Lord Xina's cell.

She draped Lord Xina's arm over her shoulders and raised him up. His body was a bloody lattice of cuts and bruises, pus oozing out of his wounds, but once he saw her, his charcoal eyes flickered to life, and he coughed.

Lady Sarnai's frown eased, the only sign of relief she gave. "Can you walk, Xina?"

He looked haggard, his wide face longer than I remembered. But he gritted his teeth, got onto his feet, and gave a curt nod.

Blood dribbled from his mouth, which was swollen and had many teeth missing. He was too hurt to speak, but it was clear my presence displeased him—whereas he seemed not the least bit fazed about Sarnai's changed appearance. As fleeting as it was, for that moment, he'd won my respect.

"Quickly then," said Sarnai tersely. "We must make it to the river before dusk."

"The river?" I echoed. The Leyang River was south of

the Autumn Palace. "Shouldn't you bear north, toward your father?"

"My father?" Lady Sarnai spun to face me.

"Aren't you going to fight him—and his demon?"

She stared at me, her dark eyes narrowing, making me feel very naïve and very stupid. "What do you think I could do against them? Oh yes, you think I'm the hope of A'landi."

A dry laugh escaped her. "I've done nothing but bleed for this country. Its peace and salvation mean nothing to me. Not anymore."

"But—"

"My father won't stop until he secures the throne," she snapped. "He and his demon will tear this country apart if that's what must be done. I'm leaving before that happens." She raised a sword she'd plucked from one of the defeated guards. "If you've any wits, you'll go too."

For the first time I noticed that, unlike most ladies', her nails were cut short and square, her knuckles rough, calluses running along her fingers worse than even mine. An archer's hands.

A survivor's hands.

"There is no hope for A'landi," she said. "Consider that advice my repayment to you, tailor. And may we never meet again."

With that, she and Lord Xina slipped away, leaving my heart heavy.

If Lady Sarnai would not save A'landi, then war between the emperor and the shansen was inevitable. Thousands would die, brave young soldiers like my brothers Finlei and Sendo, and countless other innocent lives would be lost. The rift in my country I'd sacrificed so much to mend would never heal.

"Coward!" I shouted after her, even though I knew she couldn't hear.

I clenched my fists, hating myself for believing in Lady Sarnai and for hoping she might do what I could not—I thought she would bring peace to A'landi.

I was wrong.

. . .

The only guards I encountered on my way out of the dungeon were dead ones, a trail of bodies that Lord Xina and Lady Sarnai had left behind in their escape.

Once outside, I fished through my pouch, searching its endless folds for my carpet. I pulled it out and began to unroll it, when—

"Halt!"

I spun, whipping my rug open just as the whack of a spear hit the back of my skull.

My knees buckled.

Another hit. This time harder.

My rug slipped from my fingers. I crumpled, and a dark tide washed over the edges of my world.

CHAPTER TEN

Three days after the disastrous wedding banquet, the shan-sen returned—with an army of a thousand men. Their footsteps made the hills quake, and smoke from their cannons grayed the skies. Sensing the earth would bleed once more with war, the heavens wept.

Rain poured from the skies, falling first like needles, then in sheets. Thunder beat the sky, so loudly it swallowed the sounds of the emperor's soldiers.

I pressed my ear against a boarded window.

Nothing.

I'd waited all day for the guards to come for me. Every morning since I'd been caught, two of His Majesty's strongest guards dragged me to the Hall of Dutiful Mending. They forced me to take my breakfast while thirty seamstresses watched, their stomachs growling, their dry throats denied tea or water. They were allowed no food or drink until their work was done.

Then came the worst part. After my breakfast, the seamstresses were beaten.

The girls cowered behind their stations. A few whimpered, "Please, Master Tamarin. Help me."

Their pleas tore at me, but I schooled my features to remain as still as stone. On the first day, I had tried to stop the guards, but in response they took one of the seamstresses' hands and broke her fingers. Now I knew a kind word from me would only make things worse. There was nothing I could do to help them.

Khanujin was punishing them to hurt me. Every girl reminded me of myself: a talented seamstress who was here to provide for someone she loved—her parents, her children, her village. Had I successfully remained the imperial tailor, these women would have been under my supervision. I would have gotten to know each of them like a sister, a mother, a grandmother.

But that would never happen now.

Every five lashes, one of the guards barked at me, "Where have Lady Sarnai and Lord Xina gone?"

All I could do was repeat the truth: "I do not know."

So the lashes continued. Ten a day for each seamstress. I forced myself to face the stinging resentment in their eyes, the injustice that they were being punished for *my* disobedience.

If not for Bandur's curse, my heart would have broken. It frightened me how cold I had become.

Never was a finger lifted against me. Not until Khanujin himself came.

If not for his imperial robes and golden crown, I would not have recognized him as my emperor. He'd shrunk so much his clothes devoured him. His outer coat bunched up in folds, hiding the dragons embroidered on them, and the train of his jacket trailed him in a puddle. His sleeves skimmed the ground, with so much excess fabric he kept his arms raised so no one would notice.

But I noticed.

His frame had thinned to that of a child, his face aged to a man's twice his years. His hair, once thick and glossy, was now thin as paper, and his lips became downturned, twisted with cruelty.

"I should have you killed for what you have done." The words were quiet, but they dripped with acid.

I hadn't bowed to him. At that moment, I decided I wouldn't. So what if I had freed Lady Sarnai and her lover? Without me, the emperor would be dead.

I met his icy stare. "Then kill me. Be done with it."

He flushed with anger, turning purplish red, and he slapped me.

My head jerked back, more from shock than from the strength of his blow. I recovered quickly and returned my gaze to the emperor.

That angered him, and I could tell he was about to strike me again.

"You are afraid," I challenged him. "Your ministers have noticed the change in you, and your enemies in court, the ones that used to fear you, now plot against you. You know your throne is in danger. Even if the shansen weren't a threat, someone from within would overthrow you. Betray you."

"Speak another word and I will have your tongue cut out."

"You won't," I taunted. "You need me. You cannot lead A'landi looking like—"

"Like *this*?" Khanujin barked, pointing at his face and making a grotesque expression. "The shansen brings his army to my gates. We are at war, and I will lead no matter how I appear."

Desperation leaked from his voice. Despite his bravado, he knew A'landi wouldn't follow him like this. Not when he looked more like a ruthless child than the benevolent ruler everyone had been deceived into revering. I nearly felt for him. Maybe some part of him did care for our country.

"You won't win against him. Not without my help. *I* can restore Edan's enchantment. *I* can make you what you once were." As soon as I'd uttered the words, I stopped. Where were they coming from? I *didn't* know how to restore the emperor's enchantment. But I couldn't stop. I spoke as if possessed.

You can, Sentur'na. We will help you.

I clenched my jaw, willing the voices to go away. The effort cost me my calm. My eyes blazed, their scarlet sheen coloring my vision. Khanujin drew a shallow breath; I could tell my appearance unnerved him.

"What are you?"

"The dresses give me power. *Only* me."

I refused to say any more.

"You are no enchanter," he said, staring at me. "You're a . . . a . . ."

Demon? I lifted my pendant, pinching open the walnut slightly so it shone with the power of the sun, the moon, and the stars.

Was it a demon's amulet? I still couldn't bring myself to believe it was. Its power seemed to weigh heavier on me every day, not fighting against the darkness inside me but not embracing it either. Yet.

"I harness the power of Amana," I said, though the words clung to my throat, feeling only half true. "Her magic is even greater than Edan's. How else do you think I defeated the shansen?"

"You are the reason the wedding fell apart," Khanujin growled, but he made no more threats. I could see from how my pendant drew his eyes that I'd tempted him.

He believed me.

"Give up your search for the Lord Enchanter," I said, seizing the silence. "His oath to you is broken, and he is powerless. In return, I will help you."

He gave me a glare so withering it would have sent any of his ministers onto his knees, quivering with fear.

At last he said, "If you are successful, I will consider clemency for your family. But *not* for the Lord Enchanter."

"I'll need the pouch your men took from me," I said, pushing forward. "Everything inside will aid me with the enchantment. And I'll need fabric enough to make a new set of robes."

"A cloak," he decided. "You will enchant a cloak for me. Have it ready by dawn. If it is not, I will have a seamstress killed for every hour longer it takes."

The doors slammed shut behind him. Minutes later, a guard barged into my room and threw my pouch at my feet.

When I looked inside, all I glimpsed was my scissors and my sketchbook. Panic rose in me, until I turned the pouch's soft leather inside out. The meteorite dagger tumbled out, along with my carpet, the mirror, and Edan's flute.

I hugged the pouch to my chest, sighing with relief.

I'd barely returned everything into the pouch when one of the older seamstresses arrived. Her back was hunched as if it'd been recently whipped, and she wouldn't look at me.

In her arms was a bundle of material and threads with which I was to make His Majesty's garment.

"I'm sorry," I wanted to say before she left, but the words wouldn't part from my lips.

I worked through the afternoon, fashioning a cloak with a gold-inlaid hood, then embroidering a dragon onto the back of the garment.

But how to restore the emperor's former glory to him? I did not have any more magic from my journey—no more tears of the moon or laughter of the sun—to weave into the garment.

Even my scissors would conjure no magic on his behalf.

"Amana, help me," I whispered, praying over and over.

She did not heed my plea. My plight, to sew an enchanted cloak for the emperor, was not one worthy of the mother goddess's attentions. The pendant around my neck remained still, the dresses silent.

Even my scissors did not hum. What was I to do?

You know precisely what magic will bring the power you need to restore Khanujin.

My head snapped up. I reached for my meteorite dagger, raising it at the shadows slinking across the floor. I half expected to see Bandur there, his laugh echoing against the walls.

But there was no one. No one but the demon inside me.

My fingers tightened around the dagger's hilt.

"Jinn," I whispered. The veins of meteorite on the blade gleamed to life. As before, touching the stone edge stung. But this time, the blade was warm instead of cool. This time, my fingertips flinched at the pain—as if tiny thorns had bitten them.

I studied the double-edged weapon, stroking the iron half, then touching the meteorite side and laying my fingers flat against the stone.

"Don't use the amulet," Edan had warned me. *"The more you rely on its magic, the harder it will become for you to resist the change."*

But if I didn't, the shansen would win. A'landi would be lost.

Had Lady Sarnai stayed, things would be different. But it was left to me. I had to fight the shansen alone.

"I have to protect A'landi," I murmured to myself.

My pendant thrummed against my chest, its light writhing and boiling as if Amana's children within—the sun, the moon, and the stars—sensed that I was trying to summon a demon.

I removed the pendant from my neck and set it on the ground. My body gave a sudden heave, my pulse quickening as Amana's strength left me.

I wrapped my hand around the sharp edge of the blade and whispered, "Edan, forgive me."

A hot flash of pain cut off my breath. I opened my hand slowly, taking in the thin line of blood arcing across my palm. The color was bright against my skin, but as it seeped out of the wound into the loose lines of my palm and settled there, it darkened like black ink.

Demon's blood.

In shock, I accidentally closed my hand over the dagger again. The pain was worse this time, and I bit my lip to keep from crying out.

Angrily, I flung the dagger to the side, my hand now oozing with dark, shadowy blood.

That's it, my demon urged. *Don't fight it. Use it.*

I raised my fist above the emperor's cloak and squeezed. A few drops were enough for the silk to become awash with the darkest black, the color of a velvet night. My demon's blood shimmered into the veins of the garment, infusing its fibers with a forbidden enchantment that I hoped would be strong enough to save A'landi.

I pulled back my hand, wrapping my cut with a scrap of cloth.

I prayed I hadn't gone too far, muttering aloud: "I'm still me. I'm still Maia."

You're not finished, my demon prodded. *Seal the darkness inside the cloak.*

My fingers shaking, I touched my pendant to Emperor Khanujin's cloak. The light from the walnut, still writhing, ricocheted off the stone walls around me as I began to focus it on a spot of blood, already sinking deeper into the cloth, a stain that would not stop spreading.

Dark shadows enfolded the pendant's two walnut shells and the glass crack in the center, painting the entire piece black. The darkness lingered for a long second before it vanished, and my pendant was restored to how it'd been before.

Inside me, the voices of Lapzur whispered triumphantly, *Sentur'na, Sentur'na—our guardian.*

You are coming home.

At last.

CHAPTER ELEVEN

By nightfall, the earth trembled no more. The heavens ceased their weeping, and the sky god painted his canvas the purple-blue of an iris in bloom. But beneath his strokes of twilight, the acrid smell of cannon fire thickened the air, and swords clanged against the wind.

After sundown, the shansen's army breached the city walls and began their march up the hill to the Autumn Palace. By morning, the war would be at the palace gates.

It was during this eerie interlude, just before dawn, that the emperor summoned me to his war council. He wanted his cloak.

Something told me I might never return to my room, so I brought my pouch, slung over my shoulder. I made it ten paces into the imperial audience chamber before a minister snatched the cloak from my arms and handed it to the emperor.

Khanujin held it up. The hem draped down the wide carpeted steps leading to his throne. The cloak's creamy marigold silk shimmered in the young sunlight, the bold threads of the dragon I'd embroidered a sharp complement to the black brocade embedded into the fabric—dyed by my demon magic.

"It is done?" he asked me. A hint of precaution colored the question.

"Yes."

With a grunt of satisfaction, Khanujin stood and tossed the cloak over his shoulders. Almost at once, the wilt in his shoulders squared, his hollow cheeks and sunken figure broadening until he stood tall and full, and his sable hair, swept under the hood, luminous.

A miraculous transformation. All the ministers drew sharp breaths and fell to their knees. A small smile curled across Khanujin's lips. The same smile that had once enthralled me—had made me worship him as the most magnificent ruler of all kingdoms—now made me loathe him.

"Now we are ready for battle," he said, raising his sword. "Let us claim victory over the shansen."

The ministers fawned over him, praising Amana. Even the minister of war, who had looked weary and anxious only moments before, declared the battle all but won.

"Master Tamarin, you shall come with us."

I jerked up, ears ringing in shock. Outside, lightning flashed, and the rain had started again, rattling against the roof tiles.

"Our army is in position. We ride now."

I didn't struggle when his soldiers threw an armored vest meant for someone twice my size over my tunic and jostled me onto a horse.

Khanujin, too, was in armor, the cloak I'd sewn draped over his shoulders. Soldiers and servants cheered him as he passed, even as the gates rumbled with the shansen's men trying to get in.

"Son of Heaven, bring us victory!" they shouted. Rain beat their temples and streamed down their cheeks. "Khagan of Kings, destroy the traitor!"

Red banners flailed against the wind, embroidered dragons flying among the troops. My horse moved so fast to keep up with the others I hardly noticed we were heading toward the gate, and into battle.

When I heard the first explosions of cannon fire, I mistook it for thunder. But thunder did not hurl stones and tiles into the air like fireworks or make trees erupt in brilliant plumes of black and amber smoke. Every subsequent burst rattled my heart.

My demon sight flickered, making my eyes burn as it soared beyond the Autumn Palace to the valley below. *A slab of wood, a sign for what had once been an apothecary, clattered from a broken roof. The entire town had been destroyed. Ash rained from the sky, and corpses—mostly civilians, whose brows were still wrinkled with fear—littered the roads.*

My head hurt. So this was war—this was why Keton woke up in the middle of the night, screaming and sobbing, after he'd returned home. The ache in my heart, which had dulled since Bandur had claimed me, flared for just an instant. And with it, the old Maia.

A spark of hatred ignited in me.

Outside the palace walls, the shansen's banner flew, the tiger's snow-white fur glistening against jade-green silk. With a shudder, I thought of how the warlord had changed on the night of the banquet. How his demon's amulet had smoldered, smoke billowing in the form of a tiger before it devoured him.

Not *it. She.*

Gyiu'rak.

Arrows spat up from the palace ramparts, arcing above me in a neat line, so high they looked like dots, and a flock of birds bolted at the approach of the shansen's army.

The warlord and his men raised their shields and charged

through the hail of arrows. Men fell on both sides, and more arrows flew. Then the gates roared open, and the emperor and his legions spilled outside.

The emperor's soldiers barreled forward at the enemy, horses' teeth gnashing as they galloped past me. Forgotten, I kept to the shadows of the gates, watching the shansen and his sons cut down every man who dared get in their way, watching Khanujin glow with the enchantment from my cloak as he exhorted his men to fight and die for him.

But it wasn't the emperor or the shansen who captured my attention: it was a woman among the warlord's ranks—one whom I had never seen before, mounted on an ivory steed.

A smile graced her lips as she rode serenely into battle. Even on horseback, she appeared taller than was natural, her sinewy limbs bare, a cloak sailing behind her shoulders. Long white hair striped with black at the temples flashed behind her, rippling like the pearlescent armor she wore over her wrists and torso. Like Emperor Khanujin, she was beautiful and strange, so mesmerizing some of the soldiers stopped to stare at her. The bile rose to my throat when I saw the gleaming claws handling her horse's reins, the sharp teeth behind her smile—more feral than serene as she drew close—and her eyes.

Rimmed with the liquid gold of amber and honey, and red as blood in the center.

A *demon's* eyes.

"Gyiu'rak," I whispered. This was her human form.

With supernatural speed, she struck three of the emperor's soldiers dead. Bodies fell around her as she darted between swords and spears, too fast for any human hand to touch, her claws sharp enough to slice through flesh—through bone.

I'd seen what Gyiu'rak had done to Khanujin's soldiers the

98

last time I'd encountered her. It didn't matter whether she was tiger or woman; all it took for a demon to kill was a touch.

There was no way Khanujin would win this battle.

I spurred my horse forward. At my command, its hooves thundered toward the emperor.

"You cannot win!" I yelled at him. "We must retreat."

Khanujin brushed me aside with a flap of his sleeves, and two of his guards flanked me so I couldn't go after him.

Cannon fire drowned my shouts, but then I heard Gyiu'rak's deafening growl and the slice of her claws against the wind as she hurtled toward the emperor.

Strength bubbled in me with violent potential. *You can save him.*

I had only a second to decide. I'd already broken my promise to Edan, so why not heed the voice? Why not give in?

Do nothing, and the emperor will die.

I ducked between Khanujin's two guards and grabbed the emperor by his shield, pushing him off his horse.

The demon slammed into me instead, the impact so brutal I flew off my saddle, landing hard on my back.

My horse collapsed, dead. Gyiu'rak pulled her claws from its flank and sprang to her feet, ready to launch herself at the emperor again.

"Run!" I shouted to Khanujin.

Before Gyiu'rak could leap after him, I caught the hem of her cloak and yanked to hold her back. She spun, lashing at me with her tiger claws.

I was a tailor; I had no warrior's training. Dance as I did to avoid her attack, I felt the swipe of her fingertips bite my flesh.

Were I human, her touch would have killed me. But my leg bore no wound. Not even a mark.

Gyiu'rak's scarlet pupils constricted. "Impossible."

The emperor forgotten, she circled me, ignoring the battle raging around us. Her movements were slow and languid, meant to make me feel like prey.

We both knew I couldn't run away. She was faster than I was, and far stronger.

I reached for my dagger, hidden in the back of my tailor's belt.

Gyiu'rak seized my arm. "You," she rasped, recognizing the weapon as the one I'd wielded against the shansen in the Autumn Palace. The demon looked at me, realization darkening her features.

"You don't belong here," she said into my ear. She hissed, "Sister."

A chill raced up my spine. I shouted, "Jinn!" and unsheathed the blade, then stabbed the glowing meteorite into the demon's chest. Gyiu'rak's mouth stretched into a scream, her white hair billowing around me as her flesh blistered and burned. I shoved the dagger deeper, watching the demon's red eyes darken to cinder—until she finally shriveled into a cloud of smoke.

The cloud took on the form of a tiger as it drifted across the battlefield, seeking its home—the shansen's amulet.

I didn't watch for long. My pulse was a martial thrum, the dagger's blade still singing in my hand.

Around me, the god of death reigned. There were barely any of the emperor's soldiers left. If I didn't do something, all would be lost.

I wove my way through the battlefield, up to the ramparts where Khanujin's remaining archers frantically rained down arrows upon the shansen and his men.

But no matter how many arrows pierced the warlord's back,

he only grew stronger. Soon he'd be at the gates of the Autumn Palace.

Let us help you, Sentur'na. The ghosts of Lapzur will win this fight for you.

Tempting. So tempting. All it would take was a word. A thought.

No.

Drawing on my demon magic would bring dire consequences.

I clutched my pendant. Its warmth radiated uncomfortably against my chest, making me aware of how cold my skin was.

Earlier, when I'd worked on the emperor's cloak, the pendant had been silent. Amana wouldn't come to my aid. But now it trembled, faintly aglow with the light of the sun.

The laughter of the sun would overpower the shansen's army and force him to retreat. It would win the battle for Khanujin.

But did I dare call on Amana?

The power of her dresses was with me, locked tight in my pendant. Before, I hadn't hesitated. Now I remembered what had happened when I made Khanujin's cloak, how the darkness had spilled across the pendant, briefly painting it black as a demon's amulet.

My dresses were the only shield I had against my demon self. If I called upon Amana's magic—if I sacrificed the dress of the sun to save the emperor—then I risked weakening my own defenses.

The only alternative is far worse, I realized grimly. I trusted Amana more than I trusted any demon, even my own.

Taking the pendant in my hand, I released the dress of the sun. It spilled out like shimmering sand, its wide skirts flaring over my legs, the bodice tightening against my waist. My tailor's clothes vanished under the magnificent power of the dress, and the strength of the sun filled me, silencing the whispers from Lapzur that haunted me.

Arrows arced toward me, but the dress of the sun swallowed them all. Flames burst from the seams of my dress, flaring whenever anyone dared get too close.

The heat scorched me and yet imbued me with incredible strength; the power was irresistible. But did it come from the dress of the sun or from the demon blood flowing in my veins? Or worse yet, from both?

I'd soon have my answer.

Shadows gathered at the hem of my skirts, slowly slinking into the folds of my dress. The laughter of the sun fought them off, flaring brighter than before, but my demon was strong. She knew how to play on my fears.

The dress of the sun won't be enough, she whispered huskily. *What can it do, blind the shansen's army? You'll need more to save your emperor from Gyiu'rak, but Amana will not heed your plea. I am here. The ghosts of Lapzur are at your command. By the power of the sun and moon and stars, they will obey us. They will decimate the shansen's army. They will defeat his demon.*

She was right; I did need her. But at what cost would she win this battle for me?

Deep inside, I already knew. Edan's concerned face bubbled up in my memory. Baba's and Keton's too.

The cost was me—Maia.

I lowered my arms. *No.* I refused to twist Amana's powers.

I tore at the dress, but it would not come off. My fingers fumbled for the scissors.

I cut and cut, ignoring the pain bursting inside me from my

mutilating the wondrous creation I had labored over for so many months.

But I had created a living force, and as I stepped out of the dress, its broken seams began to come back together again.

I didn't need Amana to help me. I had the laughter of the sun, the tears of the moon, and the blood of stars with me: three pieces of magic as old as the world itself. I just hadn't known how to use them—until now.

Once more I activated the dagger and, biting my lip through the searing pain, with one, precise slash, I stabbed the dress of the sun in its fiery bodice, drawing the blade down, down to the edge of the skirts until I had ripped the gown in half. Then I threw the dress, the first of Amana's legacy, into the sky.

Let the laughter of the sun aid my people, I prayed, watching it burn brighter and brighter. *Let the power of Amana save them and bring hope for another day.*

In a single burst of light, the dress exploded into the clouds and was no more.

Darkness swept across the Autumn Palace, silencing the arrows and the swords and the spears. As the weapons burned into ashes, the shansen hollered for his army to retreat.

My pendant knocked against my chest, sending a surge of agony rocking my mind from my heart, my heart from my body. Somewhere in the back of my consciousness or in the hollow chambers of my soul, I saw my own blood-red eyes gleaming at me amid a fury of smoke.

And I screamed.

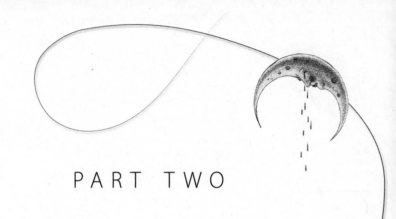

PART TWO

THE TEARS
OF THE MOON

CHAPTER TWELVE

Frost crusted my eyelashes, flecks of ice flaking off when I tried to open my eyes.

I am not dead.

My heart stuttered, still beating.

And I am not a demon.

My thoughts were mine. I was still Maia.

I sat up, relieved to recognize my own hands and arms, the tangled black hair brushing my cheeks.

Yet I felt different. Everything ached, a numb sort of pain, vestiges of the agony that had nearly killed me when I destroyed the dress of the sun. And my head . . .

Sentur'na . . . , a chorus of voices beckoned.

My heart throbbed, trying to fight off the calling. *No, I'm not Sentur'na. I'm not a demon.*

Sentur'na.

The voices rose up, growing stronger, gnawing hungrily at the hollow inside me.

A thick strip of bandages hugged my waist; it smelled fresh, lightly scented with ginger. My fingertips grazed my abdomen as I unwrapped it, and I winced.

My skin was scaled with white and gold bruises, so luminous and pearlescent they would have looked almost pretty if not for the stains of dried pus. The dress of the sun had hurt me, but unlike Lady Sarnai, its power couldn't kill me. I was already healing.

I touched my pendant. The walnut half that had once carried the laughter of the sun no longer sparked gold when I touched it, yet the pendant weighed more heavily on my chest than before—despite the fact that there were only two dresses left inside now.

The tears of the moon. And the blood of stars.

I planted my feet on the ground, surprised when they met rough stone instead of wood. Birds I had never heard before chirped outside my walls. Where was I?

My breath turned to steam in the chilly air, and I inhaled. It smelled different here. A wave of homesickness rushed over me when I heard the unmistakable rhythm of tides washing onto the shore. I was near the sea.

I peeked through the cracks of a hastily boarded window. All I could make out was the full moon hanging in the sky. She had been a slender crescent last time I'd seen her.

By that count, I'd been asleep for two weeks. *Two weeks!* I let out a heavy breath. Every day I remained free of Bandur's clutches was a victory.

"Maia?"

Startled, I turned. I hadn't even heard Ammi come in, carrying a tray of ginger water and more bandages.

"You're awake!" she exclaimed. The water on her tray trembled.

"What's happened?" I asked. "Where are we?"

"The Winter Palace."

The Winter Palace. I should have guessed. Built on a cliff overlooking the Cuiyan Ocean, it was the most naturally protected of His Majesty's palaces, more a fortress than a palace.

"Why not go to the Spring Palace? The army in the capital is far stronger."

My friend lowered her voice, and I understood there were guards outside the door. "His Majesty is wounded. They feared he wouldn't survive the trip to the capital."

"Oh." I breathed in. "How many dead?"

Ammi's face darkened. Her full cheeks looked thinner, and new ghosts haunted her eyes. She reminded me of Keton, of what experiencing war had done to my once carefree brother.

"Over half the Autumn Palace's army."

"Half the army?" I repeated, dumbfounded. The number was far more than I had imagined. "And the shansen?"

"He disappeared. His army retreated."

A victory, then. But a hollow one, given how many casualties we'd suffered.

Still reeling over the losses, I suddenly realized I was missing my scissors. "Where are my things? I was carrying a pouch—"

Ammi reached behind her skirt. "You mean this?"

She held out my pouch. Its folds sagged, the leather more ragged than it'd been before.

"Thank the Nine Heavens," I murmured. I dug into my bag, taking inventory of what was inside. My carpet, tightly rolled, Edan's mirror, my dagger, my scissors. All there.

"Thank you, Ammi. I hope it wasn't too dangerous for you to keep."

"No," she replied. "Everything has been in disarray since the battle. Cooks are now guards, maids are now nurses." She gestured at herself. "I traded shifts with a friend so I could see you, but I can't stay long." She lowered her voice. "Once the emperor learns you're awake, he'll double the guard. Soldiers from the capital are to arrive tomorrow to reinstate order."

Tomorrow.

That meant I'd woken up just in time. I fished out my scissors and reached for my tunic, tucking them in their usual place on my tailor's belt. I couldn't stay here. *But where should I go—to Lapzur or to find Edan?*

Ammi was staring. "When *I* looked in the bag, there was nothing inside. You *are* an enchanter."

"I'm not."

"Everyone saw you fight against the shansen. You saved us."

I faltered. I owed Ammi an explanation.

"I've a little magic," I confessed, "but it isn't like an enchanter's. It's dangerous. It's why Khanujin is keeping me a prisoner. It's why I have to leave."

Ammi flinched at how casually I'd used the emperor's given name. I wouldn't refer to him as my ruler ever again.

"Let me come with you."

I shook my head. "You wouldn't be safe. Besides, I don't even know where I'm going."

"You're going to look for the Lord Enchanter."

My head jerked up. "Who told you that?"

"No one. It just . . . makes sense he'd help you."

Wait for me, Edan had said. *Don't go to Lapzur.*

Guilt prickled me. I'd already broken one promise to Edan, and now I was considering breaking another.

Should I try to find him? When I closed my eyes, I could see him. I could hear him calling my name. But the sharp angles of his chin, the bend in the bridge of his nose, the slight lilt in his voice when he called me *xitara* . . . those memories were beginning to blur.

Soon they'd be gone.

Ammi watched me, her dark eyebrows slanting into a frown. "Something is eating away at you, Maia, and it's not the wounds from your magic. You shouldn't go alone to find the Lord Enchanter. I'm coming with you."

I wanted to say no, but I hesitated. A part of me knew she was right: who could say what state I would be in, in a few days? Whether I could even trust myself. It would be good to have a friend with me. Besides, she'd be harshly punished if Khanujin discovered she'd played a hand in helping me escape and in freeing Lady Sarnai.

Still, I wondered whether she'd be safer with the emperor than with me.

"No," I said. "You should stay here. It'll be dangerous."

Ammi crossed her arms. "It's not a request. After months of lying to me, you're not allowed to refuse. I still haven't forgiven you, you know. If you don't want my help, then at least take me away with you. I've spent too many years working in the palace—I want to go home."

Didn't we all? But her words struck a chord in me, and, in spite of the sting from learning she still hadn't forgiven me, I finally nodded.

"I have to leave tonight," I warned her.

"How? There are soldiers all around the Winter Palace."

I drew my carpet from the pouch and unrolled it. "With this."

Ammi gasped, amazed that it had fit into such a small bag. But her expression changed to skepticism as she examined my carpet. It had become a shabby thing, more a rag than a rug.

"Trust me," I said.

"We'll need food," she said slowly. "And warm clothes. It's getting colder."

"You get the food. I'll take care of the clothes," I said, holding up my scissors.

When she left for the kitchen, I tucked my fingers inside the scissor bows and parted the blades. At once, their magic bloomed; my scissors could make the simplest cotton silken and the dullest material shine, but that was not what I required of them tonight. I made gloves out of a bandage, and out of my bedsheets, the scissors fashioned simple peasants' garb. All I needed to do was touch the clothes to the stone floor, and an unremarkable shade of gray permeated the fabric. Within minutes, I had our disguises.

Within an hour, we left the palace.

. . .

The winds were not in our favor. Powerful gales buffeted my carpet, whose magic had grown feeble over the last few weeks. It limped across the sky, unsteadily rising and dipping without warning when the gusts grew strong. But riding my rug was still far safer than taking the Spice Road. I had a feeling that I could spark the carpet alive with demon magic if I wanted. But I did not dare.

Thankfully, Ammi was too enraptured by the world below us—and the changing landscapes as they flashed by—to notice my troubled silence.

"We're going so fast," she kept marveling. She let out a squeal as the carpet dipped unsteadily. "Will it take us to the edges of the world?"

A smile loosened my lips. I remembered how thrilled I'd been when I first experienced Edan's magic.

"Not *that* far," I replied. "I was told it's ten times faster than His Majesty's speediest stallion. Maybe three now, given the headwinds."

I studied the quilt of landscapes below. Edan was at the Temple of Nandun, deep within the Tura Mountains. From what I remembered, the Tura Mountains were south of the Winter Palace. The same direction as the Forgotten Isles of Lapzur.

"But it'll take us far enough," I murmured. "Someplace the emperor and the shansen won't be able to find us."

I pursed my lips. I couldn't tell her I was bound to the demon guardian of Lapzur, that his call tugged at me more violently than Edan's to the Tura Mountains.

We made our way south, making camp far from the Road, usually in the woods. For Ammi's sake, I wished I had found Edan's feast blanket in his chambers, the one we'd used in the Halakmarat Desert to conjure a twenty-course meal out of thin air.

We subsisted on what she had taken from the palace kitchens, and our tent was the carpet pitched up with a flimsy rod of bamboo. Once it grew colder, we'd have to find shelter in a village and pray His Majesty's soldiers did not recognize us.

Ever since I'd woken, something *had* changed. Even when the winds were biting, I never felt cold. Or hot, when I tended our fire. Ammi had to remind me to eat, or I'd forget. The burns from my dress left only the memory of pain, not pain itself. All of me was numb.

If Ammi noticed, she never asked what was happening to me, never asked why my eyes would suddenly glow red, or why, in spite of the cold, I never needed a cloak, or why sometimes, when she called me Maia or Master Tamarin, it took me an extra beat to respond.

At night, the voices grew stronger. I whispered to myself

sometimes, when Ammi was asleep, to try and drown out the noise. I'd tell myself the stories Sendo used to regale me with or pretend I was writing a letter to Baba and Keton. Sometimes, when the moon was bright, I tried to draw in my sketchbook, but I hadn't brought a brush or ink, and sticks with dirt could only get me so far.

"Dear Baba and Keton," I murmured to myself one night. "You must leave A'landi. War is coming again, and I fear you will not be safe. Please don't look for me. I am going far away, and I do not know if I can return.

"Your Maia," I ended, lingering on the sound of my name.

Ammi rustled at my side. Sitting up on her elbow, she rubbed her eyes. "Who are you talking to at this hour?"

"My father and brother," I replied sheepishly. "Sorry if I woke you."

"Your father and brother?"

"They're far in the South. Sometimes when I miss them, I pretend to write letters. I want to warn them that war is coming again, but even if I had a brush and ink, it would be too risky to send."

Ammi didn't reply. She was so still I thought she'd gone back to sleep, until finally, she said, softly, "I heard your father was a tailor, and your brother was injured in the war. That's why you lied, isn't it? To me, to everyone. You were trying to protect them."

"Yes." I bit my lip. "I'm sorry, Ammi. Really, I am."

"I know. I suppose I would have done the same for my family."

Her family. She'd said she wanted to go home, but she'd never told me where home was. "Where are they?"

"No one's looking for me," Ammi said, ignoring my question. "I could do it for you. Post the letter, I mean. I can't write. Or read."

Most women couldn't. I'd been lucky Baba made me learn.

"I'll teach you," I offered. Eager to rekindle any spark of our old friendship, I drew a few strokes in the earth. "This means *sky*."

Ammi tried to copy it, but she missed a stroke. "Maybe it'd be best if we continue in the morning," she said, making a face. "It's too dark to see."

I'd noticed how every time a shadow moved over our tent, she jolted. After years in the palace, she wasn't used to such darkness. I'd been the same once, but little frightened me anymore. When Edan and I had camped in the forests, I'd grown used to the symphony of sounds, the dance of shadows bending under the moon, the lurking of the unknown.

"You should go back to sleep. It'll be morning soon."

"What about you?" asked Ammi. "You've hardly rested. You need to. Ever since you returned from your journey, you haven't been the same. You look . . . different."

I pursed my lips, unable to deny it. "How *do* I look?"

"Thinner," she began, "and more melancholy; at least I thought so at first. Then I saw the way your eyes lit up whenever someone talked about the Lord Enchanter." She gathered her cloak over her shoulders. "Are you sad because he had to leave?"

My throat tightened with emotion. How could I tell her that he had to leave because of me? That I had lied to him—to *everyone*—about what was happening to me?

"I'd rather not talk about him."

"Oh," said Ammi, looking stung. "My apologies, Master Tamarin—"

"*Maia*. And it's not your fault."

Let her believe we'd had a lovers' quarrel. I didn't care what she thought. As long as it wasn't the truth, it didn't matter.

"You sleep first," I told her. "It takes me a while . . . these nights."

Ammi did the opposite and opened a flap of our tent. A pocket of moonlight spilled inside. "Do you see the stars?" she said, shuffling closer and pointing. "See the seven lights, all the way up north? They're Shiori and her six brothers."

"Shiori?" I repeated. "Was she a goddess?"

"No, she was a Kiatan princess who lived hundreds of years ago. It's just a legend, but there's a statue of her in my district, a gift from Kiata. It's always been one of my favorite stories." Ammi pointed again at the sky. "If you look closely, the stars that make up Shiori and her brothers come together in the shape of a crane."

I couldn't quite see the crane. "In Port Kamalan, we call that the water dragon. My brother told me stories about it when I was young."

"It looks more like a crane than a water dragon! I'll show you." She outstretched her hand. "Can I borrow your scissors?"

"My scissors?"

After a moment's hesitation, I passed them to Ammi. I watched her snip a small square off the inside layer of her tunic, unaware of the power my enchanted scissors possessed.

"These scissors are quite rusty," she said, folding the scrap of cloth. "You should get a new pair from the—"

"They work fine," I interrupted. My voice came out harder

than I'd meant it to. I softened my tone. "They've been in my family a long time."

"An heirloom?"

"Of sorts," I replied, taking back the scissors from her.

"Maybe it's my fault, then. One usually uses paper to fold the crane."

"I have a few pages left in my sketchbook."

"Save them for your letters. Paper is expensive." Ammi held up the cloth bird against the moonlight. Its two wings hung off the edges of her palm, and its soft beak pointed up. "Each point of the crane is in the stars."

I still didn't see it, but I nodded anyway.

"An evil enchantress turned Shiori's brothers into wild cranes, and Shiori folded thousands of birds to bring them back. There are many versions of the tale—maybe your brother told you a different one."

"Maybe," I mused, trying to recall Sendo's many tales. "There was one he started, about a sea dragon who saved a princess—and, come to think of it, her brothers. But he never finished it; not many Kiatans visited Port Kamalan, and Sendo got most of his stories from listening to sailors talk about their voyages." I stopped there, hoping Ammi didn't hear the pain in my voice.

"Is he a tailor like you?"

"No, he died a few years ago." I forced a smile before she could react. "But he loved the sea the way I love to sew. I wish you could have met him. You would have liked him."

"I'm sure I would have," Ammi said softly. "I've only been on a ship once, when I was a little girl. It frightened me, not being able to see land anywhere. I can't swim."

Neither can Edan, I remembered. I clung to that memory, making a note to write it down somewhere. I'd never been one for keeping notes about things, but I'd started sketching again, at night when Ammi was asleep.

They were little drawings in the dirt, of Edan and me climbing Rainmaker's Peak, riding camels in the Halakmarat Desert, and soaring over Lake Paduan toward the Thief's Tower. I drew Baba's smile from the last time I saw him, Keton standing with his cane, dyeing dresses green instead of purple. But much as I tried to draw Mama or Sendo or Finlei, my hand would suddenly cramp, and I could not.

That night, I decided, I would draw Ammi. She was happiest when she had a cup of steaming tea in her hand and a plate of cookies at her side. A few crumbs clung to one corner of her lips, and she wiped them off with the back of her hand.

"You said you wanted to go home. Where is your family?" I said again. She hadn't responded the first time.

"I don't know."

"Don't know?"

She hugged her knees to her chest. "My parents sold me to the palace when I was five years old. I was the youngest daughter, and they couldn't afford to feed me. They were so poor we used to bathe in the water we used to wash our rice." She swallowed visibly. "One day, they put me on a ship with half a dozen other girls, and it sailed to Jappor. I don't even know where they live."

"Oh, Ammi . . ." I wanted to help her find them, but I wouldn't make any promises I couldn't keep. That much of the real Maia was still intact.

"The only times I've left the palace were to travel to the next one when the seasons changed," she continued. "I've never even been to the city outside the Summer Palace."

I fell silent. A few short months ago, I'd been the same. Before I'd left home for the Summer Palace, to compete in the emperor's trial, I too had felt trapped.

"This is all I have left of my family." Ammi held the bird up, but its head drooped in her fingers, flagging in the wind that drifted through the open slits of our tent. "My sisters used to make them for me when I was small. Back home, they were charms for good luck."

During the Five Winters' War, I too had made paper charms for luck. They hadn't been anything like Ammi's crane, but this small reminder of my past warmed me.

I wrapped my arms around my knees, the flap of my carpet beating against my back from the wind. "Tell me what you remember about them."

"My parents were rice farmers. They worked on a paddy with a dozen other people and grew fish in the ponds. My sisters and I would try to catch the fish with our hands, but we were never quick enough. Back then I was so small the water reached up to my waist, and my fingers would get caught in the nets we used to catch fish." She tilted her head, looking wistful. "My family was very poor.

"For years I was angry at them for selling me, but now, if I could just see them again, I'd forgive everything in a heartbeat. After the emperor imprisoned you, I realized I might never see you again either." She held out the bird to me, as if it were a peace offering. "That's why I forgive you, Maia Tamarin. I might need some time before I trust you again, but you're my friend, and I forgive you."

"Thank you," I whispered, balancing the bird on my palm. I didn't tell Ammi it was better that she didn't trust me, but somehow, I could tell she knew.

She offered me a smile. "You should rest, Maia. Maybe a story will help. The story about the Kiatan princess, perhaps?"

I leaned back against the ground, the grass and dirt soft against my elbows. "Yes."

"Shiori was the youngest child of the emperor," she began, "and his only daughter. She had six brothers, and she loved them more than anything in the world."

I listened to Ammi's story, her words tugging at my heart-strings. Edan loved me. Edan was searching for a way to break *my* curse.

Everything that was still right and true inside me wanted to go to the Tura Mountains and reunite with him. Yet everything that was still right and true inside me compelled me not to. Every morning, I woke a little colder, a little less Maia. My eyes burned red longer every day, and Ammi was too kind to point it out—or too frightened. I'd caught her staring, but when I looked at her, she quickly averted her gaze.

No, I couldn't go to him. I would find a safe place to leave Ammi, and I would return to Lapzur alone. Before I lost myself.

Before I lost everything.

CHAPTER THIRTEEN

I dreamed of Lapzur, of its ghosts waiting for me back at the haunted islands. Their voices were like scratches against my skin, cutting deeper with every word.

Sentur'na, they called.

Again with that name. Even in my dreams, I did not know what it meant.

Sentur'na, you grow weak. Come back to us. We will make you strong again.

Every night since I'd left the Winter Palace, it had been the same promise, over and over, until the voices grew so loud I couldn't bear it anymore. Only then did flames scorch the sky of my dreamscape, and a bird with demon-red eyes lit the ghosts afire.

Their screams still echoed in my ears as I shot up, awake. My heart raced, sweat dribbling down my temples.

Ammi was still asleep, her feet poking out of our tent. Gently, I folded my cloak over her legs. I wouldn't need it. The wind raised goose bumps on my arms, and the hairs on the back of my neck bristled, but I wasn't cold.

I headed for the nearby creek. A frosty morning dew laced the foliage, and the soft crunch of fallen leaves under my feet reminded me that a new season was beginning. Fall was changing into winter.

But for the changing colors of the autumn leaves, I had never experienced much of the four seasons in Port Kamalan. What brilliant oranges the cypress trees would wear! It'd been my favorite thing to paint in my sketchbook, the challenge of re-creating the fire of the leaves enough to engage me for hours.

"Why do the trees change color?" I had asked my brothers.

Sendo had paused, no doubt trying to think of a poetic answer for me. But the ever-blunt Finlei beat him to answering, *"Because they're dying."*

"He means," said Sendo, seeing my stricken expression, *"that as the green fades, the leaves die and fall off the trees."*

Their answers had quieted me. I'd studied the vibrant smears of paint on my fingers, then looked to the trees by the sea. *"If dying is this beautiful, then I wish I were a tree too. I'd be happy to die and be reborn in the spring."*

How they'd laughed at me. I laughed now too, bitterly. I'd been so innocent back then, believing in past and future lives. Most A'landans did, including Mama and Baba and Sendo, so I hadn't thought to question it—until now.

If I became a demon, a part of me would die. But it wouldn't be a beautiful death, and there would be no spring, no rebirth, for me.

What would happen to the Maia that died? Where would she go? Had she had a life before this one?

I wrapped my arms around my chest, knowing there was no answer.

Leaves crunched under my heels, the brisk cold seeping deep into my lungs. We'd only been gone a few days, flying south toward the Tura Mountains and Lake Paduan, but winter had followed us. By the creek, the edges of the bank were already beginning to freeze, an early sheet of ice lacing the moist dirt.

At this rate, we wouldn't be able to camp much longer. The cold wouldn't kill me, but Ammi . . . she would do better with a roof over her head and a proper fire.

Crouching beside the creek, I cracked the ice with a branch and washed my face, trying to shock some life into my tired eyes. Once I'd filled our canteens, my freezing fingers fumbled into my pouch for the mirror of truth. My reflection glimpsed me wearily, and I set the mirror against the bank's damp soil.

"Edan?" I called. The glass rippled with the sound of my voice. "Edan?"

Nothing.

My heart sank. Every morning, I'd tried to reach him. Always unsuccessfully.

"If you can hear me," I whispered, "I'm not coming to the Temple of Nandun. I'm . . . I'm going to Lapzur instead." My throat ached, and I forced my next words to sound firm. "Don't follow me, Edan. Stay where you are."

I echoed myself, "Stay where you are."

Fresh ice glittered across the mirror glass. My shoulders slumping, I wiped it clean with my knuckles, then slipped the mirror back into my pouch. For days, I'd heard nothing from Edan. I only hoped he wasn't still waiting for me, and that I'd have a chance to tell him—even if only in the mirror—that I was returning to Lapzur alone.

Back at our camp, Ammi huddled beside the remains of our fire, shivering. How thin she'd grown in these last few days.

"Out for water again?"

I felt a flicker of guilt as I passed her a water canteen, my daily excuse for my disappearances every morning.

Seeing her teeth chatter as she drank, I made up my mind. "We'll stay in an inn tonight."

"But the shansen is looking for you. And so are the emperor's men."

"If we stay out here, you'll freeze."

I'd meant to say *we'd* freeze, but the words came out wrong. Far too honest. Luckily, Ammi didn't catch it.

"But what if they—"

"We'll be careful," I rushed to add. I couldn't say what truly worried me about staying in the villages. Not that someone might recognize me as Maia Tamarin, but that my demon eyes might reappear and give me away for what I was becoming.

A monster.

· · ·

Disguised as traveling brothers, we found a suitable inn along a forgotten spur off the Road. Centuries ago, the town might have been a bustling oasis for weary travelers, but if so, it'd shrunk into a small village since then. Inside, several men were slurping noodles with hot oil, and others drank and gambled with tiles. Business was healthy enough that the innkeeper barely glanced at us when we paid for our lodging.

Our tiny room had two moth-bitten cots beside the window, cobwebs slung across the corners, a lone candle on a rickety table, and a pot of incense for prayer. The ceiling creaked every time a loose tile on the roof rattled, but no wind leaked in through the window cracks, and we had a kettle full of hot water.

This was luxury compared to our tent.

"There's a peddler selling fruits and steamed buns on the street," Ammi said, glancing out the window. "It'll be cheaper to buy from him than to eat at the inn. Do you want anything?"

I peeked outside too. Behind the peddler, someone wheeled another cart, selling honeycomb cookies and peanut cakes. My stomach grumbled with a familiar longing for something sweet.

"Maybe a honeycomb cookie if you have spare change left over," I suggested.

The hint of a smile lifted Ammi's lips. "You like honeycomb cookies? I like them too." Then her smile vanished, and her brow furrowed.

"What is it?" I asked.

"All the food I took from the palace is gone. We have enough money for the room and dinner tonight, but . . ." Her voice faltered. "If you made something, I could sell it. Nothing fancy. A simple handkerchief might be enough."

Since making His Majesty's cloak, I had barely touched a needle. I was afraid my fingers had forgotten how to sew. I'd never gone more than a few days without them itching to work. I bit my lip. "I didn't bring any—"

"Use this," she said, pushing a handful of red silk cloths into my hand. The color was washed out from the storm, but I recognized them as napkins from the wedding banquet.

A flush deepened Ammi's cheeks, as if I had accused her. "The maids steal every now and then. There's a whole black market for items from the palace. I've never taken anything before. Never. Except for these and the food we needed for our journey. Besides, His Majesty owes us ten thousand jens for our help finding Lady Sarnai. . . ."

Her voice trailed off, and I knew we were both thinking the same thing: that it was money we'd likely never see, given we'd aided Sarnai's escape from the Autumn Palace.

"I wasn't rebuking you," I said. "I'm . . . impressed."

"Oh." She reached into her pocket and produced three thin spools of thread and a needle. "I asked the innkeeper for these."

The color was a dull red and the thread coarse, clearly meant to be used for mending. It would have to do.

When she left, I unwound the thread from the spools, ignoring the scissors throbbing at my hip. They yearned to work again.

"Not now," I murmured to them. It had been so long since I'd sewn without magic. *I* needed this task more than my scissors did.

I picked up the needle, rolling it between my thumb and first finger. The two weeks I'd slept after defeating the shansen had made my fingers stiff and clumsy. My first stitches on the napkin were crooked and uneven, some petals of the flower I was trying to embroider bigger than others. Frustrated, I picked them apart, then tried again.

I loosened my grip on the napkin and slowed down, letting each dip of the needle match the steady rhythm of my breath. As I worked, I hummed the tune Edan used to play on his flute. A twinge of regret fluttered in my chest. If I went straight to Lapzur, I'd never get a chance to give his flute back to him.

Ammi returned just as I was finishing the last handkerchief. In her basket were sand pears, a box of steamed buns, and one large honeycomb cookie fresh off the griddle.

I held the cookie on my palm, the heat seeping through the thin banana leaf that wrapped it, and inhaled. Not one of the hundred dishes I'd sampled during the royal wedding could compare to the sweetness of this treat.

"It's all yours," she said, grinning at my blissful expression. "I ate mine on the way back."

I wasted no time and took a bite, sinking my teeth into the crispy golden edge, then savoring the syrupy honey as it melted on my tongue. After days of salted meats and leftover banquet food, how wonderful it felt to eat something hot, fresh, and simple.

I licked my fingers clean and let out a contented sigh.

"My cookies are better, to be honest," Ammi said slyly. "I'll make you some one day."

"I didn't know you baked."

"The emperor's bakers get overworked sometimes. I'd help when I had a spare moment. You don't get such prosperous cheeks by serving tea all day." She patted her face. "Used to dream I'd open my own shop, if I ever got out of being a maid. Maybe it would become so famous my family would hear about it."

She pursed her lips.

"Is that why you wanted to win the ten thousand jens?" I asked her gently.

Ammi shrugged, not wanting to talk about her home anymore. "Baking makes me happy." She picked up one of the handkerchiefs I'd made. I hoped she wouldn't notice the dropped stitches on the earlier ones, how some of the petals were uneven. "I've noticed two things make *you* happy. Sweets and sewing."

I laughed. "Very observant."

"You ought to sew more," Ammi continued. "You look happier than I've seen you in weeks. The Lord Enchanter will be glad to see it."

At the mention of Edan, my shoulders sagged. "He won't. I should tell you, Ammi, I've made up my mind not to see—"

Ammi raised her finger to her lips and darted to the side of the window, closing the curtains with a jerk.

I heard shouting outside, and horses neighing. Nothing out of the ordinary, given that the inn was on the village's main street.

"What's the matter?" I whispered.

"Soldiers."

The muscles in my jaw stiffened. "Here?"

She nodded grimly. "That's not all. The peddler mentioned that mercenaries had been spotted in the next province."

The shansen's men.

She looked at me, her expression beseeching me for answers. "The emperor's men are looking for a woman with red eyes. An enchantress. But people are saying she's a demon."

What could I say? She'd seen my red eyes before. I couldn't deny I was who they were looking for.

"I'm not a demon, Ammi." I swallowed, about to add "Not yet," but she looked so relieved I couldn't bring myself to undo the lie.

"The shansen's demon must have cursed you somehow. You seek the Lord Enchanter to help you."

My mouth went dry, the sweet aftertaste of the honeycomb cookie turning sour.

I didn't reply. She wasn't that far from the truth. Maybe it was better that she believed the shansen's demon had cursed me.

Ammi flinched as we heard men shouting downstairs. "What should we do?"

"We stay tonight, leave first thing in the morning. People think we're brothers, and His Majesty's men couldn't possibly know our true identities."

Besides, I thought, *I'd much rather face Khanujin's soldiers than the shansen's mercenaries.*

Ammi took the handkerchiefs I'd embroidered. "I'll see if I can learn more."

"You're a true friend, Ammi" was all I could manage. *I pray you won't regret it.*

. . .

While Ammi was gone, I lit a candle to ward off the coming dusk, but the shadows that danced along the dented walls stirred my nightmares. Wolves with sharp teeth. Tigers with crooked claws. Birds with broken wings.

Under the waning flame, I studied my old drawings of Edan, memorizing the sharp angles of his face, the tiny crook of his nose, and wishing I'd taken the time to paint the black of his hair, the blue of his eyes.

I should try to summon him again, I thought as I flipped the pages of my sketchbook. But after passing my portraits of Baba and Keton, I stopped at a blank page.

Edan could wait. I needed to draw Ammi first, before I forgot her too.

I got as far as outlining the contours of her face, when the door rattled open.

"Look, fifty jens," Ammi said proudly, showing me the coins in her hand. "It's not much, but it'll pay for another night here, and tomorrow I can buy more food." She noted my sketchbook and hovered over it. "Is that me? I want to see."

"It's not finished," I said, hastily shutting it, but Ammi put her hand over mine, her nails digging into my flesh.

I jerked away from her. "Ammi?"

A sneer formed on her lips, twisting her kind face into one I hardly recognized.

"What? You don't like me this way?" Bandur spoke through Ammi's lips.

"Get out of her," I said, grabbing my friend by the neck. I didn't realize the power of my strength until I was holding her up high, her boots kicking above the ground.

Bandur laughed, a giggly sound that sliced through me like a knife.

I set Ammi down, and she slumped into the chair.

"Enough, Bandur," I said icily. "Let her go."

Ammi looked up, the whites of her eyes bleeding a red so bright I flinched. The color washed out of her face, her skin becoming so pale it matched the alabaster walls behind her.

"*You* are the danger to her, not I," said Bandur. He tilted Ammi's head so I could see the bruises my fingers had made on her neck. "Look—see what you've done."

Shame rippled inside me. "No," I whispered. "That was you. . . ."

"The longer you stay among these mortals, the greater the harm you will bring to them. You would do well to tell your enchanter that." The demon forced Ammi's mouth into a coy smile. "He searches for you day after day."

My breath caught in my throat. Edan was looking for me?

"But even he knows he cannot save you, *Sentur'na,*" Bandur continued. "You will kill him before he can even try." The demon paused, reveling in my pained expression. "Return now to Lapzur."

"I *will* return." My hands flew up to the walnut pendant hidden beneath my tunic. "But when I do, I will fight you."

130

Bandur snorted. "You will lose. Your pledge is unbreakable, and not even your precious dresses can save you. Accept your fate, Maia Tamarin. There is nothing you can do to change it."

A red string appeared, connecting me to Bandur. Seeing it, I gasped.

"Nothing," he whispered. Then a haze of smoke lifted from Ammi's limp form, and he was gone.

Ammi didn't wake when I shook her, but she was still breathing. Thank the gods for that.

I slammed my fists on the table so hard that the walls shook. Anger swelled in my chest, fury choking me. "I never, *never* should have brought her with me."

I tore off my pendant, ignoring the wash of dizziness that came over me, and placed it on the table beside the mirror of truth.

I thought hard of Edan, searching for him to tell him I was going to Lapzur and that he must not come for me. I was going to Lapzur alone.

My blood still pulsating with rage, I picked up the mirror. Then the walls of my room in the inn disappeared, and the glass misted.

Edan.

He sat in meditation, but his eyes flew open before I called his name. At the sight of me, his lips formed a faint smile.

"Maia," he said softly, slowly lingering on the music of my name.

"I'm not coming to you," I said abruptly. "I have to go to Lapzur before . . ." My voice trailed. I didn't need to finish what I was going to say.

The softness of Edan's tone vanished. "Let go!"

The edge in his voice startled me. "Don't use the amulet.

The more you rely on its magic, the harder it will become for you to resist turning into a demon."

"It's not a demon's amulet," I argued. "It's a pendant, full of Amana's power. The dresses will help me defeat Bandur."

"The power of Amana sings through the dresses you have made. But now that power has been exposed to your pledge to Bandur. You must not use it, you must not corrupt its magic. Be strong, *xitara*. You're stronger than this."

My eyes were starting to burn, and I turned away.

It was the truth I'd been afraid to confront—to even think about. Sometimes, when a shadow fell over me, I looked down to see my pendant bathed in darkness, the way it had become when I'd made Emperor Khanujin's cloak. One day, I feared, it would blacken forever, like the amulets belonging to Bandur and Gyiu'rak.

"You're already changing, aren't you?" he said.

The words stung, but I couldn't deny them. "I summoned you to say goodbye," I said. "I'm not going to meet you at the temple."

"I don't care what you're becoming, I want to see you." Even through the cloudiness of the mirror's glass, his cool blue eyes pierced mine. "Meet me in the forest with the poplar trees. I'll find you."

There were hundreds of forests with poplar trees in A'landi, but I knew which one he meant. We'd been happy there, before we had journeyed to Lake Paduan.

"If you won't come see Master Tsring, at least come for me."

One last time, I thought, and nodded just before the mirror fogged and the vision of Edan left me. My pendant rattled against the mirror, the crack in its center gleaming.

Sentur'na, Sentur'na, Bandur mocked, his voice creeping into my mind. The shadow of a wolf prowled my walls.

"GO AWAY!" I yelled.

Your enchanter cannot help you. Neither can his master. This is my final caution: come to Lapzur. Now.

"Or what?" I retorted. "You'll send your ghosts to fetch me?"

Worse, Sentur'na. Worse. I'll take away everyone who matters to you. Perhaps I will begin with your friend here. Bandur's shadow eclipsed Ammi's sleeping figure, a claw stroking her cheek. *She has such a sweet and caring disposition . . . a true friend.*

"Leave Ammi alone!" I lunged for my pendant, which flared hot with power.

Bandur's laugh grew louder and louder, boiling from the walls until I thought I might burst with rage. Sparks of light hissed from my fingertips, but I was too furious to wonder what was happening. Angrily, I hurled a stool at the wall, until his shadow disappeared.

From behind, Ammi grabbed me and a tide of relief washed over me. She was herself. Except terror was twisting her face, and darts of light flashed in her eyes as she shouted something I could not hear.

Then the edges of my vision came into focus, and my hearing returned.

"Fire!" she was shouting. "Fire!"

Our room had burst into flames.

CHAPTER FOURTEEN

The fire snaked ruthlessly across the ceiling and raced down the walls. I lunged for my pouch, stamping out the sparks that clung to its tassels.

Ammi bolted for the door, and I was right behind her when I remembered Edan's mirror still on the table. I needed it, and I spun back, only to be greeted by a flash of blistering heat.

A high wall of flames shot up, dancing around the perimeter of the table. No coincidence that the shape of a wolf emerged from the blaze, eyes glimmering, milky-white teeth in its jaw stretched open in a silent laugh. *Come into the fire, Sentur'na.*

Smoke bled into my eyes and scorched my cheeks, but it wasn't the heat that made me hesitate. Nor was it Bandur. . . .

"Leave it!" Ammi yelled, pulling me toward the door. She couldn't see Bandur, couldn't hear him taunting me.

I yanked my arm away from her and turned back for the mirror.

Bandur vanished, leaving only his wall of fire behind. It roared at me hungrily, the high flames blackening the edges of my sleeves and my trousers to near-ashes.

No more hesitation. My fingertips closed over the mirror's handle, and its glass shimmered, glazed with heat. Touching it should have seared my flesh, just as rushing through the fire should have killed me—yet I felt no pain. If anything, the fire was feathery and soft, its warmth melting the cold inside me. This was what I had feared. This was why Bandur had wanted me to come into the fire. . . .

Did I imagine it, or was my skin glistening as if ignited by a thousand sparks? I watched, mesmerized, as my nails became as pale as the blue heart of the flames—

"Hurry, Maia!"

Behind me, the fire gathered in intensity. The walls were about to cave in. Grabbing the mirror, I took a step back, toward Ammi's voice—and I tripped.

The mirror tumbled out of my hand and shattered.

NO! A strangled scream came out of my throat as I fumbled on the floor to gather the broken shards. Sparks flared at my face, ashes flying into my eyes. I coughed into my sleeve. The smoke was getting thicker, the fire stronger.

Ammi yanked me to my feet. "We have to go! Maia!"

I reeled at her angrily, nearly wrestling her, but she hooked my arm through hers and pushed me out of the collapsing room.

My anger faded. It'd nearly gotten us both killed.

I covered my mouth with my sleeve, but the smoke was already so thick it coated my lips and lashes. It was harder on Ammi. She was choking on it. If we didn't get out, she'd suffocate. She'd die.

We stumbled down the wooden stairs, one step ahead of the flaming falling beams. The altar by the door had crumbled, the painted faces of the gods melting, and the oranges that had been offered in prayer were charred like the dark side of the moon.

When at last we made it outside, Ammi sucked in a desperate gulp of air. I did the same, the cold stinging my throat before it settled into my lungs.

The other guests stood, helplessly watching the fire devour the inn, its flames roaring against the cloudless black night. None of them knew how it had started, or where it had come from. But some were starting to speculate.

"The forests in the North have fires like this. You see the red tips?"

"Demon fire."

I whirled and looked at the fire more closely, watching the edges dance with an unnaturally red sheen. My fingers still burned. No more sparks danced from their tips, but my nails were blackened and burnt. And suddenly I knew.

I had been the one to start the fire. Not Bandur, but me.

He was right. This—all this—was a warning that I was changing. That if I didn't come to Lapzur, I would hurt those I cared about.

"We have to go," I said to Ammi. My voice crawled from my throat. I needed to get out of here, as far from what I had done as possible. Before I hurt anyone else.

"We have to help them. The inn, all these people—"

"Nothing can help them now," I replied crisply. "We must go before the emperor hears of this and finds us. Or the shansen."

As soon as I'd said it, I wished I could take the words back.

Ammi looked at me as if she didn't recognize me.

I tugged Ammi away from the blazing inn when my demon's sight flared, showing me a little girl screaming inside. Her mother crouched over her, shielding her with her body.

The roof of the inn cracked, and my heart clenched.

My eyes burned with the same terrible heat before they

turned red. Not caring who saw, I barreled into the inn, threading through the flames as if they were gusts of wind, not torrents of fire. My lungs shrieked for want of air, but I kept going.

The girl and her mother were barely conscious, huddled in the corner of the room, heartbreakingly close to the window—their means of escape. When I reached them, they hardly acknowledged me. The little girl let out a groan.

The human Maia couldn't carry a mother and her child to safety. Couldn't even drag both of them the few meters across the room to the window.

But the demon Maia could.

A laugh echoed inside my mind—or was it the crackle of the fire around me? I could not tell. I hurried toward the pair and rushed them to the window. It was already open, but the fire had progressed to the roof, gnawing hungrily at the gray tiles. We'd have to get down somehow. Before the inn collapsed and the girl and her mother perished.

Each second mattered. I tore the enchanted rug out of my pouch and set the mother and daughter on it. I wouldn't fit.

"Fly!" I yelled as it quivered to life. "Take them down!"

Once the rug spiraled out of sight, I leapt after it onto the roof. The fire sprang after me, needling my ankles, and I danced along the clattering roof tiles to keep my shoes from burning. I felt no pain. I did not burn.

Once I saw the carpet deliver the mother and girl to safety, I circled to the back of the inn where no one would see me and jumped to the ground, my arms held out as if they were wings.

I landed silently, with impossible grace.

Well done, Maia, Bandur purred. *But it is just the beginning. Will you put more innocent lives at risk? Or have you learned your lesson? Will you face your fate at last?*

"I'll come to Lapzur," I whispered. My throat burned. Everything tasted of ashes. Of doom. "I'll come to Lapzur, but on my terms."

My voice hardened. "I'll be there before the next full moon. I'll not come before I see Edan."

A claw of fire bit into the inn's roof, and I stifled a scream as tiles smashed down onto the ground.

You have nerve, to bargain with a demon.

"You want your freedom, don't you? Then let me relish the last of mine."

You do not seem to understand that it is you *who are the danger. The longer you stay away from the isles, the more harm you will bring to those you love.*

He laughed. *I will give you two weeks. Bring the enchanter if you wish, but I won't promise he will be safe on Lapzur. If you do not arrive by sundown, no one you love will be safe anywhere.*

"I'll be there."

No sooner did the promise leave my lips than rain poured down in sheets. Steam rose from the inn's walls, a sudden wind chasing away the smoke. As fast as it had come alive, the fire began to die.

The villagers fell to their knees, thanking the gods. I watched from afar as they took in the stranded guests and gave them shelter.

No one had died in the fire, yet guilt writhed in my chest.

Whatever consequences I'd have to face for agreeing to go to Lapzur were worth it. I'd never been so relieved to see rain. I couldn't help but feel it was washing away the blood on my hands.

Ammi found me, hiding in the shadows.

"How are they?" I asked. "The mother and the child."

"They'll live. Thanks to you." She knelt beside me. "You told me you'd be more of a danger than help to A'landi if you stayed in the Winter Palace. Is this what you meant by it?"

"Yes," I whispered. My pulse pushed into my throat. "We should part here. I'll only get worse. The fire, I think I started it because I was angry—" I stopped. How to explain it to her? I didn't know where to begin.

"I've noticed your eyes," she said. "They burn red sometimes. It frightened me at first, but I know you, Master Tamarin. *Maia*. This isn't you."

This isn't me. That was what I'd been telling myself all this time. But soon it *would* be me. Soon I wouldn't be able to hide from myself any longer.

"Ammi, I . . ." I wanted to tell her what was happening to me. She'd already guessed and come close, but still, I held back the truth.

She seemed to understand. "I'm not going to leave you. Whatever is happening to you, it is against your will."

My mouth tasted bitter. "I don't think even Edan can help me now."

"He can," Ammi insisted. "Keep your faith. If you can't, then I will for you."

I said nothing. I couldn't even thank her.

"We should go now." She lowered her voice, which quivered when she spoke, "People saw your carpet, and those two men— the ones with the Northern accents—they've started asking everyone questions about you."

I went still, remembering the two who'd commented on the fire earlier. So they were the shansen's men.

"You'd be safer without me," I told Ammi.

"I can't go back to the palace." She was afraid; I could hear it in the unsteadiness of her words. But she lifted her chin bravely. "Maybe I would be safer, but you wouldn't be. This isn't a fight you win alone, Maia. Until you're reunited with the Lord Enchanter, I will take care of you."

"Then, let's go." The carpet had returned to me, and I unrolled it, holding it up. It juddered and shook before it finally lifted, hovering just above the rain accumulating at my ankles.

But as Ammi jumped onto the carpet, I couldn't shake the feeling that she'd be safer here, that I should insist that she stay.

You do need her, I reassured myself again. *You need a friend.*

But you might hurt her.

It chilled me that I couldn't tell whether the voice was mine or the demon's inside me.

CHAPTER FIFTEEN

The storm followed us. Ribbons of lightning streaked across the darkened sky, and thunder boomed in long, shuddering rolls. It was hard not to think of Bandur's laughter as Ammi and I wove through the clouds, but I had other concerns. We had little money and no food. Worse, both Khanujin's soldiers *and* the shansen's were looking for me.

Ammi slept, curled into a small ball on her side of the carpet.

I left her alone, grateful she was finding rest, while a part of me envied her peace. Even if I were able to sleep, my mind wouldn't let me rest. I couldn't stop reliving my last conversation with Edan.

Meet me in the forest with the poplar trees. I'll find you.

The forest wasn't much of a detour on the way to Lapzur. I could easily stop there with a few days to spare—as long as the magic in my carpet didn't run out.

So why did I hesitate? I wanted to see him. Gods knew I did.

And yet . . . Bandur had agreed too easily to let me bring Edan. Far too easily.

I gripped the ends of my sleeves tight, twisting their burnt edges with my fingers.

Who would I even be by the end of the fortnight? Someone who couldn't feel love? Someone who couldn't be loved?

I felt more of myself slipping away. No matter how hard I

tried to hold on to my memories, they were like water, leaking through the seams of my fingers. When I thought of Edan, I remembered how my name on his tongue would send a rush of warmth and joy surging through me, but I couldn't remember how it felt to touch him. I couldn't even remember what his voice sounded like.

It wasn't just Edan. Baba and Keton, too. Soon their drawings in my sketchbook would not be enough to remind me how much I loved them.

Dawn touched the threads of my carpet, its misty rays illuminating the world below. The rain was finally abating, and I lifted my cloak to glance at Ammi. Her eyebrows pinched together in a restless sleep, her cheeks flushed in spite of the cold.

I laid my palm against her forehead. "Demon's breath," I muttered. She was burning up. "Ammi?"

She rolled her head to the side, shivering under her damp cloak.

"Hmmm," she slurred. "Let me sleep."

I had to get her somewhere warm and dry. But where?

We were flying over a cluster of sandstone pillars; the mist-covered landscape extended for miles of gorges and ravines, the cascades of rushing waterfalls so far below they looked like a painting. I squinted, making out a large city ahead, not far away. From the unusual landscape, I guessed it was Nissei, one of the richest cities in A'landi.

Nissei sat on the south bank of the Changi River, surrounded by the famous Sand Needle Forests. Although it wasn't along the Spice Road, many merchants came to trade for its famed porcelain. It was said that the secrets of bone china rivaled the secrets of silk, and certainly, since porcelain was so valuable, every child in Nissei learned to paint china before learning to write.

I was wary of stopping in such a busy city, but there was no time to search for a better option. The storm had relented, but more dark clouds gathered on the horizon. And Nissei was in the Bansai Province.

"Master Longhai's home," I murmured to myself. He had always been kind to me, even though we'd been competing against each other to become His Majesty's tailor. He would take us in.

If I could find him.

It was early enough that fishermen were still coasting the river, so I landed the carpet near an empty part of the port.

"Ammi," I said, hoisting her arms around my neck. "Ammi, I'm going to take you to see Master Longhai."

I dragged her to one of the side streets and yelled for the first wagon I saw, pulled by two mules and driven by a boy with a straw hat and dirty fingernails.

"What's wrong with your friend?" the boy asked.

He wouldn't take her if he knew she was sick. Big cities feared plague, and with winter near, people were bound to be more vigilant.

"Too much to drink," I lied, forcing a hearty laugh. "I need to get him home. Master Longhai will be so worried. Could you stop by his shop?"

The boy frowned. "I'm not going into the city. . . ." Then his eyebrows rose at the thought of a reward from the wealthy tailor. "But I suppose I could make a detour."

I was already loading Ammi onto the wagon.

I pretended to sleep so the driver wouldn't ask me any more

questions, but I stole glances at the city when he wasn't looking. Cobblestone streets, washed clean by the rain, with curly green moss growing between the stones, brick houses with wooden balconies decked with strings of lanterns, a serpentine canal whose stench offended my nostrils.

Imperial scrolls hung on every street, but we moved too fast for me to read them. I tensed, hoping they weren't posters seeking my whereabouts. Or Edan's.

Finally, we arrived in front of Longhai's shop. A board hanging on the door announced that he was not open for business this week.

Please, I pleaded, pounding on his door. *Please, Longhai, please be here.*

Someone answered. A woman with a long face, wearing a tightly pulled bun and a measuring string coiled around her neck.

She gave me a hard look. What a sight I must have been—rain-washed, sleep-deprived, and dressed in tattered clothing.

"We don't answer to beggars."

"I'm not a— Wait!" I grabbed the side of the door before it closed in my face.

The seamstress glowered at me. I couldn't risk saying I was one of the tailors from the trial.

"It's urgent." I gestured at Ammi, still in the wagon. "My friend needs medical attention."

The door began to close on me. "The hospital is on Paiting Road."

"Please!" I burst out desperately. "It's—"

"Madam Su, what is this din?" a familiar voice interrupted. "I am trying to work."

"Master Longhai!" I shouted. "It's me!"

Longhai's portly form appeared in the hallway. "Master Tamarin," he said, stunned, pulling me inside. "What are you doing here?"

"I'm with a friend. She . . . she's ill, and I didn't know where else to go."

"Say no more." He ushered me into the hall, waving a thick hand at the seamstress. "Madam Su, pay the driver and bring the girl inside."

Outside, the rain was starting up again.

"I didn't think I'd see you again for a long time, Tamarin. You are welcome here. I'll see to it that your friend has proper care."

I nodded my thanks.

"Now we'll get you some clean clothes—and lunch! I remember you always forgot to eat. We'll have to fatten you up while you're here."

Madam Su and her assistants returned into the shophouse with Ammi, and motioned for me to follow them.

"She has a fever," I said, intercepting Madam Su. "Please take good care of her."

The old woman's stern face finally softened. "I've had four daughters who've been through worse. As long as we get her dried and warm, she will recover."

After I washed and changed, Master Longhai gave me a tour of his shop. There were workrooms for cutting, embroidering, and tailoring, and a room for storing fabrics and threads, as well as the garments Longhai's staff had prepared for his clients: brocade skirts, sashes embroidered with golden carp, and robe after robe of richly dyed silk, tunics trimmed with gold-inlaid designs so fine they shimmered.

Longhai was a master at painting silk, so he had a studio

for himself with a dazzling array of paint pots and inkstones. Hand-painted fans rested on a pine table opposite his workspace. A scroll with the seal from the previous emperor, Khanujin's father, hung on the wall, commending Longhai for the mastery of his craft.

Seeing all this, I felt a heaviness in my heart. Only a few months ago, all I'd ever dreamed of was becoming an imperial tailor, of one day having my own shop and my own family.

Now I wasn't sure that would ever happen.

Longhai didn't ask me any questions. What I was really doing here, why I wasn't still working for Khanujin, why I hadn't introduced myself with my real name to Madam Su at the door.

Guilt bubbled up my throat, a confession spilling out before I could stop it.

"About the trial," I began, "I'm sorry I deceived you—about being a man."

"I don't care whether you're a mare or a stallion, young Tamarin. You are too skilled. Even if I were blind, I would hire you in an instant. I've never met your father, but I imagine he must be quite proud of you."

I wished I could beam from his praise, but it was hard enough to summon a smile. "I'm not so sure of that anymore."

Hesitation creased Longhai's brow, and he closed the door behind us. "I received this a few days ago," he said, unrolling a sheet of parchment from his desk drawer.

It was a drawing of me. Quite accurate, too. The artist had captured my freckles as well as how I usually parted my hair, and I was even biting my lip the way I tended to when I was nervous.

Maia Tamarin, age 18. May be traveling under the identity of her brother Keton Tamarin. If found, bring to authorities immediately, alive. Reward of 10,000 gold jens.

"Master Longhai, I can explain—" My tongue groped to find the right words.

Longhai ripped the drawing in half. "I'm sure it must be a misunderstanding. If you wish, I could speak to the governor on your behalf. I have some influence in this city, and he will listen to me."

"It is not that simple," I said. "But thank you."

"Then you are welcome to hide here as long as you wish. My staff can be trusted, but be wary. Even the most honest man will turn into a viper for a sum of ten thousand jens."

Ten thousand jens. Not long ago, I'd never even dreamed of seeing such a sum. Now it was the reward for my capture.

I swallowed. "I noticed the scrolls hanging from the buildings in Nissei. Are they notices about me?"

"No, they're conscriptions." Longhai's tone turned grave. "Haven't you heard? His Majesty is drafting men into the army once more." He leaned against his desk. "My sons were taken along with many of my workers."

The floorboards tilted, and the edges of my vision blurred. The whole shop could have collapsed and I would have stood there, immobilized by shock. All I could think about was Keton. Gods, if the emperor came for him again, then everything I'd done would have been for nothing.

"I knew the war had resumed." The muscles in my throat were so tight it hurt to speak. "But if it's reached this far south already . . . I thought we'd have more time."

"Unfortunately not," replied Longhai. "There was a battle in the Jingshan Province, not far from the Winter Palace. His Majesty lost a thousand men. He needs more."

I balled my fists, trying to ignore the anger gathering under my skin. There was no hope of a truce, not with Lady Sarnai missing. Not with Edan powerless.

The shansen had Gyiu'rak on his side. He was too strong. He'd rip apart my country thread by thread.

A'landi would fall.

Rain and thunder filled the silence between us, and I breathed in. Slowly, my shoulders fell.

"We can do nothing," Longhai said, answering his own question, given my silence. "You have nothing to worry about while you're under my care—"

"His Majesty's soldiers are *here*?" I asked, my blood turning cold.

"They left a few days ago, after it was announced the war had begun again. They are marching north to defend the Winter Palace. It's said the shansen's army is gathered there."

A mix of relief and dread came over me. "I was there."

"They won't be back to look for you," Longhai assured me.

All I could manage was a meager smile. I'd expected a hundred men and women under his employ, but there were only a handful of seamstresses tittering by the cutting tables. Now I knew why.

"Do you know where the conscription officers are headed next?"

Please don't say south, I silently pleaded. *Not to Port Kamalan.*

"I don't know," Longhai replied. "You look worried, Master Tamarin."

"For my brother. The only one I have left."

The older tailor eyed me. "The real Keton?"

"It was he who was badly injured in the war," I said grimly. "I took his place to come to the trial. I've already lost two brothers to the war. I fear if there's another . . ." I couldn't finish my thought. My hands fell to my sides.

"The war took my companion as well," said Longhai quietly. "He was dearer to me than anyone in the world."

I looked up at him. I hadn't known. "Oh, Master Longhai . . ."

He spoke over me, "Time eases all wounds, even ones to the heart. All I pray now is that my sons will have a kinder fate. And your brother."

I didn't dare pray. Who knew whether it would be gods or demons that listened to me? But I nodded.

"You should write to Keton and your father. Even a few words will ease their worry—I speak as a father, and as a friend. I will have the letter sent discreetly."

"Thank you, Master Longhai," I said softly. "I don't know how I can ever repay you. For letting us stay here . . . and for being so kind to me during the trial. You should consider yourself fortunate you did not win."

"I heard she asked you to make the dresses of Amana," Longhai said slowly. "Did you truly succeed?"

Now I hesitated. "I did."

"What I would give to see them."

I didn't tell him I had the remaining two with me in my amulet. That secret I kept even from Ammi.

"They were supposed to bring peace," I said at last. "But I'm beginning to believe it would have been better if I'd never made them at all. If I'd stayed in Port Kamalan and never come to the palace."

"With your talent?" Longhai chuckled. Then, seeing how grim I looked, he sobered. "We do not choose to be tailors; the cloth chooses us. There's a feeling in our fingers, a feeling in our heart. The gods saw fit for you to bring Amana's dresses back to this earth. You must believe there is a reason for that, young Tamarin. A good reason."

I responded with a numb nod. Once I would have believed him.

But it was far too late for me.

CHAPTER SIXTEEN

Under Madam Su's care, Ammi made a steady recovery. I wished I could sit by her bedside all day, but I'd promised Longhai I would help with his shop. So, while Ammi rested, I joined his staff in the workroom.

My scissors hummed at my hip while I worked, but I ignored their call. No magic for me today; sewing calmed me, and I needed the distraction. My fingers weren't as nimble as they'd been a month ago, but the tasks Longhai gave me were simple. I stitched a shirt for a scholar and embroidered butterflies on a pair of slippers for a merchant's daughter.

No one paid me any heed; there was too much work to be done, and the seamstresses were too busy chatting with one another.

"Ay, I heard Scholar Boudi took on a third concubine last week."

"Another one? How he's able to afford his household is beyond me."

"Yes, yes. And think what will happen if war comes. The price of silk will go high!"

As I sat, listening to their gossip, I thought of the seamstresses I'd left behind in the Hall of Dutiful Mending. I hoped they had survived the shansen's attack.

At noon, the seamstresses cleared the workroom for lunch. I stayed behind. I hadn't been hungry in days.

"Aren't you going to eat, my friend?" asked Longhai, seeing I was still at work. "There's beef stew with rice noodles for lunch today, a shop favorite."

I didn't look up at him. "I'm nearly finished."

He took the stool next to me and observed my work. "Your skill never fails to impress me, Master Tamarin."

I held up the slippers I'd been embroidering. "There's nothing impressive about this."

He pointed at my tight, even stitches and the nine colors I had labored the last two hours to integrate into the design. "Even when your heart is only half in the work, you're better than most masters out there. I should thank your father for keeping you in Port Kamalan. If you'd grown up in the Bansai Province, you'd have put me out of business."

I chuckled. "Was your father also a tailor?"

"By the Sages, no. He was a porcelain painter, as was his father before him, and so on. Five generations of fine bone china in my family. Our shop was the first stop merchants made in Nissei. He nearly disowned me when I showed interest in becoming a tailor, but my grandfather saw I had some talent and permitted my mother to teach me embroidery in secret." He gestured at a painting of his mother, which hung in a place of prominence, presiding over the workroom.

"My younger brother owns the porcelain store now. The war nearly destroyed both of our businesses; if not for each other, we would not have survived. Still, compared to others, fortune has been kind. I've my reputation, my health, and my shop." He paused, and I knew he was thinking of his companion who'd been lost to the previous war and his sons who had recently been called to bear arms.

Lightning cracked the gloomy sky, and Longhai glanced out the window. "The dragons must be out to play," he murmured.

"The dragons?" I repeated. "Is that a saying here?"

"You haven't heard it before? I suppose Port Kamalan doesn't get many typhoons during the summer. Bansai does, and heavy rains in the winter too." Longhai opened a silk fan. "The Kiatans say that the dragons in heaven bring about mischief to the earth by causing rain and quakes. Their porcelain traders always used to mumble about it when they came during the summers, and we locals picked up the phrase. I rather like it."

"It's poetic."

"Luckily for you, this is a little dragon. Makes travel inadvisable, but it'll pass."

The tailor reached into his pocket for some coins. "Now, this is going to be nothing compared to your salary in the palace, but—"

"I couldn't take your money." I shook my head. "Please. Especially not after you've been so kind to Ammi."

Longhai set the money on the table, leaving it up to me to decide whether to take it. "Ammi?" His belly shook as he laughed, remembering. "Ah! The kitchen maid who used to serve you breakfast."

"She's become a close friend," I replied. I'd been thinking about my next words ever since I'd arrived at his shop: "I wonder if she might stay on with you."

Longhai folded up his fan. The amusement fled his eyes, and his features became solemn. "Going somewhere?"

I bit my lip. What could I say, that I was on my way to the

Forgotten Isles of Lapzur to battle its guardian? That unless I defeated Bandur, I too would become a demon?

Or should I say I was looking for Edan?

Since Ammi had fallen ill, I'd avoided the thought of Edan. Was he already waiting for me in the forest? What if when I found him, I was more monster than Maia?

"I displeased Emperor Khanujin with my service," I replied evasively, "so we've been trying to go as far from the Winter Palace as possible. Ammi's done nothing wrong."

"I see," said Longhai quietly. "The Tambu Islands might provide sanctuary. Once this storm passes, I could help arrange passage—"

"I don't plan on hiding," I said firmly. I wouldn't elaborate.

"What of the Lord Enchanter?"

My fingers stopped, and I pulled too hard on a thread, causing the fabric to bunch. With a frown, I started undoing the stitches I'd made too tight. Try as I might, I could not set them straight again.

Longhai placed a hand on my work, urging me to look up. His voice softened. "I have many friends who come and go from the palace. A little while before you arrived, news came that he is missing. And I heard he aided you in making the dresses of Amana."

"He did," I said. I didn't want to talk about Edan.

"Master Tamarin . . ."

At the sound of my name, I bolted up. I wasn't hungry, but I clutched my stomach, pretending to be suddenly famished.

"What was that you said about beef noodles, Master Longhai? Keep your coins, but I will have some lunch after all."

Before he could respond—or ask me any more questions—I hurried out of the workroom.

. . .

The wind howled, a low guttural cry that made even the sturdy walls of Longhai's shop tremble. The bowl of pins on my worktable rattled, and I bent over to relight my candle.

The seamstresses had left hours ago, and I sat alone by the weaving loom, watching the sheets of rain cascading outside.

I lifted my carpet from the loom; I'd repaired the holes and some of the tattered tassels, but its magic was threadbare. If I was lucky, it might give me a few more days of flight, then I'd have to make the rest of the trip on horseback.

But how to find the forest where I was to meet Edan?

I had no maps, no mirror of truth, and my demon sight had been utterly quiet since I'd made my bargain with Bandur.

A part of me wanted to renege on my promise and go to Lapzur without Edan. That had always been my plan—to go alone—but if I could still be honest with myself, it wasn't because I was trying to be brave or honorable or true.

It was because I was afraid. Of myself.

Edan's presence at Lapzur would only endanger his life—from Bandur *and* from me.

Yet . . . I'd made a promise, and the part of me that was still Maia *wanted* to, *needed* to, keep it . . . for the sake of clinging to whatever humanity was left in me. When and if I gave in to my fear of the demon in me, Bandur would already have won.

I need to find Edan, I thought. *But how?*

I'd been thinking about the story of the Kiatan princess Ammi had told me, and the paper cranes the princess had folded and enchanted to help her on her quest to find her brothers.

I would make a bird to find Edan.

With my scissors, I cut a small scrap from the carpet. The

magic Edan had imbued into its fibers had weakened, but my scissors had magic enough to send it on a mission.

Carefully, I shaped the scrap into a bird. A knot of thread for eyes so it could see, and two wings so it could soar, strong and powerful, through this storm.

I touched the bird to my walnut amulet, painting its wings with a sliver of light from the tears of the moon, then I placed a gentle kiss on its head.

"Find Edan," I whispered. "Search the forests and the mountains. Then come back to show me the way. And hurry."

If I didn't make it to Lapzur by next week—the full moon—Bandur and his ghosts would take away everyone I loved.

I would willingly surrender myself to him before I would let that happen. But not yet. Not if I might see Edan one last time. Not if together we stood a chance of defeating Bandur.

I opened the window a crack and sent the bird out, watching it weave between the needles of falling rain.

Then I waited.

CHAPTER SEVENTEEN

"*If you leave, you will not be welcomed back here.*"

Edan didn't hesitate. He pulled off his temple robe, folded it, and returned it to the old man—the master of the Temple of Nandun.

"*You were meant for magic,*" *said the master, warning him one last time.* "*Do not undo the progress you've made here by going after this girl. Darkness consumes her. Do not let it doom you as well. Stay and finish your training.*"

"*I was meant for magic, once,*" *Edan agreed,* "*but because of Maia, I am no longer the enchanter I was before. I am meant for her now. Her above all else.*"

Without waiting for the master to reply, he went to the stables for the stallion he had stolen from the Autumn Palace, and took off into the woods.

The Tura Mountains faded into the distance as Edan barreled through the forest. Every tree was a poplar, spines straight as bamboo rods, like a kingdom of needles.

Under his breath, I heard my name. "*Maia,*" *he murmured.* "*Wait for me. I'm coming.*"

At the sound of my name, whatever this was—a dream or my demon sight—disintegrated, and in its place appeared an image of my cloth bird. It fluttered against the wind, searching for Edan. It began to flap wildly when it found a pocket of poplars, deep within the woods, and my enchanter weaving through thickets.

My cloth bird had found him! Starlight shimmered over its wings as it shot up into the sky, making its way back to me, asleep in Master Longhai's shophouse.

But then, the stars began to shatter. The ground shuddered, swallowing the trees and the mountains and the moon. Out of the dark chasm flew shadows with charcoal eyes and cloudy white hair.

Sentur'na.

My cloth bird pierced the crowd, wings flapping at the ghosts to fend them off. But there were too many. They surrounded my bed, skeletal arms outstretched. Their fingers circled my neck, squeezing away the last of my breath, and my pendant began to blacken. . . .

"Wake up!" my bird shouted at me, suddenly able to speak. "Wake up!"

. . .

"Maia, wake up!"

I jolted upright on the bed, breathing hard.

A warm hand rested on my shoulder. "Breathe," Ammi said, sitting on the edge of my bed. "Breathe."

My heart pounded wildly in my chest. "What . . . what . . ."

"You were shouting in your sleep." My friend's eyes shone with concern.

"Just a bad dream," I said shakily.

"You've been having a lot of bad dreams."

"What did I shout?"

Ammi let go of my shoulder. She looked tired, her blankets half tossed onto the ground. I must have disturbed her rest.

"You were speaking in a language I didn't understand. It sounded like someone was trying to kill you. In the end you kept shouting one word."

"One word?" I whispered, even though I already knew.

Shadows folded out of the candlelight, and Ammi's face blurred.

Sentur'na.

I could still hear the voices in my head, relentlessly calling for me, *Come back to us.*

The wooden ridges of my amulet scraped against my skin, rough and warm, clashing with the cold that clenched my insides. My nail dug into my pendant, trying to pry open the crack to let some of Amana's power seep out and silence the voices.

No. I forced my hand away from the pendant. *That's what Bandur wants. He wants me to rely on the dresses. He wants them to become corrupted, like me—*

"What's that?" Ammi asked, interrupting my thoughts. "Can I look at it?"

No, I wanted to balk, but I forced myself to pass it to her.

Ammi held the pendant to the light, so the glass crack in the center caught the glint of the sun.

"I've never seen anything like this!" she exclaimed. "Where did you get it?"

I wasn't listening. My throat had closed up like I was being strangled. White-hot barbs of fire pricked the corners of my eyes, which burned redder than ever before.

"Maia!" Someone grabbed my shoulders. "Maia, are you all right?"

I jerked away. "Don't touch me," I snarled.

"I'm sorry—" The girl beside me let go. I looked up at her round face, her kind but frightened eyes. "Maia?"

Maia? I backed away, confusion roiling in my gut. That name sounded familiar. Her face looked familiar. Why couldn't I remember?

Demons devour you piece by piece. Memory by memory. Until you are nothing.

When I looked at the girl again, her white teeth gleamed in the candlelight, fangs protruding through her parted lips and gray fur bristling over her skin.

Bandur.

I slammed him against the window. The iron latticework shuddered behind his back, and he let out a cry of pain. I dug my nails into his arms, sinking through his fur into his flesh.

"Maia!" he squealed at me. "Maia, please! Stop! You're hurting me!"

He wasn't fighting back, but I knew better than to trust Bandur's words. Behind the whimpers and the scarlet eyes thick with pain, he was leering at me—he had my amulet!

"Give it back," I rasped.

Bandur's eyes widened in fear. "Here."

I threw the amulet's chain over my neck and backed into the corner of our room, breathing hard. It hurt as if someone had ripped my heart from my chest. But why? This had never happened before.

Because it is your demon's amulet, I could hear my demon voice explain gleefully. *And inside, the power of the moon and the stars. Once your pledge to Bandur has been fulfilled, the dresses too will be consumed by darkness.*

The figure I had mistaken for Bandur slumped, whimpering

on the ground, blood trickling down her arm. The shadow of a wolf danced along the wall beside her, baring its crooked fangs, a deep chuckle rumbling out of its belly.

My knees buckled. Everything snapped back into focus.

Ammi. I'd just attacked Ammi.

"Gods," I whispered, crawling toward my friend.

She shrank from me and wouldn't look me in the eyes.

Now she knew why they burned red.

I lifted Ammi gently and brought her back to her bed. I knelt beside her. "I'm sorry, I'm sorry. Please forgive me."

"It . . . it was an accident. I'm not hurt."

An accident. A lump rose in my throat, for it had been no such thing, and we both knew it. I was getting worse; Bandur was playing tricks on my mind, and I couldn't tell what was real and what was not.

Shakily, I rose to my feet. I didn't trust myself to help her. Didn't trust myself to sleep in the same chamber as her.

"I'll ask one of Master Longhai's servants to help you."

Before Ammi could protest, I rushed out of the room and closed the door behind me. I pressed my back against the wall, catching my breath.

Rage coiled up inside me, twisting so tightly my lungs squeezed.

When I finally worked up the courage to return to our room, I saw that Ammi had lit a candle while I was gone, as if she were afraid of the dark.

"I'm sorry," I said to her quietly. "That's never happened before. It won't again. I promise."

My promise sounded hollow, even to me. But thankfully, Ammi didn't hear me. She'd fallen back asleep.

I crumpled to the ground and reached for the pouch that

held my dagger. Ever since I'd given up the dress of the sun, my body had been numb. I hadn't felt the cold or the heat, pain or hunger. I'd barely slept.

"Jinn," I whispered.

The meteorite came to life, veins of liquid silver gleaming and glimmering. I didn't remember such heat emanating from the dagger. My pulse raced as my fingers slid over the blade—

"Agh!" I cried. A jolt of searing pain shot up my hand, and my fingertips leapt off the meteorite as if they'd tried to grab burning coals.

Cradling my wounded fingers, I returned the dagger to my pouch. I pushed the window slightly open, taking in the cool air. Watery moonlight trickled in, dancing across my bare knees. I rocked myself back and forth, squeezing my hand to numb the pain.

It took a long time before the hurt subsided and I could feel my fingers again.

One thing was certain: my time was running short.

CHAPTER EIGHTEEN

Sunlight dappled the bamboo window frames, patches of cerulean blue seeping through between the clouds. The storm had finally lifted.

For the first time since I'd attacked her, Ammi arose from her bed. The floorboards creaked under her steps as she tiptoed toward the door. I started to sit up in my bed to call out to her, but she stilled at the sound of my rustling.

I stilled, too. After what felt like a long time, she let out a quiet breath and closed the door behind her. I heard her footsteps rush down the stairs.

Nothing had ever made me feel so wretched. Was she avoiding me?

I dressed to meet her for breakfast. In my mind I rehearsed the three things I needed to tell her. That she'd be safe from me, that I was leaving to find Edan. That I was sorry I'd hurt her.

But when I saw Ammi helping Longhai's cook knead dough for making steamed buns, I fled before she noticed me.

"Are you not taking breakfast?" Madam Su asked, passing me in the hall.

"I already ate," I lied. I glanced at the bandages on her tray. "Is someone hurt?"

"Ammi is, didn't you know?" Worry gathered in the head

seamstress's temples. "She had a bad fall last night. Luckily, it's just a few scratches."

Something rose in my chest, strangling my words. "Did she say how she fell?"

"Yes, but I practically had to pry it out of her," Madam Su said with a laugh. "She said she tripped over a kettle. But, funny, I didn't leave a kettle in your room."

My insides churned with guilt. Maybe Ammi would never speak of what happened last night, maybe she would pretend nothing had happened. But in the same way that the old me hadn't been a good liar, Ammi was not, either.

No wonder she hadn't been able to look at me last night or talk to me this morning about what had happened.

She was frightened of me. It stung, but I couldn't blame her.

I was afraid of me, too.

· · ·

"Is everything all right?" Longhai asked me, later that day. "Madam Su mentioned that you looked troubled, though truth be told, you haven't been yourself since you arrived."

I concentrated on my embroidery. Today's project was stitching a mountain landscape for a nobleman's scarf.

"Look at me, my friend."

I clung stubbornly to my work. "I'm sorry, it's just that I got off to a late start this morning. If I don't continue, I won't finish this scarf in time—"

"Oh, damn the scarf. It can wait. What's wrong, Maia?"

Finally, I regarded him. It was the first time he'd used my real name. Did it sound foreign because I'd never heard it com-

164

ing from his tongue, or because the name was starting to feel less like my own?

Longhai sighed. "Come with me."

I put down the scarf and followed him back to his personal studio. This time, instead of drinking in the sight of his paintings and his tools, I took in the rosewood desks and chairs cushioned with expensive brocade, the priceless embroidered scrolls hanging on the walls, the hand-painted vases sitting on scarlet-lacquered shelves. In spite of all the finery around me, what caught my eye was the jacket hanging behind Longhai's desk.

It was a ceremonial military uniform. Bronze tassels dangled from the seams, the intricate swirls and patterns of the brocade inlaid with coral and studded with jade buttons. Embroidered on the left sleeve—was a tiger.

"Did this belong to the shansen?"

"Yes," he informed me. "To the twenty-third shansen."

The current shansen, Lord Makangis, was the twenty-seventh. That would mean this jacket was from the Qingmin dynasty. Little craftsmanship had survived the wars during which the last Qingmin emperor was overthrown. "It must be—"

"Priceless?" Longhai said. "Yes, I spent a foolish fortune on it. But it serves as a good reminder to me of what is lost war after war. Art is lost. Art, and our children."

He lowered his voice. "These are dangerous times, Master Tamarin. There is good reason to believe that Emperor Khanujin's dynasty is coming to an end and that the shansen will take his throne, but only the gods know what will come to pass." He leveled his gaze at me. "You are in a precarious position, wanted by both sides. Not many have the ability to help you, and you would not ask for help even if you needed it."

Edan had observed that about me during the trial.

Well, I did need help. Desperately.

"The storm has passed" was all I could say. "I meant to leave this morning, but . . ."

"Ah, I heard your friend had a fall."

My voice came out hoarse. "Yes."

"You haven't told her you're leaving," Longhai deduced, reading the guilt on my face. "Will you consider staying on?"

After what had happened with Ammi, nothing would change my mind. She couldn't come with me to Lapzur, or even to the Tura Mountains to find Edan. I couldn't risk it. "No, I can't. I must go alone. The soldiers . . . no one is looking for her."

Longhai nodded gravely. "She will be safe here. But you . . . Maia, you can't expect to get very far on foot."

I pursed my lips. "I could use a horse. I . . . I can't promise I'll return it. And any maps you can spare."

"I'll have my swiftest steed ready for you by this evening. You will stay for dinner, won't you?"

"I must leave as soon as my work for you is done," I said, shaking my head. "Before dusk. I fear I've already stayed too long."

Longhai's face darkened at my words, but bless him, he didn't ask any more questions. "May the Sages protect you, young Tamarin. And may the gods protect us all."

I echoed his words, but I didn't have the heart to believe them.

• • •

Now that the storm was over, the streets outside Longhai's shop came alive. Carriages scraped along the roads, and I heard Madam Su greeting customers in the front of the store. Not wanting to be seen, I ducked out of the workroom to find Ammi. I'd been trying to muster the courage to speak with her before I left.

I found her in the kitchen, stirring a pot of soup.

"Some soup, Maia? Come, have a bowl before the other seamstresses drink everything up. Longhai's regular cook has the day off, so it's just me in the kitchen."

She was prattling on more than usual, and despite how calm she sounded, I knew she was nervous about being around me. "Ammi, I . . . I'm sor—"

"You don't have to lie," she blurted. "I know it wasn't you. It was the shadow inside you."

The shadow inside me. That was one way to put it.

Ammi bit her lip to keep it from trembling. "What's happening to you, Maia? You didn't even know me."

I didn't even know myself, I thought, but I didn't say it aloud.

It was time I told her the truth.

I asked, "What do you know of demons?"

She hesitated, setting her spoon back in the pot. "I grew up with stories about demons. Our shaman said they used to roam free in the world, creating mischief and spreading misdeeds before the gods intervened. He said magic was wilder then."

"I came across a powerful demon during my travels with the Lord Enchanter." I inhaled. "When I sought the blood of stars, the demon who guarded the Isles of Lapzur marked me and claimed my soul as his own. Edan bargained with him to take my place, but because I made the dresses, the demon no longer wants Edan. Now it is I who must assume guardianship of the isles."

Ammi drew back. "You're becoming a demon?"

I wouldn't lie to her. "Yes. Edan is waiting to go to Lapzur with me."

I stopped there, waiting for Ammi's reaction.

"Then we must leave as soon as possible. Tomorrow morning at first light." She touched my shoulder, still hesitant, but when she faced me, some of the fear in her eyes had gone. "Thank you for telling me, Maia."

I didn't have until tomorrow morning. I'd leave tonight, as soon as the sun began to set.

"I'll help you," she was saying. "The Lord Enchanter will, too. If magic is what got you into this mess in the first place, then magic can save you."

She truly believed it.

Edan can't save you, disagreed the shadow inside me. *No one can.*

I ignored the voices and nodded to my friend. "I hope so. I hope so."

I wouldn't lie to Ammi, but that didn't mean I wasn't willing to lie to myself.

. . .

I was upstairs in our room packing when something knocked at the window. I ignored it.

Another knock. "Strange," I murmured, going to the window and opening it.

There! I spotted my cloth bird stuck in the latticework. Gently, I eased it through the wooden slats, and it burst inside, circling around me before it landed on the back of my hand, wings still flapping wildly.

"Did you find him?" I asked.

The cloth bird leapt off my hand and fluttered to the window.

"I'm coming. I'm ready."

My belongings were few. Edan's flute, my sketchbook, my scissors. My dagger.

There was no time to say goodbye to Ammi, and even if I left her a note, she wouldn't have been able to read it. So I ripped a page from my sketchbook and folded it into a paper bird like the one I'd sewn to find Edan. At the last minute, I yanked a fiber from my carpet and sewed it into the bird's wings, then I left the paper bird on my desk.

As I turned to leave, voices outside my window sharpened my ears.

"This is the tailor's street?"

I glimpsed out the window. A band of men were rounding the corner. At first glance, they did not look so different from any other residents of Nissei, but my tailor's eyes picked apart their clothes.

The styles were not of this province, and the clothes weren't those of traders. Traders didn't cover their belts with coats to hide their weapons, nor did they wear dirt-crusted boots that peeked out from the hems of their robes. Nissei was a clean city, and the streets were paved with stones, not dirt. These men had come from the woods.

The shansen's spies.

Apprehension bristled in me. These men were clearly looking for Longhai's shop.

Hurriedly, I threw my carpet into my pouch and went down the back stairs.

As Longhai had promised, a horse waited for me at the back of the shop, saddled and packed with a bag full of food.

The mare reared, frightened by the sight of me. She snorted and kicked when I approached.

"Shhh . . . ," I said, stroking her mane gently. "Please. It's Maia. Just Maia."

I started to hum to her, scratching behind her ears so she'd know I wasn't dangerous.

That I wasn't a demon.

Still humming, I pressed my forehead against her neck and waited for her pulse to slow. Once she was calm, I kissed her neck and mounted.

"Thank you," I whispered.

As we edged onto the street, taking cover under the long shadows from the wall around Longhai's shop, I heard the shansen's men at the front door.

"There's no one by that name here," Madam Su was informing them. She lifted her head slightly, noticing me creep my way to the front of the shop.

"We know the imperial tailor is here," one of the soldiers said gruffly, trying to push past the seamstress into the shop. "I warn you to stand aside, woman. I've killed for less."

Madam Su held firm, even when the soldier unsheathed his dagger and held it threateningly at her. But I froze, pulling back on my horse's reins.

"Looking for me?" I shouted. With a hard kick to my horse's side, I charged toward the street.

"That's the tailor!" they yelled, running after me. "Stop!"

Before they could reach their horses, Ammi ran out of the shop brandishing a large iron pan and whacked the back of one soldier's head, and Madam Su knocked the other to his knees.

I caught my friend's eyes for an instant. Understanding flooded hers, and she nodded.

I didn't look back again.

After that, no more of the shansen's men followed. My cloth bird perched on my shoulder, I raced onward—making for the Tura Mountains on the distant horizon.

CHAPTER NINETEEN

My bird flew quickly, bouncing from gale to gale. With the wind pushing me, I barely noticed Nissei disappear behind me, the mountainous pillars of the Sand Needle Forests and the Changi River blurring until the landscape looked like faded watercolors.

I concentrated on the spread of trees coming into view before me, the forest Edan and I had spent our last days traveling through before we had gone to that cursed place, the Forgotten Isles of Lapzur. How different it looked in the teeth of winter. Just months ago, the trees bore leaves as vibrant as the greenest jade. Now the forest blazed yellow, so bright it hurt my eyes.

I couldn't stop to rest yet, and though my legs burned from riding and my throat was dry from lack of water, all I could think of was that Edan was somewhere near, closer to me than he'd been in weeks.

Winding deeper into the forest, I followed my bird into a valley of trees with crisp golden leaves and ashen spines. To the west, the sun began to sink, leeching color from the world around me.

The air grew chillier. I was getting closer to Lapzur. My cloth bird directed us south, but something kept urging me east instead—toward the Forgotten Isles.

Not something. *Me.*

The demon inside me displaced the voices of the ghosts in my head. Unlike theirs, her voice floated down into my thoughts, soft and alluring.

Why bother seeing the enchanter? she asked. *Your reunion will only pain you when you have to leave again. Best to go to Lapzur now. You're so close. Once you become the guardian of Lapzur, you can call for the enchanter—you can be together again.*

When I ignored her, she took another approach. *Bandur is weak,* she said seductively. The words slipped into my mind, like silk too smooth not to touch. *You have the dresses of Amana. You will be stronger than him.*

Think on it, Maia.

I drew a shaky breath, hearing the demon use my real name, and I tried to forget what she had said. But her poison brushed against my ears, gentle as a kiss. The possibility her words promised haunted me, lingering in my thoughts long after she went silent, which made her far more dangerous than the ghosts or Bandur. It was becoming harder to distinguish her thoughts from mine, to navigate the difference between what I wanted and what *she* wanted.

While my thoughts drifted, my cloth bird disappeared into a canopy of leaves, and my horse let out a tired grunt. I dismounted to let her rest, then whistled for my bird.

Strange, where had it gone?

I started to whistle again, when an arrow ripped past my sleeve, and my horse panicked and bolted away.

Terror shot to my heart.

Soldiers.

Dark green plumes bobbed from their helmets—sharp bursts of color against the gray of their armor, their horses, and their stony faces.

The shansen's men.

"Demon's breath," I muttered.

The call for another attack came from behind me, just enough warning for me to run.

Another volley of arrows flew high above the trees, then showered down in my direction. This time, their shafts were tipped with fire.

A shock of heat flew past me, and the moist dirt sizzled with steam inches from my heels. I barreled through the forest, twisting around the densely packed trees. I wouldn't be able to outrun their horses or their arrows.

But my carpet would.

"Fly!" I cried, retrieving it out of my pouch. "Fly!"

The carpet remained limp. In desperation, I angrily grabbed its edges and yanked on one of the tassels. My amulet grew hot over my chest.

"Fly," I commanded the carpet again. My voice came out low and guttural this time. A voice I barely recognized.

I jumped on the carpet, and it shot forward.

I didn't get very high before a net tumbled over me. Thick, sturdy ropes dug into my skin, and my carpet plummeted. As soon as it hit the ground, I burst up, trying to cut my way out.

A boot shoved me back down.

"Got you!" one of the men shouted. His sword slid out, the flat of the blade heavy against my back. "Don't move."

Two men held me down while the others lifted the net.

I lay on my stomach, heart pounding, knees chafing against

my carpet. My mouth tasted of mud, of grime clinging to my lips. Rage swelled within me. The veins in my neck pulsed, and my cheeks burned, a rush of heat bringing my blood to a boil.

How dare they! the voice inside me screamed.

I agreed. With a flick of my wrist or a flash of my eyes, I could have them all writhing on the ground. The shansen's men would be no more.

Do it, the monster purred. *Let them come closer. Let them touch me. I will burn them all.*

Show them your power, Sentur'na.

I bolted up onto my knees, so fast I barely felt the blade scraping my skin. Blood trickled down my arm, staining the edges of the ripped cloth. Anger burned in my eyes.

They gasped. "D-d-demon!"

The soldiers came at me with more force and desperation than before. *I'm not a demon yet,* I reminded myself. I was still flesh and bone. I leapt away from their swords, astounded by my own swiftness.

A rippling cold crept over me, hardening my skin like a thick armor. With each strike against me, the armor thickened.

I picked up a fallen sword and stabbed the next man who grabbed me. I spun, swinging for another man sneaking up behind me. But he went rigid and fell forward, an arrow lodged in his neck. Same with the other two soldiers—arrows stuck out of their chests and backs like they were pincushions.

I was so preoccupied looking for who had helped me that I didn't notice the two soldiers rounding on me from my sides. One hooked his arm around my neck, trying to choke me into unconsciousness, and the other grabbed my arms, twisting until I let go of my sword.

My amulet slid out of the folds of my robe, warm against my skin.

I focused my mind, trying to access the power tingling inside me. But the dresses wouldn't answer to me, not while a demon's rage rattled within, swelling in my chest. My lungs squeezed, breath growing tight. I clawed at the man's arm. Fire bubbled in my blood, ready to boil over if I would let it.

I let it.

In a burst of force that shocked even me, I flung the men aside, sending them reeling a dozen paces back.

I scooped up my carpet. It was in shreds, a threadbare mess of knots that I only vaguely remembered weaving. I clutched it under my arm and ran.

This way, Sentur'na. Through these trees.

The ocean, in the east, sparkled, as if beckoning me toward it. But east was the way to Lapzur. I ignored the directions and went the opposite way. I couldn't tell south from east or west.

The shansen's men followed. I slid down a slope, skating across the leaves, and hid behind a rocky outcrop.

The men passed above me.

I waited until the rush of their clothing and weapons faded into the forest. Then I let out a sigh and sagged against a tree. Finally, safe.

A leaf dropped onto my shoulder. As I brushed it off, another fell onto my palm. I stared at it, its heartlike shape oddly familiar.

"A poplar leaf," I breathed.

A rush of excitement bubbled in me, and I whirled to face the endless grove of poplar trees around me, when—

Someone grabbed me. A man in a tawny cloak, with a near-empty quiver of arrows on his back and a slender walnut staff in his left hand. The man who had intercepted the shansen's soldiers.

He held me against him, so close I could feel his breath on my hair. I tightened my grip on my scissor bows, at my side.

"They're gone," whispered the man. "All clear."

I spun out of his grasp and brandished my scissors. His eyes widened, and he backed away, raising his hands to show he wasn't going to harm me.

His heels hit the trunk of a poplar tree, and the creamy little buds fell like snow over his black hair. Aside from his clothes and the walking staff he'd dropped, he looked no different from the other soldiers. He could be one of Khanujin's men, sent to bring me back to the Winter Palace. And yet . . .

"Maia? Maia, it's me."

I didn't put the scissors down. My vision was blurred from the men choking me earlier. My hands still throbbed with power.

"It's me," the man said again, softly this time. The intensity of his gaze tickled me, but not in an unpleasant way. He reached for my hands, his touch achingly familiar.

Edan?

I'd wished for so long that we'd be reunited again, and now here he was. But was this Edan *my* Edan? Or was he an illusion sent by Bandur to torment me?

I could not tell.

My hands trembled. I exhaled, the steam of my breath curling into the cold air, and I looked up at him. His expression was tense, lips pursed and brow knotted as my eyes roved over his face.

"Do you not know me?" he whispered. Hurt flashed in his clear blue eyes. "Maia."

Maia.

Even my own name sounded strange to me, stranger than it ever had before.

I grasped my amulet, now cool against my chest and glowing with the silvery tears of the moon. Holding it calmed me.

Steadying my fingers, I reached out and touched his cheek. Slowly, I traced my fingers over the shape of his face, brushing my thumb over his thick eyebrows and down to the corner of his eye.

Its color, blue as the sea by home, convinced me. No ghost could take that from him.

Faster now, I swept my touch down to his lips, pursed with anticipation, then over to his nose and the small dent on its bridge, where it had been broken.

"You never told me what happened to your nose."

A familiar grin eased the worry on his face, and his eyes flickered—tentatively, hopefully.

"A soldier broke it when I was seven or eight," he said. "He'd been aiming for my teeth, but was so drunk he missed. Said my smile was too smug for someone my age."

The ice around my heart thawed, and I wound my arms over his shoulders. "Edan. You found me."

Relief bloomed in his eyes, and his shoulders, which had carried all the tension in the world, released. "I'd find you anywhere, *xitara.*"

Xitara.

In Old A'landan, it meant *little lamb*. But also something else—in a language I'd never learned.

"Brightest one," I whispered. *Brightest one,* in Nelrat, the language Edan had grown up speaking.

He leaned in to kiss me, but I put my hand against his chest to make him wait. I wanted to look at him first. His chin was stubbly with little black hairs, something I'd never seen during our months of traveling together. He did the same to me, thumbing the dirt off my cheeks, his fingers following the lines of my cheekbones to my shoulders, to the chain that held my amulet.

A war broke out on his face, like he didn't know whether he was happy to see me or pained by the state he'd found me in. Happiness won out, and he kissed me.

I placed his hand on my cheek. His fingers were warm in spite of the chill.

"I'm not sorry I lied to you," I said. "You wouldn't have left otherwise. The emperor would have killed you—"

"I know why you did it," he interrupted. "I've had time to think about it, and I understand." He took my hands. "Just don't do it again."

"I won't."

"Good." His fingers brushed across my cheek to my chin, lifting it so our eyes were level. If the coldness of my skin startled him, he did not show it.

He kissed me, so tenderly that all the love I had for him flooded back into me. I returned the kiss, hungrily, almost desperately, parting his lips with my own and digging my fingers into his back. Bringing him closer.

Edan let go first. "There'll be more time for that later," he said mischievously.

The crooked grin on his lips faded when he saw I wasn't returning his smile.

There was so much still unspoken between us.

"I've been looking for you for days," he said. "Wandered off the Tura Mountains, then a hawk said it had seen you."

I tilted my head. "You can still speak to hawks?"

"After centuries of being one, I still understand a squawk or two."

I couldn't tell whether he was being serious or playful. Or both.

I pointed at the staff he'd dropped. Edan had told me once that walnut had magical properties, so I knew it had to be special. "What's that for? I've never seen you carry it."

"It's to help channel my magic," he replied, picking it up. "Makes enchantments a little easier these days."

A wooden hawk, roughly whittled, perched on the top end of the staff. Fitting.

"Come," he said. "We're not too far from the temple. We should go before more of the soldiers come looking for you. And for me."

He must have seen me tense up, for he added, lightly, "If we hurry, we might make it back in time for dinner. For a temple that's been forgotten for centuries, the food is quite outstanding."

His stomach rumbled, not mine. I laughed quietly at the sound, but still I hesitated. "Why does everyone try to ply me with food? You and Master Longhai and Ammi . . ."

"The Maia I know never passes up good food."

Concern crept into his voice, no matter how hard he tried to hide it.

"I'm still the Maia you know," I assured him—it wasn't a lie, I hoped. I couldn't even tell anymore. "But I can't go with you to the temple. I have to be in Lapzur in a week's time."

"Lapzur is on the other side of the Tura Mountains," said Edan softly. "The temple is on the way. Let Master Tsring help you. And if he cannot, I will come with you to Lapzur."

My eyes glared red in the reflection of his gaze. Seeing them, I covered my face. I wasn't even angry; I was happy for the first time in weeks. So why had my eyes changed?

"I . . . I can't. . . ."

Edan caught my hand, pushing it away from my face. "Now that I've found you again, Maia, I will never leave you. I will stay by your side until the fire in the sun grows cold and the light in the moon is no more. Until time blots out the stars."

"You've gotten more poetic since I last saw you," I said mildly.

Edan's expression did not change. "I know you would do the same for me."

Seeing him again, feeling his arms around me and his breath warm against mine, I found my resistance wavering. "How could Master Tsring help me?"

"Bandur was once an enchanter. And Master Tsring knows more about the oath than anyone else in the world. Perhaps he can find a way to break your pledge to Bandur."

My brow furrowed. "Why is he at the temple of the beggar god?"

"Nandun is not the most beloved of the A'landan deities, true, but he's one of the most important. He had compassion for the humans he'd been instructed to punish, so he renounced his heavenly state and became a beggar like the poorest of humankind. He gave strips of his golden skin to the humans, until he too became flesh like them, and quite nearly mortal. When drought and famine came, he dissolved into the Jingan River; his blood became the water to irrigate the land for crops, his bones, fish to feed the hungry A'landans."

"I've never heard the tale of Nandun told in this way," I reflected. "Often, he's made out to be a fool."

"A fool to the other gods, perhaps. But we are taught otherwise: it is said that Nandun's disciples were the first to be touched by magic. To control the greed and hunger for power that some of his students developed over the years, he created the oath—to bind magic from those who would disrupt the world's natural balance and overpower the gods."

"*He* created the oath?" I asked.

"The origins of magic are unknown," Edan replied. "You'll find the story changes depending on who you ask. But Master Tsring is a disciple of Nandun's teachings, and the keeper of many of magic's mysteries." A pause. "He was also Bandur's teacher."

A flare of hope lifted my brow. "His teacher?"

He nodded, extending a hand for me to take. "Come, let's see him."

No one can help me now, I thought, looking toward the water glittering in the east. Lapzur was that way, beyond its mist, waiting for me. *I'd already bought as much time from Bandur as I could.*

But if this Master Tsring had truly been Bandur's teacher, maybe I did stand a chance. Maybe there was hope.

Maybe.

Above us, dusk was falling. Amana was winding up the threads of the day, unspooling shadow and moonlight across the aging sky. And my cloth bird had returned—she fluttered from tree to tree, making percussion of the rustling leaves before she landed on my palm. As I patted her soft head, I sighed. Maybe her return was a sign of better things to come.

Against my better judgment, I took Edan's hand. "All right, I'll go," I told him. "But just for a day."

CHAPTER TWENTY

A pair of inky eyebrows darted up at the sight of me, drawing creases in the monk's broad forehead.

"Your kind is not welcome here," he said, waving me away from the temple doors. "Go now, before my master arrives and banishes you to the fiery pits of Di—"

The last thing I needed was a reminder of what I was becoming. "Summon your master," I said, cutting him off. "I have come to speak with him."

The monk opened his mouth to protest, but he noticed Edan beside me.

"You!" he cried. "You are not permitted to return here either. Master Tsring specifically—"

Like me, Edan wasn't in the mood for the doorkeeper's games. He pushed past the young monk, and I followed.

The monk scurried past us, shooting warning looks at Edan. "Once he hears you're back, Gen, you'll be in trouble yet."

Edan and I ignored him and continued along the corridor. The Temple of Nandun was ancient, its structure carved into the underbelly of the mountain so skillfully one could not tell where the temple ended and the mountain began. We passed several chambers, sparsely occupied by the master's acolytes, their eyes half closed in concentration.

"Are they practicing magic?" I asked Edan.

"Most are."

I tilted my head at a lone plum tree in one of the open-air courtyards. "How does it flower so late in the year, and so high in the mountains?"

Edan led me to stand under its branches. "Nandun took refuge under a blossoming plum tree," he explained. "Magic is what keeps it alive here. The disciples take turns tending to it, and it blooms always, even in the dead of winter."

"Plum blossoms are the first flowers to bud after winter," I remembered. "They're a symbol of hope and purity."

He plucked one and set it in my hair, the way he'd done on our travels with the blue wildflower I now kept pressed in my sketchbook. "And new beginnings," Edan said quietly.

We found Master Tsring meditating in the garden. His eyes were closed, and if he heard us approach, he made no gesture to acknowledge it.

Copying Edan's movements, I sat cross-legged on the ground, and waited.

Master Tsring looked so old and frail his robes practically swallowed him: his pants hung slack, the hems discolored with age. His shoulders were pinched, narrowing his gaunt frame. Yet when he spoke, his voice was strong.

"You disobeyed me, Gen," he said. His eyes snapped open, pupils sparking like burning coals. "I forbade you to leave the temple."

Edan touched his forehead to the earth, remorsefully. "Forgive me, master. It is entirely in your right to expel me."

"Quite so!" Master Tsring huffed. "The audacity of you young enchanters—"

"—is inexcusable," Edan finished for him. "However, I implore you not to punish my companion. She—"

184

"I know who she is," said the old man irritably. "Even if you had not spoken about her all these weeks past, I would recognize the demon's kiss upon her. You do the temple grievous harm by bringing her here."

"She hasn't yet succumbed. There is still a chance for her. Please, help her."

Master Tsring looked at me, his gaze holding mine. He muttered, "Trouble always comes from enchanters who take the oath."

"It is because of this girl that my oath is broken," Edan said softly.

"I would hardly call her a girl," Master Tsring said, pointing at my red eyes.

I squared my shoulders. I'd done enough hiding and cowering in my time at the palace; I wouldn't cower anymore. "I am here for your help, not your reprimands."

He harrumphed, twisting the ends of his long white beard. "Long has it been since an enchanter has broken his oath and sought out my counsel. When Edan came to me, I should have realized his freedom came at a price. Though I would not have expected it to take the shape of one such as you."

His tone provoked me. "A girl?" I challenged. "Or a demon?"

"Both," replied the master curtly. He harrumphed again and stood, circling me deliberately, his cane tapping the stone ground between each step. It was hard to imagine that this wizened, shrunken figure had once been Bandur's teacher, a great enchanter.

Edan waited, and I shifted uncomfortably.

"Interesting," he grunted, once he'd inspected me from every angle. "Gen is correct—you haven't yet succumbed. Surprising, given how long ago it has been since Bandur marked you."

"Does she have a chance?" Edan asked.

"That, I cannot ascertain just yet." Tsring threw his beard over his shoulder, then poked at my ribs with his cane. "They say the belly has a better memory than the heart, and I must agree. Let us eat." His cane thumped the ground. "One cannot unravel a demon's curse on an empty stomach."

. . .

I couldn't shake the feeling that lunch was a test.

Though I hadn't eaten for days, I was not hungry. The monks served me a steaming bowl of carrot soup, with soymilk and bean curd and pickled cabbage, a meal I should have consumed greedily. But I had to force down every bite, as if I were eating paper. Even the tea they served, a famously bitter brew called Nandun's Tears that grew sweeter as one drank it, had no flavor to me.

Master Tsring did not speak during lunch, nor did Edan. Their silence made me anxious, and I found my attention wandering to the table next to us, at which the master's students clustered together on two long benches.

Only a handful were A'landan. They wore faded blue robes, and each was accompanied by a creature: a turtle, a cat, even a young bear. Their stares weighed on me, though they quickly looked away.

It was my red eyes they were staring at, I knew. My eyes unnerved even Edan.

I saw a student enchant her soup into black sesame paste, a dessert Finlei used to love. She drank it quickly, before anyone saw. But Master Tsring cleared his throat and pounded his fist

on the table once. "Enchantment is to be used during your studies, not at meals."

The girl's face flushed with embarrassment. "Yes, sir."

That was all Master Tsring said during the meal. He was
lost in thought otherwise, chewing on a steamed bun, flavored
lightly with spring onions. I'd left mine untouched.

When the disciples cleared their table and left, he scraped
his spoon against his empty walnut bowl. "I have come to a
decision about your companion, Gen."

My shoulders hiked with tension.

"There is no hope left for this one," Master Tsring said
gravely. "Take her to Bandur immediately, before she brings
ruin upon us."

"But you agreed she has not yet succumbed."

"That matters not." Tsring's wizened fingers gestured at my
amulet. "She has already been named."

"Named?" I echoed.

His voice was low. "Sentur'na."

Hearing it spoken aloud, I felt my blood turn cold. That
word had haunted me for weeks. *Sentur'na*.

"Breaker," translated Edan slowly.

Master Tsring grunted. "Or, more literally, *cutter of fate*."

A shiver ran down my spine. "No. That isn't my name."

"Soon it will be. It is the name that the ghosts will obey. You
yourself will know no other. An enchanter may have a thousand names, but a demon has only one."

"It will be different for her," Edan insisted, coming to my
defense. "Bandur killed his master, and because of his heinous
act he was cursed to become the guardian of Lapzur. Maia
chose this path . . . out of love."

Master Tsring considered this. "It is rare indeed that one chooses to become a demon. Perhaps that is why her transformation is slow. But the outcome will be the same, no matter the delay."

"If I return to Lapzur, Bandur will be free," I said slowly. "What will happen to him then?"

"Only in Lapzur is his power great," Tsring replied, "but he will seek to make bargains with the foolish, spreading sorrow and ruin. My disciples and I are prepared to confront him."

"And what will becoming a demon be like for me?" I asked in a small voice.

"You will continue to change," he replied. "Your eyes are just the beginning. The rest will come, but it is hard to say what shape you will take."

"What shape?" I echoed, before I realized what he meant. An ache rose in my throat. Bandur took on the form of a wolf; Gyiu'rak, a tiger. Soon I would have my turn. What would I become?

"Demons who began as enchanters are especially powerful," went on Master Tsring, "but you have no oath, and you have no schooling in magic."

Tsring folded his arms on the table. The edges of his sleeves were stained with carrot soup. "The magic in you is wild. I can smell it. It is like wood smoldering, the smoke so thick it makes the air difficult to breathe."

He eyed me sternly. "Demon magic feeds off destruction. An unquenchable rage. The desire for vengeance. These are signs of changing."

With a shudder, I remembered my anger at the shansen's soldiers, Emperor Khanujin, even Ammi . . . how much I'd wanted to hurt them. How easy it had been to give in.

When I said nothing, Master Tsring continued. "A demon's power resides in his amulet, which can be destroyed only by the demon himself, or by a source of powerful magic such as the blood of stars. As sentinel of the Forgotten Isles, Bandur guards it zealously, for it can bring his demise."

I was fingering my amulet without realizing it. Its color had darkened, the ridges of the walnut shell were charcoal gray, and the glass crack in the center was murky instead of clear. The change in color made my heart jump. "What about the power of Amana's children?"

Master Tsring watched me, his expression unreadable. "A curious question few would ask. Gen told me you were able to sew the dresses of Amana."

"Yes."

Tsring chewed on a stalk of sugarcane, considering. "The demon grows stronger in you every day. Since you are the creator of the dresses, they will succumb to the darkness along with you. But the dresses are both your salvation and your ruin; they are the source of your power in your amulet. If you destroy them, you will be free of Bandur." A deliberate pause. "But you will also die."

I fell silent, choking back a cry.

"That is not an option," rasped Edan. His next words came quickly, as if he wanted to forget what Tsring had said. "What if we were to destroy the Forgotten Isles?"

Tsring shook his head. "Even if that were possible, there is no way to free her. Her promise is sealed twofold, by the demon, and the goddess."

His words sank into me. "I've already destroyed one of the dresses," I said tightly. "The laughter of the sun."

The master's expression darkened. "In doing so, you have

hastened your end. Those three dresses are your body, your mind, your heart."

I stiffened at the revelation. Since I'd sacrificed the dress of the sun, my body had become numb to all but extreme heat and cold. Since recovering from my wounds in the Winter Palace, I hadn't felt pain either.

"What Gen says is true," Tsring continued. "You have already lasted longer than most. Your devotion to your family, your love for Gen and his for you—these are your strength, the barrier that protects you from Bandur. But you know better than any that the wall is crumbling. Your memories will be the next to go. Without them, we are nothing but empty husks. You are running out of time."

"So you're saying I should give up and let Bandur win." My nostrils flared, a surge of anger quickening inside me.

Tsring stared into my simmering eyes. Whatever he saw there did not please him, for his lips wrinkled into a frown. "Stay tonight, but leave tomorrow for Lapzur. Any longer and you will become a danger to my disciples and the peace here in this temple. I will be forced to subdue you."

What makes you think you can win against me? I nearly spat. But I bit my tongue to keep the words from spilling out. They drummed in me, the urge to show Tsring I would not cower before him. Him, a mere enchanter.

I squeezed my hands together tightly as Master Tsring rose and left the dining quarters, leaving Edan and me alone.

"We've wasted our time coming here," I said.

Edan put his hand over mine. He'd been quiet the past few minutes. "You didn't tell me you sacrificed the dress of the sun."

I swallowed, some of my anger fading. "The Autumn Palace was under attack. Hundreds of lives were at stake."

"I should have been there with you."

My shoulders fell, and I pulled my hand away from Edan's. "It's better that you weren't. There wasn't anything you could have done."

Immediately after I said it, I wished I could take back the words. They stung him. They stung me, too.

"I'm sorry. I didn't—"

"Master Tsring is wrong about you," Edan interrupted. "He blames himself for what happened to Bandur, so much that he cannot see you are different. Talk to him again."

He stood. "I'll be in the library."

Alone, I slammed my fist on the table. If not for Lady Sarnai, I wouldn't have had to make these damned dresses, the root of everything that had gone wrong. And if not for Emperor Khanujin and the shansen and their stupid war, I would have grown up with my brothers and never had to go to the palace in the first place.

Lady Sarnai, Khanujin, the shansen. I hated them all. I even hated Master Tsring for giving Edan false hope that I could be saved.

But most of all, I hated Bandur.

I inhaled a breath.

"Remember what Master Tsring said," I murmured, working to calm myself. "Vengeance is the path to your fall."

But you're going to fall anyway, spoke the demon's voice inside me. *You might as well destroy those who've hurt you along the way.*

I felt my blood begin to chill. Groping for control, I clenched the edge of my stool, digging my nails into its stiff wood. "Go away."

But how can I do that, Sentur'na? I am you. I AM YOU.

191

I shot to my feet, heart thumping madly as my stool toppled behind me. Silence greeted me when I burst into the hall. The demon had not followed.

Relieved, I leaned against the wall to wait for my ears to stop ringing.

"Edan?" I called out then.

The hall was empty. No sign of Edan or Master Tsring.

I started toward the courtyard, when a flicker of my reflection in the window caught my eye. Against my better judgment, I stopped to look. My face had grown gaunt, my cheeks so sunken I could see the slant of my bones curving to my chin.

That wasn't all. My pupils flickered like two flames, and my skin was so pale that blue veins shone through.

All the air left me in a rush. My body tensed and tipped. "That isn't me," I insisted, rapping my knuckles against the window's glass. "Show me who I am. The real me."

I waited, but my reflection did not change. This was no enchanted mirror of truth, just a sheet of glass.

Even if it were an enchanted mirror, it would show you the same. This is who you are now.

I glared up at the ceiling, looking for the shadow of the demon that had just spoken. But it was *my* demon, the one inside me.

And she was right.

A fit of anger came over me, my fists shaking at my sides. I couldn't control it, the hot, boiling rage bubbling in my throat.

I punched the window. It cracked, but did not shatter. A thousand reflections of myself blinked back at me, every one with red eyes and sunken cheeks.

I gaped and turned from the cracked window, reeling down

the corridor. My knuckles bled, the skin underneath pink and raw. But my knuckles didn't hurt. Not at all.

"My name is Maia," I said to myself, over and over. "My name is Maia Tamarin."

I pulled on my hair, trying to grasp something, *anything*, to help me hold on to the girl I'd once been. My fingers found the plum blossom Edan had placed in my hair, and I held it on my palm.

I started to close my fingers over the petals, but a gust of wind swept in, carrying the flower from my hand. I lunged after it, but it was already too late. Over the mountain, it drifted off.

Lost and never to be recovered.

CHAPTER TWENTY-ONE

That night, the ghosts of Lapzur tormented me. They perched on the crooked trees outside Edan's window, white hair streaming from their scalps, melting into the moonlight, their voices low and harsh. It was well past twilight, the entire temple clothed in darkness. Beside me, Edan slept peacefully.

Come back, the ghosts entreated. Over and over, they made the same pleas, their hollow black eyes following my movements as I tossed and turned.

Don't fight us, Sentur'na. You will lose. You will die.

I pinched my eyes shut, remembering Master Tsring's warning to me. That the dresses were both my salvation and my ruin—if I destroyed them, I would be free of Bandur. But I would also die.

A gust of wind blew the window open. I sprang up to shut it, then curled back against Edan in bed.

"Can't sleep?"

I rolled onto my side to find Edan gazing at me. The ghosts' calls receded to the back of my mind.

He was still the same boy I'd grown to love during our travels, but he'd changed since being freed of his oath. During our few moments together, he smiled more and laughed easily. If not for the curse hanging over me, I thought, with a bitter pang to my heart, he might always be smiling.

"Nightmares?" he asked.

I didn't reply. Instead, I scooted closer to him, inhaling the warmth of his skin. "Why do they call you Gen here?"

Edan folded an arm under his head. "It was my name before I became an enchanter. They will call me by no other name until I regain enough magic to be deserving."

"So you no longer have a thousand names?"

"For now," he said, with a twinkle in his eye. "Don't worry, I'll earn them back."

We laughed, but the sound struck me as hollow. I didn't want our last days to be like this, pretending everything was the way it used to be.

At my silence, he prodded, "Are you worried about what Master Tsring said?"

"No." I hesitated. We'd searched for the master after dinner, but he was nowhere to be found. "I was just listening."

"Listening?" He flashed a grin. "To me?"

"You were snoring," I teased.

"Ah, how our roles have changed." A bittersweet note touched his voice. "I remember when we were on the Road, *I* was the one who used to listen to you. You snore a little before you fall fully asleep. I'd gotten used to the sound."

I poked him playfully in the ribs. "I don't snore."

"You don't. Except when you're exhausted." He took my hand and rubbed my bruised knuckles, a question in his raised eyebrow. The amusement fled from his tone. "What's this?"

I drew my hand back. "Nothing."

"Maia . . . tell me."

I wouldn't look at him. I stared at the ceiling, then at the grooves in the granite walls. Finally I said, "I . . . I got angry at myself after lunch."

"Why?" he pressed.

"Sometimes I see things—hear things. . . ."

"From Lapzur," Edan murmured, tightening his hand over mine. "When was the first time?"

I faltered, listening to the rustling of leaves outside the monastery, the falling pebbles against the stone walls. The ghosts had disappeared, and I eased my breath, letting my shoulders relax. Just a little; I knew they hadn't left me entirely. The shadow of Lapzur hung over me like a shroud.

Edan asked again, "What did you see just now—outside the window?"

"The ghosts of Lapzur," I whispered. "They're not happy with me for coming here."

Edan's dark eyes glittered. "Are they still there?"

"They're gone." It was my turn to grin, though it took effort. "Maybe they remembered to be frightened of you."

"How often do they visit you?" he asked quietly.

"Every night. Sometimes in the day, too. I didn't want to worry you—"

It's easier to fight them off when I'm with you, I wanted to say. *Easier to slip into my old self and make believe I have more time. Easier to look into the mirror and remember who I am.* But I couldn't.

"That's why you haven't been able to sleep."

"I don't need to."

If what I said troubled him, he didn't show it. He wrapped me in his arms, clasping me to him. "Rest now. What did your brothers do when you were little and couldn't sleep?"

I thought hard. "Sendo used to tell me stories when there was a storm. I was more afraid of thunder than of lightning. Keton used to tease me that the thunder was an evil spirit hungry for the hearts of little girls. He liked to scare me."

"I hope he got a thrashing for that."

The wryness of his tone made me smile. "Finlei gave him extra chores."

We laughed, and I rested my head on the crook of his arm, calmer now. "Do you ever miss your brothers?" I asked.

"Sometimes," he admitted. "I wish I'd known them as well as you knew yours. I like to think they're living their next lives now, with full stomachs and full hearts. Better lives than the ones we led."

"Their next lives?"

"In Nelronat, we believed that this life is only the beginning. That our souls are reborn into the next life and the next, and that those we love are tethered to us so we may find each other."

"We have something similar in A'landi." I propped myself up on one elbow and fished around in my pouch for the spool of dull red thread Ammi had given me back at the inn.

"My mother believed in fate." I unwound the thread, wrapping it around his wrist. "She told me there was an invisible thread tying me to someone else." I looked up to meet his eyes. "Someone I was destined to meet and would be bound to all my life."

I pressed my palms against his, studying his hands—the palms once stained with the blood of stars. They weren't a noble's hands. Rough along the sides with calluses like mine, but his fingers were long and graceful.

Slowly, I tied the thread around his wrist, knotted it.

"You said that I am your oath now," I whispered, "so I bind

you to me. No matter what happens, come back on the ninth day of the ninth month. Every year, I will wait for you—by the sea where I grew up, back home in Port Kamalan."

Edan drew me close, wrapping his arms so tightly around me that his heart pounded against my ear. He kissed me, the warmth of his breath melting me. "I won't let him have you."

"It isn't up to you. It's up to me." I held out my wrist for Edan to tie a thread around.

As he knotted it, he said, so quietly I almost didn't hear, "I've been thinking about what Master Tsring said. If we destroyed Lapzur."

"I've been thinking about it too," I admitted. "Bandur would be no more . . . but my pledge to him would still stand."

"Yes, but you would not be bound to the isles."

I could see a plan unspooling in Edan's mind, hope springing from despair. Did I dare to hope as well?

"It can't be easy to destroy Lapzur," I reasoned. "If it were, someone else would have done it long ago."

"Bandur is a formidable guardian," Edan agreed, "and his army of ghosts is strong. But I'm willing to take the risk."

I looked at him, then at the matching red threads on our wrists. A protest died on my lips.

Edan spoke again: "Master Tsring says I will never recover all the magic I had while under oath, but some will come back to me." Edan raised his hand, and the threads around our wrists grew warm, the ends stretching for each other. "The magic I had when I was a boy."

His forehead was moist with perspiration, a thin watery line gliding down his temples. "I fear it won't be enough to save you from Bandur. Or A'landi from the shansen's greed and Khanujin's pride."

"You've done enough to protect A'landi for a hundred lifetimes," I said. "The battle against Bandur isn't yours to fight. It's mine."

I held his cheek so our eyes were level. "You told me once that Amana's dresses were not meant for this world. Their power is in me now. If that isn't enough to defeat Bandur and save A'landi, then I don't know what is."

"You sound like you don't need me at all," he teased gently.

"You're wrong," I whispered. I needed him more than ever. It wasn't the dresses that compelled me to cling to who I was, but Edan—and my family. "Without you, I'd be lost."

I rested my head on his arm again. "Sing for me," I said softly. "I want to hear that little tune you always played on the flute when we were traveling."

"This one?" Edan started to hum, his throat vibrating that simple song I'd grown to love so much.

"What's it called?"

"It doesn't have a name," he replied. "My mother used to sing it to me when I was a boy. I sang it to remember home when I was in the monastery, then to calm the horses when I was taken to war. It's been with me a long, long time."

Together we hummed the melody, its lilting energy so wistful and simple I thought of Port Kamalan, of my brothers and of Mama. As the tune approached its end, an ache for home swelled in my throat, and I could barely hum the last note. That ache sat with me a long time, even when the rhythm of my breath finally steadied, matching Edan's.

But still I could not sleep.

I waited an hour before I dared to move. Edan had fallen asleep again, so, careful not to disturb him, I rose and sat at his desk to pen a letter home.

Dear Baba and Keton,

I'm sorry I left so suddenly.

The emperor called me back—

I pray that you are safe and far from the field of battle, and do not need the comfort of this letter. I do not know when I'll be able to write again, but I write now to tell you I am well and being looked after. Please do not worry about me.

Keton, please be careful. Baba, too.

If I do not see you again, know that my heart is with you.

My brush sagged, and I clutched my head in my hand. How could I tell them I'd come into the possession of unspeakable power and that both Emperor Khanujin *and* the shansen were combing the country for me? How could I write that their lives were in danger—because of me—and that I couldn't protect even them . . . because *I* was the last person I trusted.

Because I was turning into a demon.

What I'd written would have to be enough. There was nothing I could add that wouldn't bring Baba and Keton pain.

I picked up my brush again and reached for a fresh page. My fingers trembled, as if I could not remember how to set my brush to ink, as if my hands did not know how to form characters on paper. I squeezed the handle tight, the dripping ink smearing under the side of my palm.

This time, I wrote to Edan.

A long time ago, a foolish girl was asked to weave the sun, embroider the moon, and paint the stars, three impossible tasks she did not believe she could accomplish. But that foolish girl was lucky, even more so because those three impossible tasks freed the boy she loved.

I am lucky, Edan. I know that for every dawn, dusk must unravel its darkness. I know I have to pay a price for what I've done, yet I would not change anything about the choices I have made.

Still, I will not lie. Shadows cling to me, and darkness folds over me. Some days, I do not even remember how to set my needle to cloth. I would rather leave you now while I still remember your face, your voice, your name.

I swallowed, loosening my grip on the brush.

And should you ever feel alone, when I am gone, go to my father and brother. They will know who you are, and they will love you. Look after them and protect them, the way you would protect me.

I beg you, Edan, let me be strong. Let me go.

I blew once on the letter to dry the ink, then I slipped it into one of his cloak pockets, tucking it inside his flute so he wouldn't find it right away. If we were successful in defeating Bandur and in lifting his terrible curse from me, I would take it back and burn it. If not, then I would leave him. And when I did, at least he'd have a piece of me—of the *real* me, no matter what came.

Only one task left.

Reaching for my tailor's tools, I touched my amulet to summon the dress of the blood of stars. It was the most fickle of my dresses, and the one most connected to me. I'd held off on repairing it for so long, not wanting to remind myself of what I had sacrificed to make it.

Streams of silk curled out of the amulet, and the star-painted dress materialized in my arms. Though the bodice was ripped and the skirts torn, seeing it still filled me with wonder. As I set it over my lap, its fabric came alive at my touch, unleashing a trove of colors—most of all a vibrant, shimmering violet, like stars beaming from across the universe. And power enough, I hoped, to slay a demon.

I set to work.

CHAPTER TWENTY-TWO

A stroke of sunlight caressed my face, easing my eyelids open.

I blinked, not remembering that I'd fallen asleep. But I was back in bed, a thin muslin blanket folded over me, and Edan was gone.

On my pillow I found a fresh plum blossom, and a note written in Edan's small, elegant hand.

I'm going to look for Master Tsring. There are fried buns and peanut cakes for breakfast. You'll like the cakes. Will save you some before they're all gone.

Tucking the note into my pocket, I smiled. Trust Edan to remember my sweet tooth. I sniffed, inhaling the aroma of fresh peanuts on the griddle. The old me would have swooped downstairs to wolf down the cakes, but now they did not tempt me at all.

I dressed and hurried to find Edan, but Master Tsring himself intercepted me in the stairwell.

"Come," he said before I could stutter a morning greeting.

He motioned for me to follow him, down the winding wooden stairs into a cavernous corridor built within the mountain. The corridor grew narrower, and we exited into an outdoor alcove behind a waterfall. Despite the rush of the cascading falls, the air here was calm. Water-stained statues of Nandun, carved of stone and jade, stood along the edge of the rock.

"We call this sanctuary the Cascading Peace," Master Tsring said, sitting on the wet ground. I followed his example. The water pounded behind me, cool spray misting the back of my neck. "I tell my students to come here when the responsibilities of magic trouble them."

He gave me a moment to absorb his words. "Few enchanters walk this earth, Maia. Rare is the gift of magic, rarer still the ability to wield it. Gen was one of our most powerful, but even he failed to understand that serving a thousand years beside men and women of great destinies is as much a burden as it is a gift."

"He knows now," I said quietly. "He's known for a long time."

"He has learned to live with regret," Tsring agreed. "Still, had he not met you, it is likely he would have completed his oath."

"I—"

"Better he break it now than later," the master said over me. "My disciples here will never take the oath. Never will they taste the power that Gen possessed, and never will they endure the suffering that has befallen you."

"What are you trying to tell me?"

"Ill times await A'landi," said Master Tsring carefully. "There is much good Gen can still do, even though he will never be as powerful as he once was. I ask you to go to Lapzur alone, so that he may stay here and complete his training."

"Y-you want me to leave him?" I spluttered.

"It would be for the best. I thought I could help you, Maia. Truly." The old man paused, his attention settling on a stream of water trickling down the rocks. "But now I see you *should* have let Gen become the guardian. Armed with the goddess's legacy, you make a far more dangerous demon than he would have been."

His words made my chest tighten. A wave of irritation rippled through me, and I bit my lip, trying to subdue my rising temper. I would not be angry. I would not.

The master bowed his head, aware of my struggle. He took on a gentler tone. "My disciples complain that I am harsh. I do not mince my words because I have seen what withholding the truth can do. Perhaps if I had been harsher with Bandur, he would not have broken his oath. Perhaps he would not have taken it in the first place."

Master Tsring's lips thinned, crinkles forming along the corners. "If you fail to defeat him at Lapzur, I will be ready for him when he is freed."

"You're wrong about me," I told him, standing. "I won't turn."

"It matters not either way."

I spun sharply to face him. His statement was firm, his eyes clear. This was not what he had told us at lunch yesterday.

"I had the gift of prescience," he explained. "Its power has faded since I completed my oath, but every now and then, the sight returns to me. No matter how many times I look into the flames, no matter how many times I cast the stones or read the leaves, it is the same result. For you, Maia Tamarin? I see naught but ashes." He rose to stand at my side. "You know it, too."

Mist from the cascading falls blurred my vision, and I

lowered my lashes, trying to blink my eyes dry. "Is that why you wanted to speak with me this morning? Simply to tell me that I will die even if I defeat Bandur?"

"Whether or not you defeat him at Lapzur, you are still your own greatest enemy. You cannot survive the battle against yourself."

Tsring exhaled, lifting his arms. "Even still, all is not as bleak as it sounds. There is a rip in the heavens, created by magic. The Weaver, your ancestor, was the first to mend it, but he was careless and left a trace of his magic among his mortal descendants." He eyed the scissors hanging from my belt. "Thanks to the folly of enchanters and demons, the rip in the heavens has returned. It falls to you to mend it once more.

"Maia, two powers clash inside you now. I am certain you have felt it. The dresses urge you to heal the heavens, but the demon inside urges you to tear them apart. Whichever voice you choose to heed will determine the legacy you leave behind."

I swallowed hard. "What about Edan? Did you see his fate?"

"Gen's fate is more fluid. Whether or not he lives rests heavily on the choices you make."

"That's why you think he should stay," I whispered.

"Whatever he chooses, I will honor," replied Master Tsring. Then he hesitated. "I asked him to stay before he went looking for you. I told him that he was meant for magic. Do you know what he replied?"

The answer rang familiar, as if coming from a dream.

" 'I was meant for magic, once, but because of Maia, I am no longer the enchanter I was before. I am meant for her now. Her above all else.' "

A small smile tugged at the old man's lips. "There, that is what I wished to tell you. Go now. Choose well."

I started to turn away from Master Tsring, then paused. "Thank you," I said softly, before hurrying back to the temple.

I raced down the corridor, ignoring the looks from his disciples when I burst into the eating hall, eyes blazing red. I didn't care about their stares, or about the propriety of the temple. I ran into Edan's arms, nearly toppling him over as I hugged him close and buried my face into his robes.

"Maia," he breathed.

I looked up at him, taking in the earnest lines that furrowed his brow, the concern shining in his eyes. I knew there was no need to ask the question lingering on my tongue. "Are there any more peanut cakes left?" I asked instead.

The lines on his brow eased, and he chuckled. "I stashed a few for you." A pause—he knew me too well. "What happened?"

"I ran into Master Tsring," I confessed, the words rushing out of my mouth. "He thinks it'd be dangerous for you to go with me. He's seen—"

"That I might die?" Edan finished for me.

I bit my lip and stared at the floor. For a moment, I was my old self again.

He tilted my chin up, a spark of mischief in his eyes. "I won't let you have your carpet back if you leave me behind."

"It doesn't fly any—"

"It does now. I got a few of the disciples to fix it this morning." He twined his fingers through mine. "I'm coming with you, Maia. You'll not be rid of me so easily."

It was difficult not to melt, even for an almost-demon like me. "Everyone's watching."

"I don't care." He grinned, and kissed my cheek. "Come, eat before breakfast is over."

I barely glanced at the generous spread of food. My encounter with Master Tsring had erased any appetite I might have had. "Let's go now. I don't want to stay here any longer."

. . .

It should have taken us a week to reach Lake Paduan, but we arrived before nightfall on the third day. It was as if Bandur—the *isles* themselves—knew I was coming, and sent winds to bring me back.

The lake's icy fingers clutched my legs as I slid off the carpet and stepped ashore. Each breath tasted bitter, stinging my throat. With each step, I sank deeper, heavier, into the sand, knowing Lapzur had been waiting for me to return. Now that I was back, it would never let me leave.

I traced the crack in my amulet, summoning the dress of the blood of stars under my breath.

Inky, dark liquid bubbled out of the jet-black shell. Silk danced in ribbons of smoke and mist, flowing between my fingers and winding over my shoulders. Sleeves threaded over my arms, light as the kiss of the wind, and a skirt cinched itself around my waist before draping me, full as a bell, with a hem that flickered like candlelight.

Here, where the blood of stars fell once a year, my dress was at home.

"You should take this back," I said, passing Edan his dagger.

I'd wrapped a scarf around the weapon. Even though I hadn't uttered "Jinn" to trigger its magic, I could feel an uncomfortable heat emanating through the fibers of the cloth.

Wordlessly, Edan took it from me. We'd gone over our plan one last time before arriving at the isles, but I hadn't fully anticipated the tremendous power of this place. Already, it threatened to overwhelm me.

"Should the worst befall me," I said, "please take care of my father and my brother."

Edan stiffened. He strained to keep his tone even. "You won't—"

"And take care of yourself," I spoke over him. I grasped the folds of my dress, the dark fabric shimmering at my touch. "I'm ready."

Unlike the last time, the ghosts did not tempt me. They did not hide in the shadows, did not bother to mimic my mother or brothers. I did not hear Mama's voice, or Finlei's, or Sendo's.

Instead, they welcomed me as one of their own. Which was far worse.

Sentur'na, you have returned to us. At last.

As I walked to the Thief's Tower, the city rebuilt itself around me, crumbled bricks reassembling themselves into proud buildings with gabled roofs, dead trees sprouting leaves as verdant as springtime, and the sky above blushing with the colors of dusk. The moon, full as it had been when I'd sought its tears, hung within a net of stars. Stars whose blood adorned my gown.

I glanced at Edan, wondering if he saw the city as I did. Something about his dark expression told me he did not.

This isn't real, I reminded myself. *But how real it feels. Like I belong here.*

For the first time in weeks, I felt alive. It had been so long since I'd felt my blood rushing from my cheeks to my fingertips, stirring my heart. No longer did I feel the presence of the demon inside me, looming in my thoughts and tightening her grasp.

This was how the isles would seduce me. Not with my family, but with power. With life.

The ghosts bowed to me, their long, crooked arms outstretched. Others clamored for Edan, boldly reaching for him in spite of the dagger he wielded. The meteorite glowed brighter than I'd ever seen it, a shimmering silver that was nearly blue.

"Leave him alone," I seethed, hissing at the ghosts who drew too near. They backed away, nails scraping against the stone path as they crawled to obey.

Bandur was waiting for us at the Thief's Tower, a hideous hybrid of wolf and man flanked by a pack of wraithlike wolves. When he saw me, he bared his fangs with pleasure.

"You have finally come," he greeted me from the top of the stairs. He spared a glance for Edan. "And with the oath breaker."

I looked over and saw that Bandur's wolves had surrounded Edan, separating us. Angrily, I whirled to face the demon.

"An incentive, if you will." Bandur gestured at Edan. "To ensure you complete the ceremony. I warned you he was not invited, Sentur'na."

How I hated the way Bandur spoke that name. My name.

"Do you hear your new friends? They claim you."

I did hear. Thousands of voices, each an icy pinprick stabbing me from every direction. *Our new guardian has arrived.*

My amulet weighed on my chest, and my whole body felt like stone. My dress went dark, its fabric inky as the eternal night above. I lifted my skirts and forced my leaden legs onto the first step and the next and the next, up to the Thief's Tower.

Fear gripped my heart.

Was it truly my fate to become the next guardian of Lapzur? What if I couldn't fight Bandur?

I reached the mouth of the tower, where Bandur awaited me. Wisps of smoke trickled out of the jagged crack in his amulet, forming a dark cloud around me.

Without ceremony, Bandur yanked my amulet from my neck, closing his claws over it. Smoke drifted through the seams of his fingers into the amulet, and though my mouth was clamped shut, a rush of cold stung my lungs and chest, making me gasp aloud.

When he opened his fist, my amulet had become black and lackluster—like his. Like a demon's.

Bandur's amulet—its round obsidian surface, dull and scratched—suddenly blazed to life. The wolf engraved on the top sharpened, its fangs gleaming, its ruby eyes glittering.

"The transfer of guardianship has begun," he said, hanging my amulet over his neck.

I didn't struggle as the breath was squeezed out of me. Instead, I looked him calmly in the eye. I prayed he wouldn't notice my shaking hands reaching behind my skirt to unhook my scissors.

In one swift motion, I grabbed the scissors and stabbed him in the neck. Bandur howled, and I dug the blades deeper, until black velvety blood welled out. Then I wrenched out the scissors and snipped the amulets' chains, catching them as they fell from his neck.

The smoke abruptly stopped. Air rushed back into my lungs as my amulet reconnected itself back over my neck, and my strength returned. Smoke gathered at my feet, curling around my ankles like snakes. Flames tickled my fingertips as I tucked Bandur's amulet into my skirt.

An arrow flew past me and pierced Bandur's shoulder. He ripped it out and snarled at Edan, who'd managed to break free of the wolves.

"Go!" Edan shouted, wielding the dagger, leaping up the stairs toward Bandur. "Go now!"

I was already running. We'd planned this meticulously. He would fend off Bandur while I raced to the top of the tower.

Ghosts swarmed after me. Their airy hands tore at the train of my dress, some close enough to graze my skin. But I was already marked by a demon; the ghosts could not harm me.

I ran, my feet pounding against the stone steps, spiraling up the tower.

"Maia, stop!" my mother shouted, blocking my path.

Baba's workshop in Gangsun appeared just as I remembered it. The stool Mama had bought for me was by the window, with my basket of tools on the floor. The altar with Amana's statues, the paint barely dried.

I could hear Finlei and Keton fighting outside, Sendo trying to play peacemaker.

"They're fire and wind, those two," Mama said, shaking her head. "You and Sendo, earth and water. Like the river against the stone."

I refused to let the power of the isles devastate me. I knew it wasn't real. And yet—memories of my family flooded back with vivid intensity. It had been so long since I'd heard Mama's voice, so long since I'd seen her. Like last time, I almost couldn't resist.

"Stay with us, Maia. Isn't this what you always wanted? To be with your family again."

Gray hair tickled her temples. She looked so real, the wind that ruffled my skirts fluffed hers, too. I gazed at her, taking in the burnished glow of her cheeks, the freckles dotting her skin, the wrinkles along the corners of her lips. She was just as I remembered her, and yet—something about her eyes were too soft and watery to be human.

"Stay with us," Mama said again. She edged closer to me. "You are the strong one, Maia. The one who will hold the seams of our family together. You can do that, here."

At the sound of my dead mother's words on this pretender's lips, a surge of anger swelled in me.

"I *will* hold my family together," I said through my teeth. "But you are not my mother. Let me pass."

The ghost's lips pressed tight, and my mother's face melted off, her black hair washing out until it was wild and white, streaming down over her starved black eyes.

She wrapped a skeletal hand over my wrist.

A ghost's touch doomed a human to become a ghost. But I was no longer human. I flung up my hand, breaking her grip on me. My skirt flared angrily, spitting beams of light.

The ghost writhed, her shrieks slicing the air as her bones sizzled into smoke.

I leapt up the steps, two at a time, my dress lighting the dark winding stairway up to the rooftop, to the well that collected the blood of stars.

And there it was. How desolate it looked—like a stone bowl jutting from the earth. It hadn't been so quiet the last time I'd arrived. Then again, today was not the ninth day of the ninth month. No stars bled in the sky, no silvery dust fell into the well.

I gripped the side of the well, its rocky surface scraping against my elbow. Inside surged a fathomless gulf of darkness.

This—*this* was the heart of Lapzur. Not the Thief's Tower, not Bandur.

Not me.

I took out Bandur's amulet. The obsidian sent a shock wave roaring through me, burning icy cold. As if it knew I wanted to destroy it.

I leaned over the well.

"Stop," rasped Bandur, appearing on the other side. "The enchanter's life for my amulet."

My demon sight flickered to Edan. *He was still downstairs, surrounded by ghosts, their fingers grabbing at his throat. His dagger flashed, arcs of silvery blue sweeping furiously around him as he fended them off. One touch, and he would become a creature like them.*

"They prey on weakness," Bandur reminded me. "His weakness is you, Maia. No mortal is able to resist, not for long. And he *is* mortal now."

I flinched.

"Return the amulet to me, or Edan will die."

"No," I whispered, my eyes burning, my blood blazing with anger. With my demon sight, I traveled down the tower again to where Edan and the ghosts were.

"I am the guardian of Lapzur now!" I yelled at the ghosts. "Let him go!"

They froze, confused. *Sentur'na . . .*

"I am Sentur'na." This time, my voice boomed like Bandur's. My eyes glowed bright as two blood-red stars. "Let him go."

Sentur'na. They bowed, obeying me and backing away from Edan.

"Kill him!" Bandur screamed. "She is not the guardian yet!"

They rallied at the demon's command, but Edan had spun away and was now making for the top of the tower. The ghosts surged after him.

My heart clenched. We'd both known the risks of coming to Lapzur.

"If we go," I'd told him, "then we go with the intent to destroy Bandur. For good. Even if that means one of us—or both of us—doesn't make it."

I uncurled my fingers from the amulet, and my demon sight broke.

A flash of teeth and claws was my only warning before Bandur slammed into me. I screamed and almost pitched into the well, but the demon caught my wrist, pulling me toward him.

"Now we complete the ceremony, Sentur'na." He gashed my arm with his nail, sharp as the edge of a sword, and blood oozed from my wound. "Once the blood offering to Lapzur has been made, you will be the new guardian."

He held my arm over the well. My sleeves flailed against him, sparks shooting from the fabric as it singed his gray fur. In a beastly rage, he clawed at my dress and snatched at his amulet, but I held it out of reach over the well.

"Give me the amulet."

His words chafed my ears, cruel as a knife sharpening against bone. They echoed down into the well, ringing off the endless stone walls.

"The last time we encountered each other, I traded you your amulet for a vial," I told him. "I will not be so foolish again."

"You drop it, and you'll die along with me."

I looked down. Below was darkness, blacker than the bottom of the sea and as endless as the night. The rippling folds of my dress shimmered, but even their luminous starlight could not penetrate the abyss.

Bandur's amulet dangled, swaying to the drumbeat of my heart. Too late I saw the dark rivulet trickling across my arm, collecting into one thick bead at the slope of my elbow. I jerked to the side, and it splashed against the stones. But there was nothing I could do to stop my blood from running down, down—once it touched the bottom I'd be the guardian of Lapzur.

Knowing he saw it too, I faced Bandur with my steeliest smile. "So be it."

And I dropped his amulet into the well.

CHAPTER TWENTY-THREE

In a whirl of shadow and smoke, Bandur vaulted into the well after his amulet.

Panic knifed through me. I couldn't let him get it back.

I threw myself after him, scrabbling at flashes of gray fur. The battle, fought in the pitch black of the well's oblivion, was frantic. Bandur was stronger, but I was more determined.

Then Bandur's flesh flickered, and I dug my nails into his fur, knowing I'd caught him. I dragged him out of the well and held on until I heard the amulet break the surface and sink into the well's murky depths.

Then another plop. My blood.

Bandur twisted violently out of my grasp and seized my neck, dangling me over the well.

He held me close, so close I could smell the ash on his breath, the smoke whistling from the singed layer of his fur. The folds of my dress took on a life of their own, flailing against him, a storm of stars and light whipping at his demon flesh. His red eyes burned wild with anger, and his claws tightened around my neck.

Why wasn't he dead? I'd destroyed his amulet.

"Congratulations, *Sentur'na*," he rasped. "You are now the guardian of Lapzur."

I couldn't be the guardian of Lapzur. The well had devoured his amulet *before* it'd taken my blood. It should have killed him!

My fear escalated to terror. I grabbed the scissors from my belt and thrust uselessly at his hands, his heart, his throat.

"How—"

My question became a scream as he grabbed my amulet, scoring its surface with his monstrous nails. I bucked and went limp.

Laughing, Bandur seized the scissors dangling from my fingers. "The amulet is your heart, Sentur'na. You could have controlled me when you had mine, but you didn't know, did you?"

He held me high in the air, and I screamed again, but no sound came out of my mouth. I was choking, couldn't breathe.

"Now—you die."

Below, the well's dark waters swirled, gathering into a terrible tempest. Its stones were crumbling, piles of rocks and pebbles cascading into the water. Somehow, seeing the violence of the well, I *knew* I wasn't the guardian. If I were, I would be stronger than Bandur. I would control the power of Lapzur's ghosts, and I could have commanded them away from Edan and to my aid.

Bandur was bluffing. But why?

Seconds stretched to eternity. Frenzied, my dress attacked him, trying to snatch my amulet back before he dropped it into the well.

He launched the scissors against my dress, their metal humming and zinging with power. But the scissors wouldn't cut; he was not their master.

With a snarl, he hurled me—and my amulet—into the well.

As I fell, suddenly I understood. Destroying Bandur's amulet hadn't destroyed *him,* but now he was mortal. That's why he was so desperate to be rid of me and to get off the island.

Because he knows you can kill him, Sentur'na, whispered that dark, seductive voice within me. *You have the dresses of Amana. You are stronger than him. Give in, and kill him.*

For once, I listened.

I dove for my amulet, catching it in my fist. My skirt glittered, illuminating the dark well around me. And, overriding the fear that clenched my heart, I let go and trusted the blood of stars to catch me and lift me.

Like a shooting star, I rocketed up and out of the well and leapt onto Bandur's back.

Startled, the demon spun and tried to throw me off, but my sleeves countered the attack, whipping and wrapping themselves around his neck. I snatched my scissors from him—and stabbed him in the heart.

Bandur shrieked. Writhed. He tried to rip the scissors out of his chest. With the last of his strength, he flung me across the rooftop. I lost my grip on the scissors and fell hard on the cold stone floor.

He peeled away, smoke leaking from his lips as his body began to dissipate. He flailed, but his arms and fur had thinned into shadow, his red eyes melting into a stream of blood. Then a storm of fire devoured him.

Until he was no more.

Rocks flew up out of the well, hurtling fast toward me. I turned onto my stomach, covering my head to shield myself. Around me, the rooftop began to crumble, exposing the stairway and Edan, who was running toward me, his face shiny with sweat. Even though Bandur was no more, ghosts surrounded him.

Alarmed, I sprang to my feet, but the earth beneath me quaked, knocking me to the ground again. Out of the corner of my eye, I saw my scissors tremble on the lip of the well, then fall inside.

I let out a choked cry. "My scissors!"

"Leave them." Edan grabbed my wrist. "We need to go."

A flash of light erupted from the well, so great it swallowed the entire island. It lasted no longer than a blink, but the ghosts vanished.

Bandur's remains were a pile of ashes. The wind swept them up from the stone floor and scattered them over the raging waters below.

Gone was the well of the blood of stars, destroyed by the eruption of light. In its place was a mess of broken rocks and stones. Debris whirled across the rooftop, tiny pebbles prickling my skin. Edan shielded us with his cloak.

"We have to get off the tower!" he shouted as the winds picked up. Something roared in the near distance, like the rumble from the belly of a terrible beast. It took me a second to realize the island itself was crumbling.

Another quake. The world tilted so violently I couldn't keep my balance.

I staggered back, and Edan caught my arm.

Below, Lake Paduan's waters crashed and heaved. Edan was fumbling to unroll the carpet. With a glance, I took in the rips and tears, the holes and broken tassels, and claw and teeth marks. . . .

"It's not going to fly," I said, touching his arm. Without my scissors, I couldn't fix it. My demon's magic was destructive, and Amana's I could not control. I had understood my scissors—how to wield them and channel magic into the garments I'd sewn—but now they were gone.

"The only way is to jump into the lake."

"Together, then," he said, pulling me up toward the parapet.

The wind howled, and my hair flew wildly behind my shoulders. I looked down and was immediately grateful for the fog shrouding the waters, obscuring just how high we were. Even then, I could see the foam curling over the dark, stormy waters.

"You can't swim," I remembered. "Edan?"

"There's no other way."

Behind us, the wind grew strong, and the tower rumbled.

"Ready?" he asked.

I nodded, interlacing my fingers with his. "On the count of three. One, two—"

We jumped.

I couldn't see the water below, which made the plunge even more frightening. The water growled, alive with the wrath and fury of all those who had perished in its depths. I gasped, feeling the force of gravity pull us down, down, down.

I braced myself for landing, my stomach twisting and my heart in my throat.

At the height of my fear, the wind wrenched my hand away from Edan's, tearing us apart.

"Maia!" he shouted.

"No—" I started to shout, but no sound came out. Salt air rushed up into my nostrils, and a beat later, I shattered.

The crash into the lake hurt so much my body was in shock. I had forgotten what pain felt like. Water thundered in my ears and the cold began to numb me.

But it was the burning in my throat that reminded me to kick, to work, to live.

Reflexively, I swam for the surface.

I sucked in a gulp of air. The tides were fierce, hungrily

trying to bury me in their depths, and water splashed at my face as I thrashed.

"Edan?" I yelled. It was so dark I couldn't see anything. "Edan!"

My dress lit up with the brilliance of the stars. At once, the waters were illuminated, and I saw him, sinking into the depths of the lake.

I dove after him, grabbing him under the arms and kicking back to the surface. Then I hooked his arm over my shoulders.

"Edan?" I cried worriedly. "Edan, are you all right?"

He coughed, water spluttering out of his nose and mouth. His arms splashed clumsily until I steadied them, relief thudding in my ears.

"That's the closest I've come to drowning in centuries," he said.

"You scared me!"

Behind us, the isles sank into the lake, creating a vast whirlpool whose violent winds I could feel even from here. I watched Lapzur fold into the darkness, the Thief's Tower disappearing last. Never to be seen again.

"Well, I guess there goes our option of swimming to the nearest shore," Edan said, his tone more wry than grave. I placed a salty kiss on his mouth. Only he could find humor in a moment like this.

But he did have a point. The carpet had flown us quite a distance to reach Lapzur. Without it, we were stranded in the water—from our point in the lake, I couldn't even see any sign of land.

Yet I didn't panic. My mind was already spinning with an idea: after he had marked me, Bandur had been able to journey far from the isles through glass and nightmares and smoke. A demon that was not bound as guardian of Lapzur could probably do much, much more. I remembered how Bandur had thrown me into the well—and how I'd flown up away from its depths. Heat coursed through my fingertips, a spark I'd been struggling to hold back, igniting the flames within me.

"Wrap your arms around my waist," I whispered to Edan. "And hold on."

We shot out of the water, my skirts blooming like a lantern as it floated us to shore.

Once we landed, the fire inside me extinguished. I let go of everything and collapsed.

. . .

A familiar heart beat against my ear, steady and gentle, in a rhythm I'd heard many times before. As I stirred, a warm breath tickled my cheek. A thick cloak was draped over me, a comforting arm wrapped around my waist.

I couldn't have been asleep long, for it was still night.

I twisted to face Edan. His collar was damp, goose bumps rising on his exposed skin.

"You're shivering," I said.

"My clothes will dry," he replied through his teeth. "Don't worry about me, *xitara*."

"I'm not cold," I said, only to realize it wasn't true. The air was frigid, and for the first time in weeks, I tasted the frost on my lips when I breathed in. The only thing that kept me from shivering was the blood of stars.

"What are you—"

I pulled my dress over my head, unknotting its buttons. Without my scissors, there was no elegant way of undoing them.

I ignored Edan's protests and wrapped the dress's folds around us both, summoning warmth into the shimmering fabric.

Slowly the color returned to Edan's skin, but I helped hasten the process by kissing him. It was only dawning on us now that we'd won.

Bandur was dead. His tower on Lapzur had collapsed.

The whispers had stopped.

I breathed in, relishing the silence in my head. I could finally hear myself breathe, could hear my heart racing so fast and unsteadily every beat echoed in my ears. The throbbing in my temples had ceased, and my eyes had stopped burning. And pain—I'd felt pain when we crashed into the waters.

Did that mean I was free?

I tilted my head, lips brushing against Edan's. Heart hammering, I tentatively brought my gaze up to match his. I was sure I'd see two glowing red pupils reflected in his eyes, devastating as the blood-red seals on the letters pronouncing my brothers' deaths during the war.

But . . . nothing.

My eyes did not even glitter under the moonlight. They were earthy and brown, like the chestnuts I used to buy with my brothers in Port Kamalan. We'd roast them over charcoal and sprinkle precious cumin over the meat—Keton's favorite. Baba used to get angry with Finlei for wasting his earnings on a spoonful of cumin, just to indulge Keton. But Finlei and Keton were a pair, just as Sendo and I had been.

As I remembered all this, my eyes watered with emotion. I'd nearly forgotten.

Edan reached for my fingers, covering them with his. "Your hands are warm."

"So they are." I squeezed his hand, so happy to hold it again. I looked down at the dress of the stars. The brilliant colors of the fabric had become muted, matching the deep-violet sky. My amulet no longer sat heavy on my chest.

"I think I'm free," I whispered. "I think . . . I think it might have worked."

"So you'll not forget me again?" he asked.

"Never." I inhaled, and began humming our song. The song his mother used to sing to him, I knew now. "Not even if it means this tune is stuck in my head forever."

The song died on my lips as Edan brought my hand to his mouth. His breath tickled my fingertips. He kissed my fingers, his lips traveling across my palm, then to the back of my wrist. Every kiss sent tremors of pleasure shooting through me, like the stars that burst across the night above us.

I rolled atop him so our chests were aligned, and we sank into the sand, drinking in one another. And just before we fell asleep, for a few blissful moments, I thought that the worst was over.

CHAPTER TWENTY-FOUR

I awoke gasping.

Invisible fingers were strangling me, sharp winds biting into my lungs and choking me from inside. As my human pulse thumped, the length between each beat grew longer, longer, until—

No!

As my eyes shot open, the shadows disappeared, the fingers pressing down on my throat—gone. In their place I saw the shore, the first rays of dawn cutting across the lake, Edan beside me. It had all been a dream.

I sucked in a desperate breath. It burned, and I groped at my neck, shock rippling through me at the touch of my own skin, cold as death. Worse yet, the numbness in my chest had returned.

Careful not to wake Edan, I untangled myself from his arms and sat up. My fingers were like ice. Horrified, I saw that my nails had hardened, the beds brown like dried blood, the tips sharp and pointed.

I shoved my hands into the sand.

My heart thudded, deafening over the calm of the gently lapping lake.

I was still turning into a demon. I hadn't ended my transformation by defeating Bandur and destroying the isles; I had merely delayed it.

I didn't know how long I sat there, battling every new breath, before Edan stirred.

"Good morning," he said sleepily. On his lips rested a lazy smile, so endearing it pricked my heart to see it. "How long have you been awake?"

Hearing his voice, I tensed. I twisted to face the lake before he could glimpse me. My amulet, tucked under the folds of my tunic, throbbed against my ribs. Without looking down, I had a sinking feeling it was still black as night.

"Not long," I managed.

"Listening to the water?"

His question, so simple and innocent, made my chest ache. He sounded happy. "A little."

"Is something wrong, Maia?" I felt Edan's hands on my shoulders, his shadow melting into mine in the sand. "You sound distressed."

I dug my fingers deeper in the sand. I didn't want to tell him. I didn't even know how. "What will happen to future enchanters now that Lapzur is gone?"

Edan tore his gaze from the glittering waters before us. For what felt like a long time, he considered my question. "The sun and the moon will continue to meet once a year, and the stars will bleed when they come together. But now that the well of the blood of stars is no more, never again can an enchanter drink from it and bind himself to an oath of a thousand years. A new generation of enchanters will emerge."

"But you said the oath prevents them from becoming too greedy. That magic corrupts."

"That will always be true," he replied. "In Kiata they used to ban magic, and anyone born with it was exiled. Other lands never encouraged the tradition of oath taking. It is better this way, I think." At my silence, he gently teased, "They'll be singing songs about you in a thousand years, about how you destroyed the Forgotten Isles of Lapzur armed with nothing but a pair of scissors."

I mustered a smile, but it faltered as I remembered Master Tsring's story about my ancestor, the Weaver. "I wish I hadn't lost them."

"Is that why you are melancholy?"

"They belonged to my family for a long time," I answered indirectly. "Funny, I used to resent their magic helping me sew. But now that they're gone, I miss it. Their magic was a part of my past. Without them . . ."

I fear I'll be lost.

Gently, he thumbed sand off my cheek. I knew he sensed something more was wrong, but his concern was tempered by the joy from last night. He still believed that Bandur's death and the destruction of Lapzur might have reversed my change into a demon.

If only I didn't have to disappoint him.

For, now as I listened to my heart, I could hear myself breathe between each thump, the rhythm so relentlessly steady I wondered if anything would ever make it race again, whether I would ever feel again.

It would beat slower and slower, until one day soon, it would stop. And I would no longer be human.

No longer Maia.

Hope shriveled inside my chest, but I plastered on a smile.

Let Edan think I was better, at least for a few more hours. Let us be happy for a few more hours.

But my eyes burned with a familiar, devastating heat, and when he reached for my hand, still buried in the sand, I recoiled.

I swallowed. "I'm not saved yet."

Wrenching my hands out of the sand, I raised them. My fingers were unrecognizable, more like claws than hands.

Edan's face showed no surprise.

Which surprised me.

"Did you know this would happen?"

Shadows eclipsed his face. Rather than answer, he took my hands, claws and all, holding tight when I tried to pull back. He kissed my fingertips, the hard curves of my nails.

"Bandur is gone," he said, as if that would reassure me. "You aren't bound to the isles any longer."

I turned my head before he could kiss me again. My lips were cold, no matter how he tried to warm them with his own. Even when he touched the small of my back, tilting my chin up to face him, I couldn't bear the scarlet glint of my eyes reflected in his.

"You should leave. Before I become—"

"No. Maia." He raised his wrist, showing me the red thread still affixed there. "We are bound, you and I, in this life and the next. Wherever you wish to go, I will follow."

I wondered—where *did* I wish to go? I wanted to see Baba and Keton, but the thought of telling them the truth—of what was happening to me—that was more than I could bear. It would hurt them to know what'd happened to me. I'd rather spare them the pain.

Emperor Khanujin, no matter how much I despised him,

229

needed me. It would take a demon to stand against Gyiu'rak, and so long as there was still Maia in me, I needed to help. I needed to save A'landi. I only hoped it wasn't too late.

I pushed Edan gently to the side and angled him to face me. I had my answer, but I knew he wouldn't like it.

"In our next life, do you think you'll still be you?" I asked him instead. "Will you be a cattle herder's son and me the daughter of a tailor once more? Or will you be someone else entirely—and I'll have to find you again?" I cocked my head. "Maybe in the next life you won't even like to read."

"Oh, I doubt that," replied Edan wryly. "*Some* things can't change. Though the young Gen used to think books were better off used as tinder to roast carrots. My family was poor, and there was no civil exam to better yourself like in A'landi."

"You'd have done well on the exam," I said. "Maybe you'd be a high official. Or a minister, like Lorsa."

Edan wrinkled his nose. "At least a governor."

That made me laugh, and I tried to imagine what he'd been like as a boy. "So the monks taught you to read, after your father left you with them."

"Yes, but I wasn't at the monastery long. The soldiers came for me, for every able boy within a hundred miles." Edan grew quiet. "Sometimes I think the only reason I survived those wars was that I was too young to even carry a sword. I was to play the drums, but my arms were too weak, so I learned the flute instead."

"You hardly ever play it anymore," I said with a note of wistfulness.

"That's because I've been too busy teaching you to sing," Edan joked, but he reached into his pocket to oblige me. He took out his flute, but a piece of paper slipped out from inside the instrument's wooden body. "What's this?"

I jumped, recognizing the letter I'd written. I'd forgotten about it.

"Nothing," I said quickly, reaching over him for it, but Edan had already begun to read.

"Maia," he said, his voice thick with emotion. "Maia . . ."

I hung back. "I wrote it before we left for Lapzur. Our last morning at the temple, Master Tsring told me that the only way to be free was to destroy the dresses. . . . He told me . . ."

My voice trailed, my eyes drifting to the farewell I had written Edan. I had composed the letter before Master Tsring had confided in me my fate, and yet . . . somehow, somehow I must have already known. Perhaps that was why I had forgotten to take the letter back.

"He told me I would not survive."

A muscle ticked in Edan's jaw. I'd stung him. "And you didn't think to tell me?"

"I . . ." I didn't know what to say.

He waved the letter high so I couldn't snatch it from him. "Were you even going to tell me you were leaving?"

His voice was firm. Too firm. A flare of anger ignited in me. "It's my choice, just as it was yours to take the oath. You knew the consequences. I know mine."

"It wouldn't be the same for you as it was for Bandur, Maia. Your heart is good. We would find a way for you to—"

"Fight it?" I shook my head. "There is no way. You asked where I wished to go next. I want to go to the Winter Palace."

As I expected, my answer did not please Edan. He pursed his lips tight. "Maia, you need time to rest. Just because you're no longer bound to Lapzur doesn't mean you aren't still in danger. The last thing you should do is rush back to the palace to fight the shansen's demon."

"Would you have me hide?" I cried. "Would you have me let our soldiers die, let this war drag on for another five years?"

"Yes," he replied. "I would prefer that the woman I love not hasten her transformation. Especially not for the sake of fighting Khanujin's battles."

"I'm not fighting for Khanujin, I'm fighting for my country. A'landi is helpless against Gyiu'rak without me. Just now you promised to go with me wherever I wished. And now?"

"I meant what I said," insisted Edan. His fists clenched at his sides.

"But?"

"You might do more harm than good if you go."

There. He'd said it.

The heat in me reached a boil. My cheeks burned, and my eyes blazed with delirious fury. "You suggest that I let this war run its course? You, who's spent centuries flitting from one war to the next."

"Yes, and so I know the ugliness of war. I know that power can make things worse instead of better."

"And I know that if I do not help A'landi, then the Maia inside me will be lost forever."

"Or maybe that's precisely how she will be lost," Edan whispered. "Think this through, *xitara*."

Even hearing him call me *xitara*, the name that had once been so dear to me, couldn't quell the anger stirring in me.

"I would rather die as this Maia than live forever as a demon and watch my country fall," I snapped. My words took on a cruel edge—I couldn't help it. "You wouldn't understand. Nel-

232

ronat is gone, your family is gone, your home is gone. What have you to fight for?"

"You," he said hoarsely. "You are my family and my home."

Deep inside, I wanted to stop. I didn't want to hurt Edan. But the demon in me had other plans.

"I'm not your family," I said. "I'm not anyone's family."

"Maia—" He tried to wrap his arms around me, but I threw him off, and he slammed back hard into the sand.

He got up. Spread his arms out in entreaty. "Please."

"Don't touch me," I warned him. My control was slipping, and I spun away. I couldn't—

"Maia . . ."

As I heard him say that name again, my eyes grew so hot the ocean blurred into the sky, and a rush of fire surged through my veins. I turned on him, but my mind was not my own. My body was not my own. Everything happened too fast. One moment, I felt the wind lashing at my face, the next, I saw my claws extended, razor-sharp nails pointed at Edan's heart.

Blood trickled down his cheek.

I stepped back in shock. *I didn't mean to,* I wanted to say, but Edan already had his dagger raised at me.

Seeing it made me balk. I could almost feel pangs of the meteorite's searing heat radiating off its blade, and I waited, my breath tight, for Edan to utter his name "Jinn" and activate its power.

But he didn't. He didn't have to. The message was clear. The sorrow in his eyes was clear.

He lowered the dagger slowly. With every inch that it fell, my heart sank.

"I love you, Maia. Come back."

My fury vanished, leaving me hollow. Broken.

This was the boy who'd given himself up to a demon for me. The boy I'd given up the sun and moon and stars to be with.

The boy I loved.

I wanted to burrow myself into the earth and stay rooted there, where I would hurt no one, and no one could hurt me.

Edan dropped the dagger. It landed on the dirt with a thump, the meteorite side of the blade still glimmering. The world came into stark focus, and yet everything was spinning, spinning and unraveling. I couldn't keep up.

"I'm sorry," he said, uttering the words I should have spoken. "I shouldn't have—"

I couldn't listen. I couldn't bear the pity, couldn't bear to see the emotions warring on his face. I turned and ran. Even as Edan's voice calling "Maia!" faded into oblivion, I didn't stop.

The name meant nothing to me.

CHAPTER TWENTY-FIVE

Trees blurred into rushes of color as I fled through the forest, half running and half flying. Ribbons of smoke curled after me, and my feet were barely touching the ground.

I was moving like a demon.

How could Edan think there was any chance for us when I had almost killed him? How foolish I'd been to hope that by freeing myself from Bandur everything might return to the way it had been before.

Maybe I should go far away—where I wouldn't be a danger to anyone but myself.

I slowed, coming back to earth. Foxes and squirrels scattered, making for the bushes and the trees, but the birds did not flee. At least *they* weren't afraid of me.

My claws snagged against my sleeves, and I ripped away the excess fabric. Sparks flicked from my nails, like flashes of the fireworks I'd seen dancing above the Autumn Palace.

Where could I go, looking like this? Not Port Kamalan.

Yet it was the only place I *wished* to go. I hadn't been brave enough to say goodbye to Baba and Keton last time, and now I regretted it more than anything.

No, I had other regrets too. Fresh ones.

"You are my family and my home," Edan had said.

"And you are mine," I should have told him. I said it now,

and I curled my arms around my chest, hugging the ache inside me. The pain was like a knot holding me together, one I did not dare undo.

Didn't Edan see? He was why I needed to stay, why I needed to fight for the emperor. There would be no home for Baba, Keton, and him—no home for any of us—if Gyiu'rak and the shansen conquered A'landi.

My amulet grazed my knuckles, the walnut ridges sharper than I remembered. I clasped it, feeling Amana's power recoiling from the demon I was becoming. My dresses had been stronger when they were three; *I* had been stronger, too. But for all the tremendous power they held, they could not free me from Bandur's curse. They were doomed along with me.

And with only two left, I didn't have much time.

Edan was still far behind me. I'd wait for him, apologize, and we'd go to the Winter Palace together. Then, if the gods favored us and we won against the shansen, I would go home to Baba and Keton one last time.

Are you even sure your father and brother are still safe in Port Kamalan? a dark voice rippled inside me.

I stilled. For the first time, I didn't tell her to go away. *What do you know?*

Perhaps it is the shansen you should fight for, if you wish your family to be safe.

My eyes began to burn, so hot that I cried out in pain. All of me convulsed, and I curled against an oak tree, tendrils of bright fiery smoke unfurling from my skin.

My demon sight took me far from the forest, to an army of thousands, all sitting erect in their saddles, weapons raised, emerald banners of a tiger sailing in the wind. Ahead was the

Winter Palace, but the army had stopped just before the Jingan River. Something momentous was about to happen.

At the helm of the army rode the shansen, with Gyiu'rak beside him.

Her ruby eyes burned fiercely, and when my gaze found her she lifted her head, her whiskers perking up—as if she felt my presence.

Her mouth curved into a lethal smile. "Sister . . . you're here. Just in time."

I stiffened in shock. Why had my sight brought me here—where were Baba and Keton?

The deafening blare of a horn knifed the air, and I noticed the blackened sky, the burned structures and smoldering wreckage beyond the river. The destruction stretched on and on, an unending shroud of charred temples, houses, and trees. Fury choked me, yet I could not look away. The demon inside me was drawn to the destruction as much as I was repulsed by it.

"Demons near and far," boomed the shansen, his voice speaking in unison with Gyiu'rak's, "I summon you from the dark recesses of this world."

I summon you.

The power of his words slammed into me, pulling me into a tide of darkness. I clutched at my head, unsure of what was happening.

"I have paid my blood price and bound Gyiu'rak to me," the shansen continued. *"Hear me and aid me. I will conquer A'landi and bring you back in glory."*

I summon you. Hear me and come to my aid.

The earth rumbled, my vision going in and out as the shansen and Gyiu'rak repeated their call. I tried to fight the summons, but my blood was blazing to answer, and my limbs began to fracture into smoke. My amulet glowed, and the power of my dresses held me in place, but I feared it would not be enough.

Another call from the shansen drew a scream from my lips. *I summon you.*

Like an invisible dagger, the words stabbed my chest, and I doubled over. I dug my nails into the dirt, to keep my flesh from scattering into smoke and shadow.

Come, Maia, beckoned Gyiu'rak, her blood-red eyes glittering in the smoke swirling around me. *We have your father and your brother. They're waiting for you.*

I went still. My father and brother?

My sight burned, and I saw Baba and Keton, chained together, a pine board loaded over their shoulders. Keton struggled to march fast enough, and Baba could hardly bear the weight of his shackles. The walls I'd built around my heart crumbled when I saw them shuffle forward together as the soldiers bellowed for them to move faster.

"Can't you see he's an old man?" Keton yelled. *"Let him go."*

A soldier beat my brother's shoulders with a thick lash. "Another word, boy, and those broken legs are what I'll thrash next."

Keton collapsed, but as Baba helped him up, my brother's eyes shone with defiance.

"Don't," Baba warned.

"Does the shansen not have enough men that he has to abduct them from the emperor?" Keton said, his lip bleeding from the blow.

The soldier sneered at him. "Fool, they don't want you two for soldiers."

My brother's brow furrowed. "Then?"

"You'll find out. Once we reach the Winter Palace." The lash cracked the air again. *"Now walk!"*

I blinked away the vision, my eyes stinging as if I'd rubbed them with salt. As everything came back into focus—my sight, my hearing—my heart sank. I knew what I'd seen just now hadn't been a dream.

The shansen had my family. Baba and Keton . . . they didn't even know why they'd been taken.

Answer the call, Maia, Gyiu'rak rumbled, *or your family will pay.*

What could I do?

If I went, I'd make the shansen stronger; I would become part of his demon army.

But if A'landi fell, Baba and Keton would die anyway.

My thoughts raced. Last I had faced Gyiu'rak, I'd sacrificed the dress of the sun to defeat her.

I clutched my amulet. *"Those three dresses are your body, your mind, your heart,"* Master Tsring had said. What would it mean for me to lose my mind?

I knew what Edan would say. He'd tell me that the dress of the moon was too great a sacrifice to make.

But the shansen wasn't only summoning *me*. If I had trouble resisting his promises of death and ruin, then who knew how many legions of demons and ghosts would gleefully come to his aid? Such an army would decimate the emperor's forces.

I had no choice.

Still gripping my amulet, I sprang up. Smoke bled from my fingertips, and every second I resisted the summons made my insides scream with agony. But I needed the dagger.

I didn't need to search far. Edan had nearly caught up; he was panting, his cheeks flushed from racing after me. When he saw me, he shouted, but I couldn't hear what he was saying. I was somewhere else, stuck halfway between the real world and the darkness of the shansen's summons.

He was a mere hundred paces from me, but I couldn't wait.

I let go of my amulet and stretched out my hand to him. The smoke from my fingers traveled quickly, thickening until they curled around the dagger on his belt. And in a snap, the weapon flew to my grasp.

"Jinn," I breathed. The dagger slid out of its sheath, and the meteorite sizzled alive, its power against me so strong that I nearly dropped it. Simply holding the hilt was like putting my hand into a pile of burning coals. But I could bear it; I had to.

I gripped the amulet hanging over my chest. "Help me stay strong," I whispered, pressing it to my face. If the goddess of the moon was listening, perhaps she would take pity on me. "Help me. Please."

It took only a thought for me to call forth the dress of the moon. The moon's soft beams enfolded me, and for the last time, my moon dress coursed out of the walnut, its shimmering silk flowing over my arms. The cuffs and cross-collar sparkled with white-gold floss, the flowers and clouds I'd embroidered glittering like tiny crystals. Light bathed me, and tears misted in my eyes—tears of the moon.

Before I could change my mind, I raised my dagger and stabbed the heart of the dress. Silvery ribbons unraveled, dancing and swirling around me as I dragged the dagger down to the hem of the skirts until I'd torn my creation in half.

Unlike the sun-woven gown, whose death had been fiery and violent, the dress of the moon remained serene. Remorse clotted my throat, and the last of my tears streamed down my face when, finally, I threw its remains into the air.

Amana, I prayed, watching my dress skim the clouds, its light beaming across the sky. *If you can hear me, I return the tears of the moon to you. In return, I ask that you sever the threads that bind me—and all demons—to aid Gyiu'rak and the shansen. Give me the strength to stay Maia—long enough to help A'landi.*

No sooner did my prayer end than the tears of the moon disappeared in a bright white flash.

The summons ended abruptly. The shansen and Gyiu'rak were gone.

I grasped my amulet, feeling lightheaded. I'd won a victory against the shansen today, but at a terrible cost.

I still have one dress left, I reminded myself. *The strongest dress: the blood of stars. My heart.*

Was it enough to save my family and A'landi?

"Maia, Maia." A boy was running toward me out of the forest, breathing hard. He wrapped his cloak over my body and stroked my hair. "It's all right. He can't have you."

"The tears of the moon represents the mind," I murmured. "I've lost it. My memories, my—"

"Then I'll remind you. You still remember me, don't you?" He touched his nose to mine, his eyes so blue. Blue as water, as the glittering sea by . . . I could see it, but I couldn't name it.

I squinted. His face was familiar, but I couldn't remember why.

He pressed a kiss on my lips, soft and warm as a breath of sunshine on my back.

Edan. The boy with a thousand names and yet no name. The boy whose hands were stained with the blood of stars. He was coming back to me.

But in his place, other memories fled. My dearest memories,

as if handpicked from my mind to hurt me most with their loss. No matter how I tried, I could no longer recall the blue of the waters I'd grown up with, the stories my brother used to tell me of sailors and sea dragons. I'd had three brothers once. Which one had chuckled when he tried to get me to go out into town with him on an adventure? Which one wore a crooked smile, laced with mischief, whenever he managed to swindle me into doing *his* chores?

"My father and brother . . . ," I said hollowly. "The shansen has taken them hostage."

"Then we must go to them."

I shook my head. "*I'll* go." I shot up, a wisp of smoke shadowing my movement. "I have magic. You don't."

Edan flinched at the reminder. "I have enough. This is what the shansen wants. He wants you wild with grief and anger."

A ragged breath caught in my throat. When I tried to picture my father and brother, their faces were blotted out, as if by a wet brush. They might as well have been strangers, but I knew I needed to save them.

"If you want to save your father and your brother," said Edan, "then you need a plan, like the one we had for Lapzur. Let me help you wield your magic. The magic in here." He pointed at my amulet. Then he pressed his fingers to my chest. "And the magic in here."

"How? I don't think I can."

"You need to control your anger," he said. "It will grow stronger every day, like Master Tsring said, feeding on your desire for vengeance. The more you give in to it, the faster you will forget yourself. The faster you will turn."

Fury coursed within me, but I picked up the threads of Edan's reasoning.

"You're right," I said at last.

I reached into my pocket, searching for the cloth bird I'd stashed there days ago. "We can't do this alone, Edan. The shansen has an army of thousands, along with Gyiu'rak at his side. And possibly other demons." I paused, a name on the tip of my tongue that I fought to bring forward. It belonged to someone important—someone who would bring hope.

"Lady Sarnai," I said, snatching the name before it fled me. "We must find Lady Sarnai."

"The shansen's daughter?"

"He still cares for her. She's the only one who can fight him." I lifted the bird's beak with my finger. "She's the hope of A'landi, Edan. Not you. Not me."

He tilted his head. "You sound as if you admire her."

"I always have," I admitted. "The problem is, she escaped the palace after her father attacked. Even if I knew where she was, I don't know if she'd help us."

Taking a deep breath, I ironed out the wings of my cloth bird, which had become crinkled in my pocket, and held it out to Edan. "We can use this to find her."

"Clever," Edan said, inspecting my work. His long fingers traced the threads I'd sewn into the wings, and I knew he recognized them from our enchanted carpet.

A thick eyebrow arched as he mused, "The folds are Kiatan."

"You know it?" I asked.

"I've been to Kiata many a time," he replied, "when I was much younger."

"Someone told me a tale about the Kiatan princess who folded such paper cranes to search for her brothers. Mine don't look so much like cranes, more like ducks—"

"Or phoenixes," Edan suggested. "Not the A'landan ones,

with the eagle head and all the peacock feathers. In Nelronat, phoenixes had wings of fire, and they were born from the ashes of their previous lives. I caught one once, brought it with me everywhere—even to Kiata—until it flew away."

"I'd thought those were legends." My next words clung to my throat. "Fairy tales, like Shiori's tale. I hardly remember hers now. Or who told it to me."

"Then I will tell it to you again," said Edan. He stroked my cheek. "Tonight."

My skin warmed at his touch, and the wink of his eye made me blush. My bird sprang to life, its soft wings tickling my palm.

"Find Lady Sarnai," I whispered to it. "Tell her that the kingdom is in danger, that we need her. Ask her to meet us at the Winter Palace."

The bird wriggled to life, its pointed beak nodding in assent. Then I lifted my hand and it fluttered off into the sky.

I watched it disappear, weaving its way through the trees until I saw it no more.

CHAPTER TWENTY-SIX

We were too late.

The Winter Palace was burning, its sharply curved roofs abloom with fire. Smoke threaded through the emerald pillars and devastated courtyards, and heavy clouds loomed across the sky, which had turned from azure to charcoal.

There was no sign of Lady Sarnai.

Despair gnawed at me as my demon eyes swept through the palace and its surroundings from afar. I took in the helmets, broken spears, smashed lanterns, and spilled canteens. Several corpses lay in the streets: mostly soldiers, frost glittering on their toes, their boots and cloaks stolen by local peasants who couldn't afford to have scruples about how they survived the coming winter. The dead numbered no more than several dozen.

"Where are the emperor's soldiers?" I asked Edan. "He sent for an army to defend the Winter Palace. They couldn't have just disappeared."

Edan's expression was grim. "I don't know, *xitara*."

The gates were bolted shut, shadows flickering behind the scarlet-painted doors. The shansen's guards.

"We'll have to go over the gates."

Edan made a face to show exactly how he felt about me

using my demon magic, but he took hold of his walnut staff and wrapped his arm around my waist.

I leapt into the air toward the palace. My cloak billowed behind me, and flames scorched my shoes, the wind dangerously fanning the sparks that danced at my soles.

I was not so practiced at moving like a demon that I actually flew; it was more like taking giant leaps. Still, as I swam through the sky among the birds, I almost felt like one myself. And, not for the first time, I wondered what shape I would take when I finally succumbed to Bandur's curse.

"A demon!" exclaimed the shansen's guards once we approached the palace. "And the enchanter!"

Arrows rained upon us, faster than birds—like tiny daggers cutting the sky and making the air sing. I panicked. My feet stuttered in midair, struggling to get us higher.

"Keep flying, *xitara,*" said Edan. "I'll take care of the arrows."

The next attack came, and he raised his staff, muttering something under his breath. The arrows bounced off an invisible shield.

"Ah, so his magic has not left him entirely," I heard the shansen remark.

I should not have heard him, not over the crackle of the fire devouring the Winter Palace, or the howl of the winter wind.

But my demon ears were sharp, my demon eyes even sharper.

Whatever injuries had ailed the shansen after the battle in the Autumn Palace had long since healed. He continued, "But the Edan I knew would have sent those arrows flying back at my men, multiplied tenfold *and* with their wings aflame." He turned to his men. "Call off the attack. Let them come. I want to have a word with Khanujin's demon."

No more arrows flew, and I cleared the gate in a rush of smoke.

I looked down at the shansen's soldiers. At their helm rode the shansen's sons—their dark eyes devoid of mercy, and their mouths wearing variations on their father's cruel sneer. The eldest carried Sarnai's ash bow, and I wondered what it had been like for her to grow up among them. They reminded me nothing of my own brothers.

Behind them rode the shansen's generals and his Balardan mercenaries. The waiting soldiers had their swords drawn and arrows nocked. Did they expect me to surrender?

My mouth set with irritation. I could burn their weapons to ashes with a thought!

I landed on the stone floor of the palace courtyard with a *thud* so resounding the shansen's soldiers staggered back. They parted ranks, and the shansen came forward to greet me.

"Have you come to beg for your emperor's life, Maia Tamarin?" he rumbled. "He has been waiting anxiously for you to return."

So, he was still alive.

I raised my chin. "Where are my father and brother?"

"Gyiu'rak tells me you were able to refuse our summons," said the shansen, ignoring my question. I wondered if he knew that I'd thwarted Gyiu'rak's attempt entirely, preventing all demons from coming to his aid. His demon was nowhere in sight.

"Impressive. I had hoped you might join us. That invitation still stands. Accept it, and I will reunite you with your family."

His cordial tone unnerved me. At the wedding, he had been gruff and unpleasant. But now he was trying to win me over. That meant he viewed me as a threat.

I was. I could pierce his chest with my claws and spill his

blood upon the ash-covered ground—before a single one of his guards could react.

If it weren't for Baba and Keton, I might have done it.

"Enchanter," the shansen continued. He affected a small bow. "I must thank you for breaking your oath. I could not have accomplished any of this if you had been by Khanujin's side."

Edan's breathing stilled, but he said nothing.

"History will record that the Five Winters' War was fought between me and Emperor Khanujin," continued the warlord, "but this is a lie. The war was between me—and you, enchanter. A pity your magic is so weak now."

"I want to see my father and brother," I snapped.

"You'll see them soon enough." The shansen turned. "You have arrived in time for the passing of thrones."

He signaled to his three sons, who promptly disappeared into a chamber behind the courtyard. When they returned, they dragged forth a cowering figure.

I hardly recognized the emperor. No headdress, no armor—the cloak I'd sewn for him was torn and tattered. His black hair was a tangled mass, and he looked like he hadn't washed in days. Rope bound his wrists and ankles, and he was gagged with one of the shansen's banners, a pop of bright green.

A chill crawled up my spine as realization dawned. The army would not have abandoned Khanujin here. Not unless—

No. I spun, taking in the palace's ashen remains. The air was too still, too quiet.

And in that moment, I knew what had happened to Khanujin's army: it had been destroyed—by Gyiu'rak's ghosts.

What price must the shansen have paid for such power?

"Let him go," said Edan, breaking from my side, his shadow tall and commanding.

"The Lord Enchanter speaks," mocked the shansen. "Curious, Edan, that you continue to serve Khanujin even after your oath has been broken. Even more curious, that you should arrive with the imperial tailor. I never took you for an ally of demons."

"She is not a demon."

"Not *yet*," spoke a new voice.

In a tempest of pale glittering smoke, Gyiu'rak materialized from the shansen's amulet and took her place beside him, shifting into human form. Her white hair, striped with black, was knotted up like a court lady's.

"Sentur'na," she greeted, baring her teeth as she spoke my demon name. A wicked smile curved her mouth as she regarded Edan. "Jinn."

At the title, Edan stiffened.

"You have arrived in time for the end of the Ujin dynasty."

Khanujin's eyes bulged at the sight of the shansen's demon. He twisted his hands, trying to free them from the ropes.

"Enough," said Edan. "You've captured the emperor and claimed your victory. Let him go. You dishonor your legacy by killing him."

"Dishonor?" the warlord snarled. "You think Khanujin would spare me if our roles were reversed? No. He will be sacrificed to my demon. His blood is the price I pay for a new A'landi."

"I will pay it," I spoke up impulsively. "Let the emperor go."

"You?" Gyiu'rak rasped. "A demon cannot pay my blood price. But your father and your brother . . ."

With a hiss I'd never heard myself make, I lunged to attack her, but Edan held me back. His eyes beseeched me not to do anything rash.

249

Gyiu'rak laughed. "Very well, then," she said. And in a movement so quick it was but a whirl of color, she sliced her nails across the emperor's pale throat.

Blood welled out, as bright as the rubies dangling from his wrists.

The violence of it—the suddenness—shocked me. The air froze in my lungs, my body growing taut as a string.

Then, *snap*.

Khanujin crumpled. Edan caught him, laying him gently on the ground.

I knelt by his side. My ruler's lips were gray like the ash that had showered his skin. I swept it off his face and held his hand. I had no love for him; nothing I said would comfort him. And yet, for this moment, I wished I could do something to ease his passing.

His cheeks puffed with one last breath, and his eyes went hollow. He was the last of his dynasty, and with him passed the end of an era. He had been selfish and ruthless, but in a way, I understood. He had even been cruel, but when it came to his country and his people, he hadn't been devoid of heart. Not like I knew the shansen would be.

When Khanujin's father had died, the entire country had spent a hundred days mourning him. Every shop and home had covered its windows with ivory sheets to honor Emperor Tainujin's death, and I had tied a white band around my sleeve as a little girl.

Khanujin would have no such honor.

The shansen's men hoisted the warlord's banner. "Long live the emperor," they chanted. "May he live ten thousand years!"

To my surprise, the shansen did not puff up his chest with

pride, nor did he spit on the emperor's corpse, as I half expected him to do. Instead, while his soldiers celebrated his victory, the shansen circled me, his boots leaving indents in the dirt behind him.

Crimson veins glittered across the warlord's amulet. I wondered how much blood he had promised Gyiu'rak in exchange for her magic.

"For one so devoted to her country, you do not seem to understand that A'landi's future lies with me. I extend my invitation to you one last time, Maia Tamarin. Accept, and I will spare your family. Refuse, and they will die."

The ultimatum resounded in my ears.

I did not succumb, but neither did I resist. "Where are they?"

The shansen tilted his head, and my father and brother were brought to the square.

I watched apprehensively. At first glance, I wasn't sure it was them. All I saw were two men, one younger and one older, chained together, rice sacks over their heads.

"You don't know them," observed Gyiu'rak, the words cutting me like a knife. "You've already forgotten."

Anguish gnawed at my heart. I shouldn't have needed to see my father's and brother's faces to recognize them, but she was right. I did not know them.

A guard struck the back of Baba's legs, and he cried out in pain.

"Do you recognize his scream, Sentur'na?" Gyiu'rak taunted.

I recoiled. I did not know the sound of Baba's scream because I'd never heard it until now.

But I did know the sound of his voice. "Keton," he uttered

weakly when my brother tried to defend him. Snow-covered boots pinned my father and brother to the ground, and I heard Baba whisper, "Don't fight."

Slowly, the memory of Baba came back to me. Even now, under these terrible circumstances, he was calm. He was tender. At last I recognized the slight bend in his frail back, the defined knuckles on his hands—hands that had spent years teaching my own how to sew.

I recognized my brother, too. The way his heels rocked back and forth when he limped forward, the uneven cut of his pants—hemmed awkwardly by himself while he wore them— the elbows that jutted out whenever he was frightened or on edge.

I faced the shansen. "Free my father and my brother."

Gyiu'rak snorted. "Or else?"

"Or else I'll kill you," I said coldly.

Gyiu'rak's eyes flickered with amusement. Sharp tiger fangs protruded over her bottom lip, and as she stalked toward me, I could see the muscles swelling across her arms and legs. She made a point of dwarfing me. "I'd like to see you make good on that threat."

"Don't," Edan said, touching my arm. "If you go down this path . . ."

He didn't need to finish his warning. I knew what he meant. If I let Gyiu'rak goad me, I'd be surrendering to my demon's desire for vengeance.

I would become like Gyiu'rak.

But how I wanted vengeance.

I whirled toward the shansen, ignoring Gyiu'rak. "Let them go."

"You try my patience, tailor," he replied. "I gave you a chance to join us. You were unwise to dismiss it." He inclined his chin at Gyiu'rak, whose eyes had darkened with bloodlust. "Kill them."

My heart shot up to my throat, and I choked back a cry, lunging for Gyiu'rak before she could get to Baba and Keton. She blocked me easily with her arm and threw me aside.

I'd never been hit by such strength before, not even from Bandur. All of me folded, nerves wincing from the blow. My knees wouldn't unbuckle, and she laughed as I struggled to pick myself up.

"Pitiful," she rasped. "Worry not. I'll make their deaths quick."

I closed my eyes, conjuring the image of Emperor Khanujin's death—the gash Gyiu'rak had drawn across his throat, so swiftly he had not realized what had happened until the broken seam on his neck began to spill blood, draining the color from his face and the life from his body.

I wouldn't let that happen to Baba and Keton.

Pushing up, I threw myself on the demon, grappling her from behind and wrapping my arms around her neck.

She swerved and twisted, springing into the air to fling me off. I held on tight, digging my nails into her neck and chest. Her flesh was cold, her bones hard as iron. I couldn't tell if my attacks were having any effect.

When we landed, she rushed into the fire that still blazed in the center of the square, with me hanging on tightly. Over and over, she charged into the flames, trying to drown me in their heat, but I felt nothing. The fire tickled my skin and singed the tunic on my back, but it did little else to me.

I couldn't say the same for Gyiu'rak. The flames scorched her human skin. I could see the pain register on her face, the way she clamped her mouth tight, her lips pressing against her fangs. Were other demons vulnerable to fire? The realization stunned me; Bandur had often traveled to me through flames, but never in his human form.

Once she realized that her effort had been in vain, she bared her teeth. "Maybe you are more advanced than I thought, changeling."

She slammed onto her back, forcing me to leap off before she crushed me. I fell hard on my side, my ribs giving under my weight. Gyiu'rak pounced for me, and I rolled away toward the fire, grabbed one of the logs crackling within, and swung it at her face.

Sparks from the sizzling wood spat into her eyes, and she let out a tiger's roar, her arms shooting out in another attack. I ducked, then pushed her into the fire.

An arc of silvery blue swept past me. Edan, wielding the meteorite dagger. He barreled toward the fire and plunged the blade into the demon's chest.

Gyiu'rak screamed, her body spasming with pain. In a storm of smoke, she vanished, swirling back inside the shansen's amulet.

The fight wasn't over. Hundreds of soldiers surrounded us. Grimly, I turned to face them. Edan and I had no chance of defeating them all, but I would do what I had to—to free Baba and Keton.

"Kill the prisoners!" the shansen shouted at his sons.

Bows lifted, arrows pointed at my father and brother. Terror seized me, and I leapt to shield them.

Then a familiar scarlet arrow struck one of the shansen's

sons neatly in the heel of his hand. Another arrow, then another, until all three sons collapsed, gravely injured.

Could it be? I craned my neck, searching for Sarnai.

Horses pounded through the gates, bursting past the flames, their hooves kicking up embers and ashes. More scarlet arrows flew, and I heard shrieks and cries, the last sounds of soldiers before they fell.

With the shansen's men distracted, I hurried Baba and Keton to a corner away from the fray.

I tugged at the rice sacks covering my father's and brother's faces, but at the last moment, I decided not to lift them. I didn't want them to see me like this, more demon than girl.

"Stay here," I said, touching Keton's shoulder, then Baba's. "You'll be safe here."

"Maia?" Baba said. "Is that you?"

I bit my lip so I wouldn't reply. Hearing him call my name brought the ghost of a pang to my heart. Just enough to make it ache for an instant, then the feeling was gone.

I returned to the battle to find Lady Sarnai and Lord Xina flanked by a small battalion of warriors.

I'd never seen Lady Sarnai in combat. She was faster than any man and just as strong. None of the shansen's soldiers could match her skill with a bow; she shot a dozen men, clearing a path for Lord Xina to attack her father.

But the shansen, imbued with a demon's strength, easily overpowered the man who'd once been his favored warrior. He snapped Xina's spear in half, flung him at one of the fortress walls, and let out a triumphant roar, more tiger than man.

My eyes tracked the amulet swinging over his armored torso. The obsidian gleamed with Gyiu'rak's magic, and I feared I knew what was coming next.

The shansen spun to face his daughter, who was advancing on him with her bow raised.

Dropping Lord Xina's broken spear, he opened his arms as if to welcome her attack. He waited until she was twenty paces away before he touched his amulet—and then, melding with Gyiu'rak, he transformed into a tiger, white fur bristling over his human skin.

I'd seen the warlord transform before, but Lady Sarnai had not. She yanked back on the reins and folded her body forward, shoulders curling in to brace for her father's attack.

I had to do something! But I was across the battlefield, too far to help.

With dizzying speed, the tiger tackled her. Her horse shrieked, and Lady Sarnai toppled from her saddle, disappearing from view. Most warriors would have died instantly, and at first, I feared Sarnai had. Then she surfaced, wrestling the tiger with her bare hands.

The shansen raised his claws to her throat.

Stop! I shouted into his thoughts. *She's your daughter. You taught her to fight like this.*

A flicker of hesitation glimmered on his brow. He growled, but he was listening.

Your demon has warped your thoughts. Don't let her murder your daughter.

While I spoke to the shansen, Lady Sarnai struggled to inch away from his claws and regain her footing.

Kill her! Gyiu'rak screamed from the shansen's amulet. The demon's shouts overpowered mine, and the hesitation on the shansen's brow vanished. *Kill her.*

The shansen's claws hovered in the air. My stomach twisted with cold fear. I was sure that by the next beat of my heart Lady

Sarnai would be dead. Down his paw came, but his daughter rolled away, and Lord Xina charged. The warrior drove his broken spear into the shansen's side.

The tiger roared with pain, writhing and twisting. Lady Sarnai raised her sword. Unlike her father, she did not hesitate. But it was too late. The shansen leapt over the fire and disappeared.

Immediately, the flames subsided, and Lady Sarnai stabbed her sword into its remains. I could not see her face, but her shoulders heaved in frustration. She'd missed the chance to defeat her father.

She spun from the embers and strode to the banner the shansen's men had hoisted. She broke its pole over her knee and ripped the flag in half.

"The shansen has retreated," she declared. "Shut the gates!"

And at her command, the doors of the Winter Palace thundered to a close.

The battle was over.

CHAPTER TWENTY-SEVEN

It was not a victory.

Lady Sarnai knew, as I did, that the shansen only conceded the Winter Palace because it held no strategic value for him. The smallest of Khanujin's residences, it had been built during more peaceful times for the purpose of housing the royal family during A'landi's bitter winters. It relied on its position on a cliff for its defenses, and the military barracks had been depleted of its resources during the Five Winters' War. It did not even connect to the Great Spice Road.

Emperor Khanujin had made a mistake staying here. The Spring Palace was only a week's journey from the Winter Palace, and, seated along the eastern coast of A'landi, it was protected by both the imperial navy and Jappor's army—the strongest in the nation. Now that Khanujin was dead, no one could stop the shansen from conquering the capital—and A'landi.

No one, I wanted to tell Lady Sarnai, except her.

Her three brothers were in chains; her scarlet arrows jutted out of their hands and legs, their ribs and shoulders. Each wound looked calculated to bring severe pain, but not to kill.

She ignored their pleas for forgiveness and reclaimed her ash bow from her oldest brother.

"Take them to the dungeon," she told Lord Xina. "I'll decide what to do with them later."

Terrified by the dark demon magic they had witnessed, many of the shansen's troops were willing to pledge themselves to Lady Sarnai, who had fearlessly led them in battle during the Five Winters' War. Those who would not defect were thrown into the dungeon without food or water. A few spat at her, shouting, "I've more honor than to follow a woman!"

They were also thrown in the dungeon, but with a note to the guards to have their tongues cut out.

No one else dared question her command.

By noon, Lady Sarnai had restored order to the Winter Palace. Her men had extinguished all the fires, and she'd enlisted the emperor's surviving ministers to inventory what weapons could be salvaged from the armory and what food the palace had in its granary and storerooms.

"She's really something, isn't she?" Keton asked while I cradled Baba's head on my lap. "Even more frightening than I remembered her during the war."

"Yes, she is." I didn't want to talk about Lady Sarnai. Seeing my brother and my father again, all I wanted was to memorize their faces. To hear their voices and fill the widening gaps in my memory.

Baba's sleeves were torn, and when I rolled them up I saw welts on his arms.

"They only hurt us when we resisted," said Keton thinly. "When they came to Port Kamalan, I tried to fight them. They nearly burned the shop down."

I paled with wrath. Just thinking of Baba being torn from his worktable, of soldiers looting the shop my family had strived so hard to keep, of seeing my father and brother in chains, and of Keton, who had only just regained his ability to walk, pushed down and whipped—how dare the shansen!

"I'm sorry," I whispered. "This is my fault."

Keton touched my arm, a sign of forgiveness, but I could see the questions forming in his head, made evident by the crease of his brow. Why *was* this my fault? Why was I so important that the shansen had sent soldiers to Port Kamalan to capture him and Baba? These questions I wasn't ready to answer.

I pressed my lips tight and hid my hands in my pockets.

To my relief, Edan appeared.

"The main apartments in the south courtyard were untouched by the fire," he said quietly. He sounded tired; using magic had drained him more than he was willing to let on. "It'll be warmer there for your father."

Keton's eyes widened, recognizing Edan from the stories I'd told about him, but this wasn't the time for introductions.

Together, Edan and I lifted Baba and carried him inside. We found a bed in one of the ministers' chambers, and as we set Baba on it, his hooded eyes peeled open.

He clasped my arm. "Maia."

I flinched and kept my eyes lowered, hoping Baba wouldn't notice them if I stayed in the shadows.

"You're safe, Baba," I told him. "The shansen is gone. Lady Sarnai has taken the Winter Palace."

"And the emperor?"

I hesitated. "Dead."

"Dead. So many dead." Baba's eyes glazed over and stared off at the ceiling. He said nothing for a long while. "May the gods watch over him."

He started to sit up. "Who is that behind you?"

Edan had returned with a steaming bronze kettle.

"Baba, Keton . . . ," I started. "This is Edan, His Majesty's Lord Enchanter."

"*Former* Lord Enchanter," said Edan, clearing his throat.

Any other time, I might have smiled at how nervous Edan looked, but not today. He set down the kettle to properly greet my family. First a bow to Baba, then to Keton, who balked.

"We're the same age," said my brother. "Stop bowing. Please."

My father eyed the enchanter with distrust. "Ah, yes, I've heard a great deal about you. There are many who believe you are the reason for the Five Winters' War."

Edan inhaled a deep breath. "And they would not be incorrect," he replied, "sir."

"So you are the one to blame for the deaths of my eldest sons. For the thousands of sons that died, and the many more that are marching to their deaths as we speak."

"Baba—" I tried to interject. I offered him the water. "Drink."

At the sound of my voice, Baba's shoulders trembled.

He let out a sigh of remorse. "I am tired," he said at last. "Save these introductions for another time. I wish to rest."

His eyes closed, dismissing us all.

With heavy steps, I followed Edan and Keton out of the room. My brother touched my shoulder and said, so softly only the two of us could hear, "It's been a difficult week for both of us. I'll stay and speak with him when he's better."

I nodded numbly, trying to hide my disappointment.

"Thank you, Keton," I said, and I left him to join Edan.

"Don't worry, *xitara*." Edan kissed my cheek. "I was never very popular among A'landans, but I managed to win over the most important ones."

I forced a smile, but that wasn't what worried me. If Baba distrusted Edan for his magic, what would he think once he knew the truth about me?

What would he think, once he discovered his daughter was a monster?

. . .

In the aftermath of the battle, Khanujin's corpse had been forgotten. His imperial robes lay in tatters, the enchanted cloak I'd made for him almost unrecognizable under the grime and dirt and blood. When I saw the emperor's corpse defiled and overlooked, the resentment I'd once held for him faded.

"He deserves to be buried," I said. "Many loved him . . . even though they didn't know how cruel he could be."

"He wasn't a good man," agreed Edan, "or a great ruler, but he cared for his country enough to make sacrifices for it."

He crouched beside his former master. The sneer that used to twist the emperor's mouth had eased into a gentle line, and he seemed more regal now that he was pale and gray in death.

Among the talismans on his belt, I spied Edan's old amulet.

Edan picked it up and held it, running his thumb over the hawk engraved on the bronze surface. I thought he might keep it, but after a long pause he placed the amulet back on Khanujin's belt.

"Even without the oath, I felt an obligation to protect him. I promised his father I would protect A'landi. I've failed them both."

"A'landi hasn't fallen yet," I replied. "We won't let it."

Edan nodded and started to reach for my hand again, but the arrival of Lady Sarnai and her entourage of soldiers cut off whatever he was about to say. The shansen's daughter stood strong as any king, one hand on her hip, and the other on her sword's hilt.

"What are you two doing here? With that—" Lady Sarnai couldn't bring herself to acknowledge the dead emperor. Her expression hardened at us. "There's work to be done. Make yourselves useful."

Still kneeling next to Edan, I rose. I didn't care to look up to her.

No doubt I was expected to obey immediately, but I did the opposite. "He deserves to be buried, Your Highness. You cannot leave him here to rot."

"Who are *you* to give commands?"

"He was the emperor," I reasoned. "Whatever you felt about him, he died for A'landi."

"A dishonorable death," she spat. "His army was slaughtered. He allowed himself to be taken prisoner—"

"Would you rather he have run?" I countered. "Emperor Khanujin was no great man, but he was not a coward. He chose to stay with his country to the end."

Whereas you did not, I left unsaid.

Sarnai's face darkened at the insult I'd intentionally left hanging in the air.

"Have him washed and cleaned," she ordered her men. As if an afterthought, she added, "Tailor, make him a suitable shroud for burial."

She barely spared me a glance as she spun on her heel. Something flittered behind her, even as she tried to swat it away.

My bird.

"Come with me," I said to Edan, and we trailed her to the Winter Palace's audience chamber, which Lady Sarnai made her own simply by laying her bow on the pine table. Lord Xina and Khanujin's surviving ministers were already there, waiting for her.

"Tamarin," she said, glowering when she realized we'd followed her, her irritation heightened by the fact that her huntress's ears hadn't heard us.

She crossed her arms. "I thought I gave you orders to work on a burial robe for your Khanujin."

Instead of replying, I whistled softly, and the cloth bird, which was darting about the hall, fluttered to my palm.

The shansen's daughter sniffed. "So the bird is yours. I should have guessed. Trouble seems to follow wherever you go."

I squared my shoulders boldly. "When do we march on Jappor?"

"March on Jappor?" she repeated. The entire council looked at me like I was mad.

"The window for saving A'landi is closing," I said. "We have to go now."

"And why would I save A'landi?" Sarnai growled. "The emperor is dead, thousands of his men are dead. I won't throw away another thousand lives when there is no hope of winning against my father." She turned away. "We retreat west, take our survivors with us."

"But—"

"Nations rise and fall. The enchanter should know that better than any."

"You're angry," I said. "You have a right to be. Khanujin has taken much from you. He's also taken much from me—from

264

all of us. But think of what will happen to A'landi should your father become emperor. You yourself said he is not the man you remembered, that he's been corrupted by his demon. What is to stop Gyiu'rak from becoming the true ruler of A'landi?"

Sarnai's shoulders tensed. "We cannot win against my father's army. With Khanujin dead, if the shansen's declared himself emperor, the army in Jappor will be at his side. The other warlords will not dare rise against him."

"Can you summon them to help us?"

"There isn't enough time," replied Lord Xina. "The shansen will reach Jappor in a matter of days. He'll have control of the imperial army."

"*Gyiu'rak* will have control over the imperial army," said Lady Sarnai tightly. "Her power over my father grows stronger every day. Once the blood price is paid, it will be complete."

"I thought the blood price was the emperor's life."

"The emperor's life, yes." Lady Sarnai's voice became hollow. Her scars shone pale under the watery light. "And ten thousand others."

My stomach sank. This was not only news to me, but also to the ministers. There was a shocked silence, and then everyone began talking at once. Sarnai raised her hands and stomped her boot on the wooden ground.

"Enough! To my father, it is nothing. Thousands already died in the Five Winters' War. He sees it as a chance to depose a corrupt dynasty and begin his own. I've fought enough battles to know when I must retreat and when I must fight on. There is no way we can win against Gyiu'rak."

"I disagree, Your Highness," Edan spoke up.

Lady Sarnai's voice was hard. "Then enlighten us, enchanter. How can my father be defeated?"

"He will need a few days to recover from his wound," Edan reasoned. "The imperial navy and Jappor's army will resist his rule; the Five Winters' War was not so long ago that they have forgotten he was the enemy. They will try to defend the Spring Palace from him. But his demon will be even stronger in Jappor, given its proximity to the North. I would say we have a week. Two, at most, before the capital falls."

Lord Xina's eyes, dark as glittering black stones, turned to Edan. "And why should we trust you? You, whose loyalty can be bought—"

"Bought?" Edan repeated. "Do you think I wanted to help Khanujin fight against the shansen? To tear your country apart in war? I was bound by an oath I could not break. I had no choice. The shansen's men have a choice; they follow him only out of fear, not out of loyalty. Show them they should fight for you—to save their country."

"They fear Gyiu'rak," Lady Sarnai said thickly. "No one can stop her."

"I can," I spoke, my voice deadly calm. "I am like her. A demon."

The room went quiet. The ministers staggered back—as if the distance made them safer from me. Some muttered prayers or curses. Lord Xina pointed his spear squarely at my throat.

I ignored them all and looked steadily at the shansen's daughter. If my admission took her aback, she did not show it.

"Enchanter, tell me why I shouldn't have the tailor executed."

Surprise flickered across Edan's brow. Lady Sarnai and he had never gotten along; she had never sought his opinion before.

"It is true the imperial tailor has been cursed to follow the path of demons," he said quietly. "And it's true that in due time, her actions will no longer be those of Maia Tamarin, but of the monster inside her. Yet I believe that even as a demon, she will do all she can to protect A'landi."

Grave as Edan sounded, his faith in me warmed some of the ice around my heart. I bit my lip, hoping Sarnai would believe him.

The war minister stood. "This is preposterous. We cannot allow a demon in our midst. Arrest her at once. Lord Xina, I beg you to listen to reason—"

"This is *my* army to command," Lady Sarnai said sharply. "Not Lord Xina's. I give this warning once, Minister Zha, and only because you are new to my rule."

While the minister cowered, Sarnai's cold gaze returned to me. "Tomorrow morning, I will announce whether or not we march to Jappor. And I will decide the fate of Maia Tamarin. You are dismissed."

• • •

"Do you think she'll change her mind?"

Edan knew I wasn't asking whether Lady Sarnai would spare my life, but whether she'd see the sense in marching to Jappor.

He considered my question. "She is a brilliant warrior, but an inexperienced leader. The shansen never gave her command of his troops during the Five Winters' War. She was but a girl of fourteen when the war began—very young, and in awe of her father's reputation and strength. Now that she must fight him, it's hard to predict what she will or will not do."

I thought of how the shansen had hesitated before attacking Sarnai. "Do you think he loved her?"

"Before Gyiu'rak corrupted him? Perhaps, in his own way. But the shansen has always loved power above all else. He saw Sarnai's potential and promised her command of his armies when she came of age."

"He also promised she wouldn't have to marry," I said, remembering what Lady Sarnai herself had told me long ago.

"He bought her loyalty. She served him, and she truly believed that he could make A'landi better by deposing Emperor Khanujin. But when he began dealing with Gyiu'rak, their relationship was poisoned. And when the truce was sealed and he sent her to marry the emperor, her faith in him was completely destroyed."

"And her faith in A'landi as well," I murmured with a frown. "How can I help her? We need more men, and we have so little time."

I paused. The emperor's banner lay before me. I had intended to sew it into a burial robe, but another idea had been pricking at me.

"The bird I made to find you—and Lady Sarnai. I can make more. Hundreds more." I swallowed, touching my amulet. The walnut halves felt hollow under my palm. "I only hope I remember how to sew." I looked at my claws and winced.

Edan took one edge of the banner, so we held it together.

"I'll help you," he said.

We set to work, cutting the banner into a hundred squares. Edan folded, and I sewed. I could only manage the most basic of stitches, the ones Mama had taught me when I was a girl. It was enough.

Into each bird, I sewed a thread from the remains of my enchanted carpet to give them the gift of flight. The threads twitched as I worked, awoken by the magic thrumming in my blood.

Why so selfish, Maia? You don't need birds to win the war. You have enough power to overthrow the shansen. If you sacrifice yourself, you would save thousands from death. Is that not honorable?

I bit my lip so hard it began to bleed.

"Are you all right?" Edan asked, looking worried.

"If I could save A'landi by giving in"—I faltered, staring at my hands; at what *used* to be my hands—"by completely turning into a demon, shouldn't I? No one would have to fight. I could save the lives of countless men and women."

"If you give in, Maia, you won't be yourself anymore." He pried the needle from my shaking fingers. "Hold on for just a little longer. For A'landi. For me."

"I fear it'll drive me mad," I confessed. "There's so much anger in me. I can't control it." I squeezed my eyes shut, wishing I could drive away all the horrible memories of what I'd done since Bandur had cursed me. Those memories were much sharper than anything from my previous life.

"What if I forget you again?" I whispered. "What if I—"

"Attack me?" Edan took in a tight breath. "You might. Enchanters and demons are natural enemies."

Seeing my horrified reaction, he kissed me softly. "If you forget me, I'll find a way to make you remember again. And if you attack me"—he flattened my hand against his chest—"I'll hold you until you stop."

I wasn't convinced, but Edan wasn't finished.

"I believe what I said to Master Tsring, about you being good." His fingers brushed my hair, sweeping it away from my eyes and to the side of my face. "Every day you're changing. You look more and more like a demon, and I know the voice inside you is growing stronger. But your heart is *yours*, Maia. That will not change as long as you hold on to it."

"I hope you're right."

"I know I am." His gaze fell to my growing pile of cloth birds. "Would you believe me if I told you I knew her? The Kiatan princess who folded a thousand cranes?"

"You're not as old as that!"

He made a face at me. "The *story* isn't as old as that. I met Shiori only once, and briefly, but she wasn't so different from you. Even when a terrible curse befell her, she stayed strong. Her paper birds brought her hope."

He pressed my hand against his heart. "You are not alone, Maia. Not now, not ever."

His pulse beat steadily against my palm. I nodded, and I gathered the first batch of my cloth birds onto my tunic. The red threads sewn into their wings glimmered in the moonlight.

I leaned on Edan as I climbed onto the windowsill, crouching before the vast view of the forests and ocean below the Winter Palace. Still holding his arm, I turned to face him.

"For luck," he said, his breath tickling my nose before he kissed me.

I leapt into the sky, a rush of air propelling me higher and higher. There, among the clouds, I suspended myself as long as I could—as if I were treading water.

"I am not alone," I repeated. "And not all is lost."

Hugging the birds close, I forced a small smile. Hardly a consolation, without the laughter of the sun, my body could not feel the cold of the night icing over my skin, and without the tears of the moon, my heart did not quail at anything.

Especially not at the inevitable future, at the cost for saving A'landi—that I would die.

Sensing I was about to fall, I raised my amulet and pressed my lips to the glass crack, releasing the tiniest drop of the blood of stars, just enough to bathe my birds in its light.

Then, against the white sickle moon, I flung up my arms, sending the birds off to find anyone who might fight for the future of A'landi.

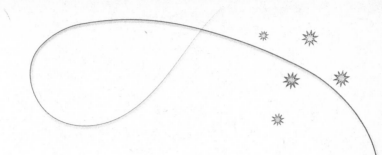

PART THREE

THE BLOOD
OF STARS

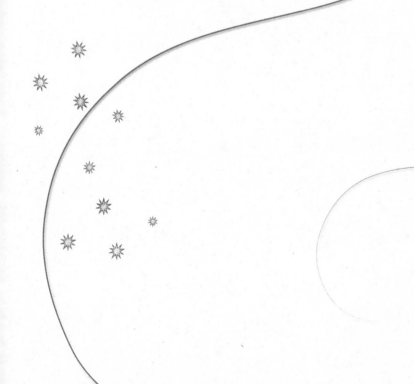

CHAPTER TWENTY-EIGHT

Amid the ruins of the shrine in the Winter Palace, Emperor Khanujin was sent to the heavens. No priests or monks were present to preside over the ceremony—only Lady Sarnai's soldiers and the few ministers who had survived the shansen's attack. They built a modest pyre of rust-colored bricks and knelt before the emperor once they'd laid him upon it.

Edan would not attend the funeral. When I asked why, he replied, "These rites are some of A'landi's oldest traditions, meant to honor Khanujin and to wish him safe passage to his place among the gods. Enchanters and religion have never been in harmony with one another. It would be an insult to him and to your people if I attended."

I bowed with Keton and Baba to pay my respects, then lingered a few moments, watching the wind lift the emperor's ashes away from the pyre. My fingers were sore from sewing all night.

After making hundreds of birds with Edan, I'd attended to the task of fashioning Emperor Khanujin's burial robes. I'd used his banner, along with whatever scraps I could find in the palace—old curtains and tablecloths, even the rice sacks used to cover Baba and Keton's faces—to sew my birds, and without my scissors, I couldn't spin coarse linen blankets into silk.

Only what was left over went into Khanujin's robes. So, the

emperor was buried plain as a villager. No embroidery, no jewels studded into the humble cloth, no inlaid gold or brocade. Not so much as a patch of silk.

No one said a word about it.

"Where are you going?" Keton asked me. When I turned, he flinched. "Your eyes, Maia. They've been red since yesterday. You—"

"They're just bloodshot," I lied quickly, waving away his concern with a gloved hand. A veil of unease fell over me. My brother used to tell me I was a terrible liar, and I had been. But things had changed. *I* had changed.

I hurried ahead to avoid his questions. But as my brother followed, I couldn't help but listen to the quiet landings of his footfalls, the graceful skid of his cane from one step to the next. The last time I'd seen him, he had only just begun to try and walk again.

My chest tightened. Not long ago, all I had wished for was to see Baba and Keton so I could embrace them. But now that we were together, all I did was keep my distance. I didn't know what to say to them that wouldn't be a lie.

And how that pained me.

I slowed my steps and walked beside my brother. My hands sunk into my pockets, the piecemeal gloves I'd made barely concealing my claws.

"I haven't been sleeping well," I said at last, a meager attempt at an explanation.

"Me neither." Keton tilted his head, listening to the flames still crackling from the funeral pyre. "I heard Lady Sarnai held a war council yesterday. Do you think the rumors of a march to Jappor are true?"

That was the reason I wanted to see her. "I don't know."

"There are men willing to fight," said Keton. "I will fight."

I bit my lip, trying to ignore the surge of alarm rising to my throat. "No, you should stay here. With the wounded."

Keton frowned at me, and I wished I could take back my words. "My legs are getting stronger, Maia. I may not be as fast as the others, but I can figh—"

"You've already fought. You've already seen too much of war."

"Says my *younger* sister," he chided. "I didn't know what I was fighting for back then. Now I do. The other soldiers feel the same."

"What are you fighting for?"

"The emperor is dead, and the shansen is halfway to the capital. You've seen his demon." Keton swallowed. "If we don't defend A'landi against him now, then heavens help us. We are doomed."

How could I dissuade him without cheating him of the same opportunity I'd wanted for myself—to help save our country?

I wanted Lady Sarnai to march to battle. I wanted her to defeat her father, to slay Gyiu'rak and send her reeling into the underworld.

Ten thousand lives! How could any man crave power so much he would bargain the lives of his people in such a trade?

I unclenched my jaw, reining in my wrath. When I looked at my brother and saw the fire in his eyes, I recognized the same determination that burned inside me.

"I'm going to find Lady Sarnai" was all I could manage, putting a hand on his shoulder. "Take care of Baba."

. . .

Neither Lady Sarnai nor Lord Xina had attended the funeral, but I knew where to find her. She'd slept outside by the kitchens, giving up for the wounded her claim to one of the palace's limited rooms.

I heard her before I saw her, sparring with Lord Xina. They were so engrossed in their match they barely noticed me, and I slipped behind a pillar to watch.

Sarnai still hadn't taken off her armor. It must have been a third her weight, yet she carried it proudly, with her shoulders squared and sweat glistening on her brow. Lord Xina was at least twice her size, but she moved with deadly grace, her fighting stick dancing to the beat of battle the way my fingers used to dance with a needle. Spying an opening in Lord Xina's side, she jabbed him in the knee and whipped her pole to hook his ankles and bring him down to his back.

"You've grown slow, Xina," she said before helping him up. "You're going to get yourself killed if you keep lumbering around like a bear."

"And you've grown weak, Sarnai. So if I lumber like a bear, at least I don't swing my sword like an ax. What happened to your training?"

Instead of taking her hand to get up, Lord Xina pulled her down, and for the first time, I heard Lady Sarnai laugh. He'd never been handsome, but after his time in Khanujin's dungeon his face had become a patchwork of nightmares: his front teeth cracked, his nose smashed, and his upper lip torn. Yet the way they looked at each other made my heart heavy, and I turned away from the scene, giving them a moment of privacy.

When I finally looked again, they sat together beside a fire burning in a brick pit, once used to roast meat. They weren't alone.

Edan had beaten me there.

"If you have come to beg for the tailor's life, you are too late," said Sarnai, barely acknowledging him as she wiped the sweat from her temples. "My mind is made up. She cannot be allowed to live."

"Then you are not the warrior I knew during the Five Winters' War, Your Highness."

"And you are not the enchanter I knew," Sarnai retorted. "Perhaps I should have *you* executed as well. After all, what can you offer now?"

Edan raised his walnut staff, and the campfire shot up, taking on the shape of a hawk. Only if I looked closely could I see the sweat glistening on the nape of Edan's neck. Such a display would have been as easy as breathing for him before, but now it took much effort.

"You will not defeat your father without Maia Tamarin—"

"She will stay in the Winter Palace," Lady Sarnai said over him, surprising even me with the sudden reversal. "That is more mercy than she deserves."

Edan began to speak, but I stepped forward and interrupted, "Take me with you to Jappor. I would give my life to save A'landi. To save my family."

All three looked up, surprised that I had managed to creep up on them. Had I been that much clumsier before, as Maia, or did becoming a demon give me the gift of catching everyone unawares?

Lady Sarnai's gaze pierced mine. "Your enchanter already pleaded the case for you. I've come to believe that along with the loss of his powers comes the loss of his reason. The only reason you still stand free, tailor, is because of what you did for me and Xina in the Autumn Palace." She paused deliberately, so

I'd understand even that generosity was more than I deserved. "But you will not be leaving the Winter Palace."

"You cannot keep me here," I said, the edge in my tone sharp as a knife.

At that, Lady Sarnai stiffened. Lord Xina reached for his sword, but she stopped him.

"Can't I?" she said, rising. Her long black hair, freed from its warrior plaits, flew behind her back. "Edan says that your heart is still good, but I've known demons all my life. The seed of all magic is rooted in greed."

"I don't believe that."

She scoffed at me. "That is what my father used to say. You know, he was still a young man when the old emperor, Tainujin, united A'landi. Every shansen must make a mark for himself through war, and my father worried that with a united country, there would be little chance for him to bring honor upon his name.

"My father craved war. It was not his intent to divide A'landi in two. Far from it. But he was angry that so many of my grandfather's victories for Tainujin were attributed to the Lord Enchanter, and he vowed the same would not happen to him.

"Gyiu'rak came to him, offering to help him defeat Tainujin's enchanter and usurp the throne—for a price."

"Ten thousand lives."

"Yes," Lady Sarnai said grimly. "I was there that night—it was the first time I ever saw a demon." She stared into the fire. "My father refused to pay, but she'd planted a terrible desire in him, one that couldn't be quenched even after he'd assassinated Tainujin and his heir. He grew greedy; he wanted Edan's amulet so he would control the enchanter himself. But Khanujin discovered their plans and took it first, and my father was forced to retreat to the North.

"Gyiu'rak lurked in the forests there, and preyed on him when he returned. She extracted a blood oath in exchange for her dark magic to defeat Khanujin and his enchanter and take the throne."

Sarnai lifted her gaze from the fire, her hard eyes meeting mine. "My father was never the same after that day. During the Five Winters' War, I hardly noticed the change, but slowly . . . he was overtaken by bloodlust." Her voice became thick, her features twisting from the memory of something terrible. "I tried to show him what was happening to him; I begged him to stop. But he would not listen."

I swallowed, understanding in my own way how good the anger felt. I could still taste its sweetness.

"You have no choice but to bring me," I said evenly. "None of you is a match for Gyiu'rak."

Lady Sarnai's nostrils flared. "Didn't you hear anything I said? I don't trust you."

She was wise not to. Little did she know it, but I could have easily slipped into her mind, the way Bandur had with Ammi, and compelled her to do as I wished. The possibility floated in me now, muddying my own restraint with its appeal. But I held back.

"If you're worried I will betray you," I said, "Edan has a dagger that can be used against demons."

"Maia," Edan whispered. "Maia, that's enough."

I pretended not to hear him. "He has it now."

Lord Xina raised his arm, beckoning Edan to hand over the weapon. Reluctantly, he passed it to the warlord, who, in turn, gave it to Lady Sarnai.

"An ordinary-looking thing," she commented.

As she surveyed the dagger, taking in the intricate lines

carved onto the scabbard, I continued, "Should I begin to turn against A'landi's cause, hold the hilt and utter the word 'Jinn.' That will unsheathe the blade. And then you must pierce my heart—" I held up my amulet, for it was my true heart now, more and more with each day.

There was a crack in my voice, but I wasn't finished. "I will be wearing the last dress of Amana when I fight for you. The dress of the blood of stars." My throat closed up. "It is the source of my strength. If you wish to kill me, you must destroy it as well as my amulet, and I will die."

It was obvious from the grimace on Edan's face that I was telling the truth.

"You must not blame Edan for withholding this from you. He believes there is still good in me. But I know better."

For the first time, I knelt before Lady Sarnai. "Now you know how I may be slain." I thought of my last dress, the one that protected my soul from the demon's grasp. "Let me help you with Gyiu'rak."

To my surprise, she rose from beside the hearth and gave the dagger back to Edan. Without explanation, she said, "We will march for Jappor, and you will join us." She lingered on the words, adding, "Do not disappoint me, Maia Tamarin. If you do, I swear upon the Nine Heavens that you will not live to regret it."

CHAPTER TWENTY-NINE

We followed the coastline of the Cuiyan Ocean upward, and gradually the terrain eased into steppes and grasslands, lightly laced with snow. Violent winds tore across the grass, the bitter chill whistling into my lungs. In the far distance, I could make out the famous northern forests—where demons were said to lurk.

During our march to Jappor, I scanned the sky for my birds. Only one returned, alone, which made my heart sink. But then I saw more, soaring above a convoy of ships along the northern coast of the Cuiyan Ocean. Fishermen's boats with ragged sails, merchant ships, and, praise the gods, a fleet of dragon battleships flying Emperor Khanujin's banner.

Soldiers came on foot, on horseback, in wagons, and in carriages. Some brought their wives and sisters, who in turn brought food, blankets, tools for making bows and spears, for sharpening daggers and swords. Most found us thanks to my birds, but others were men Lord Xina had summoned. Reinforcements arrived by the hour. By the end of the day, hundreds had joined Lady Sarnai's forces.

I'd seen what fighting in the Five Winters' War had done to Keton, how it had dimmed the light in his eyes. These soldiers' faces were the same as my brother's, hardened by war. Now I viewed them with respect rather than pity.

But still, how cruel I felt asking them to fight again.

"Their coming here isn't magic, is it?" I asked Edan worriedly. "I didn't force them to come, or summon them the way the shansen tried to summon me?"

"No," he assured me. "The people know a united country is something to hope for, and fight for, with or without an emperor."

Among the crowd of new arrivals, I spotted a familiar pair of pigtails. A girl's face came into view: full cheeks, bright round eyes, and a small, round mouth.

"Maia!" Cheeks flushed with excitement, the girl ran toward me, dangling one of my cloth birds by the fiery red thread I'd sewn into its wings to make it fly.

When she dropped the bird into my hand, I held it close. The thread, still warm with magic, tickled the base of my thumb.

"You look better," she greeted me warmly. She cocked her head at Edan. "Was the Lord Enchanter able to help you?"

For the life of me, I could not remember her name. It teased the tip of my tongue, like silk that kept slipping out of my grasp. I frowned. "We were able to buy some time."

Understanding flooded her kind eyes, and she grasped my hands, ignoring the feel of sharp nails and warped fingers under my gloves. "It's me, Maia. Ammi. I'm your friend."

"Ammi," I repeated, hugging her. The name did sound familiar. Threads of an escape from the Autumn Palace and a journey across A'landi unspooled in my memory. This girl was important to me, but I couldn't entirely place why.

Her shoulders relaxed, a smile widening across her full face. She swung a large bundle over her shoulder; she looked warmly dressed, with a quilted vest and a pair of thick woolen trousers.

"I brought extra clothes and supplies—compliments of Master Longhai. I left his shop a few days after you. Once I heard that you were off to fight the shansen, I knew I had to help. I might not be much good with a sword, but I'm handy with a knife and a good fire. Soldiers have to eat."

"So they do." I glanced at the hundreds of newly arrived men. "I'm afraid you'll have your work cut out for you."

I grabbed one of her bundles and motioned for her to follow me. "Come, I'll introduce you to my family."

. . .

Ammi quickly established herself as our head cook. Having women at the camp did miracles for the soldiers' morale. Even Keton smiled more.

"A happy belly makes a happy man," Ammi would say. I hoped the high morale would last. We were getting closer to the Spring Palace.

We had marched so long that the soles of Keton's shoes had become worn, I noticed. He never complained, and I didn't bring it up as I walked beside him, keeping him company as he pushed Baba in a supply wagon.

"You should stay in the Winter Palace," I'd tried to convince my father. "It'll be safer."

"Where my children go, I go."

"But—"

"I'm not staying behind," Baba insisted.

So we brought him along. He mostly slept, still recovering from his time in the shansen's captivity.

"What do you think will happen to the emperor's concubines

now that he's dead?" Keton asked, trying to make lighthearted conversation with me.

"Emperor Khanujin did not have any concubines."

My brother snorted. "Of course he did. All emperors do. I bet he kept the prettiest ones in the Spring Palace. The women in Jappor are famous for their beauty. That's why they say the capital's never been conquered, because the ladies will charm A'landi's enemies into defeat."

"Even if that story were true, I don't think their charms will work on the shansen," I said dryly.

Keton's tone shifted, becoming darker. "Maybe not." He fell silent for a moment, before he shook off whatever was bothering him. "You know, I wish battles could be fought with rice pots instead of swords. We'd certainly win if that were the case."

My brother had never showed much interest in food before. "Why do you think that?"

"Ammi said Jappor is the capital of A'landi's best food. Nothing like it in the North, she said. She's quite the cook, your friend."

I tilted my head in surprise. "You talked to Ammi?"

"A little. To thank her for her good work." Keton stole a glance at Ammi, who was weaving her way through the army, passing out cups of tea and bamboo leaf–wrapped rice dumplings. Then my brother cleared his throat, and an unexpected blush tinged his cheeks. He immediately tried to change the topic. "Why isn't the enchanter walking with us?"

I glanced at Edan, who'd kept half a dozen paces ahead during our entire march. My lips pursed, and I didn't reply. Keton knew as well as I did the answer to that.

Baba was still wary of Edan; he thanked him politely when

Edan came to help us pitch our tents or bring us food, but Baba never invited him to stay and eat with us.

Every time I tried to defend him, a dark look passed over Baba's face. I closed my mouth, following Edan's advice not to say anything—to give Baba more time. But deep down, I was afraid of the questions Baba would ask if we broached the subject of magic; I was afraid that he already knew what I had become.

My brother wore a sly look, one I had never learned how to read.

"Enchanter!" Keton called, waving Edan over. "Why don't you walk with us?" My brother caught my startled expression. "Don't worry, Maia. I'll be nice. Edan! Join us."

Edan blinked, looking momentarily stricken by the invitation. But he obliged.

"We were just talking about the Spring Palace," said my brother. "Tell us about it. Are the women as beautiful as they say? Or do you prefer the women from the South?"

"Keton!" I elbowed my brother, horrified. "Have you been drinking?"

He laughed, and I hid a smile when I saw Edan's expression. I'd never seen him look so tongue-tied.

"All right, all right—just tell us about the Spring Palace. Why is it so far north?"

"A'landi wasn't always as large as it is now," Edan replied. "When the first emperor ruled, the Spring Palace was his only residence, and he built it in the North so that the shansen's armies could defend A'landi from invasion. As the empire expanded east and south, his descendants built three more palaces as a way to divide their time among the kingdom.

"Not until Emperor Tainujin's time did people begin to

worry the capital was too far north. Too close to the shansen's territory, where the Northerners held more loyalty to him than to the emperor. Those worries would turn out to be prophetic."

Keton said nothing, which Edan must have mistaken for disinterest, for the next thing he said was, "Maia tells me you fought in the Five Winters' War."

A shadow suddenly fell over Keton's eyes. "I fought in the same regiment as my two brothers. They were far better soldiers than I was. Finlei told me he fought with you once. Said you felled a hundred men with a swoop of your arms."

Edan's face was unreadable. "That was a long time ago. A lifetime ago."

The two men fell silent. I walked between them, until Keton mumbled an excuse to check on Baba.

"I shouldn't have mentioned the war," said Edan quietly, after Keton left. "That was a mistake."

"You were nervous. You shouldn't be—he likes you."

"He *wants* to like me. Wanted."

"Talk to him again," I said. "It would mean much to me if you two became friends. He's the only brother I have left. You are both my family."

"Maia . . ." Edan's voice trembled. "You talk as if you're going to—"

"I'll take over pulling the wagon," I interrupted, not wanting to hear the end of what he was going to say. My heart might be numb, but it wasn't dead yet, and I would spare him whatever pain I could.

"Try again," I said. "Keton will appreciate your company."

With a nod, Edan left and went to speak with my brother. I pulled Baba, alone, listening to the crunch of my shoes against the grass. Such a human sound, despite the curling of my claws with each step. My feet longed to fly, but I suppressed the urge and walked on.

A few minutes later, I heard my brother laughing.

"She did what?" Keton exclaimed. "I told her to keep to herself. No wonder you saw through her disguise."

Though my ears yearned to hear what they were saying about me, I focused on the road ahead. My amulet thumped against my chest, and I thought of the three dresses I had sacrificed so much to make.

What little I had left of my tailoring gift wasn't for sewing with needle and thread, it was for crafting a future, stitch by stitch, for the people I loved. That future would hold tight, even as I unraveled. It had to, or else the choice I had made—the choice that Master Tsring had told me was inevitable—would be for naught.

. . .

Two days later, we crossed into the Northern Plains. To the east was Jappor, and to the north were the forests and woodlands where Lady Sarnai had grown up.

Lord Xina drilled the soldiers, teaching them to fight as a unit while also testing their physical strength and stamina. Edan taught them what he knew about demons and ghosts.

"Ghosts cannot wield physical weapons; they are not fast like Gyiu'rak, and they are not clever. Their only means of attack is to lure you toward them. They will speak in voices that are dear to you. They will take on the faces of your loved ones, and they will know things that are buried deep within your heart. Do not fall for these traps. Do not touch the ghosts. If you do, you will become one of them, and your spirit will wander forever between the heavens and the underworld, until the demon you serve is vanquished."

Meanwhile, I sat with the women, peeling a modest bounty of radishes and potatoes one of the farmers had brought.

The women stole glances at my eyes and my gloved hands, and whispered behind my back when they thought I couldn't hear. It was easy to ignore until Baba came to help; then I quickly made an excuse to leave. I didn't want him to see the looks they gave me, and I didn't want to finally have to face his questions. I didn't want to hurt him with the truth, not yet.

My presence stirred gossip in the camp, so I kept mostly to myself, except for when I joined Lady Sarnai's nightly war council.

"Four hundred men," Lord Xina said grimly. "Not nearly enough."

I wanted to shout that it was more than we could have hoped for, but Lady Sarnai beat me to it.

"We've survived worse odds. The women could fight. Several of them have expressed a desire to."

"They wouldn't add much," said Lord Xina. "You'd only be sending them to their deaths. Your father will have thousands of trained men."

"This is not a war between armies. It is a war against my father. He commands his soldiers through fear, through his alliance with Gyiu'rak. Once he and the demon are defeated, the army will surrender. The challenge will be killing Gyiu'rak. Twisted though my father may be, he is still human—with a human's weaknesses. He could have killed me at the Winter Palace, but he did not." Her voice fell soft, but her tone was hard. "He remembers me."

I drew a labored breath. If it weren't for seeing Baba and Keton daily at the camp, I would not remember them either. Their faces would be lost to me, the sounds of their voices a familiar song I'd heard before but could not sing.

I'd lost Sendo's stories and the sound of Mama's laugh. And the words Finlei used to say when I lacked courage or faith in myself.

I tried not to panic, but the hollow ache inside me grew sharper with each new day.

Tonight, I decided. I would tell Edan what had been lurking in my mind for days.

I prayed he wouldn't hate me for it.

· · ·

When dusk fell, we built a village of tents in the middle of the plains. It had not snowed yet, though the grass beneath our boots crinkled from frost, and with each passing hour the chill of the wind bit deeper. There weren't many women at the camp; we slept within a handful of tents near Lady Sarnai. Few noticed when I snuck out to visit Edan.

I kept a hand on his chest, taking in the slow steadiness of his heart. Not long ago, I used to worry about him becoming a hawk every evening, but now that felt like a distant memory. He didn't shout out from his dreams anymore. Now that was me.

Sometimes, in the middle of the night, he would reach for my hand. How I wished it would always be so.

But staying Maia was a fight. Every second, every minute, every hour, I battled against myself to distinguish my thoughts from my demon's. The blood of stars kept enough heart in me to sustain some inkling of who I was. But if I were to lose that dress . . .

"Was it like this for you?" I asked when Edan woke me from a nightmare. "Being away from your oath? When we were traveling, and you felt the tug of dawn and the pull of dusk?"

"It was different," Edan replied. "The battle wasn't against myself. I could feel my magic leaving me, but I knew that reuniting with my master would bring it back. For you, your magic is turning against you . . . and . . ."

"And there's nothing I can do," I finished for him bleakly. "It's only a matter of time."

I pursed my lips and stared at my nails. Thick, hard, and sharp. Even my knuckles had become gnarled, my skin growing scaly and parched.

"How did you end up a hawk?" I asked suddenly.

"Maybe we shouldn't talk about this anymore, Maia. You—"

"I want to know," I said. "I've been thinking about what form I'll take on. It'll help me to know."

He inhaled a deep breath. "Demons take on the form they had when they were enchanters, but not every demon began as an enchanter. Some demons have no spirit form, and others are powerful enough to take on any form they choose.

"I prayed for a creature with keen eyesight," Edan confided. "Mine was getting poor from reading so much by moonlight. Soldiers didn't have much use for candles."

"So, a hawk?"

"Early on, when I discovered my talent for magic, one landed on my head."

"On your head?" For a precious second, I forgot my troubles and chuckled.

Edan smiled. "I tried to shoo it away, but it followed me the rest of the week, screeching so loudly the other boys in my troop threw pebbles at it. I couldn't understand what it was saying to me then, but I've always thought it could understand me. I never saw it again, yet I never forgot it. I wasn't surprised when a hawk was what was chosen for me."

I had no inkling of what would be chosen for me. No such creatures had come to me; in fact, all feared me at this point. But I did not say this to Edan.

I traced the lines on his palms. "These last few weeks have been hard for me. Not knowing whether you were safe, not knowing whether my country would go to war, not knowing whether I'd wake up the next morning as Maia, or as someone else." I swallowed, wrapping Edan's arms tighter around my shoulders. "But I know now I'm strong. Because I have someone to be strong for—Baba, Keton."

"And me?"

"Especially you."

My fingers crept up his chest to his neck, twirling a loose curl. But as soon as I wound it around my nail, I let go and stared at our hands, his on top of mine, the curve of his palm fitting perfectly over the back of my hand. His long fingers covering my sharp black claws.

"I want you to promise me something," I said, trying to keep my voice as even as I could. "I've gotten better since finding you again and seeing my family. But it will not last. I can feel myself slipping a little more each day. If I should . . . become dangerous, you must stop me."

"Maia . . ."

"When I do finally become a demon, Edan." A lump hardened in my throat, making it painful to speak. "I want you to take the amulet. Take it away to the far corner of the earth and trap it in all the magic you can. Do what you have to do—bury it, throw it to the bottom of the ocean—just make sure I never find it again."

"What good would that do?" Edan said gently. "You would spend all your hours searching for it. You are bound to the dresses inside—"

"One dress. I only have one dress left." My throat felt raw, but I pressed on. "Please, Edan. I don't want the demon me to have it . . . for her to abuse its power."

For her to hurt anyone more than she already has.

"Demon magic cannot be contained that way, Maia." Edan's voice was grave. "Not even for you."

Deep down, I had already known that. But I had hoped all the same. "Then end me. Promise me you will."

I shook my head, preempting any protest.

He gave a numb nod. "If it comes to that, I will."

Without another word, he left the tent. It took all my restraint not to follow him. I waited, sure he'd be back soon.

He did not come back.

CHAPTER THIRTY

$\mathcal{L}$ady Sarnai saw my shadow outside her tent before I had a chance to announce myself.

"Don't loiter, Tamarin. Come in."

She was bundled in thick layers of fox fur, and she narrowed her eyes at how little clothing I wore. The wind seeped through my thin muslin sleeves, but I wasn't cold.

Her tent was spartan, furnished with a cream-colored candle, a worn burgundy blanket, and two bronze pots—one for water, one for fire. Her bow lay on her bed, beside a quiver of freshly chiseled arrows.

"What is it?" Her tone was curt.

"I've come to ask a favor of you." The words came out hoarse.

Lady Sarnai set down her sword, which she'd just begun sharpening. "You are in no position to ask favors."

"I apologize, Your Highness. I'll—"

She harrumphed. "Passive as ever. I don't know how I ever took you for a man. What is it you want?"

My shoulders squared at her insult. "I asked Edan to kill me if ever I should lose control. But I don't believe he will."

Now she leaned forward, interested.

I took a deep breath. "I want you to complete the task if he fails."

An elegant eyebrow arched, and she sat on one of her trunks, her back rigid. "I knew what you were the moment I saw you. I've known it since you made me put on that cursed dress and nearly killed me."

I bowed my head.

"But no real demon would give up the secret of how to kill her. That is why I gave Edan back his dagger. Why I let you live. But your days are numbered, Tamarin."

"I'm not—"

"Don't interrupt me. You haven't the right, and I haven't finished speaking." She flexed her sword hand, and her frown deepened.

"I've told you what magic did to my father," she said. "I witnessed him transform from the emperor's most loyal general to a traitor desirous of power above all else. He thinks he is in control of the demon at his side, but Gyiu'rak has him fooled. She will bleed him dry; it is her nature—a demon's nature. And I see it in your eyes."

Her voice turned cold. "You cannot control it if you are weak."

Weak? my demon voice spluttered in disbelief. *Yes, you are weak. But only for resisting. Imagine, Sentur'na, what you could do for A'landi if you gave in. You would truly be Gyiu'rak's match. You would—*

Go away. I snuffed the voice with my mind. *I'll not listen to you.*

"Why did you come back?" I asked Sarnai. "You said there was no chance of beating your father."

"There isn't," she said. "But better I lead A'landi against him than *you*."

It was meant to be an insult, but I did not flinch. "Then you've given me a reason to be glad of what I am becoming."

I didn't give her a chance to respond. Spying the ash bow behind her, I gestured at it. "When I was impersonating you, your father said it was a testament of your strength."

Lady Sarnai ignored the bow and sniffed. "My brothers were trained from birth to be warriors, something I wanted above all else. My father said I could train with them if I could draw his bow. He knew it was an impossible feat, even for my brothers. I could throw a knife and hit a dragonfly from a hundred meters away and stomach the poisons that my brothers meant for each other and slipped me instead, but I did not have enough strength to draw the bow even halfway. My father only thought of me as a pawn to be married off.

"I wouldn't have it. So I joined my mother for embroidery and dancing lessons, but at night, I went into the woods and carried logs on my back from the forest to the castle to build strength.

"I did this for half a year, until my soft hands grew rough, my back stopped aching from the weight, and my bones grew strong. When my father found out that his only daughter, the Jewel of the North, was doing hard labor in the middle of the night, he ordered the woodsman hanged. What good would I be to him if my beauty was compromised? I could hardly become an empress if my face was scarred and splinters marked my skin."

She touched her cheek. The violet bruises were faded, all but ghosts against the flush of winter on her cheeks. The silver-white scars on her skin were there to stay, prominent reminders of her encounter with my dresses, but they weren't what must have chased away the soft elegance she once had as a young girl. War and loss were to blame for that.

She drew a breath. "But I stole my father's bow and drew it, easily, as if I'd been pulling a sash around my robe, and my arrow cut the woodsman free.

"I was allowed to join my brothers from then on. When I bested them all, my father gave me to Lord Xina to train." She trailed off, pursing her lips. "Then to Khanujin to marry."

A long silence fell between us. Finally, I broke it by asking, "Are you relieved he is dead?"

"Khanujin was not a good emperor. Not even a good man." She lingered, as if what she wanted to say next vexed her. "But I thought about what you said, tailor, and there was truth to your words. Much as I hated him, he put A'landi before all else. Now that I see it, I have no choice but to respect him." Her expression turned grim. "So, yes, I am relieved that he is dead, but I wish he weren't. Now his burdens fall to us."

Us.

"Perhaps even he, the emperor we both came to loathe, had some good in him after all."

"I wouldn't go that far," Lady Sarnai scoffed. But, for once, she had no harsh words to say about Khanujin.

"You're an odd one, Tamarin," she said after a pause. "Perhaps in a different life we might have been friends. But not in this one."

What could I say to that? I bowed my head. "Thank you, Your Highness."

"Enough with the titles. We are all soldiers now." She gripped the hilt of her sword, sweeping a cloth over the blade to clean it. The bow behind her remained untouched. "If you have the magic and the will to call so many to our aid, you can find the strength within to battle whatever it is that ails you."

I blinked in surprise. "Yes, Lady Sarnai."

"Good. Go now and work on it." Her voice hardened, regaining the harsh tone I was used to hearing from her. "You must not fail."

. . .

Every morning, Keton got up before the other soldiers to exercise his legs, and the next day I followed him. He could walk without his cane now, but not for long, and wielding a sword was difficult for him. Yet when he saw me, a hint of his old grin returned, and for a moment, he was my mischievous youngest brother again, with a gleam in his eye that meant he was up to no good.

"You know, I never thought I'd relish the day the shansen's right-hand warrior gave me a sword," said my brother. "Never thought I'd be fighting for his daughter, either."

"How do the others feel about it?"

"We all have mixed feelings. We didn't trust Lord Xina at first, but he wouldn't spend so much time drilling us just to get us all slaughtered in battle."

"What about Lady Sarnai?"

"Many distrust her, and some even hate her. You can't blame them. She was just as ruthless as her father during the war, even more brutal on the battlefield than Lord Xina. But we all hate the shansen most, and we know the best person to defeat him is his daughter." Keton cocked his head. "Will you ask me next what we think about the enchanter?"

I held my breath. "I wasn't planning to."

Keton grinned at me. "The enchanter is growing on us. I'm beginning to like him." His grin widened. "Your friend Ammi's growing on me, too. I'm guessing more radish soup today?"

"Onion," I replied.

"Ah, onions." Keton chuckled and tested the balance of his sword, passing it from one hand to the other. He'd been practicing; I could tell the simple act wasn't easy for him, even though he made it look so. "Remember how much trouble I used to get into over them?"

I forced a laugh so my brother wouldn't see that I didn't remember.

"I'd cut open an onion to help me cry, then take some of Baba's red dye and pour it over my sleeve to pretend I'd cut myself. What a fit Mama threw, thinking I was injured."

"And when she found out you weren't," I said, slowly piecing it together, "she made you cut onions all day. Until your eyes were so red you couldn't see straight. And Finlei and Sendo would call you pickle face."

Keton laughed. "We used to have fun, the four of us. Didn't we?"

My throat went dry. What memories I had left were like wild birds trapped in a cage. One by one, they flew out, never to return.

"You remember how Sendo and I used to pretend to be Balardan pirates?" Keton sheathed the sword and swung the scabbard at my backside. To his disbelief, I evaded it neatly.

"Where'd you learn that?" he asked.

"On my travels."

His eyebrow rose. "From the enchanter? Baba asked if he's made his intentions known to you."

Hearing that brought a wave of heat over my face again. But it chilled as quickly as it came. All I could say, guardedly, was, "And?"

"He said he has." Keton's mouth twisted wryly. "What, no smile? Maybe my advice to you was too good. I think you spent too long pretending to be a man at the palace. Nothing seems to ruffle you anymore."

"Maybe," I allowed. *Or maybe I know that future will never happen.* "What does it matter? Baba doesn't trust him."

"Baba wouldn't trust a monk. It has nothing to do with him being a foreigner; his A'landan is even better than mine. Even if he were the emperor himself, Baba would still have reservations. He doesn't think anyone is good enough for you."

"Me?" I twisted my hands, gloved to hide their hideousness. "You have always been Baba's favorite."

"I'm the favorite, but you're the one he sees the most of himself in." Keton set down his sword and leaned against it; he looked tired from training. "He wants you to be happy. Like he was with Mama."

I thought of the red thread I'd tied to Edan's wrist and reached for the strand around my own. Still there.

"Edan makes me happy."

"Anyone can see that," Keton said quietly. "Baba will, too. It's just the magic that worries him. Sorcery is deception, and the enchanter had everyone fooled about the emperor."

"That was Khanujin's doing," I said. "Besides, Edan's not an enchanter anymore. Most of his magic has left him."

"Then who is this other . . . enchanter the shansen spoke of?"

"*Enchantress.*" I bit my lip, pressing extra hard—but there was no pain. "It's me."

I'd expected my brother to reel back in shock, but he merely nodded. "I had a feeling you were hiding something. Baba did too."

"I—"

"I'm not pressing you to tell us. But there are rumors in the camp. . . . Baba would want to hear the truth, from you."

"I know." I hung my head. "I know."

Keton touched my shoulder. "What was that saying Finlei used to tell you?"

I faltered. My stomach twisted and churned—I could almost feel the words spilling off my tongue, but Keton spoke them before I remembered.

"Seize the wind." My brother smiled sadly. "Don't become the kite that never flies."

I repeated the words, knowing he meant them as encouragement. But it wasn't so simple. Some things Baba was better off not knowing.

Lady Sarnai appeared suddenly, coming up the short grassy hill behind my brother. As usual, she scowled at me. "Exchanging stories with your brother isn't what I meant by finding your strength, tailor."

At the sight of her, Keton dropped to his knees. "Y-your Highness," he stammered.

My brother couldn't take his eyes off the shansen's daughter. Silvery white scars kissed her once flawless skin, and dark gray veins branched across her cheeks and neck. Her beauty was changed, hardened, but perhaps it had never been Lady Sarnai's beauty that arrested people. Even more than before, she exuded a warrior's spirit, her steely eyes showing enough mettle to make even the strongest of wills flinch.

"Get up," Sarnai said to Keton. As he struggled, she acknowledged his past injury with a slight jerk of her chin. She raised her arm to stop me from aiding him.

"He'll never become strong if you help him." When Keton stood again, barely able to heave his sword over his shoulder, she frowned.

I knew what she must be thinking: he wouldn't survive against the shansen's men, not while simply holding his sword unsteadied his balance and worsened his limp.

And yet it would crush him if he were discharged. I opened my mouth to say a word in his defense, but she spoke before I could:

"A needle is to a tailor as a sword is to a warrior. It is not that different." Sarnai reached for the bow slung over her shoulder. "But the needle is not the only tool a tailor wields, and a sword does not make the warrior." She passed her bow to Keton. "Give me your sword."

Keton obeyed, and Lady Sarnai watched him shift his balance, adjusting for the lighter weapon.

"I did not say to try to draw it," she said sternly. "That bow is not for you. Hold it still. Like this."

It was impossible to read what she was thinking as she showed him. But after what felt like a long while, she muttered, "I don't know what fool gave you a sword." She clicked her tongue. "We have more need for archers than swordsmen, and your arms and back are stronger than most. Report to Lord Xina, and he will equip you with a bow."

At that, my brother brightened, and I stiffened in surprise. "Thank you, Your Highness."

"Don't thank me yet," she said. And then to Keton: "You've never even wielded a bow before, I can tell. You'll have to train hard, from now until the battle begins."

She glared at my lowered head, the only gesture of thanks I could summon.

"And you, tailor. You could use a lesson as well—I've seen you with that dagger of yours. Pitiful technique."

"I'm the least of your worries," I said. There was no point in telling her I no longer needed a weapon. Should I truly wish to cause harm, I had other means of doing so. "The women need training in how to fight. Those who wish to."

A light sparked in Lady Sarnai's eyes. She regarded me, and for a flicker of a moment I thought she saw me more as an equal than as a servant. "Those who wish to join the army will be trained. We'll begin after lunch."

By evening, nearly every able woman in the camp had volunteered for Lady Sarnai's training, including Ammi, adding dozens more soldiers to her army.

We all knew our chances against the shansen were slim, that it took months, not days, to make a soldier. But hope was a valuable weapon, and we were sharpening its every edge.

CHAPTER THIRTY-ONE

The last morning of our march to Jappor, it began to snow. The flakes fell gently at first, frosting the yellow grass. Within an hour, every tree branch glistened with white, like there were pearls hanging from the boughs. The change in the landscape was so mesmerizing that no one saw the smoke from the dying campfire twist into the shape of a tiger.

No one, except me.

The hairs on the back of my neck bristled. "Gyiu'rak." I cursed, spinning to warn the others. I didn't get a chance. She sent an invisible blast of demon wind, rocketing to my lungs.

My throat seized, punctured by a thousand needles, and I lurched forward trying to catch my breath.

"Maia?" Ammi said, running to my side. "Maia, what's wrong?"

I clutched at my chest, choking and pointing at the fire.

Powerful limbs emerged from the shadows, condensing from smoke to flesh. But by the time Ammi and the others realized what was happening, it was too late.

With an earth-shattering roar, Gyiu'rak burst out of the flames.

Terror descended on the camp, everyone scrambling for weapons and for cover. I pushed Ammi behind a wagon and grabbed the nearest spear, even though I knew it would do little good against a demon.

Gyiu'rak prowled the camp, snarling at the cowering soldiers. Her fur glistened, white as the snow, with burnished stripes like carefully considered strokes of ink.

She was searching for someone. I shouldered my way toward her, but it wasn't me she wanted; it was Lady Sarnai. The shansen's daughter appeared, her ash bow raised, with a scarlet arrow nocked in place—aimed at the area between Gyiu'rak's eyes.

A laugh tumbled out of the demon's throat. "Your pitiful weapons cannot harm me, little jewel," she mocked. "But keep them raised if it makes you feel safer."

She turned to address the rest of the camp, slicing the tension in the air with her every breath. "By request of His Excellency, *Emperor* Makangis, I bring you warm tidings. As you all are citizens of A'landi, he offers you this one chance—to surrender."

Lady Sarnai pulled her bowstring back. I tried to catch her attention, to warn her not to attack.

She ignored me.

Her arrow sang, straight and true, piercing the demon neatly in the forehead. Smoke sizzled from Gyiu'rak's fur, but she plucked the arrow out as if it were a burr in her coat, and flicked it away.

Within seconds, the demon's wound closed bloodlessly.

Shock rippled across the camp. Soldiers shrank behind their shields, knees trembling violently. Even Lady Sarnai staggered back.

I moved closer to Gyiu'rak. An arrow couldn't hurt her, but *I* could.

"We have ten thousand against your pathetic army," the demon announced. "Lord Makangis welcomes your surrender now. If not, the battle will commence tomorrow—and we will show no mercy."

Some of the men wavered, taking tentative steps forward. Then I heard someone cry, "We will not surrender!"

It was Ammi. She and the other women blocked the soldiers. They repeated, "We will not surrender!"

"Your blood price will not be paid." The words boomed out of me. "Not while I fight by Lady Sarnai's side."

"And I," declared Edan, joining me.

"We fight for Lady Sarnai. We fight for A'landi."

Soon every man and woman chanted the words, their strength gaining momentum across the camp.

Gyiu'rak threw me a baleful glance. "Curious, that they should listen to *you*, Maia Tamarin," she rasped in a low voice. Her head tilted. *They don't know yet, do they? Shall I tell them?*

I went very still. My nails had grown so sharp that simply curling my fists made my palms bleed.

What are you afraid of? Gyiu'rak spoke without making a sound, sliding into the inner crevices of my mind. *Are you afraid that they'll try to kill you? That they will fear you? Let them. Soon they will all be dead—*

"Leave!" I barked at the demon. "Go now."

My words hung in the air, the sound of my voice so thunderous that snow trembled off the trees.

A smile curled over Gyiu'rak's tiger lips. "Very well."

Without warning, she lunged, attacking the soldiers nearest her. As their screams pierced the air, a plume of smoke enshrouded the tiger and she vanished.

The chanting had stopped, and the air was thick with fear and uncertainty.

No one had surrendered to the demon, yet she had triumphed. Before, the soldiers had only heard stories about her power and invincibility. They hadn't witnessed it until now.

But Lady Sarnai has a demon, too, I thought. *Me.*

"How can we fight *that*?"

"She can't die. What chance have we?"

"We're doomed."

"We still have the Lord Enchanter!" I heard Keton shout. "And—" My brother's eyes met mine, and I shook my head.

"The enchanter did nothing while we fought for our lives at the Autumn Palace. He no longer has power."

At my side, Edan tightened his fists.

"Show them," I urged him. "Show them they're wrong."

"It is not my magic that will save us," he replied. "It's yours."

Much as I wanted to deny it, I knew he was right. *I can't hide forever. Not if I want to save A'landi.*

Flicking off my gloves, I stepped into the middle of the camp and raised my claws. The wind swallowed the gasps that followed.

"Many of you have wondered about my eyes, why they glow red as a demon's. And my hands." I raised them, extending my claws. "They are part of the price I paid to make the dresses of Amana."

Keton stood at the front of the soldiers, a mass of hundreds, all waiting to hear what I was going to say next. I inhaled, avoiding my brother's gaze.

"I am a demon." I let the words ring in the air, taking care to look as many men and women in the eye as I could. To show them, in whatever way that I could, that I was still Maia. That I would not harm them.

I swallowed, taking in the fear in everyone's eyes, the curled lips and tense jaws. Edan touched my elbow, nudging me onward.

"In our legends," I continued, "the first demons were created by the gods themselves, gods who grew restless in heaven and wanted an immortal race to do their bidding. So they soldered parts of men and beasts together to create a new kind of creature. When the mother goddess learned of them, she sent her children—the stars—to chase the demons from heaven onto earth. Since then, the stars have stood guard over the demons to make sure they never return to heaven."

I held out my amulet. "Demons and ghosts are vulnerable to the power of the stars, which I will harness to keep A'landi safe. To keep all of us safe."

Cracking open my amulet, I released a beam of starlight, silver and gold, and dazzling with all the colors of the heavens. It was not a true show of my power, merely a gesture to ease their fear, but it worked. Heads lifted, eyes glimmered. Threads of hope wove through the crowd.

"It isn't my magic that will save us from Gyiu'rak!" Edan shouted to the crowds. "It is Maia Tamarin's!"

"I will fight Gyiu'rak," I pledged, "and Lady Sarnai will defeat her father. But the shansen's army is strong. We need all of you to help us, so we can win back A'landi's future."

At that, murmurs of agreement swelled across the camp, and I stepped to the side as Lady Sarnai came forward to rally the soldiers.

I would do my part. I only prayed I would not let them down.

Baba sat on a log, huddled beside a small fire over which a brass kettle hung, rubbing his hands together for warmth. Despite his recent captivity with the shansen, he looked sturdier than he had in years. Over the past few days, I'd heard him laugh with Ammi and some of the older men and women at camp. I'd even seen him attempt to help with the mending.

Yet whenever he saw me, his good spirits faded.

I lifted the kettle and poured hot water into the wooden cup at Baba's side. If he'd heard my confession, he said nothing about it.

"I didn't think I'd ever see snow again," he murmured, sifting it through his fingers. "Did you know I grew up near Jappor? I was a lazy boy, didn't want to learn my father's craft—or any other, for that matter. One year, there was a terrible blizzard in the middle of autumn. No one expected it, so we were unprepared. It lasted days, and since there was no business to be had during a storm, we ran out of both food and money."

He regarded me. "Since I was the oldest son, my father sent me into town to beg. I trudged from house to house through the snow, which was waist-high, offering to mend torn sleeves and patch up pants in exchange for rice. Just as you did in Port Kamalan when times were hard for us. That was when I discovered I loved my needle and thread, as my father did and his father before him." He touched my gloved hands. "As you do."

"Did you know the scissors had magic?" I asked, after a pause.

Baba inhaled the steam from his cup before sipping. "I suspected. My mother never spoke of them. She was a talented tailor herself, like your grandfather. But she stopped sewing

310

when I was very young. She gave me the scissors when I moved to Gangsun with your mother and instructed me to take care of them. I think she knew they wouldn't speak to me. I take it they spoke to you."

"They did," I replied. "But I've lost them. I had to give them up."

Baba could tell there was more to the story than I was telling him. "You've gotten so pale, Maia. I worry about you."

"I was sick for a while," I said. It wasn't a lie, not entirely.

"The enchanter . . . he took care of you?"

"He did his best. I wish you would give him a chance."

Baba sighed. "I want to, but then I ask myself—where was he when the shansen attacked the Autumn Palace? How can he say he loves you when he abandoned you to the mercy of demons and the enemy's soldiers?"

"Is that what bothers you, Baba? That you think he left me to die?"

From his silence, I knew it was. "Maia, I want what is best for you. A man of magic is not—"

"Edan left because I lied to him," I interrupted. "I didn't tell him what I'd become. Just as I've been avoiding telling *you*. If there's anyone you should distrust, it should be me."

Baba stared at me, stricken. The color drained from his face. "Now is not the time for stories, Maia. This is unlike you."

"You know it is the truth. Baba, you've noticed the changes. . . ."

"I noticed when you came home," he said quietly. "As if all the light from your eyes had vanished forever." He stopped. "I blamed the enchanter for your unhappiness."

What could I say to comfort him?

"They aren't rumors," I whispered. "It was my choice."

"Your choice? First your mother, then two sons," Baba choked. "A father shouldn't have to bury his children, Maia."

My throat burned with sorrow. I wished I could cry with him, but no tears would come. The brisk air fogged at my lips, a tendril of steam twisting from my breath.

"I'm sorry, Baba," I said. "If I don't return, be good to Edan. Keton could use another brother, and Edan . . . he has no one in this world."

Baba's eyes clouded with the tears he'd been trying to hold back. "You love him," he said. "He is the one your mother spoke of, then. The one you are tied to, from this life to the next."

"Yes."

Snow began to fall, and I held out my hand, watching the flakes melt as soon as they touched my palm. Below, the fire smoldered, its sizzling the only sound aside from birds. The embers at my feet blinked like dying stars.

"Then let your heart be at peace," Baba said at last. "No matter what you become, you are always my Maia. Always my strong one."

Something in me lifted, knowing my father understood. "Thank you, Baba. Thank you."

CHAPTER THIRTY-TWO

The shansen's horn blared from the other side of the Jingan River. Three calls, each deafening enough to unsettle the snow from our helmets.

An invitation to battle.

I stared fixedly ahead, ignoring my reflection in a soldier's shield as I rode alongside Edan, behind Lady Sarnai and Lord Xina. We'd left Baba behind in the camp this morning, but I'd chosen not to say goodbye.

It was for the best. I'd woken up *different* today. Overnight, my black hair had deepened into the darkest shade of gold, my eyes burned red as molten fire, and my nose had sharpened to a point as fine as an arrowhead.

I hadn't greeted Edan when he came to me. I had recognized his tall frame, the square edges of his jaw, the slant of his shoulders. But I didn't know why I recognized him. Why I loved him.

A bridge divided our army from the shansen's, ten soldiers wide. Engraved on a stone pillar at its base was a greeting from A'landi's first emperor, welcoming all to the capital, Jappor, where the Great Spice Road began and ended, where fortunes and misfortunes were made and reversed. I wondered if the first emperor had ever imagined that this bridge, the only way into Jappor, would also become the doorway to war.

Plum trees edged the capital's walls, pale pink buds drooping from snow-covered branches. Untouched by war for centuries, Jappor was considered one of the most beautiful cities in the world. But now that the shansen had conquered it, I doubted it was so beautiful anymore.

Beyond Jappor loomed the Spring Palace, its sea-green roofs so tall they pierced the clouds. There was no sign of mourning for Emperor Khanujin—only the shansen's banners draped from every roof, bursts of violent green that slithered down the walls.

His army awaited us across the river.

"This is what we are fighting for," Lady Sarnai was saying. I'd missed most of her speech to rouse the soldiers, but when she spoke my name, I snapped to attention.

"—Tamarin will wear a legend we all know, the gown painted with the blood of stars."

I touched my amulet, summoning the last dress of Amana. It spun over my shoulders to my ankles with the splendor of a midnight tempest. The brilliance of the stars weighed little, the never-ending folds of night swirling like clouds around me.

Gasps of wonder echoed behind me, but I kept my eyes on Edan. Out of all the crowd, he was the only one looking at me, not my dress.

At Lady Sarnai's signal, we galloped onto the bridge. A storm of footsteps thundered past me, swordsmen rushing for the shansen's men, and I glanced back, just once, to see Keton among the archers. His bow slung over his shoulder, he was helping a fellow soldier lift a hand cannon, trying to find an ideal place to fire it at the shansen's army.

They didn't get the chance.

Twenty paces on, a cold mist shivered up from the raging river below, suddenly thickening into an impenetrable fog.

Through the haze, I saw him.

The shansen stood alone, no army behind him. He carried only a broad sword, sheathed at his side. He bowed slowly, his fur-lined cloak billowing behind him. Over his uniform, he wore golden armor, the head of a tiger blazing in the center of his torso.

Something wasn't right. Why weren't the shansen's soldiers on the bridge with him?

"Edan," I murmured, pointing at the warlord.

"Draw back!" he shouted to Lady Sarnai. "It's—"

Too late.

The shansen hadn't come alone. Hundreds of ghosts accompanied him. They emerged out of the mist, dead flesh hanging off their exposed bones, and what little skin they had was milk-white like the snow, their eyes black as onyx.

"We push forward!" Lady Sarnai shouted, charging toward her father.

Ghosts surrounded her and Lord Xina, closing her off from the shansen. Our soldiers panicked, forgetting Edan's training as the ghosts blocked escape in every direction.

Sentur'na. You know you cannot win. Join us.

I ignored the ghosts and turned back to our soldiers. "Remember what Edan told you!" I shouted. "Don't listen to them! Brace your minds against whatever they say—it isn't real!"

Edan sent a flare of fire through the fog, lifting it momentarily and sending the ghosts staggering back. But one by one, the soldiers froze, arms hovering in the air with weapons raised.

They're listening to the ghosts, I realized with a sinking heart. Lady Sarnai's army would be decimated without a single casualty on the shansen's side.

I gripped the folds of my skirts, willing the power of my

dress to turn the ghosts away, but nothing happened. Why couldn't I summon its magic?

Because Amana rejects the darkness in you, my demon voice replied. *You are too far gone, Sentur'na. But all is not lost. You've other magic in you powerful enough to wield the dress.*

Yes, use the thirst inside you—the anger and hatred for the shansen—to call upon the blood of stars. Amana's magic and our own should not be at odds with each other. Unite them, and you will be a demon far more powerful than Gyiu'rak—

"Enough!" I pushed the voice away and glided into the fight.

The ghosts turned on me, their thin fingers latching on to my limbs and my dress.

I yanked it from them, my anger sparking the blood of stars alive. Veins of hot, shimmering crimson snaked across the skirts, a pattern I had never seen before.

Remembering my demon's words, I snuffed my anger immediately. There had to be another way. If this dress was my heart, surely it could sense my need.

But no. When the spark from my anger died, the dress did not come to life. The fabric remained dull as ink. As dark as death.

I saw Edan attacking the ghosts with his dagger. Lady Sarnai and Lord Xina focused on the shansen. But every arrow fired at him rebounded, every spear thrown barely nicked his armor.

"Give this up!" the shansen shouted. "You cannot win, Sarnai. Surrender, and I will spare your pitiful army."

I could not hear Lady Sarnai's reply.

What could I do? I was not the guardian of Lapzur. I couldn't call upon its ghosts to aid me. And yet, Gyiu'rak's ghosts had to have come from somewhere, from the shansen's fallen soldiers. Perhaps I could call upon the ghosts of people I'd known and loved. Their spirits.

My heart swelled in my throat. "Help us," I whispered, silently wishing for anyone who would listen.

Over and over I reached out, until pain needled my eyes and hot tears streamed down my cheeks.

Then—two familiar figures loomed from the darkness.

My brothers. Finlei and Sendo. They looked older than when I'd seen them last. There was a crooked scar across Finlei's left eye and cheek that I'd never seen before, and Sendo's freckles stood out in stark relief, the once boyish curves of his face hardened by hunger and war.

My lips parted, but my oldest brother had anticipated my question.

"This isn't a trick," said Finlei. "We're here. You called for us."

I turned to Sendo. My second brother, my best friend.

"We've brought help," he spoke. "Soldiers who fell with us during the Five Winters' War. We won't be able to stay long, but we can fend off Gyiu'rak's army."

"How?" I breathed. "How are you here?"

Before they could reply, a scream pierced my ears, so thick and full of grief that I reeled to see where it had come from.

Lady Sarnai?

I'd never seen such terror on her face. Such anguish. She swept through the crush of soldiers and ghosts with broad, wild strokes of her sword—like a brush wielded by a storm. But she was too late.

Lord Xina had fallen.

The shansen rammed his blade deeper into the warrior's ribs, holding him by the shoulder. When he saw his daughter storming toward him, panic and anger rioting on her face, he smirked.

Then he yanked out the sword, wiped the blade on Lord Xina's cloak, and kicked him to the side.

Arrows snapped from Lady Sarnai's bow. They did nothing to the shansen, which only fueled her rage. She barreled toward her father, drawing her sword and raising it high above her head.

"Sarnai, stop!" I cried.

If she heard me, she did not listen. She was no match for her father, not while he wielded Gyiu'rak's power. Only she was too blind with rage to see it, to care.

I hurled myself after her, knocking her off course.

Angrily, the shansen lunged for me. I grabbed Sarnai's sword from her hands and blocked him, but he was strong. He shoved me away, then signaled a legion of ghosts to surround his daughter.

Ghosts besieged me, too. Hundreds of them, scrabbling at my flesh and trying to block me from Lady Sarnai. My amulet growing warm on my chest, I swung her sword at them, trying to fight my way back to the shansen.

Sarnai was already up, but her weapons were useless against the ghosts. By the shansen's command, they advanced on her slowly, one torturous step at a time, until they had her cornered.

"You were always my favorite child, Sarnai," I heard the shansen tell her. "A pity you chose the wrong side."

She glared at him, backing up toward the edge of the bridge.

"The ghosts will devour you soon. It won't hurt. Then you'll return to my side, where you belong. *Daughter.*"

"You stopped being my father the day you sold your will to

Gyiu'rak," she seethed. Then, before the ghosts could touch her, she threw herself off the bridge.

I lurched for the rails, but I needn't have worried. Not even the mighty Jingan River could swallow the Jewel of the North, and Sarnai burst from its waters, cutting across the tides.

The shansen roared for his ghosts to follow her, but I'd had enough. I dropped Lady Sarnai's sword and bunched up my skirts, ignoring the whiplash of ghosts striking at my arms and back.

I let the ghosts overwhelm me, let their whispers and taunts grow and grow in my head, threatening to undo me with hopelessness. I gathered my fear and anger, letting it grow inside me in a storm—

"Maia!" Sendo called. My brother's spirit appeared behind me, his hands weightlessly gripping my shoulders to relax them. "Let go. That isn't the way."

I spun, startled to hear him. "What is, then?"

"Try again, with the dress."

I had tried, I wanted to tell him, but Sendo lowered his hands to take mine. I met his gaze, taking in his freckles that only we two in the family shared, taking in the eyes that had once been earthy brown mirrors of my own.

This last dress is my heart. Was that why I could not bring forth its magic, because I was afraid of losing the only thing that kept me Maia Tamarin?

"Your heart is strong, sister," said my brother, hearing my thoughts. "It always has been."

Let go, he had said. Slowly, I did. I released the fear I had locked around my heart, and in its place love rushed forth— love for my family, love for my country, love for Edan.

With a burst, my dress sprang to life, the blood of stars rippling in surges across the lustrous silk. Beams of light flickered across my long sleeves, darting out like needles of silver. Power wreathed me, its glow coursing through my sleeves so they fanned like wings. No longer was I a humble seamstress from Port Kamalan: I was the tailor of the gods.

The ghosts shrieked, vanquished by waves of light. I attacked without mercy, aided by Sendo and Finlei's army of spirits. Until Lady Sarnai's soldiers finally outnumbered the ghosts.

I saw Keton, aiming his bow and relentlessly shooting arrows alongside Edan. Sweat beaded his brow, his face ruddy from the exhaustion of fighting an enemy he couldn't beat. Ghosts clamored around him, screaming. He couldn't see them, but he could feel them; he could hear them.

Sendo and Finlei's spirits dove past my brother and my enchanter, their swords ripping through the ghosts around them. How I wished Keton could see them.

How I wished we could all be together.

My dress was a furious storm of silk and light. I raised my arms, the sleeves swirling around me in endless ribbons, tearing at the ghosts and clearing a path toward my true target: the shansen.

He moved with a demon's speed and a tiger's power. Each swing of his sword ended a life, and whenever someone dared run, he shifted into the tiger form he shared with Gyiu'rak and pounded after them.

I flew across the bridge and landed before the shansen. My sleeves shot out, wrapping around his muscular throat, to choke him.

His fur singed under the brilliance of my dress, his black

eyes becoming glassy. With a growl, he ripped through one of my sleeves with his claws, but the fabric mended itself and clung to him stronger than ever.

"Yield," I commanded.

"If you think this war is won, you're sadly mistaken," the shansen rasped. "Half your men are dead, while I've not sent a single soldier into battle."

The realization was a punch to my gut. The shansen was right; we'd only fought an army of ghosts. Thousands of his men awaited on the Jappor side of the bridge.

"It doesn't matter," I said through my teeth. "Without you to lead them, the battle is won."

"Then you should have killed me."

Before I could stop him, the warlord reached for his amulet. In a rush of pearlescent smoke, he dissipated into the mist.

"No!" I slammed my fists on the bridge's stone railing.

The ghosts were gone. My brothers' army of spirits was gone too. Our surviving soldiers were awakening from the enchantment the ghosts had cast over them.

Lady Sarnai had climbed back onto the bridge and was bent beside Lord Xina's fallen form. Everyone was waiting for her to decide whether we'd retreat back to camp or push forward into Jappor.

"Maia," a hoarse voice called to me.

"Your brothers," Edan said, pointing at the two spirits floating above us.

Waiting for me.

I sprang into the air. "Don't go. The fight isn't over."

"Ours is," said Finlei gently. "Amana let us heed your call this once, but we cannot help you again, sister."

"Please. Once you leave, I'll—"

"Forget us?" Sendo shook his head. "You won't."

"How could you forget two brothers as memorable as we?" Finlei teased. Then his face grew somber. "Punch Keton for me—extra hard—for following us into war even though we told him not to . . . and tell Baba we miss him very much."

When I heard the crack in his voice, my heart wanted to burst. *Stay*, I wanted to beg them once more, but I knew they couldn't. My throat swelled. It hurt to speak. "I will."

"Always seize the wind, sister."

"I will," I whispered.

Finlei turned to go, but Sendo hesitated, his forehead wrinkling with concern. He placed a hand on my arm. I couldn't feel his touch, but the gesture warmed me, like a gentle caress of sunlight on my skin.

"I've missed you, Maia." He offered me a sad smile. "You remember that last day Finlei and I were at home?"

"I was painting," I said softly. "I spilled Baba's most expensive indigo on my skirt. I was so foolish then . . . so, so foolish."

"No, not foolish." He touched my nose, and I blinked even though I couldn't feel it. "How far you've come from that little girl with the paint on her nose and fingers. The one who'd cling to my stories when we sat on the pier—you've become so strong." He swallowed. "I'm sorry we never made it home."

I blinked back my tears. There was so much I wanted to tell him—I had five years' worth of news and worries, of joys and realizations—and stories I'd dreamed of sharing with him, but now that he was here, no words would come.

"I have to go," he said, pressing a phantom kiss onto my cheek.

"Wait—" I started.

"This isn't farewell, sister. Our paths will cross again. Perhaps not in this life, but Mama, Finlei, and I will be watching you. Until then, take care."

Sendo nodded at Edan, acknowledging him before he returned to Finlei's side.

Then my brothers were gone.

My lips parted, and I sucked in an unsteady, ragged breath.

"We retreat to the camp!" I heard Lady Sarnai shout. Lord Xina's body was folded over her horse, and she led the way across the bridge. "Carry anyone you can. We will bury them tonight."

My skirts fanning behind me, I lowered myself back onto the bridge. Edan wove his arm under mine, finding my hand.

The instant my feet touched the cool stone deck, everything exploded.

. . .

The world slanted, and my stomach plummeted as the bridge folded in on itself.

I couldn't see. Dust clouded my vision. Everything was a blur of stippled gray, human screams, and cataclysmic roars from the river.

Bodies tumbled into the water like marbles, and I dove after them, saving as many as I could from the Jingan's icy clutches.

I frantically searched for Edan, my brother, and Ammi. Keton was downstream swimming toward Jappor, Ammi already clambering to shore not far from him. Edan was safe too, standing on the Jappor side of the bridge—the only piece that had not collapsed—using his magic to delay its destruction.

Relief washed over me. Then I glimpsed Lady Sarnai in the river. Her horse couldn't navigate the debris and tumbling rocks, not while it carried Lord Xina's body.

I leapt after her, fighting the hungry river.

Lord Xina's body slid off Lady Sarnai's horse into the river, and she started to dive after him, but the waters were fierce. They swallowed Lord Xina, and Lady Sarnai thrashed against me as I grabbed her by the arms, leaping into the air to reach land.

There, on the banks of Jappor, her father and his demon were waiting. Hundreds of his soldiers surrounded us, and thousands more awaited beyond the city walls.

We were trapped. The bridge was gone; we couldn't retreat to our camp. We were at the shansen's mercy.

"Welcome to Jappor, Sarnai," greeted the shansen. "Half your army is lost. You've no food or shelter. Don't you think it's time to surrender?"

Lady Sarnai rose to her feet, anger and hatred twisting her features. She lunged at her father with a dagger, but in her grief, she was unfocused, reckless. The shansen fought her off easily, and threw her to the ground.

He spat at her in disgust. "Pathetic," he rumbled. I started, certain he was about to kill her, but the shansen withdrew. Without Gyiu'rak at his side, his eyes still flashed black and cruel, but there was something about them . . . the slightest, most infinitesimal glitter of humanity.

"I give you tonight to mourn your losses. You have until dawn to surrender."

The shansen and his men receded through the gates of Jappor, leaving us by the river in the bitter, bleak cold.

. . .

By nightfall, the river had gone still, a thin layer of ice subduing its currents. Snow fell, blanketing everything in white. As we made a meager camp along the banks outside Jappor, torches danced above the city walls, a brutal reminder that warmth and comfort were so close and yet so inaccessible. The soldiers huddled together to stave off the cold, but there was little to be done for food; some grew so hungry they began to eat the snow.

The mere thought of having to fight again in the morning broke some of our soldiers. It didn't help that Lady Sarnai, their commander, was nowhere to be seen.

After dusk, I sought her out and found her kneeling by the river, holding Lord Xina's helmet.

"Go away, tailor."

I crouched beside her. What I'd come to tell her was that the men needed her. She needed to rouse them. But seeing her so forlorn, I said instead, "Come back to camp. You'll freeze out here alone."

Her teeth were clenched, and she shoved me away. "What does it matter?" she growled, straining between the words. "I will not surrender. We will all die in the morning"—she spat— "and without honor."

I understood her pain. The shansen had thrown Lord Xina's corpse into the river. Lady Sarnai couldn't bury him, couldn't mourn him properly.

"Lord Xina wouldn't want you to believe that."

"In the North, there are demons. . . ." Her voice broke bitterly. "If the dead are not honored, their spirits will become ghosts."

I regarded her. During the trial, she'd seemed older than I. Now I felt older. Like I'd lived eighty years instead of eighteen.

"We will not allow that to happen to Lord Xina," I replied. "If we defeat Gyiu'rak, his spirit will be free of her." I hesitated. "He was a great warrior. One of the greatest of his generation. Let his death not be in vain, Your Highness."

For a long time, she gave no indication she'd heard me. Then she reached into her quiver for an arrow and set its feather aflame. She placed it atop Lord Xina's helmet, watching it burn.

Together we watched the ashes rise, curling up into the clouds.

When there was nothing but embers left, she finally stood. Her eyes were dark, as if smoke clung to them.

"Tomorrow," she said through her teeth, "I will kill my father."

CHAPTER THIRTY-THREE

The shansen did not come at dawn.

He had the cruelty to make us wait until dusk, when our toes had frozen in our boots, and frost rusted our weapons as well as our spirits.

The air smelled of gunpowder and snow. Of despair.

Finally, as the sun disappeared into the river, a pearl sinking back into the watery depths of its home, we heard a rumble of thunder: the shansen's army was coming. Their footsteps made the city walls shudder, and soon they surrounded us like a snake that had coiled around its prey.

The shansen arrived last, with Gyiu'rak at his side. A familiar emerald cloak rippled from her shoulders.

Lord Xina's, I recognized after a tense beat. How wrong it looked on Gyiu'rak's broad tiger frame, the crisply dyed wool like a trophy over her white fur. The demon had also claimed his gauntlets and shield, with his family's crest emblazoned in scarlet lacquer. She flaunted them for all to see.

I darted a quick glance at Lady Sarnai. Her jaw was tight, knuckles whitening as they gripped her reins. What could be going through her mind, seeing her lover's armor on the demon who brought about his death?

She let out a cry, and her horse charged for the shansen. As her soldiers followed, I stayed.

I had my own plan.

Edan's arm brushed against mine, the red thread I'd tied around his wrist peeking out of his sleeve.

"Watch over my brother," I said, "and Lady Sarnai. She cannot defeat the shansen alone."

"Maia . . ." Edan reached for my hand. The red thread on his wrist glowed, as did mine. Careful not to hurt him, I curled my clawed fingers against his, sliding each one into place between his. Wishing this moment could last forever.

Wrapping his arms around my waist, I kissed him to silence his protests. In the middle of battle, it was a foolish thing to do, but I didn't care.

"I love you," I said, tilting my head close to his.

Then I let him go—and burst into the sky, the dress of the blood of stars folding over me in layers of twilight and stardust.

My amulet thrummed in my ears, a silent song only I could hear. My scissors used to hum to me this way, beckoning me to use them. It hadn't occurred to me until now that maybe the scissors had been sent to prepare me for this very moment. To show me how to trust the magic singing inside me, to turn my burgeoning darkness into light.

With a spark, my amulet flared to life.

The two powers within me—my demon darkness and the light of Amana—clashed, their battle visible in the bursts of light dazzling from my dress as it clung to my skin, the silk stitching itself into my flesh to protect me from darkness. To save me.

My skirts swelled as full as the moon above, lifting me high above the ground and gliding toward the clouds.

What I saw from above confirmed my worst fear. We were

losing badly. Already, our dead were piled high. We would never take the Spring Palace.

At the center of the battle, Lady Sarnai struggled against her father. She was no match for his demon's strength.

Seize his amulet, I urged her, sending the message in a plume of smoke that took the shape of a bird and flittered off toward the shansen's daughter.

Meanwhile, Gyiu'rak was prowling the battlefield.

If I could disrupt the link that was channeling her power to the shansen, Lady Sarnai might stand a chance.

Drawing a sharp lungful of air, I threw myself at Gyiu'rak and knocked her down. My skirts swept against her powerful legs, burning her with their touch. Smoke curled from her wounds, blistering against the backdrop of falling snow.

"I don't have time for you," she snarled, but I launched myself at her again. Gyiu'rak fended me off easily, grabbing my wrists. I thought she might crack my bones, but what she did was far worse. She sank her nails into my amulet.

The sharpest pain pierced my chest. My heart was being squeezed, crushed. I couldn't breathe. My mind went gray, and I choked, my lungs hacking. I pummeled Gyiu'rak, trying to fight her off.

She only smiled, and dug her nails deeper into my amulet. Thick black blood oozed from my lips, filling my mouth with the taste of charcoal.

As I screamed, she yanked on the amulet's chain. I'd learned from Bandur not to let her have it. If she possessed my amulet, she could control me.

Let yourself go! the demon growing inside me commanded.

I didn't understand. My dress was flickering and careening

329

in a panicked tempest. I couldn't control it. The pain was too much. All of me was on fire.

What happened next was a blur of blinding heat and whirling darkness. The demon Maia overwhelmed me, brutally shutting off my senses. For a numbingly long moment, I was nothing. I saw, I heard, I felt—nothing.

When the world came rushing back at me, Gyiu'rak no longer held my amulet. Her white fur was scorched, and she growled, hoisted me high, and hurled me into the river.

The world flashed deliriously behind me as I flew backward. My body was too light, like a leaf caught in the wind. Yet my head was heavy. It pounded; I could feel my demon grappling for control over my mind. She knew I was weakened, that I wouldn't be able to resist her for much longer.

I don't need much time, I told her. *Just give me a few more minutes, then you can have me.*

I sailed across the battlefield, thrashing against the wind until my dress overpowered the demon in me. Its skirts flared, and I caught myself in midair. Once I regained my balance, I searched for Gyiu'rak.

There she was—a blur of white fur, pounding across the frosted battlefield toward a tall figure on horseback.

Terror stung me back to life, and I tore after Gyiu'rak.

Edan! I shouted, smoke leaking from my lips as I tried to communicate with him.

He did not hear me. His walnut staff was raised, summoning a storm of birds that soared above him before diving into the battle to attack the shansen's soldiers.

"To the walls!" Edan yelled at our men, waving them to push toward the city as more of the shansen's men fell. Then he powered his way toward the warlord.

Watch out! I sent a desperate warning hurtling toward Edan. *Gyiu'rak is coming for you.*

Edan turned as if he heard me. Alarm registered on his face when he saw the demon closing on him, but he didn't change course. He urged his horse forward, racing against the tiger and charging at the shansen.

Gyiu'rak sprang for Edan, but he made a sharp turn left, ramming his horse into the shansen. The warlord tumbled off his mount, and Edan advanced, swinging his staff. The shansen feinted with ease, punching Edan on the side and unseating him from his horse.

Before the shansen could finish him off, Lady Sarnai furiously struck at her father's neck, his torso, his knees. But no matter how she attacked, her sword could not breach his armor.

Gyiu'rak's fur began to blur, and in a haze of white, she swooped toward the shansen's amulet. If she returned inside, she would endow him with her full demon strength, including the ability to shape-shift.

"The dagger!" Sarnai yelled at the enchanter. "Give me the dagger."

Edan pitched the weapon to her, the meteorite-and-iron blade dancing in an arc that curved blue in the air. The hilt landed neatly in Lady Sarnai's grasp, and she spun the blade to slice her father's amulet off his neck. Enraged, he slashed at her.

She ducked, and his sword sliced her horse's neck instead. Her steed screamed and reared, then collapsed on its knees, letting out a last, terrible groan. Lady Sarnai leapt from the saddle, and ran.

Gyiu'rak launched after her, but Edan tackled the demon. I could either save him—or take the amulet from Lady Sarnai.

Snow stung my eyes, and I bit my lip until it bled. Only one choice would end the war.

Making a sharp turn to intercept the shansen's daughter, I leapt so she would see me. "Give me the amulet!" I shouted. "I'll destroy it!"

She didn't hesitate. The shansen's horse was hard at her heels, and she flung the amulet at me.

I dove for it, my nails piercing its glossy black surface as I clasped it tight in my fist.

The amulet sizzled in my palm, smoke simmering from the carved tiger on its surface. I could feel Gyiu'rak's wrath as she threw Edan to the side and pounced on me. The shansen's entire army turned on me.

The clash of swords, the swoop of arrows. At the warlord's command, hundreds of arrows assaulted me. Sharp edges pierced my skin, grazing my calves and elbows, puncturing my back. I didn't feel any of it.

My time as Maia had ended.

This was the moment I'd dreaded, the moment I became a demon. But now that it was here, I wasn't afraid. I could hear my demon voice trying to calm me.

It won't hurt, she soothed. *See how powerful you will be? Even more powerful than Gyiu'rak.*

But her words had nothing to do with my state of calm. She had no idea what was coming.

My chest heaved. I felt no pain, only a rush of heat melting away the cold I'd endured these last few months.

I surrendered to the fire. Gyiu'rak's amulet still burned in my grasp, the tiger head on its obsidian face melting until it was no more than a pile of sand, sifting through my fingers.

Two screams pierced the air. First Gyiu'rak's, then the shansen's, as his sword slipped from his grasp and fell to the ground.

Caught in mid-leap, Gyiu'rak began to smolder, ribbons of smoke bleeding from her flesh until only her ruby eyes were left. Then they too dulled, until finally the wind swept them away in ashes.

The shansen's mighty strength was gone in an instant, leaving him a shriveled old man far more aged than his years. He fell into a position of defeat: his knees sank to the ground, his back folded forward in a crouch, his fists curled at his sides. For what seemed an age, he did not move. Then the shansen lifted his helmet. His hair had gone white.

"Daughter," he rasped.

A storm raged in Lady Sarnai's dark eyes as she held her father's gaze. I could tell she was trying to decide whether to finish him or show mercy. She lifted her sword so it kissed the side of his neck, the weight of her blade too heavy for his frail shoulders to bear. "Yield."

The shansen lifted his chin and dragged one foot forward so he knelt on only one knee. I took it as a sign of acquiescence—until a dagger flashed from his calf.

He knifed at his daughter's ribs.

Lady Sarnai's blade fell from her hand as she danced back, rolling to the side. The shansen lunged again, but Sarnai was ready this time. She reached into the quiver on her back and jabbed a scarlet arrow into his chest. Fulfilling the promise she'd made last night.

I did not see the shansen fall. My body would wait no longer.

The change began. Fiery wings burst out of my spine. My skin was no longer skin, but feathers of the palest blue-gold fire. My eyes rounded and sharpened into a bird's. I folded my arms over my chest. Not even the finest weavers could have imagined the brilliance of my wings, layers upon layers of individual flames interlaced with threads of rippling sapphire and violet.

Air rushed out of my lungs. My heart slowed nearly to a stop.

I had to act now, before the demon inside me won, before *she* became the legend Baba would hear one day. That couldn't happen, not when I'd given so much to spin a new dawn, to bring the sun and the moon and the stars to A'landi. Not while my heart still beat, not while I still breathed.

I turned to Edan. He was shouting my name, but I couldn't hear him any longer. I held up my wrist, touching the red thread.

The end of the thread is you, Edan, I wanted to tell him. *It's always been you.*

His eyes, blue and beseeching, were the last thing I saw before I released the blood of stars. The dress wrapped around me, scintillating waves of starlight smothering the demon inside. Soon we would all be gone.

Up I shot into the sky, high into the stars. Until A'landi was covered in clouds, and Edan and I were separated by the firmament of the heavens.

And there at last, with the blood of stars seeping from my wings, I erupted into flames.

CHAPTER THIRTY-FOUR

My dress unfurled into the night, a blanket of stars unfolding across the sky as far as I could see. The clouds grazed my ankles, soft as blossoms of snow.

When I looked down, I could not see the earth. Could not see Edan or Lady Sarnai or Keton, or the aftermath of the battle, or whether A'landi was saved.

But somehow, I knew we had won. Somehow, through a tickle in my heart that was little more than a flutter of joy— I knew that the demon inside me and the shadows that had darkened my soul hadn't followed me here. I was finally free.

All was still. Quiet but for the unsteady beating of my heart, the warmth of my blood rushing to my head as I flew on, losing myself in this endless fabric of starlight.

Then, I heard a gentle laugh. It tinkled like the soft strokes of a dulcimer. A sound I never thought I would hear again.

I strained to see the familiar silhouette against the glowing full moon. "Mama," I breathed.

My wings melted into hands and arms, my feathers softening into skin with the burnished glow of the fire in me. I flew to embrace my mother.

"I've waited for you a long time, Maia," she said, stroking my cheek. "It's as I predicted: you *are* the greatest tailor in A'landi. A tailor worthy of the gods."

"That is more than I ever wanted," I replied. She drew me close, her hand sweeping over my forehead, stroking the crease lines away.

I closed my eyes, feeling like a little girl again. The girl who'd spend all her days in the corner of Baba's shop, hemming pants and embroidering scarves. The girl who used to dream about becoming the emperor's tailor.

"How foolish I used to be," I whispered, lifting myself out of Mama's embrace. "If I could do it all over again, I'd never wish to leave home."

"You don't mean that," replied my mother. "If you hadn't left home, you wouldn't have found the other end of your thread." She gestured at the red thread on my wrist. It tickled my skin, so light I'd nearly forgotten about it.

I licked my lips. They tasted sweet, not like the ash I had tasted in my nightmares, but of the cookies Ammi had given me to eat before going to battle. Before I had died.

The corners of my vision blurred, and I looked away so Mama wouldn't see the tears misting my eyes.

I felt different. Weightless and free—which made sense, since I was probably a spirit like Mama. Below my feet was sky instead of earth, but my body did not panic. Instead, I marveled. I marveled at the evenness of my heartbeat and my breath, and at the serenity of this place.

I marveled that I could *feel*. The cold that had seeped into my soul over the last few months was gone, and so was the burning heat, replaced by a gentle warmth that sang within me. It'd been so long since I'd been warm. And when I stopped to listen to my thoughts, there were no voices but my own.

All around, stars glittered, each as vibrant as the most

precious jewels on earth. The sky was a dazzling blend of colors, a mix of dawn and dusk, not unlike the dress of the blood of stars.

Mama held out her hand to me, and something glimmered on the face of her palm.

"My scissors!"

"Amana asked me to return them to you," she replied. "They've been in our family a long, long time."

"So it's true," I murmured, taking my scissors from Mama's hand. They were brighter than before, and the sun and moon engraved on the shanks sparkled from every angle. "I'm a descendant of Amana's tailor?"

Mama nodded. "Much of the story has been lost over generations, but yes, the first to make the dresses was your ancestor."

I passed the scissors back. "Then they belong to him, not to me."

Mama touched my arm hesitantly. I sensed whatever she was about to say next wasn't easy for her. "I don't know whether it pains me to see you here, Maia, or whether it fills my heart with joy. I've missed you. . . ." She paused. "It is Amana's wish for you to join her in heaven, but . . . but I know it isn't your time yet, my daughter."

"What are you saying?"

"Your brothers and I pleaded your case, and Amana listened. She offers you a choice." Mama took a deep breath, and my heart hammered through the silence.

A choice.

"To stay here with us, as a tailor to the gods." Mama's voice was hoarse. "Or go back, to be with Baba and Keton, and with your enchanter."

Heat burned into my nose, shooting up to my eyes. I couldn't stop the tears from falling. "What I would wish is for you and Finlei and Sendo to be home again."

"Maia, you know that cannot be."

Even though I'd anticipated her answer, hearing it still drew a choked sob out of me.

"Baba needs you," said Mama. "So does Keton. And your enchanter." With her thumb, she wiped away the tears shimmering on my cheeks. "I already feel lucky to see the woman you've become—beautiful and strong and brave."

She reached for my wrist, touching the red thread I'd tied there. "See? Even life and death cannot break the bonds of fate. Edan is waiting for you."

I nodded, but before I turned to go, Mama pushed the scissors into my hands.

Holding them again made me falter. I brushed my fingers over the sun and moon on the shanks, and the blades thrummed under my touch. Even here, I could hear them humming with power.

My fingers clasped the bows, eager to be reunited with the scissors, before I shook my head. "I haven't changed my mind about them."

"They are the source of your magic."

"I was happy before without magic, and I will be happy again without it. The scissors served me well, but I don't need them anymore. Keep them for me, Mama."

My answer seemed to please my mother, for she threw her arms around me in an embrace. But she did not take the scissors.

"Before you go, you must use them one last time."

She gestured at the blanket of stars beneath us. There was a tear in the middle, a trace of glittering sunlight seeping through the seams.

The rip in the heavens.

I was to mend it, the way the first Weaver had in what was now legend.

"Together, Mama," I said.

She placed her hand over my arm, guiding me as I set my scissors against the sky, letting loose its magic to stitch together the heavens. Then, when at last it was done, my mother eased the scissors from my grasp and clasped my hand, drawing me close.

She kissed my forehead. "Farewell for now, my Maia."

When she let go, the entire world blazed, the sky ripening into a sea of flames. I watched Mama fade into the stars, the silhouettes of my brothers appearing to escort her back to heaven. Then the sea engulfed me, and I burst into flames.

And I suddenly realized what form I'd taken: a phoenix, meant to rise again.

. . .

The sound of water rippled in my ears, a misty spray tickling my face.

My first breath was full of the ocean, and I drank in its freshness. Then I started to wake.

Blood rushed to my arms and legs . . . and my toes dug into warm, moist sand.

Someone held me, a heartbeat other than my own softly thumping in sync with mine. I opened my eyes, lashes clinging stubbornly to my skin.

A hazy face hovered above me, features sharpening against

the glimmer of the sun. A nose, slightly crooked at the bridge, a square chin, finely chiseled along its edges, more bristly than I remembered it. Hair, black as cinder, with tousled curls that desperately needed trimming, and thin, uneven lips—parted now in a quiet gasp.

"Edan."

Relief spread across his face, and he dropped to his knees beside me.

"I thought you'd want to see the ocean one last time," he started. "We thought you were dead."

"I'm here." I pressed my finger to his lips, shushing him. His eyes were moist and swollen, his cheeks stained by tears. I blotted them with my sleeve, then took his face in my hands.

I kissed his cheeks, his nose, his eyes. His lips. I lingered there, inhaling the familiar warmth of his breath. Letting it seep into my own and stay there, as it had when I first loved him.

The warmth of the rising sun touched my face. "It's morning," I said. "Where's Baba? And Keton—"

"They're safe. They're on their way from the capital."

Now I bolted up. "The capital? Does that mean—"

"The war is over." Edan nodded. "Gyiu'rak is no more. The shansen is no more. And Lady Sarnai is empress."

"Empress?" I repeated.

"Yes, the people want her. The ministers had a fit at first, over a woman ruling A'landi, but she *is* the rightful ruler."

"Empress Sarnai," I murmured again, letting the words ring. "A'landi is whole again."

"She'll be here soon," Edan said. "We were going to . . . to bury you here, by the water. It was what your brother said you would have wanted."

No sooner did he speak than Sarnai approached us, accompanied by an entourage of men and women, their faces worn from the strain of battle. It was easy to see her as empress now, though she still wore her battle armor. Yet in spite of the losses still haunting her eyes, there was something about her—the grace with which she commanded those around her—that made me think she'd always been destined to lead A'landi.

Surprise flickered across her face when she saw me.

"She's alive." Sarnai pointed at me. "Why did no one tell me she's alive?"

"I only just returned," I replied, scrambling to my feet and bowing, "by the goddess Amana's grace."

Lady Sarnai sniffed, quickly regaining her poise. "Stand straight, Tamarin. Enough with the bowing." She looked me up and down.

As I rose, she lowered her head slightly, clasping her hands at her chest. It wasn't a bow, but from her, I took it as a sign of great respect. I supposed it was an even greater sign of respect that she had come all the way from the battlefield to the beach to ensure that the body of a mere tailor would be properly sent to heaven.

She'd make a fair ruler, I was sure of it. Perhaps not one who was beloved by all, but she inspired loyalty and respect. That was already more than most could do.

With a flick of her wrist, she dismissed the priests. "We have no more need of your service."

Then she turned to Edan and me—looking so stern I thought she was about to deliver a rebuke.

"The late emperor's tailor and the former Lord Enchanter are invited to attend the coronation," she said instead. Then she paused, as if she'd given her next words much thought but still needed to consider them. "Provided Maia Tamarin is no longer touched by enchantment, she is invited to stay on in my court as adviser and chief imperial tailor. And—" She searched for Edan's proper title.

"Edan," he replied. "Just Edan. I'm a Lord Enchanter no longer."

"*Edan* is welcome to stay on in my court as enchanter and adviser."

"Thank you for this chance to serve you, Your Majesty," I began. "It is a great honor, and Edan and I will always come when you need us. But I believe I speak for us both when I say we wish to return home."

Her brows furrowed. "Return home?"

"Yes, to Port Kamalan. My family needs my help with our shop, Your Majesty," I explained.

Lady Sarnai crossed her arms. She looked weary. "You shall not return home empty-handed. What do you wish for, in return for your service to me?"

"Noth—"

Edan nudged me with his elbow and threw me a sidelong glance that read: *The empress is offering you anything. Don't refuse it.*

What would I ask for? I had no need for jewels or fine dresses, or a large manor with a hundred servants.

"I'd like a shop," I said. "One in Port Kamalan, not too far from the sea. I'd like one big enough for my father and brother to live with me, but not so big that I will become indulgent with success." I paused. "And, I'd like one of A'landi's finest steeds for Edan."

Sarnai glowered. "You wish a simple life, when I am offering you a seat on my council?"

"Yes, Your Majesty."

She considered me, as if to determine whether I was joking. Then she sighed. "I suppose I'd expect nothing less of you, tailor." She fluttered her fingers at the advisers flanking her. "See to it that her wishes are fulfilled."

Sarnai started to turn on her heel, but she lingered one last moment. "I wish you well, Master Tailor." She inclined her chin at Edan. "Enchanter."

Edan and I bowed, not looking up until the wind had erased her footsteps in the sand and I could no longer see her shadow stretching across the shore.

And then I rushed into his open arms—hardly able to believe that at last we were free.

CHAPTER THIRTY-FIVE

Midsummer arrived, and I was gathering silkworm cocoons in the garden, so many that my basket overflowed. Baba and I had no need to make our own silk anymore; a steady stream of materials arrived every week from our suppliers in the capital, and our shop employed half a dozen workers. But I let myself indulge in this project—it gave me pleasure to collect the cocoons.

Ever since I'd returned to Port Kamalan, I relished plying my craft from start to finish, gathering the raw silk and spinning it into thread, as Mama had taught me. I liked weaving it into cloth and feeling it change in my hands into something beautiful. Something whole. Something mine.

Merchants stopped by the store every day, trying to sell Baba and me their wares. "Silks spun by the masters of the Yunia Province," they'd entice me. "Look at this marvelous satin, brought here from the heart of Frevera."

"I've pearls from the Taijin Sea, all the way from the Kingdom of Kiata!"

Baba and I always shook our heads. We weren't interested in their wares.

The merchants learned to wait until Keton was alone in the shop, for though my brother had grown a keen eye for selecting fabrics and restocking materials, his heart was the easiest to tug. Any story from a former soldier would loosen a few jens from his pocket.

I never chided him about it. A smile usually touched my brother's mouth these days, and it had grown wider ever since we'd made the decision to visit Jappor in autumn.

Ammi lived there now, and she'd started a bakery near the main road that specialized in honeycomb cookies and lotus paste buns. Under Khanujin's rule, women hadn't been allowed to own property, but things were different since Empress Sarnai had come to power. I'd heard Ammi's bakery was doing quite well. Well enough, I hoped, that her family might one day hear of it.

"We should visit," Keton suggested at least once a week. "You love honeycomb cookies, don't you, Maia?"

"Yes, but I've never known you to have a sweet tooth, brother!"

At that, he'd clamp his mouth shut. Even though he wouldn't admit it, Keton was counting the days until we saw my friend again. The ghosts in his eyes were nearly gone. Nothing would banish them forever, but light danced in them more often now than not.

So today when he found me in the garden, looking far too solemn, I worried something had happened. "Keton, what's—"

"You have a visitor," he said.

Oh. I returned my attention to my silkworms. "If it's Mister Chiran, tell him his jacket will be ready by eve—"

"It's not a customer."

Now I looked up. "Then who is it?"

"You'll have to come see."

My brother disappeared into the shop, and by the time I followed, there was no trace of him. I passed Baba, who was instructing the seamstresses to take a break.

"It's almost lunchtime," I muttered. "Who could possibly be visiting at this hour?" I hoped it wasn't Calu, the baker's son. While I'd been away, he had married a farmer's daughter, and though he, thankfully, no longer turned his attentions to me, he pestered Baba and me for free mending.

It wasn't a customer. And certainly not Calu.

I nearly dropped my basket when I saw him. I would recognize his silhouette anywhere, tall and lean, a slight bend in his back as he stooped to avoid hitting his head on the low doorframe. Black hair longer than I remembered, more than a few stray curls lingering over the boyish face I'd so dearly missed.

He was waiting for me to greet him, to run into his arms and plant a kiss on his mouth. It took all my restraint to hold back and say, instead, "You need a haircut."

There. His expectant smile curved into the crooked grin I so loved, and amusement flecked his eyes.

"I wanted to make a dramatic entrance," Edan replied. "Maybe fly through your window the way I used to, or send a thousand birds to write out your name in the sky."

"But?"

"But then I wouldn't be able to do this." He bent down and kissed me. The basket in my hand fell to the ground with a quiet thump.

After the Six Winters' War ended, I'd insisted Edan return to the Temple of Nandun to finish his studies with Master Tsring. It had been hard for us to part again, but I knew he loved magic

346

the same way I loved sewing. I couldn't deny him the chance to earn it back.

Besides, I needed a little time on my own. My customers knew better than to speak of my past as a demon, but even as the world forgot, I could not. Demons and wolf-shaped shadows still haunted my dreams every few nights. They were less regular now, but I didn't think they would ever vanish completely.

I told Edan of my dreams in the letters we wrote each other every week. A slew of paper birds were exchanged between us, each a letter. Many days I'd awake at dawn to catch a new letter at my windowsill, and it helped ease my nightmares. Each letter, Edan signed with one of his "thousand names."

"I didn't expect you to return until the fall."

"I finished my studies early," he said, not without a hint of pride. "Seems after all these years, I still make a good pupil. And, I wanted to surprise you."

I rolled my eyes at him. "So you're done?"

"I'm done. Here to stay. As long as you'll have me." He opened his hand. A seed rested on his palm, and when I touched it, it bloomed into a plum blossom. Its petals, soft and fragrant, tickled my fingers.

My hand jumped to my mouth.

"I practiced for a month to do that," Edan admitted. "Just to get that reaction from you."

"Was it worth it?"

"Most definitely," he said, scooping me up before I could protest. I squealed, laughing as he spun me around the shop. Then he set me down hastily, and a sheepish look passed over his face as he saw Baba standing stern-faced at the door.

My father greeted Edan with a warm clasp on his arm. "Welcome back. Now that you have returned, my daughter can spend more time at the loom and less time composing love letters."

"Yes, sir."

"Are you ready to take on your role in the shop?" he asked Edan.

"I've been practicing changing my reds to blues, and I—"

"Reds to blues? I've dyes for that." I wrinkled my nose playfully. "Best not to waste your magic. You can tend to the horses or help with the finances. Didn't you mention something about a money tree once?"

"You said you didn't care about money."

"I lied."

Edan laughed. "What a terrible liar you are, Maia Tamarin." He bent down to kiss me again, but Baba cleared his throat and gave me a sidelong look.

"You both could start by making a run to the market," he said. "I've placed an order with Mister Geh, whose ship should have arrived this morning. Go pick it up, will you?"

Picking up orders was usually Keton's job, but Edan bowed his head and muttered, "Yes, sir," as he ushered me out the back door.

"Wait, we're going out the wrong way. Mister Geh's shop is down the street. There's nothing out the back except—"

My words died on my lips as soon as I saw the boat. Tethered to a wooden pole I was certain hadn't been there yesterday, floating gently atop the waves.

"The ocean?" Edan finished for me.

I nodded mutely.

Yes, all that was behind Baba's shophouse was the ocean.

Sendo and I used to sit in the back, watching the ships coast toward the port and dreaming that we too would sail on one someday. But we'd been too poor to buy a boat, and the fishermen always refused our requests, saying they were too busy to indulge our childish fantasies.

I drew in a deep breath. "What is this?"

"You said you'd never ridden on a ship before," Edan said. "I thought about hiring one, but what's the fun in sailing for an hour or two only to have to bring the boat back?" He leaned against the boat's canopy, which was my favorite shade of blue.

"So I built you one, with some help from the disciples back at the temple . . . and some input from your brother. It isn't much to look at, but it's enchanted not to sink and it'll fit your family comfortably, and—"

I pressed my fingers to his lips, shushing him. Then I pressed my nose to his. "Have I ever told you that you talk too much?"

He caught my fingers, kissing them one by one while he continued to speak. "And there's an hour until sundown, so if the currents are kind, we should be able to take it out to see the Summer Palace from here."

"I don't care about the palace," I said, clasping Edan's hand as he helped lower me onto the boat. It rocked gently under my heels, and I saw a chest stuffed with Edan's maps of A'landi, Samaran, Balar, and a dozen other places I'd never been.

"No compass, no maps, no navigating north, south, east, or west. We'll have a thousand other days for that." I grabbed the rope anchoring us to shore, using it to steady my balance as I stepped onto the small deck. "Let's seize the wind and let it take us where we ought to go."

"We can do that. It might take longer than an hour, though."

"We have time," I said, letting go of the rope and stumbling toward him. Edan caught me, pulling me with him behind the wheel. He gathered me close, his arm around my waist.

The sea shone before us, full of possibility. Not long ago, I'd thought my story was like a fairy tale. After all, there were demons and ghosts, an emperor ensorcelled, and a princess who'd become the greatest warrior of her generation. Sometimes I didn't quite believe that I'd ever left my corner in Baba's shop, that I'd sewn the sun, the moon, and the stars into Amana's legendary dresses.

My tale was over. Perhaps fate had more magic in store for me in the future. But for now, I was content just to drift in the glittering sea with the boy I loved.

I leaned against Edan, slipping one of my hands into his cloak pocket. My fingers brushed against a small leather-bound journal, and I took it out. "What's this?"

"Notes." Edan looked sheepish. "Some famous poets have begun writing about us, and they've taken an alarming number of creative liberties."

"Such as?"

"Calling me a cowherd."

I blinked, confused, until I remembered: "But you *were* a herder's son."

"That was ages ago." Edan made a face, but his eyes were smiling. "After so many years of service, I don't even get to be remembered as the most illustrious, illuminating, and formidable enchanter in all of A'landi? Thankfully, your name is far more fitting."

I laughed. "What does the poem call me?"

A beat, and then Edan reached for my hand, clasping it. "The Weaver."

The Weaver. That name meant so much.

350

I looked to the stars, wondering if my ancestor the Weaver was there, watching over me with Mama and my brothers. Then I looked to the red thread on my wrist and that on Edan's.

Astonishing, that a cowherd's son and a simple weaver, separated by centuries of starfalls, should find each other. If Edan hadn't taken his oath as an enchanter, and if I hadn't dared to step beyond the path that was laid out for me and gone to the palace, we might never have met. Whatever history remembered of us, whether it likened us to the sun and the moon—only permitted to meet once a year—or simply to a boy and a girl touched by the stars, fate had danced to bring us together.

I touched my red thread, content that I had finally found its other end.

"Maia," Edan was saying, "shall I read one of the poems to you?"

"Later." A smile touched my lips, and as Edan raised an eyebrow, wondering what I was thinking about, I kissed him, then opened my arms to the glittering waters. "I've had enough of the stars for now. Take me to the sea."

ACKNOWLEDGMENTS

Thank you, dear reader, for making it to the end. It's been a bittersweet experience writing the conclusion to the story I always wanted to read and tell. Sequels are infinitely harder to write (at least for me), and though I will miss Maia and her journey deeply, I'm also grateful and relieved to have finished her tale and sent it out into the world. Most of all, I am grateful to the many wonderful people who made *Spin the Dawn* and *Unravel the Dusk* a reality.

My perpetual thanks to Gina Maccoby, my agent, for being with me from the beginning and guiding me through the thickets of publishing with her wisdom and ever good sense.

To Katherine Harrison, for once again whipping my book into shape with her sharp edits, and never failing to amaze me with her patience, enthusiasm, and professionalism. I am so lucky to have her as my editor. A huge thank-you to everyone at Knopf BFYR, including Alex Hess, Alison Impey, Melanie Nolan, Gianna Lakenauth, Janet Wygal, Artie Bennett, Jake Eldred, Alison Kolani, Lisa Leventer, Judy Kiviat, Julie Wilson, and Barbara Perris. Thank you for being the most supportive team I could ask for and for bringing Maia's story to more readers. You all make me feel incredibly fortunate to work with you.

To Tran Nguyen, for yet another breathtaking cover. Someone on Instagram called it Maia 2.0, leveled up, and I completely agree. I love it more than I have words to express. And to Kim Mai Guest, thank you for lending your beautiful voice and narrating Maia's tale in the audiobooks.

To my critique partners Doug Tyskiewicz and Leslie Zampetti, for lending their keen eyes and ears and for entertaining Charlotte when I needed to bring her to our meetings. A shoutout to my fellow writers Liz Braswell, Bess Cozby, Lauren Spieller, June Tan, Swati Teerdhala, and the Electric Eighteens, for being dear friends and for commiseration in dire times (especially about Book II woes). To my beta readers, Amaris White, Eva Liu, Joyce Lin, and Diana Inadomi, for being my dearest friends and, often, most critical readers.

And, of course, thank you to all the fellow writers, readers, booksellers, Goodreads librarians, bookstagrammers, and bloggers who've been so supportive of *Spin the Dawn* and *Unravel the Dusk*. Special thanks to Catarina Book Designs, Rachele Raka, and Yoshi Yoshitani, for the gorgeous art that was part of *Unravel the Dusk*'s preorder campaign.

Lastly, thank you to my family. To my parents and my sister, for helping organize and moderate my book launches, for giving me their honest opinions on everything from dialogue to the food my characters ought to eat, and for nurturing my imagination when I was a child so I could have the courage and determination to become a writer.

Thank you to Charlotte, for being the joy who makes me laugh every day, and for reminding me that children are the future of books!

Most of all, thank you to my husband, Adrian. Thank you for listening to me constantly worry about my books, for rigorously reading over my drafts while the baby is asleep, and for being my faith that love is real.

ABOUT THE AUTHOR

ELIZABETH LIM grew up in the San Francisco Bay Area, where she was raised on a hearty diet of fairy tales, myths, and songs. Before becoming an author, Elizabeth was a professional film and video game composer, and she still tends to come up with her best book ideas when writing near a piano. An alumna of Harvard College and the Juilliard School, she now lives in New York City with her husband and her daughter. *Spin the Dawn* (book 1 in the Blood of Stars duology) was her first original novel, and *Unravel the Dusk* is her second.

elizabethlim.com